NIGHT OF THUNDER

This Large Print Book carries the
Seal of Approval of N.A.V.H.

A BOB LEE SWAGGER NOVEL

NIGHT OF THUNDER

STEPHEN HUNTER

WHEELER PUBLISHING
A part of Gale, Cengage Learning

GALE
CENGAGE Learning

Detroit • New York • San Francisco • New Haven, Conn • Waterville, Maine • London

GALE
CENGAGE Learning

Wheeler Publishing Large Print Hardcover.
The text of this Large Print edition is unabridged.
Other aspects of the book may vary from the original edition.
Set in 16 pt. Plantin.
Printed on permanent paper.

LIBRARY OF CONGRESS CATALOGING-IN-PUBLICATION DATA

Hunter, Stephen.
  Night of thunder : a Bob Lee Swagger novel / by Stephen Hunter.
    p. cm. — (Wheeler Publishing large print hardcover)
  ISBN-13: 978-1-59722-923-4 (alk. paper)
  ISBN-10: 1-59722-923-7 (alk. paper)
  1. Swagger, Bob Lee (Fictitious character)—Fiction. 2. Vietnam War, 1961–1975—Veterans—Fiction. 3. Marines—Fiction. 4. Snipers—Fiction. 5. Fathers and daughters—Fiction. 6. Automobile racing—Fiction. 7. Tennessee—Fiction. 8. Large type books. I. Title.
  PS3558.U494N54 2009
  813'.54—dc22   2008048211

Published in 2009 by arrangement with Simon & Schuster, Inc.

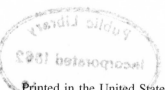

For my daughter, Amy, as the wonderful person she is, but also as the symbol for the young American reporter

Speed is of the essence

— ANONYMOUS

■ ■ ■ ■

PART I:
PRELIMS

■ ■ ■ ■

ONE

Brother Richard liked it loud. He punched the iPod up all the way until the music hammered his brain, its force beating away like some banshee howl from the high, dark mountains hidden behind the screen of rushing trees. He was holding at eighty-five miles per hour, even through the turns, though that took a surgeon's skill, a miracle of guts and timing. The music roared.

Sinnerman, where you gonna run to?
Gonna run to the sea
Sea won't you hide me?
Run to the sea
Sea won't you hide me?
But the sea it was aboilin'
All on that day

It was that old-time religion, fierce and haunted, harsh, unforgiving. It was Baptist fire and brimstone, his father's fury and

11

anguish, it was Negroes in church, afeared of the flames of hell, it was the roar of a hot, primer-gray V8 'Cuda in the night, as good old boys in sheets raised their own particular kind of hell, driven by white lightning or too much Dixie or too much hate, it was the South arising under the red snapping of the flag of the Confederacy.

He rode the corner perfectly, left-footing the brake and coming off it at the precise moment so that he came out of the hairpin at full power. It was late, it was dark, it was quiet, except of course for the thunder of the engine. His right foot involuntarily pressed pedal to metal and the car leapt forward, breaching the century mark, now 110, now 120, right at death's edge, right near to and within spitting distance of oblivion, and he loved it, a crack in the window seal sending a torrent of air to beat his hair.

Sinnerman, where you gonna run to?
Gonna run to the moon
Moon won't you hide me?
Run to the moon
Moon won't you hide me?
But the moon it was ableedin',
All on that day

A climb and then a sudden turn. It was Iron Mountain, and 421 slashed crookedly up its angry hump. He hit brake, felt the car slide, saw the great whiz of dust white in the head-lamp beams as he slipped to shoulder, felt the grit as the stilled tires fought the gravel and ripped it free, but the skid was con-trolled, never close to loss, and as the car slowed, he downshifted to second, lurched ahead and caught the angle of the turn just right, pealing back across the asphalt and leaving the dust explosion far behind as he found the new, perfect vector and powered onward into the night.

If you thought you were in the presence of a young prince of the South, high on octane and testosterone and the beat of an old and comforting spiritual, you'd be wrong. Brother Richard was by no means young; he was a thin, ageless man with a curiously dead face — a recent surgery had remolded his physiognomy into something generally bland and generic — and he was well enough dressed to pass for a preacher or a salesman or a dentist, in a gray suit, white shirt, and black tie, all neat, all cheap, straight off the rack at Mr. Sam's big store near the interstate. You'd never look at him and see the talent for driving that was so special to his being, or the aggression that fueled it, or the hatred that explained the aggression, or the bleakness of spirt and utter capability, or even his profession, which was that of assassin.

"Nikki Swagger, girl reporter." It was funny, it was corny, but she liked it and smiled whenever she conjured it to mind.

Nikki Swagger, girl reporter. It was true enough. Nikki, twenty-four, was the police reporter for the Bristol *Courier-Herald,* of Bristol, TN/VA. "TN/VA" was an odd construction, and its oddity expressed an odd reality: The newspaper served a single city set in two entities, half in the Volunteer State, half in the Old Dominion State. The border ran smack through the city, a burg of one hundred thousand set in the southernmost reaches of the Shenandoah Valley, where one state became another. It was horse country, it was farm country, it was quarry country, but most of all, and especially this time of year, it was NASCAR country. Race week was coming and soon one of Tennessee's smaller cities would become one of its larger as three hundred fifty thousand citizens of NASCAR nation — some would call it Budweiser nation — came to town for the Sharpie 500 a week and days away, one of the premier Sprint

14

Cup events on the circuit. Nikki couldn't wait!

But for now, Nikki drove her Volvo down Tennessee's State Route 421 from Mountain City, Johnson County's county seat, twenty-odd miles out of Bristol. She drove carefully as the road wound down the slope of a mountain called Iron, switchbacking this way and that to eat up the steep elevation. She knew she had to be wary, for it was full dark, visibility was limited — sometimes interstate rigs came piling up on the verge of chaos and hurt, taking a shorter, emptier route at night between podunk destinations — and to her life was still one great adventure and she wanted to enjoy every single second of it.

She checked the speedometer and saw she was under forty, which seemed about right, and the world beyond her windshield consisted of two cones of light which illuminated the next 250 or so feet, a narrow ribbon on asphalt, and curves that came and went with breathtaking abruptness. She was an excellent driver, possibly because she'd studied the nature of vehicles in space so assiduously in her western girlhood where, besides horses, she'd spent years in tough-as-nails go-karting and had the medals and scars to prove it, as well as several roomfuls of trophies and ribbons and photos of herself. The girl in the pictures was beautiful as always but equally as always slightly disheveled, and usually posed in a caged car about quarter-size. In the pictures always were her mother, a handsome, fair woman who looked as if she stepped out of a Howard Hawks movie and should have been named Slim, and her father, whose military heritage seemed inscribed in the leather of a Spartan shield that comprised the perpetually tanned hide of his smileless face.

Down the mountain she went at a carefully controlled and agilely sustained forty per, her mind alight with possibility. She'd been in the county seat all day and talked to dozens of people, the subject being her specialty as a crime reporter, methamphetamine issues. Meth — called "crystal," called "ice," called "killer dust," called "purple death," called "angel breath," called the "whispering crazies," called whatever — haunted Johnson County, Tennessee, as it haunted most of rural America. It was cheap, it was more or less easily made (though it did have a tendency to explode in the kitchen labs of the trailers and shacks where it was manufactured), and it hit like a sledgehammer. People loved the first few minutes of the high, and didn't remember

16

the last few minutes, where they put their newborn — in the oven or down the well or just on the clothesline. They didn't remember beating their spouse to death with a hoe or a brick, or wandering down the interstate, shotgun in hand, shooting at those strange things roaring by that turned out to be cars. People got themselves in a whole mess of trouble on meth. Not after every usage but often enough so that lots of ugliness happened. She'd seen families sundered, hideous crimes, law enforcement compromised by the abundant profit, dealers shot or slashed to death in alleyways or cornfields, the whole spectrum of big city dope woe played out in no-name towns the *New York Times* had never heard of and no movies had ever been made about. She was the scourge's scribe, its Homer, its Melville, its Stephen Crane, even if no one had ever heard of her, either.

As she drove, she puzzled over several eccentricities her daylong trip had uncovered. The nominal reason for the trip was to go on a meth raid with Sheriff Reed Wells, the ex-Ranger officer who'd returned home to clean up the county, as the saying went, and who had talked the Justice Department into leaning on the Department of Defense and had somehow acquired a much-beaten but still-viable Blackhawk helicopter to permit scouting and airborne tactical consideration. In fact, she'd spent the morning airborne, sitting next to the handsome fellow, as he maneuvered his troops down brushy mountain paths, and coordinated a neat strike on a rusting trailer, which in fact did turn out to house a small-scale meth lab. Nikki had seen the culprit, a down-on-his-luck mountaineer named Cubby Holden, arrested, his apparatus hauled out into the yard and smashed by husky young deputies dressed up like Tommy Tactical action figures. They loved every second of the game, leaving behind a sallow woman, two wormy kids, and a hell of a mess in the yard.

A typical triumph for Sheriff Wells, yet the problem was that meth prices, despite his many strategic successes, stayed stable in the Tri-cities area. (The second and third cities along with Bristol were Johnson City — oddly, not a part of Johnson County — and Kingsport.) She knew this from interviews with addicts at a state rehab clinic in Mountain City. Kid told her he paid thirty-five dollars a hit yesterday and two years ago, it was thirty-five dollars a hit.

Now how could this be? Maybe there were a lot more labs out there than anybody knew. Maybe there was some kind of protected superlab. Maybe some southern crime family was running the stuff in from other places.

Then she heard a strange rumor, thought nothing of it, picked it up again, and had a few hours before dark. It held that someone in the mountains was shooting up the night. Lots of ammo being burned, blasting away, somewhere down old Route 167 before it connected with the bigger, newer 61. Now what could that be? Would that be the famous super meth lab, hidden in some hollow, invisible from the sky, its security so professionally run it demanded its own set of Tommy Tacticals to handle perimeter duties and work out with their submachine guns every night?

Rumor suggested that it lay in the pie of land around the nexus of the 67–167 routes, and, night still being a bit off, she'd poked around there finding nothing except some kind of Baptist prayer camp nesting behind a NO TRESPASSING sign that she ignored and, upon arrival, encountered a Colonel Sanders in a powder blue Wal-Mart suit who gave her a free Bible and tried to get her to stay for supper. She skipped the food, but driving back down the dusty road to the highway —

It was just a piece of cardboard, trapped

19

by a snarl of weeds and held at a peculiar angle so the sun happened to light it, yielding a color not found in forests in steamy Augusts as well as right angles, not found in any forest, ever. Her eye caught it. So she stopped and plucked it up. Something in it was familiar. It was something official looking, military, at least governmental — equipment, ammo, something like that. The scrap was torn, rent by being crushed by passing vehicles, but as her father was a noted shooter and always had boxes of weird stuff around, she knew what this sort of thing could mean, though only a bit of official print was still legible on the scrap.

But then she was disappointed, as all thoughts of ammunition and explosives vanished. She thought it might be biblical, something Baptist, for it also carried religious connotations. It had been bisected in its rough passage to its nest in the leaves, and only a few symbols remained on the piece. Who knew what started the inscription, but it ended in "k 2:11," though with dirt splashes and spots and crumples she wasn't sure about the colon. But it made her think instantly of Mark 2:11. Bullet or Bible? Weirdly, both. She remembered the crazed Waco standoff of her youth, the gunfight, the siege, the fire-and-brimstone ending. That was something that somehow combined both bullets and Bibles. Maybe that dynamic was in play here, for the world in many places had not grown beyond killing on what was believed to be God's sayso. On the other hand: It's just a scrap of cardboard by the road, that's all it is, it could have blown in and ended up here a million different ways. Maybe it's just a function of my imagination, the reporter's distressing tendency to see more than what's there. She tucked it in the Bible that the old Baptist minister had pressed upon her so it wouldn't get lost or crumpled in her briefcase and drove off in search of answers.

But a local gun store, run by a bitter old man who'd turned skank mean after a bit, was of no help, so she set about her drive home.

But now she thought: My dad will know.

Her dad knew stuff. He was a great fighter, once a famous marine, and more recently had gone away for a while a few times and then come back, always sadder, sometimes with a new scar or two. But he had a talent — and in this world it was a valuable talent — and the core of it was that he knew a certain thing or two in a certain arcane subject area. He wasn't reliable on politics or movies — hated 'em all — but he was superb in nature, could read land, wind, and sky, could track and hunt with anyone, and in the odd, sealed little world of guns and fighting with them he was the rough equivalent of a rock star. Never talked about it. Now and then she'd catch him just staring off into space, his face grave, as he remembered a lifetime of near misses or wounds that healed hard and slow. But then he shook off his pain and became funny and outrageous again. And she knew that other men respected him in almost mythical ways, because what so many of them dreamed of, he'd actually pulled off, even if the details remained unspecific. After his last absence, he'd returned with, among other things, a bad limp from being laid open across the hip and not stitched for several hours, and an incurable depression. Or so she thought. And then the depression was miraculously cured in a single afternoon when a Japanese-American civil servant had delivered . . . a new little sister. Miko. Adorable, insatiable, graceful, full of love and adventure. The family atmosphere lightened immeasurably, and the family condition became extreme happiness, even if, over two weeks, the old man's hair went from a glossy brown to a gunmetal gray, and aged him ten or twenty years.

So her dad would know.

She pulled off the road, not wanting to have the cell in her hand when a truck full of logs or canned goods came barreling up the other lane off a blind turn. She got the cellular out of her purse, the car's engine idling, the silence of a dark mountain forest all around her. She picked up the Bible and plucked the scrap out, holding it in one hand so she could describe it.

The phone rang and rang and rang until it finally produced her father's recorded voice: "This is Swagger. Leave a message, but I probably won't call you back."

His sense of humor. Not everybody found it funny.

"Hey, Pop, it's me. Call me right away. I have a question."

Where was he? Probably sitting around with a crew of marine buddies, laughing to hell and gone about master sergeants from another century, or possibly out with Miko, teaching her to ride as he had taught Nikki to ride.

So she'd have to wait. Or would she? She put the scrap back in the Bible, pulled out her laptop, along in case she had to file remotely. The question, would there be a network out here? And the answer was — ta da! — yes. Wireless was everywhere!

She went to Google and pumped in "k 2:11" and waited as the magic inside hunted down k 2:11s the world over and sent the information back through blue glow to her. Hmm, nothing in any way connected to her issue. So she went to Mark 2:11 and got Mark's words, which made no sense to her. Context. You have to have context.

Arrgh, nothing. She wanted a cigarette but had been trying to quit.

But then she thought of her good friends from Brazil who were taking over the world.

She requested Amazon.com, and instantly that empire responded.

A few tries at k 2:11 yielded nothing except some technical gibberish, a book on Russian submarines, another on World War II ships called corvettes.

Next she tried to work the bullet angle, just in case, and went to "Cartridges" and got a lot of info, maybe too much. After scanning its contents courtesy of the Amazonians, she settled on a book, *The History of Sniping and Sharpshooting,* because it seemed to offer the broadest overview of the subject, then hit the one-touch purchase option so that it would arrive soon. That was stupid. Her dad would call well before then, and explain all. Still, it made her feel that she had done something positive.

She put the laptop away and checked this way and that for traffic, preparing to edge onto the asphalt. She'd be home in an hour. Another day, another dollar for Nikki Swagger, girl reporter — whoa!

Some redneck in a low black car came whipping by, faster than light or sound. Man, was the guy crazy or what? She'd never seen a car move like that, a blur, a low hum, a whisper of streamline and chrome, there and gone and then vanished forever. Was it a dream, a vision, something out of a nightmare?

It scared her. Not that these hills were haunted or anything, but you could convince yourself of anything looking at fog-shrouded hollows, hairpin turns, the dark carpeting of trees leading up to unseen peaks, the networks of roads leading off to NO TRESPASSING signs and God-knows-what-else up them. There were rumors of militia out here or some gang of outriders or Klansmen or White Supremacists or some such. There was the business about shooters, blazing away in the night, an army of righteousness getting ready for its conquest. This guy in his muscle car bolting along over a hundred miles an hour could have been an emissary from any of them.

No, she told herself. Some kid, too much beer, he thinks he's some NASCAR hero, these people love their drivers, that's what a kid's fancy would turn to. She half-believed that in the next twenty miles she'd come across the low, black speed merchant on its side, bleeding flame in a pulse of red light, as the emergency service vehicles circled it and their crews tried to pull the hero, now a crispy critter, his soul in heaven, from the flames.

She shivered. Then she slipped into gear and pulled out.

He saw her. It was in a haze of speed, but he made out the Volvo and a young woman's face caught in the glow of dash light. She'd pulled aside on the right, nestling under trees, and had been working at some task, some continuation of the curiosity that had doomed her. He saw in that flash of light a beautiful young face and he knew how close it was, he was running out of mountain road, and she'd be a much harder kill without an iron wall of trees to drive her into on her right side.

Why had he looked to the right at that moment? Who knew? It was the Sinnerman's luck, and even the Sinnerman got

26

lucky once in a while. He slowed to eighty, then found a wayside, pulled over more deeply, to await her.

Brother Richard punched the iPod and ran through his Sinnerman options again, beginning with the Travelers 3, going to the pure gospel of the Reverend Seabright Kingly and His Hebrew Chorus (that was funky!) and on to the personality-free Seekers. Then to Les Baxter's balladeer, winding through the high-boring purity of Shelby Flint, and finishing up with the arrhythmic, antimelodic approach of Sixteen Horsepower. All interesting, with the Travelers 3 maybe the truest folk esthetic, the Balladeer the highest show-biz, and the Reverend the fanciest old–Negro church version, almost unrecognizable for all the hooting and shrilling.

Brother Richard knew himself proudly to be the Sinnerman. He would do the wrong. I can live with the wrong. I exult in the wrong, he thought. I define the wrong. I am the wrong. It could have turned out different, but it turned out this way.

He waited as the music roared in his ear. And finally, she came by him on the lonely road, not seeing him pulled off to the side, her placid, little, sensible Volvo trimly purring along at less than forty. He could see that she was tense behind the wheel, for he saw her body hunched forward to the wheel, her neck tight and straight, her head abnormally still, her hands rigid at ten and two on the wheel. She was worried about the road, about the possibility of a big truck coming up from behind her or barreling widely and wildly around a turn.

But she wasn't worried about the Sinnerman. In her version of the world, there was no Sinnerman. She had no concept of the Sinnerman and no idea of what was about to befall her.

Almost out of these damned mountains. Then a short, flat run across the floor of Shady Valley, a last splurge of hills, and then Sullivan County, civilization, as 421 took her back to Bristol, to her apartment, to a nice glass of wine.

Then Nikki saw death.

It was a blur in her mirror, just a shadow as no details presented themselves. Then it was a blur in her driver's-side window, growing exponentially by the nanosecond, full of thrust and empty of mercy. It was death in a dark car, come to snuff her out.

No one had ever tried to kill Nikki before. But she had her father's blood in her veins and more importantly his DNA, which meant she had reflexes fast as her killer's, and she wasn't by nature turned toward fear or panic. The car hit her hard, the noise filled the universe and knocked her askew, toward trees which rushed at her, signaling catastrophe as her tires bit against the skittish dust. Then she did what one person in ten thousand will do in those circumstances and she did it at a speed that has no place in time, out of certitude for correct behavior at the extremes.

She did nothing. She let the car correct itself as its wheels reoriented swiftly. She had control again.

Most, seeing trees or cliff rushing at them, will overcorrect, and when they do that the laws of physics, immutable and merciless, mandate a roll. The roll is death. The neck and its thin stalk of spine can't take the g-force and sunder under the extreme vibration. Cessation of consciousness and life signs is immediate, and whether the wreck is in flames or not, further body trauma, broken bones, sundered blood-bearing organs, whatever, is immaterial. She didn't know that the Sinnerman, with his experience in automotive assassination, had presumed she would yank the wheel for life, guaranteeing death, and was surprised as she rode the bump out, got soft control, and then accelerated, half on road, half on gravel, to escape his predation.

He hit her again, in the rear-third of the accelerating Volvo, knocking her fishtailing off the road in a screech of dust. But she didn't panic at the wheel and hard-spin it this time either (sure death), but instead let it spin free and find its own proper vector as she scooted just ahead of him. He pulled himself left, drew off, set up for another thump, this one better aimed.

Nikki was not scared. Fright is imagination combined with anticipation combined with dread, and none of those conditions described her. Instead, she accepted instantaneously that she was in a fight to the death with a trained, experienced killer, and she didn't waste any concentration on the unfairness of it all. Instead, she pushed the pedal so hard to the floor of the car that she felt the beginning of g-force, though of course the Volvo 240 with its 200-horsepower six-cylinder was no match for the muscled-up Chrysler barn-burner under her antagonist's foot. But as he struggled to find an angle, she put surprising space between the vehicles and yet was astute enough to see in supertime a turn approaching. So *now* she finally braked, softly turning into a power slide that would get her around the turn at the best angle and set her up for another dead-on acceleration the hell out of there, if such a thing were possible, and it probably wasn't.

Damn, she was good! As she control-skidded around the turn in a whine of rubber fighting for purchase of asphalt, Brother Richard saw his opening and, instead of veering outside of her, he bravely cut inside to begin his surge. His professional-quality cornering, as opposed to her gifted amateur approach, won him the inside where she didn't expect him to be. As she tried to float back into the proper lane, he revved beyond redline, closed that off from her, and delivered his blow to the front fender of her right-hand side, not so much a thud as a nudge to push her out of equilibrium. But now, damnit, she figured this one out too, and jammed hard on her brakes, pumping the wheel as she skidded left.

The world spun before Nikki, racing across her windshield, pure abstraction in the cone of the one headlamp that still burned, and she nursed the brake pedal with a delicate foot while merely making suggestions to the wheel, which kept her in a semblance of control as she stopped, alas, to find herself one-eightied in the other

direction. She was now facing the dangerous rising linkage of switchbacks up Iron
Mountain that she'd just survived. So she
punched it hard, jammed on the brakes as
he came by her a third time (how had he
gotten around so fast!), somehow got
through a reverse right-hand, backing turn
at a speed at which such a maneuver should
never be conceived of, much less attempted,
and again punched hard.

But he beat her, somehow, to possession
of the road, and this time he hit her, rode
her hard right. He turned, and she saw his
face in the glare of the dash, its plainness,
its evenness of feature, its dull symmetry, its
almost generic quality, like the father of
Dick in a Dick and Jane; it burned into her
mind. And then she was off the road, out of
control among the trees, and the world was
jerking left and right, hard as the car
slammed against or glanced off the trees.
She felt her neck screaming, her head flopping this way and that, and then she hit,
and everything stopped.

Two

It happened so fast, two weeks. His hair went straight to winter from summer, with no autumnal pause. It didn't thin, it didn't fall out, it just veered off to dull gray. He looked ancient, or so he thought.

It was a memory that did it. He had recently had an actual sword fight to the death — in the twenty-first century, in one of the most modern cities on earth — with a Japanese gentleman of infinitely superior skill and talent. Yet he had won. He had killed the other man, left him cut through the middle in a mushy field of sherbet snow, turned magenta by the man's own blood.

Bob thought often: Why did I win? I had no right to win. I was . . . so lucky. I was so goddamned lucky. It was like a worm, gnawing at his heart. You lucky bastard. Why did I luck out and that guy end up guts out in the snow?

Not that Swagger had escaped intact. The

guy had laid him open to steel bone at the hip, and he'd gone too long before stitches saved his life. It never healed right, and he didn't help by denying so fiercely that there was a problem. Somehow his leg stiffened, as if the tide of blood that the stitching dammed was still there, coagulating and about to break out in a red ocean spray and bleed him to death. Killer's revenge. But the killer had also, as another part of his revenge, turned him comical, with one of those weird bounces in his gait. Could still ride, could still walk, couldn't really run much. No talent at all for climbing. A motorcycle saved his life by giving him the illusion of freedom that had once been his strongest attribute.

"I look a hundred and fifty," he'd said, just that morning.

"You don't look a day aver one hundred forty-five," his wife said. "Honey, look at Daddy, he's turned white."

"Daddy's a snowman," shouted the little girl, Miko, now seven, delighted to find a flaw in a hero so awesome as her strange, white father. "Snowman, snowman, snowman!"

"It's gray, it's gray," Bob protested. Then he added, "I know someone's going to find her ride cut short she don't stop calling

Daddy a snowman." But the tone revealed the fraudulence of the threat, for it was his pleasure to spoil his daughters and then take pride in how well they turned out anyway.

He was a rich man. Rich in land — he now owned six lay-up barns in three western states, two in Arizona, two here in Idaho, and one each in Colorado and Montana, and was looking at property in Kansas and Oregon — and rich in pension from the United States Marine Corps. He was rich in homes, as he owned this beautiful, recently finished place sixty miles out of Boise, on land he'd cleared himself that looked across green prairie emptiness to blue scars of mountains under piles of cumulus cotton against a blue diamond sky. He was rich in wife, for Julie was handsome, a character out of a Howard Hawks movie, one of those tawny, feline women who never got excited, had a low voice, and was still sexy as hell. And he was richest of all in daughters.

He had two. Nikki was a graduate of the Columbia School of Journalism and now working her first newspaper job in Bristol, Virginia, a place her father liked a lot more than the New York City where she'd spent the last year. He felt she'd be a lot safer in the small city right smack on the Virginia-

Tennessee border. Meanwhile, his adopted daughter, Miko, had taken to western life without a hitch, and quickly became comfortable around horses, the messes that they made, the smells that they generated. She loved them, took to them automatically, and it thrilled her father to see such a tiny thing so relaxed atop such a giant thing, and controlling it so confidently, making it love and obey her. The kid was already earning blue ribbons in Eventing and might even overtake her big sister, who'd been a national champion in that sport two years running when she was a teenager.

Now it was morning, and since it was August there was no school for Miko, so they were doing what they loved: the girl on her horse, Sam, and her father watching her canter gently about the ring. But he was not dominating. For while that had been his way as a marine NCO, it was not his way with his daughter. He leaned on the fence, and you'd have thought, There's a cool cowboy type of fellow. His jeans were tight, framing his lanky legs; he wore a horseman's slouch and sucked on a weed. He was all cowboyed up — the Tony Lamas boots muddy but solid, a blue, denim shirt, a red handkerchief around his neck, for it gets hot in Idaho in August, and a straw Stetson to keep the sun off his face.

It really couldn't have been more perfect, always a signal that disturbance lurks not far away.

"Easy, sweetie," he called, "you don't want to force him. You have to feel him, and when he's ready, he'll let you know."

"I *know,* Daddy," she called back. She rode eastern, on the snooty, Brit postage stamp of a saddle, with erect posture, a crop in her hand, tall, low-heeled boots, and of course a helmet. She was equally adept with the big western rigs that were like boats upon a horse's plunging back, but both Bob and Julie agreed that she would eventually go to school in the East, that she should have riding skills set for that part of the country, and, on top of that, they wanted to keep her out of rodeos, where too many young gals flocked because they liked the string-bean boys who rode like hell and bounced up with a smile when they went for a sail in the air and a thump in the dirt. Though with Miko, maybe it would be something else. Maybe it would be to actually do some crazy rodeo thing, like leave a perfectly good cow pony for a ride on a bull's horns.

"She'll probably end up the women's bull-dog champion of Idaho, but still you've got to try," he told his wife.

"If she does, she'll have to put up with a screaming nag of an old lady every damn day," Julie said.

So far, so good — Miko had a rhythm and a patience that even a generally stoic animal like a horse could feel and love. She had magical ways, or so Bob believed, and he would have gladly given up the other hip — or anything — for Miko.

Gracefully, she took a jump, without a twitch to her posture, a tightness to her spine, a twist to her landing.

"That was a good one, sweetie," he called.

"I *know*, Daddy," she responded, and he smiled a bit, wiped his brow, then looked up at a flash of movement too fast for good news and saw Julie coming from the house. He knew immediately something was wrong. Julie never got upset; she'd stitched up enough cut-open Indian boys on the reservation where she'd run a clinic for ten years, and kept her head around blood and pain and emotional upheaval and the occasional death. So if she was upset, Bob knew immediately it could be only one thing: his other daughter, Nikki.

"Sweetie," he called before Julie reached him, wanting to bring Miko in before the bad news arrived and he lost contact with

38

reality, "you come on down now, just for a second."

"Oh, Daddy, I —"

He turned to Julie.

"I just got a call from Jim Gustofson, the managing editor of Nikki's paper —"

Bob felt constriction through his heart and lungs, as if his respiratory system had just blown a valve and was leaking fluid. His knees went weak; he'd seen violent death, particularly as inflicted upon the young and innocent, in both hemispheres, and he had a bleak and terrifying image of disaster, of his daughter gone, of his endless, terrible grief and rage.

"What is it?"

"She was in some kind of accident. She went off the road out in the mountains, ended up in some trees."

"Oh, Christ, how is she?"

"She's alive."

"Thank God."

"She was conscious long enough to call 911 and give her location. They got to her soon enough, and her vital signs were good."

"Is she going to be all right?"

"Mommy, what's wrong?"

"Nikki's been in an accident, honey."

It killed Bob to see the pain on his younger daughter's face; the child reacted as if she'd been hit in the chest by a boxer. She almost crumpled.

"She's in a coma," Julie said. "She's unconscious. They found her that way, with minor abrasions and contusions. No paralysis, no indications of serious trauma, but the whiplash must have put her out, and then she hit her head hard, and her eyes are blackened, and she's still out."

"Oh, God," said Bob.

"We have to get out there right away."

Yet even as Julie said that, Bob knew it was wrong. His oldest and darkest fear came out of its cave and began to nuzzle him with a cold nose, looking him over with yellow eyes, blood on its breath and teeth.

"I'll go. I'll leave soon as I can get a flight. You book me on the Internet, then call me as I head to Boise for the flight out."

"No. No, I will see my daughter. I will not stay here. We'll all go. Miko has to see her too."

"Come over here," he said, and when he drew her away from the child, he explained.

"I'm worried this could be linked to something I've done to someone. It's a way to get me out —"

"Bob, not everything —"

"Not everything's about me, but you have no idea of some of the fixes and the places

I've been. You have no idea who might be hunting me. You have a scar on your chest, and memories of months in the hospital when that fellow put a bullet into you."

"He put it into me because of *me,* not you."

It was all so long ago, but he remembered hearing the shots and finding her, almost bled out, along the trail, Nikki screaming, another man dead close by.

"I don't say it's my business," he said. "But I can't say it ain't. And I can't operate if I'm thinking all the while about your safety and Miko's. I have to recon this alone. If it's safe, I'll let you know."

It was gunman's paranoia, he knew it. All the boys felt it, all the mankillers, good, bad, or indifferent. At a certain age, faces come to you unbidden, and you can't place them quite, but it's your subconscious reminding you of this or that man you took down and you think: Did he have brothers, parents, cousins, friends, peers, colleagues? Maybe they were as savaged by that unknown man's death as he had been by the deaths of those he'd known himself, like Julie's first husband, Donnie Fenn, such a good young man, the best, his chest torn open by the same sniper who put the bullet into Julie. Bob remembered, I killed the sniper.

41

But maybe the sniper's brother was here and couldn't get at Bob in Idaho where Bob had friends and family and knew the land and where all the creeks were, so he figured out how to draw him onto unfamiliar land, and maybe it was his pleasure to see the pain on Bob's face by taking his family first, one by one, first Nikki, then Julie, then Mi—

He cursed himself. Every time he came home alive and more or less intact, he thought about going underground, going into his own private witness protection program. New identity, new start, new place, new everything. But another part said no, you can let it drive you crazy, it's nothing, it'll take your life if you let it. You win not by surviving but by living, by having the things you need and love: family, land, home.

"Please," he said.

"Bob, this can't be yours alone. That is my daughter. That is my daughter. I cannot stay here; I have to be at her side, no matter what it costs or what the risk. I feel that so powerfully I can hardly face it."

"Let me go, let me figure it out, and as soon as I can, at the absolute soonest, I will let you know and you can go. If it's dangerous at all, I will have her moved, I will hire bodyguards, I will set up a secure place for you to come. But I have to know first."

She shook her head. She didn't like it.

"I know I can be wrong," he said. "I'm wrong all the time. It ain't about me being wrong or me being — what was the word Nikki used?"

"Narcissistic. Someone who loves himself too much, even if he can't admit it. You're not a narcissist. No narcissist would be as shut up, cut down, beaten, bloodied, dragged, and kicked in the head as much as you. I give you that. Whatever your flaws, and God knows there are hundreds of them, you're too insane to risk your life for this or that or nothing whatever to be a narcissist. So your scars buy you two or three days. Then we're coming."

"Thank you. Now I've got to get packed."

THREE

As he'd just seen Miko atop a large, muscular horse, controlling it and taking such delight in the process that morning, he now stood next to his older daughter and remembered her atop the same large, muscular animals, how she thrilled at them, how she loved them, how she made them do her bidding, how they loved her.

But Nikki was far from horseback. She lay in the intensive-care unit of the Bristol General Hospital, monitored by a million dollars' worth of gizmos. Beeps beeped, lines dashed across screens to symbolize breathing, brain activity, blood pressure, and so forth. She was still, her seemingly frail chest moving upward and downward just a fraction of an inch to signify the functioning of her taxed respiratory system.

"Those roads can be so dangerous at night, Mr. Swagger," said Jim Gustofson, the managing editor of the newspaper Nikki worked for. "If she weren't such a good reporter she would have come home earlier, when it was light. But she stayed, she got every last thing out of the day that she could have. Oh, this is so awful. I just don't know what to say."

Gustofson was a tall man in his early fifties, with a full head of hair and a shocked expression. He had repeated this statement about ten times. It was all he could say.

Bob had received the doctor's verdict. They were in the wait-and-see stage. All the monitoring systems recorded strong life signs. She was badly bruised and lacerated, but there were no broken bones. Brain activity seemed unaltered; EKG strong, signifying no permanent damage. But she was totally unconscious and had been so now for over twenty-four hours.

"There's no telling in these cases," said the young resident. "She took a bad knock on the head and the whiplash was vicious in the few seconds the car bounced. She was rattled around pretty hard. We just don't know how long she'll be out. Classically a coma of this nature lasts a few weeks."

"Or months or years? Or forever?"

"That's an outside possibility. Yes sir, Mr. Swagger. But it's rare. Usually a few weeks and they recover, their memory is foggy but in time it returns. The brain has had a shock. It realizes how close it came to death. It wants to rest and relax for a while. It'll be back when it feels safe. She's a strong young woman. Anyhow, Dr. Crane can tell you more tomorrow."

"What do the police say, Mr. Gustofson?" Bob asked.

"I've got a copy of the report for you. But Johnson County Sheriff's Department says their assessment is that she was driving home down the road, and some teenager, possibly high on the very thing she was investigating, methamphetamine, decided to show off. You know these rural kids get NASCAR fever with the big race less than a week away."

"I noticed the traffic and all the activity driving in," Bob said.

"Yes sir. Well, one of the things we've noted is that traffic aggression goes way up this time of year. So the cops believe some punk kid was trying to be Dale Senior to the decidedly un-hip Volvo, just for the thrill of it, the kick of it, and he got carried away, misjudged his speed and instead of scaring the bejesus out of her and getting a laugh out of his buddies, he smacked her off the road, and down the incline she went. She was lucky in one way."

46

"How is that, sir."

"They say he first hit her about three miles back, much higher up the mountain. If she'd have gone over there, the incline was several hundred feet. Rolling the whole way, then smashing into trees, she'd have been dead for sure. As it was, where she finally went off, the distance was only 150 feet or so, and she didn't hit any of the trees head-on but rather glanced off them. The big thing is, she didn't roll. The roll is the killer. Somehow, she outdrove him for three miles, and when he finally hit her solid, she kept the car in traction and out of the air. I'd say she saved her own life."

Bob saw his daughter in the car, in the dark, some big punk fool in a pickup with a brainful of crystal meth and a gutful of Budweiser slamming her, laughing hard, deciding it was fun, and slamming her again and again. He'd like to have a conversation with the young fellow. He'd leave him a check for the facial reconstruction bill but not a penny for the wheelchair he'd need forever.

"Do they have any leads?"

"They have a detective on the case. I spoke to her. She's very good, she's broken some big cases. Thelma Fielding. She'd be the one to see."

Bob looked at his watch. He'd taken a 1

P.M. from Boise to Knoxville via St. Louis, rented a car, and roared the whole way up I-81 to get here this fast. Now it was nearly ten.

"I'm so sorry, Mr. Swagger. She's an outstanding young woman. We all hope for the best for her. Do you have a place to stay? The town is filling up with racing fans, it might be hard to find a room. We have a spare bedroom. The paper has rallied also and there's lots of folks willing to accommodate you if need be, no matter how long you stay."

"I'll go to her apartment and stay there. The nurse gave me her effects when I checked in and I saw the key. I hope you have the address and can give me some directions. Then tomorrow after I see her and talk to the doctors on the day shift, I'll want to go out and talk to that detective."

"Just to warn you, this big race screws everything up. It brings in millions and millions of bucks. You could say the whole region lives off this month the year long. But the downside of course is that everybody's all involved in it, and the cops especially. It's a royal pain moving around town or trying to get anything normal done."

"I'm used to waiting," said Bob. "You

48

might say, I was once a professional waiter. I can wait a long, long time without moving a twitch, you just watch."

You always fear entering your own child's private life. What if you make discoveries, learn things you weren't meant to know, find out intimacies, privacies, discretion that a child always hides from her parents, just to save them worry or knowledge. You can learn too much.

But that didn't happen. If she had a private life, or any secrets, it hadn't gotten interesting yet. Nothing indicated a boyfriend, a scandal, a secret. She was dead set on doing well in this job, moving on to another job on a bigger paper and who knows what. Maybe some fancy rag like the *Times* or the *Post,* maybe running a smaller, more focused thing. Copies of those papers lay everywhere, as did magazines like *The New Yorker* and *Time* and so forth. Her books were all by journalists and novelists. That was her talent. Bob knew: You had to let them be what they could be, just as in his way, although dying young for it, Bob's own father Earl had let his son be what he wanted, and had encouraged his talents and not held his flaws against him.

After several misturns and dead ends and

an involuntary tour of Bristol, even the line in the city where Tennessee magically turns into Virginia and vice versa depending on the direction, Bob had at last found the side road that ran just next to and so close to a Wal-Mart that you'd have thought it was the parking lot, followed it behind the giant store, down a hill, into a little glade of houses, along a creek, and then up into an apartment complex. Hers was on the third floor. He saw a sheeted Kawasaki 350 in the parking lot and knew it was Nikki's, and that she loved that bike. He wished she'd taken it to Mountain City, because on the bike no redneck high on shit and beer would have outperformed her. He'd seen her ride the damned thing. She could stay with anyone, she could stay with him — he was good — and she'd have left that cracker crashed and burning in the gully, gone home, taken a shower, had a beer and a good laugh, and then a good night's sleep. She had Swagger blood, after all.

But the squat, boxy Volvo had saved her life, he bet. It wouldn't surrender to the forces of gravity or physics as it roared down the incline in a cloud of dust, shedding itself of speed. It was designed to keep people alive by Swedish geniuses, and God bless Lars or Ingmar or whoever, because he'd

50

done his job that day. It never broke, it never collapsed, and though fenders and engine and trunk had cammed inward, the integrity of the passenger box stayed intact. His daughter lived on the slenderest of threads: that she'd been able to forestall her stalker for three miles downhill, that she'd stayed out of the roll, that she'd gone over where the incline was much slighter, that the car held together, that it didn't hit the trees head-on but rather glancingly, and that she'd been conscious enough to call it in.

Outside, trees whistled in the southern night. Was this Tennessee or Virginia? He couldn't be sure. You had to live here for years to know automatically. Whatever, it was the South, with its dark history of violence, its strange streaks of courage, its stubbornness, its pride, its love of hunting, fishing, twangy music, and fast cars. He himself had sprung from such a place, a state with a long history of clan feuds and grudges, violence on the street, youth swollen hard on aggression and let to bloom until someone was dead. It sent men in the hundreds up the Pea Ridges of the War of the Rebellion, and most went willingly and died — nobly? Bob had seen enough guts-hot men to know there was no nobility to it. But he also knew the strange pride that compelled the young men of the South onward into the grape and musket, up that bleak Pea Ridge swept by leaden blizzards, the majority to die slowly of massive intestinal wounds, screaming in the night six days after the battle was lost or won. That was something.

The South, he thought. It made me, but am I of it? Is my legendary father of it? Is my daughter of it? Or does this have nothing to do with the South, and only grows out of something I did in some forgotten neighborhood or other, in the tangled loyalties of my twisted past.

He tried to settle down. He lay on her couch, aching for booze to make the hurting go away. He called Julie, gave her what's what, told Miko he loved her, and then, after nightmares that weren't quite a product of sleep but more of memory, managed to fall asleep. It had been a hell of a long day, a day like no other. He hoped he'd never have a day like it again.

It was any strip of forested road sloping down from the mountain above, a vast, high bulk of stone, sheathed in the trees that went everywhere, like a carpet or a disease. He could make no sense of the cross hatches of the tire tracks fading on the asphalt or the messed-up shoulder dirt and gravel where the big vehicles had collided at speed, or the patch down the slope laid out by yellow accident tape, now a mite ratty three days into keeping folks off the spot where Nikki's Volvo had landed.

"I'm not exactly getting a picture," he said to the woman detective.

"Sir, I could trace it out for you. Explain it better that way. The diagrams in the report make it clear too."

"No offense now, I never mean offense, but I have to ask: You sure you're up to this sort of work? It's not a big department and all this is highly technical, it seems."

"I have investigated traffic accidents and fatalities too. I admit, our state police accident team is better set up for this kind of thing, but the trickiness of state laws keeps them from operating off the federal and state highways. This is a county highway. So there's a jurisdictional problem right at the start."

"Well, I don't want to upset nobody's apple cart. I just have to figure out for myself on what happened. I'm sure you get that."

"I do, Mr. Swagger. That is why I am here to help. I have been at this a long time. I'm a good detective. We'll get him, or them."

"Yes ma'am, I believe you."

Detective Thelma Fielding, probably forty, was a strong woman with exceptionally large eyes, man-hands, what you'd call a big-boned woman. She wore blue jeans, tight to show off a body that was not beyond desire by any means — she had large breasts — and a polo shirt, black, with a badge over her left breast. A baseball cap carried the badge motif, but what told the world she was a professional law enforcement agent was the tricked-out .45 automatic worn in a Kydex speed holster on her hip. Behind it rode three mags, double stack. So the gun was probably a Para-Ordnance, not that Bob let her know he knew a Para from a Springfield from a Kimber from a Colt from a Nighthawk from a Wilson, and all the other 1911 models that were suddenly all the rage in self-defense and sporting circles. Next to the gun and the holster was her actual badge, wreathed in a leather badge holder, worn on the belt. On the other hip she wore her two-way, with a curly cord up to the mic pinned to her shirt collar. Oh, and the Para-Ord was carried cocked and locked, ready for speed work in less than a second's notice.

"So I can't make any sense of it, Detective. Can you tell me how you read it?"

"Would you want to sit in the squad car, Mr. Swagger. It's hot here in August, and you look a mite peaked. Wouldn't want you developing any health problems on top of everything else."

My damned hair, Bob thought. Makes me seem 150.

"Ma'am, I'm fine, at least for a little while. I just see tracks engraved in the road, where I'm guessing my daughter's bad boy skidded after he knocked her from the road at whatever speed he was going."

"Sir, I should tell you what you've probably guessed by now. This time of year such a thing is hardly rare. These young boys git all het up on account of the big NASCAR race week at Bristol. They want to show off for each other. It can get out of hand fast."

"Yes, ma'am. What I remember of young men reminds me such a thing is frequent." But the young men he knew spent their aggression on jungle patrol, ready to give it all up for something this batch couldn't fathom called "duty."

"The theory is," Deputy Thelma continued, "some kid decided to put a scare into the lone gal and buzzed her. Evidently she didn't scare, so he wasn't satisfied, so the game turned rough. He kind of lost his mind and banged her too hard and knocked her into the trees. Then he panicked, saw what he had done, and got the hell out of there. She was damned lucky she had a cell-phone and called 911 before she passed out, and that we got her in less than an hour. Otherwise, she may have lain there for a week before help came."

Bob examined the skid marks and could make no sense of them. He wanted to believe, yes, that's all it is. It had nothing to do with him, it was the random drift of the universe, a bad news connection between a hopped-up junior in a pickup and his few-years-older daughter, all earnest desire and commitment. The cross-hatched skidmarks were all that remained of the accident because the highway emergency vehicles and tow trucks that pulled her car out of the gully messed up the shoulder bad.

"You see, the thicker tires are his; you can tell where he skidded, then peeled out to catch up to her. She veered off the road a bit, lost some traction. He hit her right to left, then came around the other side and hit her left to right. That's what we see here. She went off right up there, down that slope, which ain't by no means the worst slope of the road, and somehow avoided hitting the trees head-on. It's all in the tracks."

He felt briefly overwhelmed.

"Is there any, you know, scientific clues that might help you figure it all out and lead to a guilty party? On the TV, there's all this crime scene stuff, makes you think it's just a matter of shining some magic light on something."

"Yes sir. Well, let me say that many folks have a wrong idea how detective work goes," Detective Thelma said. "It's the television. We shine the magic light and take something back to the lab and blow it up a thousand times and it tells us who to arrest. Not true now, never was. We do have some scientific evidence, if you call it that. I have sent both the tire tracks imprint and a paint sample I scraped off your daughter's door to the state police crime lab in Knoxville. In a few days, I'll hear back, and I'll get a make and model of tire and a make and model of car, the latter based on the color. Amazing how much auto paint can tell you. Then I can circularize all the auto body shops around the three states, see if anybody brought in a vehicle for damage repair in those colors. I can then ask local jurisdictions to check on the tires, and if we get a match or two, we might be in business. If the tires are any way unique, I can contact tire outlets."

"What are the odds?"

"Not good. Lots of folks here don't repair

their dents and dings or they do it themselves. Or if the car was stolen, maybe he'll just dump it and forget about it, that's something these thrill drivers do. Anyhow, that's what the book says. Now I work a different way."

"I'm hoping you'll tell me."

"I'm no genius but I have a sound appreciation of human nature. I collect snitches. What I do is, when I bust a kid on meth or grass or assault, I pull him aside and I say, 'Look I can go forward or you can cooperate with me and this can go away, you get a fresh start and maybe you ain't as dumb as you look.' 'What you mean?' he says. 'I mean,' I say, 'what do you know, what can you give me, what things you heard, where'd you buy the stuff, who's moving the shit, this sort of thing.' He listens, sees where his best interests lie, and opens up. I take notes. Clear up a lot of cases that way. Who broke into the Piggly Wiggly. Who stole seventy-six dollars and fifty-three cents from the Pizza Hut. How Junior Bridger afforded his new Camaro with a 344 under the hood. Other things I hear about it factor in: Why homecoming queen Sue Ellen Ramsey dumped quarterback Vince Tagetti for seeming no-'count Cleon Jackson. The answer is that Cleon's cousin Franklin just got into the meth business big time, and suddenly the dough is rolling in. Cleon delivers to folks all over town, he's now got a Lexus SUV, and Sue Ellen has always loved the Lexus line. That sort of thing. That's how crime works in a rural zone of hills and hollows and small towns and big football and bad methamphetamine addictions and very peculiar behaviors. And the kids, the snitches, they take to it. Finally, for some of 'em, they got somebody to listen to them. So right now I have my snitches working full time. And somebody'll talk. Too much beer in Smokey's one night, he'll talk. He'll brag on it, how he bopped the Volvo and it felt good. The story'll get around, it'll get to one of my kids, and he'll let me know, and I'll get a name. Then I'll bring 'em in and sweat 'em and they'll roll over and we'll have a case. It may take a little while, but that kind of police work is worth all the CSI bullshit in the world."

"That makes good sense to me," he said. "I can see you know your profession. May I call you now and again for some kind of update?"

"Why, sure, Mr. Swagger."

"But I have to ask you one other thing," he said. "I also know that in the real world, you're dealing with a workplace. I know how workplaces are. You got a boss who wants progress. Soon enough, there'll be other, bigger, fancier criminal situations and he'll want his number one investigator on them. My daughter's situation goes on the back burner. That's not your choice, it's not my choice, that's just the way it is, right? Now, especially with this big race coming up, with all the parties, all the drinking, with your department most likely pitching in on the security arrangements for an event that attracts a quarter of a million people, I am not exactly confident that you'll have enough time to devote to this. Not your fault. I ain't criticizing you. I'm just saying, that's what happens."

"I won't let that happen, Mr. Swagger. I will work this thing out for you."

"And then there's Sheriff —" he could tell, since she hadn't mentioned by name the recently famous hero of the meth wars, Sheriff Reed Wells, of the helicopter-borne drug raid and the highest conviction rate in Tennessee, that she didn't care for his high-handed, possibly self-aggrandizing way — "he wants cases that git his name in the paper. He wants the big raid, the splash. He doesn't want slow, careful, patient development of sources."

"You do know a thing or two about the real world, sir."

"Just a bit. Anyhow, I may hire a private investigator or a lawyer with investigative skills, if that's all right with you. Or I may do some poking around myself."

"Sir, there are some fine private investigators in Knoxville and some fine ex-police attorneys who know the system. Yes, that would be your right, and I understand your concern. I would strongly recommend against any poking around on your own. It can be tough out here, and unless you're a seasoned investigator, you can make things murkier, not clearer, and get yourself in a heap of trouble at the same time. These young men, they can be tough and merciless. I've seen killings, beating victims, all sorts of unpleasantness. I'd hate to find you victim of something like that, because you went to the wrong bar and asked the wrong questions."

"Well, that's sound advice. Okay, I'll stay away and try not to get my old bones beaten to pulp and get you another case."

"Then you and I are on the same page, Mr. Swagger. Now I've got to get back into town —"

Suddenly there was a squawk of electronic noise, harsh and indecipherable, and Detective Thelma switched a button on the microphone-receiver pinned near her collar and leaned into it.

"Ten-nine, here," she said.

She listened to what Bob heard as a gibberish of squawks, now and then cut by a recognizable number. Then she pushed Send and said, "I roger and will proceed on my Ten-Forty."

She looked over at him.

"Well, we have some strange boy in these parts who likes to burn trucks. Don't know why but this is the fifth one in the past two months. I've got to get over there fast, Mr. Swagger, and run the crime scene investigation."

"Yes, ma'am," he said. "I will be in touch."

She smiled, jogged off to her car, hit the gumball and the siren, and fired off.

Bob went back to the hospital and sat around for a couple of hours. He met some more of Nikki's reporter friends and picked up on how much she was loved and respected and how angry everyone was. He told them about Thelma and was gratified to learn she had a fine reputation, had been to a number of FBI schools, had a few big cases, and was something of a local character. She'd been a raving beauty once; who

knew she'd turn up as a cop and become
the three-time Tennessee state ladies'
USPSA champion, which, he now realized,
was why she carried the fancy automatic in
the speed holster. He also was invited to
dinner and turned down the invites, being
too tired and depressed for much more
comfort. About ten he kissed his daughter's
still cheek, and headed back to her apartment. There he called Julie and reported in
on his findings.

"We'll be there tomorrow."

"No, please. Just give it a few more days. I
just don't know. I like this detective and she
wouldn't steer me wrong but I still have a
queasy feeling."

"Is someone following you?"

"No. And if they were, I sure made it easy
on them. So no, no, there's no sign it's some
old mess of mine, I agree."

"Then it's clear for us to come?"

"I got one more trick to play out. Then
I'll call you."

It was stupid, he knew. But the tracks
made no sense to him. He went to his laptop, turned it on, and called up good old
Google. He typed in "Aerial photography,
Knoxville, Tennessee."

FOUR

If he blinked, he could have sold himself on the illusion he was back in Vietnam, at some forward operating base, where the helicopter was the only way in or out, and the helicopter the order of the day: taking men to and from battle, hauling out the wounded, laying on solid suppressive fire where needed. He was back in a war zone of engines somehow, and although the sandbags were missing, the perimeter security wasn't, and the whole wide area was separated into bays so that each powerful machine was isolated from the others, and its crew and shop worked as one. No, not Vietnam, but big, powerful machines just the same. The noise of them was gigantic, a physical presence demanding ear protection, so powerfully did the vibrations fill the air and set everything buzzing to the rhythm of their firing. Everyone running about had something to do with engines, all smeared with grease, all filthy in that happy way of men who love what they're doing and don't care what it looks like.

Meanwhile, a secondary fact of life was the stench of high-test fuel, which lingered everywhere, just as palpable in its way as the grinding roar of the engines. If you wanted to continue the Vietnam game further, you could: Like the aviators of that long-ago, so-vanished time and place, the drivers were the aristocrats here. Thin young men in their specialized suits, sexy, and it seemed that everybody wanted their attention or merely to be in their presence.

Of course it wasn't FOB Maria, north of Danang, somewhere in Indian country, RVN, circa '65–'73. It was the pits, that is, the center of the track, at the Bristol Motor Speedway, Bristol, Tennessee, and what towered above wasn't mountains full of Victor Charlie, but the enveloping cup of the speedway itself, a near vertical wall of seats for one hundred fifty thousand or so fans. The seats were largely empty, but a few die-hards sat and watched or took notes or worked with stop watches.

Bob was in the pit next to a vehicle that was just as purpose-built as any Huey or Cobra gunship. It was called "USMC 44," a Dodge Charger in the new, blurry digital camouflage just like the boys wore outside Baghdad, with the globe and anchor emblazoned king-size on hood, roof, and doors. Mechanics and submechanics leaped around, each, seemingly, with a special job to do, as they struggled to bring it to some kind of mechanical perfection. They worked in puddles of oil and fuel, and tracks crisscrossed the concrete as in Vietnam, the tracks of running men, the tracks of rolling, smooth, wide tires, and a myriad of smaller-scaled tracks for various wheeled devices that serviced the big machine. The USMC 44 carried a special-built V8 Hemi engine so brawny it was bursting to get out, rode on four smooth, wide tires instantly changeable, and devoured some poison brew of chemically adjusted fuel. Like any tool, it sported no softness for comfort, but was a hard, serious bucket of bolts meant for one thing only, and that was to zoom full-bore around a mile track five hundred times, spitting clouds of exhaust. It had all the gizmos: the spoiler on the rear to keep it from going airborne, the shocks made of Kryptonite or some other wonder steel, the four-inch ground clearance, all engineered to make USMC 44 go like hell. Inside it was like a hard devotional place, also lacking any softness for comfort, with one seat bolted in, the doors bolted shut, netting everywhere.

He stood there, on the outside of the ruckus, feeling like a tourist. But this is where he had been told to be, and this was the time, and the various obstacles to his penetration of the most intimate secret places of NASCAR had fallen when he gave his name, almost as if he were important.

It was the good old USMC retired NCO network in action. Bob had gotten a batch of pictures taken by Dewey's Aviation Inc. out of Knoxville, and what he saw was mainly skidmarks down ten miles of descending road on Iron Mountain, and some skell in some kind of fast mover closing in upon and trying to kill his daughter. It was, even from the air, nonsense and gibberish to Bob. But he had friends, and he called the son of a friend, who was a lieutenant colonel in personnel at Henderson Hall, or HQ, and asked if the colonel could come up with some ex-marine who'd know a lot about car behavior, accidents, skidmarks, that sort of thing. Turned out, no, he didn't, but he had something better. Someone who was fresh off the marine PIO at HQ where he'd been a part of the team that had worked with a big New York ad agency to recruit a NASCAR driver to run the USMC emblem on his car the upcoming season. Not for charity, because there was no charity anywhere in NASCAR these days. It was all marketing, done for the money. But still, the fellow, his people, his team, they all got it, and they loved running under the globe and anchor. In fact, he was still in the running for the Sprint Cup and he'd be right there at Bristol that very weekend. Calls were made, things were agreed to, and though the USMC-Chrysler team was working 24/7, there was no problem if Bob got there at eleven today, as qualifying didn't start till tomorrow and they were still tuning.

So now Bob was standing, when a scrawny youngster in jeans and a baseball cap came up to him, smiled, shook his hand, and bid him to follow. No words were exchanged, because the noise was so loud, and Bob followed the boy through the hustle and bustle, dodging a rolling tire someone was wheeling toward the car itself, its top half — Bob wanted to call it a fuselage — visible over a wall. He ducked and bobbed and then found himself inside a trailer home that was way nice, like a hotel suite, clearly set up as some kind of relaxation area. When the door was sealed Bob popped out his ear plugs, as did the boy, and Bob introduced himself.

"Gunnery sergeant, eh? You were some kind of cowboy hero in that war all that time ago, is that right?"

"It was mostly squirming around, hoping not to get shot, was all," Bob said.

"Well, I'm Matt MacReady." Bob was stunned to see that this kid was the man he'd come to see, the actual driver himself, fourth in NASCAR standings, a real comer, had a shot at winning a few nights down the road and a shot at the big cup. So young. Freckly even, with a thatch of red hair. But then the chopper aviators were all young, and if you put a helmet on them and a bird under them, they'd go into hell to get the mission done. So he warned himself against holding the boy's youth against him.

"Pleased to meet you. Congratulations on your fine racing career. Sorry I didn't recognize you."

"Being recognized is overrated, Gunny, let me tell you. And most of the folks who do just want something from you, from a signature to an investment. They all seem to have fancy haircuts, too. Don't trust a man with a fancy haircut, all smoothed up like cake frosting, you know. Hell, I just drive cars around in a circle, don't even get to go nowhere! I end up right where I started, what's the goddamn point!"

Bob smiled at the joke and the boy tried another one. "If this don't work out, I guess I'll head back to the gas station."

"Son, from the looks of it, it's working out swell."

The boy grinned, pleased to have impressed a genuine hero.

"So far, so good. The cars don't crunch up so much no more, and I take crunching up seriously because it put my granddaddy in a wheelchair for the last sixty years of his life. And they don't burn much no more neither, that's the best thing. My daddy burned to death in one, so I take burning seriously. Anyhow, since you don't want to tell me how damned great I am, that tells me you ain't no ass-kiss haircut here who wants free tix. Or no corporate glad hander wants me at a cocktail party with some of the clients where I stand around all bashful-like and the boys come up and pet me like some kind of cuddly critter. Hate all that shit, but it is a part of the business. So we are getting off to a good start. Now you tell me how I can help you. I'm guessing it don't involve putting on the firesuit and shaking a lot of hands."

"Nor putting frosting in your hair, nor getting petted much."

"I'm liking this better n' better."

"Yes sir, well, I hope I won't take too much of your time."

"Let me get Red Nichols in here, my crew chief. He's forgot more than I know. He was my daddy's crew chief too."

"Sure."

While Matt MacReady got out a cell to call Red, a beautiful girl — say, the kid was doing well! — came out and offered Bob a cold drink. Bob took a bottle of juice, and pretty soon the door opened, and a man Bob's age, wrinkled and greasy, came in.

"Red, meet Bob Lee Swagger, of the real USMC."

"Mr. Swagger, an honor, sir. I was a motor mechanic late in Vietnam and I heard of the famous Bob the Nailer."

"That old bastard is long gone. It's just an old man with a bad leg here today."

"Matt, you realize he run just as hard as you, difference is, people shooting at him. So you mind your manners around him."

"I will," said Matt. "I already have Mr. Swagger marked down as a serious southern man, not a haircut with a soft-gal handshake."

"Well, let's see if we can help him some."

And so Bob laid it out, quickly as he could, free of nuance. What had happened to his daughter, what the police made of it, his own worries, his decision to spend $2,700 to have Dewey's photo-recon the road, the arrival of the pictures over a fax transmission a few hours ago.

"So my hope is, you can look at the skid marks and make sense of them for me. It looks like chicken scratches to me. I figure you've seen skid marks before, you know how cars behave at high speed, brakes on, brakes off, how they skid, turn, wobble, go over. So you can tell me what happened. If the cops are right, and this is some hopped-up teenager, then I can rest easy. They'll get him, I'm sure. If not, I have to dig deeper and make preparations. I will protect my daughter."

"I believe you will. Is there any reason to expect anyone might try to kill your daughter?"

"It's not inconceivable. She was investigating a criminal enterprise in a county known for its corruption and drug trade. That would be one thing. Another would be my involvement, over the years, in a number of situations where violence sometimes came into play. Those episodes may have made me some powerful enemies. So it is possible that someone is trying to strike at me through her. That one just can't be ruled out. I've been around enough not to believe in coincidence."

"We don't believe in it either," said Red. "Out here, on the track where it's all happening at close to two hundred per, we don't never believe in coincidence. So let's see what you've got there, Mr. Swagger."

The boy and the old man examined the faxes, not the clearest photos ever taken, but Mr. Dewey had gotten pretty damned low and he had a real fine camera. Bob felt he got every cent's worth of the twenty-seven-hundred-dollar dent he'd put in his credit card.

"What you'll see right away is two tracks. One is my daughter's Volvo, though she doesn't come into the picture till late in the sequence. Hers are much lighter and narrower."

"Yep, he's sailing on some heavy, wide tread, no doubt about it."

"You can see where he tries to knock her this way and that, you can see how she gets away from him twice, and how she got enough down the hill that so when he did finally whack her off the road, the incline wasn't so steep and the car never rolled. They say that saved her life."

"I think it did," said Red.

They didn't talk for a while, except in

some kind of code.

"Great traction, all the way through. He's left footing. Seems to find the ideal line a lot. Say, I really like his angle."

"His angles are damned good, considering the corners are all unknown. I also like how soon he gets to the ideal, early in mid-corner. He rides this one real good and ain't fighting it none."

"This boy's been in a hundred-mile-per slide before, I think. Like his traction. He ain't hardly ever on two."

"I think so, too, Matt."

"Mr. Swagger, you got any other pictures? What I see is a damned fine driver knocking the little foreign job off the road. I will say, this girl of yours, she's a damned cool hand. Suppose she gets it from her daddy."

"Her mommy, more 'n likely. Yes, I didn't know what to make of these. Mr. Dewey told me when he was done he one-eightied and flew back up the road to make sure he didn't miss nothing. He stayed on the road a longer time than I asked him to, and way, way back he came upon some other skids. Now, it may not be the same guy, but it sure looks like it to me. Same width of track, same density of color. You'd have to make a tread comparison to be sure, but as I said earlier, don't believe much in coincidence."

He handed the two photos over, and the two men looked hard at them, then back several times at the actual pocket-of-engagement sequence.

"Well," Red finally said, "that ties it up with a ribbon."

"It sure does," said Matt.

"So tell me what you make of it."

"As I say, where he's whacking her, it's hard to make it out, other than he's a good driver, so's she. The cars are banging together, speed's up near a hundred, she keeps turning inside him, he skids out — don't lose it though — and goes after her."

"Yes sir."

"But see these here? They're bad news, I'm afraid."

Bob didn't want to be here. He didn't want to find out the worst. The world was so much better for everybody if this was just one drunk or hopped-up farmboy who wanted to put a lick on another car, just like his hero, the late Dale Senior.

But that wasn't to be.

"Now here we are, ten miles before the accident, and see this here turn he made. And here's another one. He's running like hell to catch up to her, like he got the news late that she was there."

"But it's not like he's chasing her, in the

sense that he sees her and is closing," Bob said. "It means, in other words, miles before he makes eye contact, he's going like hell to catch her."

"Well, he's sure going like hell," said Matt. "He's not just running flat out for the fun of it, he's right on the edge of a very dangerous road, and take it from me you can't get there unless you're closing on the leader with two laps to go. Nobody goes that close to dying for the fun of it. Then here, this last curve, that's his boldest, and damn it's a fine piece of driving. He read the angle of the curve exactly, knew what his attack would be and how long, maybe to the tenth of a second, and he had to hold it. A tenth too long one way, he's in the trees to the left of the road, a tenth too short, he's in the trees to the right. He found what we call the ideal angle. It may not be the shortest angle, but it means he's reading the input at supertime, he knows his car like he knows his own face, he goes into the curve just fine, he keeps traction at maximum — traction is speed and control — he never slides or drifts, he's left-footing the brake while he right-foots the pedal, not easy, and at the ultimate, perfect moment he's set up to go to the floor and hit the straightaway, speeding up not slowing down, and never wastes no time correcting or recovering."

"That's good driving."

"No, sir. That's great driving. Most civilians don't know how to corner, even cops and good young racers. It takes time and some investment of guts and fender metal and a lot of good luck to learn the trick. You find that ideal angle that don't feel right, but it is right. You ride that angle, at a certain point you brake but as she starts to skid, you got to play left-foot-right-foot, making the car dance, so that you can be speeding up before you're on the straightaway 'cause if that's where you're stomping it, you're already too late. And in all this, if your timing ain't right you're upside down in flames and hoping the foam truck gets there before your hands and feet burn off, never mind the busted neck."

"I see."

"Gunny," said Red, "whoever drove your daughter off the road wasn't no kid. He was a damned good, experienced racing driver. He had all the tricks. He's way up there with the big boys like scrawny little tub-of-guts Matt there. He's a professional. What he was trying to do, he was trying to kill her."

FIVE

The Reverend Alton Grumley pronounced a mighty sermon, full of Baptist hellfire and damnation, in the meeting hall of the Piney Ridge Baptist Prayer Camp a few miles outside of Mountain City on old 167, just before it hit new 67.

He called upon God in his majesty to send wisdom to his young prodigal, he who had failed, send wisdom, humility, respect for elders, all those things a good Christian boy should show his religious mentor.

"Thou hast failed," he said, in a power-voice, all throb and vibration. "Thou hast failed because thou did not pray for guidance hard enough. Thou must pray, Brother Richard, and give the soul in totality to the man upstairs. Only then will he listen."

The Reverend was a scrawny old boy, with slicked-back hair, all pouf and vibrant with gray and hair oil, big, white, fake teeth, and dressed in a powder blue, three-piece suit from Mr. Sam's big store. His sons and nephews had a joke. "Daddy's tailor," they'd say, "is Wah Ming Chow of Number 38 Industrial Facility, Harbin, Szechwan Province, China!" and get to laughing up a fit.

"You damned boys, the devil will take you!" he'd howl in rage, and then laugh harder.

But the boys weren't there now. In fact only one parishioner listened to the Reverend. He was a raw-boned fella of indeterminate age — fellows like him could be thirty to sixty, all hardscrabble, southern school of hard knocks and rough roads, indomitable, relaxed, tougher than brass hobnails, not the sorts to get excited but exactly the sorts to avoid riling — who now sat in the front row of the meeting hall, in tight, faded jeans, beat-up boots, a blue, working-man's shirt, and a Richard Petty straw cowboy hat both shabby and cool pulled low over his eyes. He wasn't the sort who took the hat off indoors, church or no church. He had on a big pair of mogul sunglasses too, as King Richard commonly wore, and sported a mustache and a goatee, though the hair wasn't real.

"Old man, you do go on," he finally said. "I am getting extremely tired of all this show."

"You was given a job, and you failed. If I wanted failure, I'd have sent my own damn sons. They so dumb, they guarantee failure, God love 'em."

"They are dumb," said Brother Richard, so called for his resemblance to the real Richard Petty and what was assumed to be a common NASCAR heritage. "But that's okay, because they're lazy, too."

"They are good boys," said the Reverend.

"Not really," said Brother Richard.

"Anyhows, we in a porridge-pot o' trouble now."

"I agree. After all, she saw me. Not even you have seen me. If you had to describe me, you'd come up with, 'He looks like Richard.' So I guess they'd send out Richard on the circular. But by that time, I wouldn't look like Richard."

"Everyone knows that hair is phony," said the Reverend.

"It doesn't matter what they know. It only matters what they've seen."

"Anyhow, you were highly recommended to me by at least three sources. It was said by all, 'He's the best. Nobody like him.' Yet when I need you most, you fail."

"There are some things I can't control. I can't control the fact that the girl drives like a pro. She must have raced go-karts. You can learn a lot in the damn little things. Ask Danica. Who knew? I've done that job more times than you can know, and nobody ever fought so hard or made so many good decisions at speed. If the world were fair, I'd be marrying her, not trying to kill her."

"Yessir, but as I have noted in many a sermon, the world ain't fair. Not even a little bit."

"Anyhows, I am as upset as you. She saw my new face and it wasn't cheap, not in money, not in time, not in pain. She's the only one that'll identify me."

"You should have had on one of your disguises."

"I didn't have time. You called me and I was off. I had to kick hell to even catch her. Like to might have been smeared to ketchup by a logging truck, some of the turns I took."

"Whyn't you finish her? You could see the car didn't roll. If it don't roll, you got problems."

"I am not smashing a girl's head in with a rock or cutting her throat. Among other things, if you do that, then all the law knows it's not a hopped-up kid and is a murder and maybe you got state cop investigators, maybe even FBI, and lots of trouble. It only works if everybody agrees it's some kind of hit-run thing by some kind of speed-crazy, NASCAR-loving jackrabbit with the brains of a pea. That's what I'm selling. But there's an issue of what I do and what I don't do too. I don't kill up close where there's blood. It's my car against theirs, and I always win at that game. Nobody can stay in that game. If I kill up close, hell, I'm just another Grumley."

"Car agin' car, you didn't win this time, Brother Richard."

"Now I don't like that one, Rev. This whole shebang you've got set up — well, someone has set up, as I don't believe you got the native intelligence of a porcupine —"

"You are so insolent to your elders. You should respect your elders, Brother."

"Maybe next time. This whole damn thing turns on me. You need the best driver you can get for a certain job and if you don't have him, it all goes away. You don't want that. So why don't you stop cobbing on me, Alton, and pick two sons or nephews, if you can tell them apart, which I doubt — the two with the most teeth and whose eyes are far enough apart so that in certain lights they appear normal — you send them into that hospital. And since they're such smooth operators and nobody suspects nothing yet, they can just inject an air bubble into her vein and when it reaches her heart, she's gone. Then all our problems are solved, and we can do our job, git our money and our revenge, and move on."

"I hope God don't hear the disrespect in your voice," the Reverend said. "But if I'm so dumb, how come I already sent the two boys?"

Six

Vern Pye had the gift of gab and Ernie Grumley the talent of conviction. One was a nephew, one a son, though neither was aware of which category they fit into as names were sometimes misleading among the Reverend's brood. After all, the man had had seven wives and six boys per wife as per certain biblical instructions, and, if rumor was believed, he had spread his seed amply among the various sisters of the various wives, whether those sisters were married to others or not. He had a way about him and a hunger, and women, for some reason, were eager to give to him that which they thought he wanted.

They all — wives, formal and informal, legal and only by custom, sisters and husbands, the progeny — lived together far from prying eyes on a chunk of hilltop outside of Hot Springs, Arkansas. From there they did various jobs for various contacts around the South that the Reverend had inherited from generations of Grumleys before him. The Grumleys, foot soldiers to the Lord and also various interested parties. That is why they'd temporarily migrated to the Piney Ridge Baptist Prayer Camp on Route 61 in Johnson County, Tennessee, at the insistence of Alton, the patriarch.

Vern and Ernie were somewhat slicker than the usual Grumley progeny. Each was smooth in his way and not too tattooed, and the Reverend, noting talent where it happened to spring up (although, Lord, why do you test me so? That quality was rare enough), always urged them to develop their talent. Thus Vern was the superstar of his generation of Grumleys. He was an aristocrat, a Pye out of Grumley, and so his blood was bluer than any other's, uniting two lines of violent miscreants from the hinterlands of Arkansas outside Hot Springs. He had killed and would kill again, without much emotional investment, but he didn't consider himself a killer. He had vanities, and pride. He was the *compleat* criminal. He could forge, extort, swindle, steal cold, steal hot, do banks or grocery stores, do hits, administer beatings, all with the same aplomb. He liked getting over on the johns, didn't matter who or what the game was.

It helped that he was unusually handsome, with a dark head of hair and large, white spades for teeth. His eyes radiated warmth and charm; he was as smooth with a line of bullshit as he was with a Glock, and he was pretty smooth with that. He'd done a few years' hard time, where he'd basically networked, and he had three other identities going, two wives, seven children, girlfriends among the stripper and escort population in every southern state, and a thing for young girls, which he indulged at shopping malls, clubs, and fast food joints whenever he had a spare moment. He could con a twelve-year-old into a blowjob in the men's room faster than most people could count to one hundred.

Ernie was less accomplished. He was essentially a Murphy man, a fraudulent pimp who conned college boys out of their dollars and delivered zero in the sex department, in some of the Razorback State's seamier venues. Basically, in today's operation, Ernie's job was to support Vern and learn from him, which is how they found themselves, in medical scrubs under MD nametags, walking down the hallway of the Bristol General Hospital, headed toward their destination, the critical-care ward.

It was late; the place was nearly empty. It was big enough, however, so that the concept of "stranger" could apply. No nurse, for instance, could know all the medical personnel by name or face and could therefore be counted upon to yield before slickness, sureness of authority, and the steady guidance and charisma of an experienced confidence man.

It'll be easy.

No one suspects a thing.

The girl is an accident victim, not a murder survivor.

No security, no suspicion, no fear.

Thus the two men ambled happily, making eye contact, issuing warm "Hellos" and "Say, there, how's the boy?"s as they coursed through the fourth floor's spotless hallways. They even stopped now and then for a cup of coffee, to assure a patient on a walker, and to examine bedside charts. They took pulses, looked into eyes, felt throats, just like on the television doctor shows.

When they reached Nikki, it would be a simple matter. Vern, a little brighter and that much more ambitious, was to calmly reach into his pocket and remove a number seven hypodermic filled with air. He had practiced on the skin of a grapefruit all afternoon. He was to look for a blue artery that led to and not from the heart, plump up the flesh just a bit, gently inject the needle, draw some blood to make certain he'd hit the mother lode, then cram the plunger forward. This would put a bubble the size of a small nuclear missile in her bloodstream and it would jet to her heart and explode it. Meanwhile, Ernie would race to the nurses' station yelling "Get an arrest team STAT! She's lost rhythm!"

Then they'd quietly turn and continue their rounds.

The trick, as Vern had patiently explained to Ernie, was to do nothing suddenly. If you moved fast, if your body had a shred of fear or hesitation, it would register with witnesses who were otherwise oblivious. It was the first key of the con, to sell the mark on your authenticity, which was always done with gentle insistence, assuming correct subtextual details. For example: If you were on a job like this, you made damned certain your hands were very clean, almost pink, along with your ears, your face, any visible patch of skin. Docs become docs because they hate filth, disease, laziness, clumsiness. It's how they feel like God. So to pass as one you had to play by the rules of the game. Another issue Vern was very big on was shoes. What kind of shoes do doctors wear? People notice shoes even if they don't realize they do. Thus they'd parked for a bit outside the hospital in the staff lot, and noted men of a certain age, whom they took to be docs and not orderlies of some sort (your younger fellas), and noted a lot of Rockport wingtips. So they drove to the mall — not to Mr. Sam's where all the shoes would have been made by Wah Ming Chow when she wasn't hand-cutting powder blue suits for the Reverend — found a Rockport store, and paid for a pair each, one cordovan wing-tips, the other less fashionable, beige walkers. They scuffed the shoes against the asphalt of the mall parking lot because the docs were parsimonious and wore each pair unto death.

Now, on those new-but-old Rockports, they slowly approached the girl's room. It was so close; it was two rooms away, which they'd discovered after an earlier quick stride down the hallway, reading names on the doors while feigning to look for a drink of water.

Here was where your lesser cons would give up the ghost. They wouldn't play it out straight. They'd see that the room was so damned close and that the nurses were sitting at their stations on the floor without paying any attention at all to them and they'd sort of go into git-'er-done panic. They'd go straight to the girl's room, do the deed, and get out of Dodge. Yeah, but that's where it goes wrong. An orderly is on the way to the john and he happens to look down the hall and he sees something he doesn't hardly ever see, which is a doc moving fast. Docs don't move fast, not unless it's the emergency ward and some poor fool is bleeding out or going into advanced vapor lock. Docs have too much dignity to move fast. So he goes to investigate and walks in and sees the needle going into her arm and he says, Hey what? and Ernie has to pop him with his nickle-plated Python 2.5 inch, and the whole thing goes up in flames, and Vern and Ernie end up at the wrong end of another needle somewhere down the line.

No sir, the Reverend didn't raise no fools for sons or cousins or whatever.

So they played it out by good con discipline, riding the gag hard. They dipped in on Mr. X and saw that he was fine, then had a nice visit with Mrs. Y and noted that her color had improved and got a nice smile out of her for the comment, even if she had no idea who in hell they were, until at last, after a quick check on Mr. Z, who was comatose as well, they reached the doorway of SWAGGER, NIKKI, ACCIDENT VICTIM, and were about to —

"Say —"

They looked up, puzzled but not riled.

"Say there, excuse me, gentlemen."

The speaker was a man in a blue suit and a crewcut, followed by another gentleman in a black suit but the same crewcut. He wasn't a doc, as he was moving too fast and looked a little out of place. And when he got there, he was out-of-breath.

"Whoa," he said, "more running than I'm used to, plus a terrible drive over from Knoxville. Anyway, sorry, don't mean to be a bother, we just got here."

"You're?"

"Sorry again, Ron Evers, Pinkerton Detective Agency, Knoxville office. We're setting up security for this patient, here, let me show you this."

He struggled goofily, unsure to be busting doctors, but better safe than sorry, and he pulled out a comic-book badge just like Deputy Dawg's and some kind of photo ID with an official PINKERTON imprimatur.

"I'll have to see some ID before I can allow entrance."

"Son, I'm Dr. Torrence, I'm on my rounds," said Vern smoothly.

"So sorry, doctor, really I am, but I'll have to get an administrator here to verify you.

Pain in the ass, I know, and it's your hospital, and all that, but her father hired our firm and his instructions were very clear. No entrance without verification. I've already liaisoned with hospital security, if you're wondering. I'll call the hospital admin right now," and he lifted a cell.

Something scalding went off inside Vern's head. In his younger days, he would have hit the young security guy in the throat, then kicked the other in the balls. Then he would have kicked each in the head until he was sure they were dead. Then he would have killed the girl with the knife he carried. But Vern was mellower now. Even as he felt the frustration build and build like a steam engine about to blow, he kept it together.

"Well," he said, "no need for that. I'll go get the duty nurse and she'll get this straightened out."

"Yes sir, that's fine."

"Come on, Jack," he said to his cousin or brother or whatever kin Ernie was to him, "we'll get the nurse. I *hate* it when procedure is violated."

And the two Grumleys walked ever so slowly down the hall in their Rockports to the elevator and waited ever so slowly for it to come, Vern thinking, I need to kill something or get laid, preferably by a kid, fast!

SEVEN

He called her from Knoxville the next afternoon.

"Where have you been? My God, what is going on?"

"Sorry, it's been busy. She's fine, or as good as can be expected. The brain work is all fine, she's just unconscious. They say they usually come out of these things in a week or two, and recovery is almost always 100 percent. So it's looking very positive here, medically."

"Bob, I called the hospital, she's been *moved.*"

"That's my doing. The doctors agreed it was medically sound, and so I've got her in a private hospital here in Knoxville."

"What is —"

"Uh, there was an incident."

"I don't —"

"Unclear, and maybe I'm overreacting. But the Pinkerton agent —"

"Pinkerton agent?"

"I did some checking and I'm not sure I buy the story about the redneck kid in the pickup anymore. At least not wholly. So I hired Pinkertons to provide 24/7 plain-clothes security, three teams of two. Anyhow, as the first team was going on duty, they stopped a couple of doctors on their rounds. No big deal, nobody thought anything about it, but the docs went off to get administrative authorization and never returned. So I asked, and nobody knows who they were. Nobody got a good look at them. Only evidence they were doctors was the green scrubs and the nametags, but hell, anyone can buy a pair of surgical scrubs. It didn't sit right."

"So you moved her. That was wise."

"I think it's okay if you fly in now. I don't want to give you the name of the hospital until you're in town. But I'd stay on the north side, in a suburb. She needs her mother. She looks so sad, all banged up, all those wires and tubes, so still. Breaks my heart."

"She's strong. She'll come through this, I know it."

"Okay, you have my number. When you get in here and get booked in a hotel, call me, and I'll come by. Meanwhile, I've got some nosing around to do."

"What is it?"

He told her at length about the tire treads, the interpretation of the NASCAR fellows, the general indifference of the sheriff's department, the intensifying traffic and crowding as the big race day approached, and the town filling up with campers, celebrants, drinkers, rowdy kids, and other assorted pilgrims.

"So I mean to look into it. I know you think I'm paranoid but —"

He was surprised at what came next.

"You listen to me a moment. You have gone on many dangerous adventures, leaving me to raise the child, and now I have another child to raise. Yes, I think you can turn paranoid. But this time I am paranoid too, because it is my daughter involved. So you're not working off some crazy sense of honor or something you think you owe your long-dead father or something left over from a war nobody remembers. You're working for me. If you think someone tried to kill our daughter, Bob, then you find them and you stop them. You stop them from harming *our* daughter or anyone's daughter."

"I will do that," he said. "Oh, and one more thing."

"Yes?"

"Bring some guns."

Eight

Bob didn't really approve of newspapers and had certainly never been in the office of one before. But that's what his daughter had wanted, and as he looked at the city room, with its ranks of messy desks, its knots of insouciant young people, its phone obsessives, its listless copy editors, its harassed junior editors, its earnest techies to service the computers in mysterious fashion, he wondered why it had meant so much to her, ever since she was a child. There was nothing in his family to account for such a leaning; maybe there was a writer tucked away in some branch of Julie's, but he'd never heard of such a thing. But he knew this: She loved it, she lived, dreamed, breathed, and ate it.

Okay, sweetie, he told himself. If this is what you want, I will try and get it back for you.

He sat in a conference room — glass-walled, affording a view of the newsroom and the staff, right next to the managing editor's office — as Jim Gustofson, the managing editor, a tough gal named Jennifer something, and Nikki's immediate editor, briefed him on what she'd been up to.

The gist of it was that Nikki was the cops reporter, and her specialty was the crystal meth craze that now gripped rural America, as it played across northeastern Tennessee and southwestern Virginia. She'd done a prize-winning story on the children of crystal meth distributors, who are put in foster homes when their parents are arrested. She knew the sheriffs of most of the seven immediate counties, she knew a lot of the knock-down-the-door cops, she knew the social services people, the welfare people, the educators, for the problem impacted all these areas. The stuff was pure shit; its only advantage was that it was cheap and the high it granted was intense if short lived. Once in a while you put your baby in the oven or ran over your grandmother with a lawnmower on the impression she was a troll halfling from the realm of Zelazny. But generally, like dope everywhere of every kind, it made its users useless slackers who sat around all day figuring out how to get a few nickels together for the next fix, or kitchen chemists in trailer parks who tried to cook it up themselves, all too often blowing a crater into the earth and themselves straight to hell. A few shrewdies had big labs that made what real money was available in the down-home heroin racket.

"She was preparing another big story on the shape of the problem in the immediate Tri-cities area. She'd been visiting the local police entities, trying to get a sense of what she was doing."

"Sir, are these people dangerous?"

"Well, as they say, they only kill their own kind. Turf wars, the occasional hardhead who goes for the assault rifle when the raid team shows, bitterness over price hikes or debts owed. You know that easy money, stupid people, and hard times have a way of creating misery. Your daughter was the witness to all that. She's damned good at her job. She'll be moving to a bigger city soon, I'm betting. It has been a pleasure to work with her and watch her grow."

"Yes sir. But was there anything specific about Johnson County? Some particular area she was looking at. I think I want to go poke around. It's my nature. Annoys the hell out of people, I know, but can't be helped."

"You don't agree with the police report?

Thelma Fielding is a good cop."

"She is and I liked her very much. It just don't — excuse me — doesn't sit right with me. That's why I have moved her to another hospital." He didn't bother to tell them it was in another city. Reporters talk, people listen, that much he knew.

"Yes, she said she might have to go back," said the woman editor, Jennifer. "Johnson County is so far from everything it's a kind of a bad joke around here about the cultural tendencies of the rural working class, or these days in this economy, non-working class."

"You mean the trailer trash, ma'am. I'm proud to say I am one of them pure and simple, but you don't need to pull punches with me. I know they make the best soldiers, farmers, and family people in the world, but that same stubbornness and willingness to risk makes them sick-bad-ugly-tempered boils on the butt of humanity if they choose the dark side."

"We'd never put that in the paper, but yes, that's what we're talking about. So the meth problem is particularly bad in Johnson. That's where you see your most grotesque crimes and some of the ugliest violence. But last year they elected a reformer for sheriff, a county man named Colonel Reed Wells."

"I have heard the name."

"Handsome guy, famous because he was a Ranger officer in the war in Baghdad and won some kind of medal. A star?"

"Silver Star?" Bob asked.

"Yes, I think that's right? Were you in the army, Mr. Swagger? You have something of the military about you."

"Not in the army, no ma'am. I did a spell in another branch."

"Well, it shows. I wish some more of my reporters had the discipline and the organization that the military teaches so well. Anyhow, Reed Wells was in the forefront of the fight against the drug. He's your dynamo type. To the accompaniment of much publicity, he has acquired a helicopter from the army on some kind of Justice Department grant that passes surplus material on to police agencies. He's organized a first-rate raid team, all very gung-ho. You know, guys in black with hoods and machine guns. He searches for the labs from the air most days, then coordinates with ground, then he hits 'em from above just as the ground team hits 'em from two sides. Very commandolike. Nikki said she felt like she was in Vietnam, though I don't know how she could know anything about Vietnam."

"Maybe she saw some old books," said Bob.

"But here's the thing. Johnson County leads the region in the number of meth labs raided, the number of arrests, the number of prosecutions. But the odd part is, the price of meth in Johnson hasn't gone up, it's stayed the same.

"Now why would that be? If the supply is drying up, the price would rise. Yet Nikki had discovered from someone in an abuse program that the stuff is just as plentiful and just as economical. That means that either a) outside sources were bringing it in, or b) there were a lot more meth labs than anybody thought, or c) there was some kind of superlab, capable of taking up the slack, that nobody had discovered yet. Finding the superlab: There's your Pulitzer Prize for investigative reporting, and there's your ticket to the *Washington Post.*"

"I see," said Bob. "Tell me, if I wanted to figure out what she did the last day before the event, what would I look for? What does a reporter carry? A notebook, I'm guessing."

"She had a notebook, yes. Most reporters today have laptops that they carry with them. Then they can plug their notes straight into our computer system, and it saves copying and reduces mistakes. So there should be a computer, too. And of course a cellphone. It might have numbers registered that she called that day. The police would have recovered all those things from the accident site, though of course they may be damaged or whatever. Or they may be temporarily impounded, as a part of Thelma's investigation. But Thelma's a decent person; if you want your daughter's things back, I'm sure she'll cooperate."

"You must have some sort of list of names and numbers out there — people involved in the meth business, I don't mean dealers, I mean all the social services people, the drug rehab programs, that sort of thing. She might have talked to them."

"I can get you an official list. I'll talk to Bill Carter, he did cops before Nikki got here, and I know he gave her access to his Rolodex. I'll get a list from him."

"That would be very helpful."

"Mr. Swagger," said Jim Gustofson, "I can certainly appreciate your anger at the inability of the sheriff's department to bring this thing to a close quickly. But I'm wondering if you really want to go up there on your own and start demanding answers and kicking in doors."

"I can't just sit around. It's not my nature, sir."

"With all due respect, sir, I see where Nikki's aggressive nature as a reporter comes from. But I would caution all my reporters not to take chances and I have to say the same to you. The people up there don't like strangers, and they have, as has been noted, violent proclivities. You could find yourself in a lot of trouble fast. I'd hate to see a tragedy become a double tragedy and you end up on the front page of our newspaper."

"Good advice, sir. I wish I could follow it. Most would. But sorry to say, I can't."

Bob called the hospital to check on Nikki, called Idaho and saw that Julie had already left for the trip to Knoxville, and then started the drive out to Johnson County but soon found himself ensnarled in traffic. He pulled over, got out a map and investigated various alternative routes, but all seemed to take him too far to the west and then back around. He decided to bull through straight down Volunteer Parkway on the premise that once he passed the speedway, traffic would lessen considerably and he could make up for lost time and still get out to Mountain City by midafternoon, where he'd begin with Detective Thelma and maybe even get a chance to meet up with the hero, Sheriff Reed Wells, Silver Star winner and reformer.

The traffic crawled along, and the closer he got to the speedway, the more festive Bristol turned. He felt like he was at some gathering of clans or tribes or something. There was a feeling of celebration in the air and no shortage of alcohol to fuel the glee. Pennants hung across the road, all the street lamps had been festooned with portraits of blasting Chargers or Fusions or Camrys roaring through clouds of dust, blazing bright with primal colors, looking for all the world like fighter planes hungry for the kill. Flags of a hundred colors flapped and danced in the wind against a bright blue sky. Every lawn bore a sign offering parking, and the cost increased hugely the closer he got to the speedway. The far hills were carpeted with Rec-Vs, SUVs, and tents, as a whole new population of occupiers and spenders moved in. They were like the Lakota Sioux just before the Little Big Horn, only in vans and sleepers instead of wikiups. Crowds thronged the walkways, and seeped into the slowed traffic. Everywhere, entrepreneurs had erected booths or tents, offering souvenirs of the fun, blankets, hats, posters, rental radio sets for eavesdropping on the chatter between driver and crew chief, food of every sort, drink of every sort — no problem with liquor licensing down here, everybody just sold whatever they wanted — straw hats after the famous beat-up Richard Petty configuration, neckerchiefs, sweatshirts, T-shirts charting the rise of the Confederacy. Damn, these folks knew how to party. No wonder they called it a nation. It was a hootenanny combined with Oktoberfest with an office party with a safe return from thirteen months in the land of bad things with a Chinese New Year with a hoedown with a rock concert and, oh yeah, the VJ-Day feeling his old man must have had after surviving — if barely — five invasions on five islands across the Pacific.

He shook his head at the frenzy of it; the intensity seemed to have increased three- or fourfold since his visit with USMC Matt and his crew chief, Red Nichols, a few days earlier, and he saw that dropping by to see them now was all but an impossibility; they were sealed off by crowds and madness as the big day approached.

Finally, he topped a low hill and saw his principal obstacle just ahead. It loomed gigantically, dominating all that was before or around it, and he saw it was situated a couple of hundred yards to the left of Volunteer Parkway. He would have to pass it to get beyond. The Bristol Motor Speedway looked like some kind of huge ship from space that had crash-landed in this part of the Shenandoah. It had a kind of familiarity to it he could not again place, but then it flashed clear. Some movie with Will Smith as a marine fighter pilot, but that wasn't but a small part of it. It was about an invasion from space, and these huge ships came down and dominated the earth. The F-15s fired their Mavericks at it, and the missiles just popped on the perimeter because of some kind of magic shield. It was stupid, he realized, and wondered why on earth he'd wasted the time and money. Maybe the USMC fighter-pilot thing, but now he recalled after Will and the boys had put the old USMC boot up the ass of the whatever-they-weres from wherever-they-came, the big ships crashed and burned. That's what it looked like, a giant space ship, all chrome and sleek streamline and immense scale and circularity, some kind of man-structure, too regular by far for nature, crashed and burning askew in some place where it didn't belong, a green valley with whispers of blue mountain ridges to the east and the west.

In fact, it looked like nature had somehow been scrubbed from the scene by the thing, so dominating was the man-made structure and so active the little city that had grown up in its shadows. But then he noticed, almost as an afterthought, a high foothill, carpeted in forest, rising above the speedway. It was about a mile off, on his left, separated from the speedway by a plain now peopled with a frenzied mob, where booths and exhibits and tents had been set up. Hell, you hardly noticed the hill at all — this big lump of verticality was all but banished from vision and notice by the hugeness of the speedway and all the frenzy it sustained. He thought, Wonder why they haven't knocked that old pile of rocks and trees down and put condos in right there.

Anyhow, he struggled down through the thick stop-and-go of Volunteer Parkway until he reached its closest point to the speedway itself, and saw that here too, everything was on an upswing. The grinding buzz of the cars qualifying inside — maybe his new pal Matt MacReady was on the track now, sailing along at about thirty-five degrees at 185 per — filled the air, giving every physical thing, including Bob's rental car and his eardrums, a kind of vibration. Baby sister, the boys were burning rubber and high-test today!

What was new today was that some kind of trailer park had been constructed in the immediate vicinity of the structure itself and proudly wore a kind of midway carnival banner that said NASCAR VILLAGE.

It was all jammed up with pilgrims of the faith. He saw that it was a little neighborhood composed entirely of trailers, trucks, and vans that had the specialized capability of converting to retail outlet by opening up into a kind of high counter. From behind that counter, dozens of men and women, all in NASCAR regalia, sold yet more souvenirs, most all of it driver oriented, worshiping the cult of the guy that pressed the steel around the oval at speed and risked death in the process. He had time to examine the setup at length, because the traffic had stalled almost to a creep, and it wasn't long before he noted the Matt MacReady trailer, just as big and busy as any of them, with young Matt's face emblazoned everywhere and the USMC 44 digital-camouflage pattern spread everywhere.

You couldn't but think about the money. If it was a religion, part of the observance was the cash transaction, as dollars were traded for official NASCAR gear and the official stuff evidently demanded a premium

110

over the Chinese crap that the imitators and hustlers sold in their little stalls across the way.

Someone's sure getting rich, he thought. All that damn money. Turns people to fools.

Then at last the traffic cleared, and he sped away from NASCAR Village and the speedway toward the green mountains ahead.

NINE

Why, O Heavenly Father, why, he be-
seeched. Lord, how thou tests me. Lord, I
am thy humble servant, please send me
relief.

God was busy. He didn't answer.

So the Reverend Alton Grumley was left
to his own bitter devices, and they told him,
goddamnit, things wasn't happening as
they's supposed to. Curse that girl!

He left his tiny office off the gym floor of
the rec center of the Piney Ridge Baptist
Prayer Camp and stepped out into the
heavy, pressing heat of an August afternoon
in Tennessee, and in a yard meant to accommodate Baptist jumping jacks and
deep-knee bends, saw before him sweaty
men struggling with an entirely different set
of rigors.

"Jesus Christ, no," shouted Brother Richard to a gaggle of Grumleys who fought
with a device at the base of a large truck. It

was a graceful, but surprisingly heavy, steel construction that rode its own smallish steel wheels. It was called a hydraulic jack, and was used for lifting the left or right half of a vehicle off the ground. It was crude, old, disobedient, and annoyingly stubborn. It hated Grumleys and Grumleys hated it. What they had to do with it, they had to do fast. Getting Grumleys to do something fast was like getting cats to dance. It just hardly didn't ever happen.

"You monkeys!" screamed Brother Richard to all the sweaty, tattooed Grumley beef — the sun was high, the sky cloudless; bugs and skeeters, drawn by the stench of flushed Grumley flesh, swooped and darted. "You can't do nothing right. You, balding guy, what's your name again?"

"Cletus Grumley, Brother Richard."

"You don't come across when he's trying to get the air wrench on the lugs. You wait till he's got 'em coming out, then you git on around. It's gotta work smoothly or you get all tangled up, the tires roll away, and many a race, in fact most races, are lost in the pits where the big muscle boys like you haven't practiced enough, and it ends up looking like a Chinese fire drill."

"Yes sir. But Mosby stepped on my heel, Brother Richard, which is why I done

113

spilled forward. Wasn't going forward, wasn't meaning to, just got tripped up by Mosby."

"Mosby, you a cousin or a son? Or maybe both?"

"Don't know, sir. Heard it both ways. Not sure which gal is my real ma. Was raised by Aunt Jessie, who may have been the Reverend's third wife, or maybe his fourth. I tripped on Cletus because someone, either Morgan or Allbright, pushed me."

"Morgan, Allbright, slow down," said Richard. *"Slooowwwww downnnn."* And he tried to indicate calmness, lack of excitement, craziness by a kind of universal gesture for calming, pressing both flattened hands down as if to say, "Bring it down a notch."

"It's Morgan's sweat," said Allbright, "it stinks so it makes me want to throw up."

"Ain't my sweat," said the one who had to be Morgan, "it's your own damn farts you be smelling, Morgan farts more than any white man in this world and most Negroes."

The issue was syncopation. An air-driven power wrench and the high-strength hydraulic jack had to be dragged sixty feet, set under the edge of the truck, and the truck jacked up. The power wrench had to tear loose the lugs. The old tires had to be yanked off and dumped, the new ones slammed on, the lugs power-wrenched tight. It had to be done fast, really fast, and the boys had been trying so hard. But maybe this wasn't a Grumley sort of thing. There was no one else, though, time was short, and Race Day was approaching.

"Okay, boys," said Brother Richard, "you knock off now. We'll do it again later when it's cooler. And don't let Allbright eat no beans tonight, or cabbage neither."

Richard, wiping his neck with a red handkerchief, came over to the porch where he'd seen the Reverend watching grumpily.

"Well, sir," he asked, "you tell me. Were these boys just raised by pigs or were they suckled by them too? Or maybe sired?"

"You are the Whore of Babylon, Brother Richard. That wicked tongue will get you smitten, Brother Richard."

"Not till after you've had your Race Day fun, old man. We both know that. So I will amuse myself as I see fit until we have done our jobs, and by that time, you will be so rich you won't have any thought for Brother Richard and his sharp tongue. Now, what's going on with the girl?"

"I have just heard," the Reverend said, "that that daddy of hers has moved her."

"Damn!" said Richard.

"Damn is right. She wakes up and starts singing, we are fried in batter. Maybe she won't wake up before we move. Or maybe she'll die or something."

"You can't take that gamble. You know well as I do, that girl is trouble. She has seen my face and she knows enough to tip off your plan; she makes a single phone call to ask a single question to someone who knows a little something, and we are finished. You're supposed to be a crime lord. Do something criminal."

"Well, son, that's the problem. If we find her — she's got to be in either Knoxville or Raleigh, as he moved her by ambulance, that much I know — if we find her and make sure, then we expose completely the idea that what happened to her was part of a plan, or a necessity to protect a plan. And maybe that makes all their security go up. And the plan is based on their overconfidence that no further security is needed, as you well know."

"I do know, just as I know," said Brother Richard, "that the plan is damned smart. Don't believe nobody never did what you're trying to do the way you're doing it before, so how could they figure it out? It's so damned smart, I also know you, Grumley, didn't think it up. No sign of a Grumley pawprint anywhere on it. Your ilk may screw it up if they can't get the goddamned tires switched off fast enough and we become peas in a pod for the police shooters. But I think they'll just manage it." Like many men in his profession, Brother Richard had a clear view of what was necessary for his own survival.

"No," he explained, "you can't just hope she doesn't wake up or if she wakes up, she doesn't remember. Even if she wakes up in six months, she may know enough to lead law enforcement straight to you, and I know you'll roll over on me like a mangy dog with an itch. That, plus she saw my new face. I can't have her helping a police artist by drawing a good picture of my new face. I spent a fortune on this face and it hurt like hell for months. I need a new face to operate, you understand? Old man, you have to act on this now and permanently."

"Mark 2:11. 'Get up off your pallet and go to your house.' Rise, you cripple, on the strength of faith in the Lord. Walk, pray, work, and triumph. If the Lord is our shepherd, we shall not want."

"It ain't wanting I'm worried on. It's arresting. They git me, I go to the chair. Then it's frying."

"You think you know all, Brother Richard. Even dumb old Reverend Alton knows it's now a needle."

"Chair, needle, you still end up dead. I am the Sinnerman, as I have explained. I do not want to face a day of reckoning. I will run from the Lord and try and hide in the sea or the moon or the mountain all on that day. You, you've got no worries."

"I can face my Lord proudly."

"Of course. Because you were born a snake and someone put a mouse before you and you ate it. You liked it, and that was it. You became an eater of mice. More mice, please, that was your code and you never gave a damn about anything. More and more mice you ate, and you never thought of the family life of the mice, the culture, the fantasies and religious structures of the mice, the history, theory, and music of the mice. For you, it was an easy enough thing, it was your nature. You eat mice. End of story.

"Now me, I *chose* to become a snake, for my own born-in-hell reasons. So I know that mice have as much right to life as I do, and that they feel every pain and fear and hatred that I do, love their kids, make the world go on, fight in wars, work in or build factories or houses. I empathize with mice. So when I eat a mouse, I know what agony I release in the world and knowing that, I take pleasure in it. Your code: More mice, please. Mine: I revel in the agony I release, and it suits a certain twisted-sister part of my brain, it fulfills me. That, Reverend, and I am proud to say it, *that* is sin."

"I cannot believe a blasphemer like you, Brother Richard, thinks it appropriate to lecture me on sin. You must wear the number of the beast somewhere on your body."

"No one knows less about sin than a Grumley. Y'all are basically animals. You may not even be mammals, I'm not sure. You just do what your instincts tell you, and in a funny way, it is God's will. Lord, what snakes these Grumleys be."

"Hail, Hail, the Gang's All Here" announced itself for one moment, interrupting this important eschatological dialogue, and of course it was the Reverend's cellphone, which he took out of the inside breast pocket of his powder blue Chinese suit.

"Hallelujah," he said. "You sure? Hallelujah!"

He snapped the phone shut.

"It seems that damn girl's father has showed up and is asking questions. Oh, Lord, another test."

Fuck, thought Brother Richard.

"I will send Carmody and B.J. to watch on him. If we have to, we'll have to take him down. He is old and harmless, can't hardly walk straight, his hair's all grayed out, but you never can tell."

Another mouse, thought Brother Richard.

TEN

"Glad you came by," said Detective Thelma Fielding, putting out a hand which turned out to conceal a strong grip.

"Should have worn a gas mask," said Bob.

"Ain't it the truth. You get used to it."

She was referring to a strong scent of atomized carbon that filled the air and left a sheen of grit on all the flat, polished surfaces. Clearly it had drifted over from the coal yard next to the sheriff's department, which sat in the old train station that had been converted three years earlier when the passenger service closed down.

"Nobody foresaw that when they started dumping coal there. Now we've had OSHA in here six days a week, and they finally decided to condemn this old building. A shame, it was a nice building once. Now it's got grit everywhere and nobody can stand it. Next spring, we move into a new building across town."

"Well, that's something. Must be hell on white glove occasions."

She laughed at his joke, which even he didn't think was that funny. Then she said, "I have some news for you."

"That's great," said Bob.

He sat at her desk in the sheriff's department, seeing it was neatly kept with a stack of files in an ONGOING vertical holder. There were a couple of trophies as well, displaying a little gold man holding a pistol atop a plastic, imitation-marble pedestal, reminding him that Thelma had won some shooting competitions, which perhaps explained her fancy .45 in its strange plastic holster. He decided to try and get a gander at the inscriptions on them, but couldn't from his angle. She was the same as before, khakis and a polo shirt, her gun held tight to her waist in that plastic holster, her arms oddly strong, as had been her grip. Her ducktail blonde hair had just been worked on and her face was tan, her eyes expressive.

"Also, Sheriff Wells is in, and I think you want to meet him, don't you, Mr. Swagger?"

"Yes ma'am."

"Well, the best news is, we got a paint and tire match from the state police crime lab in Knoxville. Just came in."

She reached over, took a file marked SWAGGER NIKKI, INCIDENT REPORT CF-112, opened it, and took out a faxed form.

"They say it's a color called cobalt silver, found on Chrysler Corporation vehicles, notably the Dodge Charger, the Magnum, and the Chrysler 300, their muscle cars. The tire is a standard Goodyear 59-F, and damned if that doesn't coordinate with a stolen car of a week earlier, a cobalt silver '05 Charger. Lots of Chargers go missing this time of year, because the Charger is the big hoss of NASCAR and every punk kid or crankhead is in a Charger kind of mood. So this one was stolen in Bristol, and my guess is, whatever kid did it got himself liquored up and went out looking for someone to intimidate that night. As I say, I have my snitches working. I will circularize, but usually folks don't take stolen cars to body shops, so I doubt that will pay off. They just dump 'em in the deep woods and maybe we find 'em and maybe we don't, and if we do find 'em, maybe we can take prints and maybe we can't, and if we can, maybe we can ID the car and maybe we can't. Probably can't. But I know who steals cars around these parts, and I've got some fellas you wouldn't invite to dinner or let your daughter date looking into it. So I'm sure we'll come up with a name and then we'll go visit him."

"I hope you let me come along on that one, Detective."

"Mr. Swagger, you don't have some vigilante-kickass thing in mind, do you? We can't let that happen and if you —"

"No, no, ma'am, an old coot like me? No ma'am, I know my limits. I just want to be as involved in this as possible."

"Well, we'll see. Can't make any promises. Probably not a good idea, but I am noted for sometimes making the wrong decision. More to the point, when your daughter awakes, we'll want to interview her. What's the word on that?"

Bob gave her a brief summary of Nikki's medical situation, leaving out the detail that he'd moved her, leaving out as well the results of his independent investigations.

"You will call me when she's ready to talk, sir? I know you've moved her and I am not even going to ask where, because that's your business, but I know you will call me as soon as an interview is possible."

"You don't miss much, do you, Detective?"

"Miss things all the damned time, but try not to. Supposed to pay attention, that's what they pay me for."

She smiled, her face lit up, and Bob noticed what a damned attractive woman she was.

"Okay," she said, "let's go and see the boss."

The office said war. War was in the pictures, the officer in lean camouflages standing with an M4 next to Middle Eastern ruins or in front of huge vehicles with guns everywhere, some airborne, some tread-borne, all desert tan, all speaking of war. A plaque with medals on the wall said war, the Silver Star the biggest of them, but there were others, impressive, a collection of a man who'd been in hard places, taken his fair share of risks and been shot at much, and had lived to tell about it.

Sheriff Wells was tall, thin, hard, and tan, with close-cropped graying hair, sharp, dark eyes, and a languid way of draping himself, as if to say that having seen most things, nothing on earth would be of much surprise. He wore the brown of the Johnson County Sheriff's Department, with a gold star on his lapel, and a stock Glock pistol in his holster, as well as the usual duty getup of the police officer: the radio unit with curly cord mic attached to his shirt lapel, the taser, the cuffs; none of it taken off, because he had to set the example to his men and women that the gear can save your life. You wear it all the time, that's what you do, comfort is not a part of the bargain.

"Mr. Swagger," he said after the firm handshake and the direct look to the eyes without evasion or charm, "nice to meet you, though of course I wish the circumstances could be better. How is your daughter at this point?"

Bob told him, succinctly, keeping it tight and straight, as if he were himself back in service, reporting to a superior.

"Well, we all hope she's going to be all right. I hope Detective Fielding has kept you abreast of our efforts. If you need any help, please feel free to contact us. Sometimes a criminal act is harder on the victim's close relatives than on the victim herself. I know how the thought that someone tried to hurt your child can haunt a father or a mother. So please, feel free to call us. For our part, we'll work hard to keep you in the loop. I know how tough it can be to go weeks without hearing a thing from the police. I've ordered all my officers to call each victim or next-of-kin once a week to keep them up-to-date on any investigation or legal proceedings. That's our policy, and maybe you've guessed that although I am a sheriff by appointment I am still a full-bird colonel by inclination, and when I set a policy it is followed."

"You sound like a straight talker, Sheriff, so can I ask you a straight question or two and set my mind to ease?"

"You surely can. Go ahead, Mr. Swagger."

"I expressed this to Detective Fielding, as well. I know you're all caught up in busting meth labs and you've got this big race in Bristol and you're part of the manpower commitment for security on such a big deal, and I do worry if there'll be time to investigate my daughter's situation hard, given all that."

"It's true most of our issues are manpower issues, that plus the goddamned coal dust on everything. But given the size of the department, it's a hard thing, patrolling a county that's several hundred square miles in area, most of it wooded, much of it mountainous, what with our problems with narcotics interdiction and this damned race. So we've got a lot on our plates. But please know that I try and run a professional department, and we will give this thing our best effort as time allows. My motto is: No back burner in my department. *Everything's* front burner in Johnson County. You have my word on that."

"Thank you, Sheriff."

"Now, I did want to say something to you. Detective Fielding mentioned to me that you had these doubts, which are entirely appropriate, because I know how upsetting something of this nature might be. But she also said that you had mentioned poking around on your own."

"That is my nature, sir. I am a physical man. Though you may still hear some Arkansas in my voice, I live in the West, and in the West, we are used to doing things for ourselves. It's not that I doubt Detective Fielding, or the department. I just know, however, that there's only so many hours in a day, and there are pressures on you all the time. So, yes, it was my idea to poke around a bit. Is that a problem?"

The sheriff said, "Look, Mr. Swagger, I don't mean to be disrespectful, but that newspaper and your daughter weren't beloved among some people around here, any more than I am. I take my chances, I suppose you could say she took her chances. She was focusing a light on methamphetamine in Johnson, and folks don't like that. If I had known she was going to some of the places she went — she was a brave girl, I don't think there's any doubt about that — I might have cautioned her or sent a unit into the vicinity just in case. Now it looks like you might be poking in those places too. I'm talking the places where the meth addicts do business, where the trade is practiced, where the stuff is cooked, all of them unsavory places, all of them volatile. So I really don't want to be worried about you too. My mission is to close these places down, not look after an older fellow in over his head."

"I see what you're saying. Still, if someone tried to hurt my daughter, I'd want to get him off the street and into jail as fast as —"

"Sir, you might rile somebody, and a fellow of your age wouldn't stand much of a chance against young toughs with secrets to hide. Were you in the service?"

"Did a spell in the marines a while back," Bob said.

"Well, don't let that give you delusions of grandeur. Some of these hardscrabble Tennessee boys are tougher than nails and they can go off fast and do some bad damage. Put some liquor in 'em or some crystal or both hootch and crystal and they can be downright mean, even murderous. I'd hate to find you beaten to a pulp in a ditch or, worse, dead in a ditch."

"Me too," said Bob.

"I was a soldier for many years, Mr. Swagger. I was executive officer for an armored combat brigade and went to Iraq twice, three times if you count my time in the sand in the first war when I was a lieutenant. It's part of my brain. And I still am a soldier, only now the war's against crystal meth. But I have sadly seen a lot of violent death in my profession. There's a saying — 'When the shit happens, it happens fast' — that's entirely accurate. I'm telling you, around here in some areas, it can go to combat fast. Combat is fast and scary and it takes a trained professional to survive, much less prevail, in that environment."

Bob sat still, working hard to keep his face uninteresting. But he knew that colonels were very rarely in combat. They supervised, they controlled, they kept radio contact, they took reports, they laid plans and bawled out lieutenants and captains when things went wrong. But they didn't look through the scope, squeeze off the round, and watch a man jack hard then melt into sheer animal death. They didn't see what the shells did to the people they caught in the open, how it made a mockery out of any notion of human nobility when you were just looking at freshly butchered meat. They didn't know boys who'd never been fucked, not even once, died screaming and calling for mommy. There was a whole lot about war colonels didn't know.

"Yes sir."

"Do you get my drift?"

"You are trying to be polite, but you are telling me to keep my nose out of things or I might get eaten up."

"Just about that, yes. Let the trained professionals handle it, do you hear?"

"Well, I'll be careful, I swear to you. Fair enough?"

"I'd rather have your word that you'll go sit by your daughter's side. That's where you're needed."

"Yes sir, I hear you."

"But I don't hear you agreeing."

"I have a nature to follow, that I can't deny, sir."

"Now you are being polite and telling me to go to hell. Mr. Swagger, you can get yourself in so much trouble so fast around here. I miss my command imperative to reassign you to kitchen duties or public information. But I do know trouble comes in two forms. Trouble with them, meaning the bad guys, trouble with us, meaning the good guys. It's dangerous for an inexperienced man. Were you ever in combat?"

"I did some time in —"

"I tell you, Mr. Swagger, it's not pretty.

You cannot believe what a bullet can do to a human body."

"Yes sir," Bob said.

"Well, I'm not getting from you what I want and I can't compel you to give it to me. But I have to warn you that we don't recognize righteous lawbreaking, meaning I can't cut you any slack. I can and will arrest you on a lot of silly little things like impeding a lawful investigation or disobeying a lawful order if I find you poking around. I'm so hoping I don't have to go that route on a man of your age."

"Yes sir," said Bob again. "Now let me ask you one last thing. My daughter had personal effects with her that day. I'm guessing you retrieved them from the wreck. I'd like to have them."

"Thelma, what's the disposition on that?"

Detective Thelma briefly checked her file, then looked up and said, "We recovered a laptop, seriously damaged by the wreck, a cellphone, her purse, her keys, a Reporter's Notebook."

"Any of it part of the investigation?"

"It's all pretty much busted up, Sheriff."

"Then I think we can let Mr. Swagger have those, don't you, Thelma?"

"Yes sir," she said.

"Okay, Mr. Swagger, Thelma will get

those for you. I'll walk you out. Stop somewhere and blow your nose hard to get all
the dust before it settles in your lungs. We'll
all probably die of the black lung. Anyhow,
I'll shake your hand, sir, and tell you once
again that I hope to hell I don't run into
you in booking or the morgue."

ELEVEN

Mountain City, population two thousand five hundred, was built along the stems of the crossroads of 421, 91, and 67 in a valley between mountain ridges, and it had ridden up the mountainsides in some places. Like towns anywhere, it had its nicer side and its not-so-nice side; its profusion of fast food on the big roads leading out of and into town; its shabby, ignored old main street; but also its share of beaten-down strip malls off the main drag. But in one of them he found a computer store and went in, finding it full of bustling, earnest young geeks, exactly the kinds of boys who wouldn't end up in the United States Marine Corps. They were all gathered around a monitor that showed some kind of war scenario, mainly beefy Special Ops types with super weapons destroying giant insects with their own set of super weapons. Finally a boy looked up and lumbered over.

"Can I help you sir? Whoa, that looks like toast."

He was referring to the laptop with its spidery fracture lines knifing jaggedly across the bent screen, the scuffed and cracked plastic, the keys out of whack or sprung, the whole mess looking finished for all time.

"I don't know if we can do much with that," the boy said. "You might have to replace the whole unit."

"I'm guessing y'all have a genius here," Bob said. "All these places do. Some real smart kid — all the others dislike him he's so smart, he wins the alien games all the time and he doesn't mind letting you know what a geek you are?"

"Charlie. How did you know?"

"I just figured it out. Anyhow, Charlie should be at Caltech or MIT except he flunked out of community college or got busted for marijuana or some such and he don't mind telling you how much more he deserves."

"That's Charlie. He flunked out of Vanderbilt. Math scholarship. It was the games. He is good with the games. He's the best. You can't beat him."

"I'd like to see Charlie, please."

Soon enough, Charlie was put before him, a surly kid in a hooded sweatshirt, still wearing a smear of acne, but no needles or pins through his flesh.

"Charlie, I hear you're pretty smart."

"Know a thing or two. Can't help you with that box, though, mister. It's completely wasted, I can tell you that."

"I don't want it fixed, Mr. Charlie. I want it mined."

"Mined?"

"Yeah, I want you to dig out the hard drive and salvage what information you can —"

"Data."

"Data, yeah. Whatever you can, particularly in the last few days. It was beaten up in a car accident last Thursday. Today is Tuesday. I'm particularly interested in the day of the accident."

"Mister, I don't know. Looks like someone took a hammer to it."

"Does, doesn't it? Maybe the FBI could tell me, but maybe you know more than the FBI, wouldn't surprise me. And you're here and the FBI is in Washington, D.C."

"Are you with law enforcement, sir?"

"No, just an amateur at all this."

"Well, I can make a try. It would be expensive. I charge —"

"Charlie, wait a second."

He pulled out a stockbroker's checkbook, dated it, signed it, but left the name and amount blank. He handed it to Charlie.

"You start now. You work hard. You say goodbye to blowing up monsters from space for a while. This is a maximum effort. And anything you learn, you call me ASAP on my cell, no matter the time. And when you're done, you'll know what you're owed. You fill it in on the check and go cash it and that's all there is to it. Are we on the same page?"

"Yes sir. I'll get busy right now."

"Good man, Charlie, knew I could trust you."

Bob checked into the Mountain Empire Motel, and set about the melancholy task of examining what remained of the effects his daughter carried that day. The first, of course, was her key ring, which held the Volvo key — thank God he'd bought her a strong automobile for her first job; maybe it had saved her life — and what had to be the key to the Kawasaki he saw parked out in front of the apartment building. That one was particularly biting, as it recalled many happy hours he'd spent bombing across the prairie outside Crazy Horse on his own bike, where he'd built the new house, and she'd joined him. She couldn't keep up on horseback, so she'd bought a bike, a Honda

250, and the two of them went on bounding rides over the low hills, under the huge sky in the baking heat. Those were good days, maybe his best, and, he remembered thinking, maybe more necessary than he acknowledged.

It was about then his hair started to turn; it was about then he started having the dreams.

He saw the *yakuza* swordsman with his perfect English and his smart, feral eyes, and his swordsman's ambition, and he knew that what everyone told him was true: when you saw this man, you were looking at death.

The last face-off in the snow, on the island.

What was he doing there? What had consumed him with the idea that with his week of training, suppleness from six months of cutting back brush on his desert property, and his anger, that he could stand against this guy? It wasn't David against Goliath, it was little Davy the three-year-old against Goliath-san. But he'd waded in, delusional, and learned in seconds he was overmatched. Now and then, as the fight wore on, he'd unleash a good combination, his four-hundred-year-old Muramasa blade cleaving dangerously close to the Japanese killer.

But the man was playing with him. It was killer's vanity. It was a little game. He knew he'd die when the man tired of it, when the macho chit-chat between them no longer amused him, when the magic hour came, and civilians started coming into the zone.

There was a moment where he had nothing, he'd lost everything. His lungs were blown, he was bathed in sweat, fatigued, as the other swordsman stalked him. It was all gone. He remembered the despair: why did you ever think you could do this? Why didn't you bring a gun? Pull it out, blow a 230-grain hardball through the guy and that was it. But no, you had vanity too. You could be in this game too. Fool. Bitter fool on the slippery edge of extinction.

No, he didn't think that. There hadn't been time in the fight. That was imposed later by his subconscious as he reconstructed it in the dream state. And in the dream state, night after night, he saw the *yakuza* laugh and cut, and open him deeply. He saw his own blood spurt and felt the dizzy weakness fire through his body, felt his knees give. Then he imagined the man making a witty riposte — "Sorry, cowboy, time to catch the last stage out of Dodge" or something — and then drive forward on the horizontal (*shimo-hasso*) and take his head. More than once he awoke with a scream in a sweat, seeing the world go atilt and then to blur in the eight seconds of oxygen and glucose a detached brain holds to sustain itself, felt the separation, felt the loss.

Why had he survived? That was the mystery, as strange to him as anyone. He knew only that at a certain late moment, he realized he had a steel hip and he remembered some bit of samurai gibberish — "Steel cuts flesh, steel cuts bone, steel does not cut steel" — and pivoted and opened and the target was too great. Exhausted himself, the great *yakuza* killer took the easy way out, drove the blade through the opening and felt it torque out of control when, an inch into Swagger, it hit the metal that was harder than it was.

Bob came off the blow and cut him hard upward, belly to spine, and that was that.

You were so lucky, he thought. Gunfighter's luck, arriving in the middle of a sword fight. Or maybe it was just that his subconscious had figured out a way to beat the guy, and it e-mailed him the info just in time. Maybe it was just that he came from fighters and sired fighters and had a strange gift for fighting. But he knew this: You will never be that lucky again. Your weakness turned into your strength and you figured it out one one-millionth of a second in time. The memory came at night and each time it came, it left his hair grayer.

The cycle banished that. It buried it. So much sensation, so much freedom, so much beauty, so much damned fun. What's better than to be racing across the wide-open prairie with your child, who makes you so proud, and the sense that once again, you survived.

Then he'd come back and it would be Miko's turn and they'd work with her on the horse in the ring. He'd think, Never got rich in money but got rich in daughters, and that's even better.

He put it down when it was too much for him, and quickly called his wife.

"I'm here," she said. "We've got a room in a hotel across from the hospital, and I'm here with her now. So is Miko."

"Is there any change?"

"It's looking good, the doctors say. She could wake up any minute. She stirs a lot, more like she's asleep. It helps her, they say, to hear our familiar voices. So I'm very optimistic."

"Did you —"

"Yes."

"Good. I'm in Mountain City. I'll try and get over there soon. I don't think it'll be tonight but tomorrow sometime."

"I'll be here all day," she said.

"How's the security?"

"They're good people."

"Okay, good."

"Love you."

"Love you."

Next, he turned to Nikki's cellphone, particularly to the CALLS DIALED folder. But somehow the thing was frozen up. None of the functions yielded information. But hadn't she called the cops from the wreck before she slipped off? He made a note to check with some phone expert to see if that indicated something or if it was a common occurrence when phones were damaged.

Then, at last, he turned to her Reporter's Notebook, a standard 3 × 6 pad held together by spiral rings. At first its pages were densely covered, and he saw that it was her interview with the sheriff. Then a page or so documented the raid, mostly scattered impressions like "rush of air . . . helicopter lands just as team hits . . . kid cops seem to be having time of their life. Pathetic suspect, Cubby something, sad little mutt."

He paged through it carefully, reading items from her later interviews:

Jimmy WILSON, 23, Mtn C. Drug Rehab Clin, "It's so hard, it's everywhere and it ain't no more expensive, don't know why."

Or

Maggie CARUTHERS, Carter Cnty, didn't get address, "Used to come to Johnson for drugs, pushers everywhere. Then all the busts, stopped coming, but head price was same, came over and it was still everywhere, maybe even cheaper."

"SUPERLAB???" Nikki had written. "Where is SUPERLAB?" in another place.

But it petered out, with no next step, no list of appointments. He could glean a little. She'd started at the sheriff's department in the morning, gone on the airborne raid with the sheriff, then gone to the drug abuse center and spoken to three people, then the rehab center and spoke to four, including a supervisor. Then . . . nothing. But how long would that have been? Would it have taken up the whole afternoon? The accident was at 7:35 P.M., according to the clock in the Volvo.

Where had she gone, where had she been?

He looked carefully at the notebook, trying to determine if there was any sign of tampering, but there was nothing apparent. Then it occurred to him to count the pages.

143

Very carefully, he turned the leaves over and came up with exactly seventy-three.

Hmm, seventy-three?

Now it's possible all Reporter's Notebooks have seventy-three pages. But that struck him as odd, wouldn't it more likely be an even number, like seventy-five? He looked into the spirals for signs of, what were they called, hanging chads, little nuggets of paper residue left from some kind of tearing operation? Nope, nothing.

He went to the last page with writing on it, guessing that if pages had been removed, they'd have been at the back. He found nothing. Well, maybe nothing, maybe something. He found a light set of inscriptions, the tracks of a pen against a paper that had gone through and recorded on the next sheet. He couldn't make it out, but took it into the bathroom, where the light was stronger, and holding it a variety of ways to capture the right proportion of light and shadow, came across something interesting. It seemed to say:

PINEY RIDGE BAPTIST PRAYER CAMP

And it also said . . . "gunfire"?

TWELVE

The Grumleys were the Special Forces of southern crime. The Reverend raised them, homeschooled them, taught them the ways and means of crime, strong arm, grift, con, theft, and murder, exactly as they had been handed down through generations to him. He kept them sequestered on the mountaintop compound halfway between Hot Springs and Polk County in Arkansas, while preaching hellfire and damnation on Sundays to keep his religious education accreditation and as excellent camouflage. He only trusted family; family was the magic bond that made the Grumleys invulnerable. No Grumley had ever snitched out another Grumley or a client, as was well known and part of the Grumley magic. But to keep the enterprise going, the Reverend had to procreate heroically. His real product was progeny. Fortunately, he was a man who had found his true calling, and with women he was dynamic. He had had seven wives and none had ever left him. The divorces were pro forma to keep the law at bay, and some of the girls may not even have known they were divorced. He had children by all of them, by most of their sisters and a ma or two. He even had a thing for a bit with Ida Pye of Polk County, and out of that got his spectacular boy, Vern. Though Vern, for all his skills, had issues of pridefulness as demonstrated by his refusal to take the Grumley name. Alton's brothers contributed their own seed, and the result of all the crossbreeding and the endless nights of bunny-fucking was a tribe of criminals higher by far than scum, more disciplined by far than trash, and, perhaps best of all, not the brightest of all the boys in the trade. It was a Grumley breeding principle to eschew intelligence, and when a boy or a girl was born with an uncommon mind, he or she was sent to private school far off, then college, then exile. Those kids had prosperous, if lonely, disconnected lives, and never knew they were damned by IQ. Their superior intelligence was known to beget inferior criminality, because they had imagination, introspection, questing natures, and occasionally the worst attribute of all for criminals, irony. They were poison.

146

It was known among the crime bosses of the South that a Grumley on the team meant success. Grumleys were hard, tough, loyal mercenaries. Grumleys could kill, rob, swindle, beat, intimidate anybody. If a snitch had to be found and eliminated for an Atlanta mafia family, a Grumley could get the job done. If a bank had to be tossed in Birmingham, a Grumley team took it down. If an issue of enforcement came up in New Orleans, a Grumley fist settled the issue. If a loan was past due in Grambling, Louisiana, a white Grumley was dispatched, and it was known that he would be fair and honest in his application of force, would never use the word "nigger" and therefore ruffle no hard feelings. He would come, beat, collect, and move on. It was only business, and everybody appreciated that high level of professionalism.

It was known too that Grumleys didn't go easily, and that was part of their reputation. If he had to, a Grumley would shoot it out with the whole FBI. He'd go down with a gun in each hand, hot and smokey, just like an old-timer from the golden age of desperados; he didn't mind shooting, he didn't mind taking fire, and he didn't mind the odds against him heaping up to a thousand to one. He wouldn't be one to negotiate.

This of course meant the cops stayed away if at all possible, but if not possible, they treated Grumleys roughly, out of their deep fear. No love was lost, no sentimentality attached, no nostalgia generated. Cops hated — *hated* — Grumleys and Grumleys hated right back, hard and mean.

Grumleys were handsomely paid for their efforts, which is why it was so strange for twelve of the youngest and the most promising to have been called from prosperous enterprises in this town or that city, and gathered, under the Reverend's watchful eye, to this isolated chunk of Baptist Tennessee. Called for a caper that even they themselves didn't fully understand, under the supervision of a strange fellow calling himself — or come to think of it, called by them, for he called himself nothing — Brother Richard. Who taught them not how to bust safes or short-wire alarm circuits or tap into computer data banks, but how to change truck tires at high speed. That was really all they knew — except for all the shooting practice, which, hot sweet mama, promised some fun! — and damnit, it was beneath them to do such manual labor under so cruel and arrogant a leader. But the Reverend insisted, and in the Grumley universe, his word was law. He sold obedience and loyalty and it was their job to offer obedience and loyalty.

And thus it was that two other Grumleys, two hard ones, named B.J. and Carmody, were assigned to stay with the damned girl's daddy as he had adventures in Mountain City. What they saw was an old coot with a bristle of white-gray hair and a bad limp. They differed on what exactly he represented.

B.J.'s opinion was strong.

"Hell, he ain't nothing but an old man. This here's a waste of time. That coot can't get nothing done. Blow in his ear, he'll fall down."

But Carmody, by trade an armed robber and occasional assassin, had a different opinion.

"Don't know, brother. He *looks* old, he *moves* old, but first up, I don't like how tan he is. Tan means he's outdoors a lot and if he's outdoors, he's might to be all spry and peppy. I'd like to git a close-up look on that face and see how much age he wears. Maybe he ain't all wrinkly. I just know gray hair and a limp makes a man look old and feeble, but looking ain't being. He may have a jump or two might surprise us."

"You are a fool, Carmody. I say we go on in there, brace him hard, tell him this ain't

149

his part of the country and he'd best return to the old folks home and watch him run. He will run scared like a rabbit, I guarantee."

"He's got some sly, I'm telling you. Some men have natural sly. They see into things, they git what they want, they ain't got no need to show bull-strong like your lower-class white thug, them thick-necked fellas the eye-talians think are so tough. Man, wish I had a buck for each one of them I saw fall down and not get up —"

"You *do* have a buck for each one of them you saw fall down and not get up."

"You know what, I do. Anyhow's, I'm not at all convinced this fella ain't your natural sly."

They were parked in the parking lot of a Hardee's across the street from the Mountain Empire Motel, where the old man had gone to ground. It was boring duty, in a one-horse hick town rimmed by mountains and fueled by fast food. No decent whores anywhere in sight, though maybe a fella could get his motor oils changed somewhere in the little burg's Negro section. That may have had more to do with Grumley lore, out of Hot Springs' colorful past, however, than anything real.

"Ho-hum," said B.J. "Ho-fucking-hum."

"Oh, wait. Lookie, brother, that's him."

It was. They saw the old guy hobble out of his room, lock it solid, and limp to his dumpy rental car. In a few seconds he had it fired up and headed back down the road, turned left onto the big, wide stretch that was 421. They followed. In just a bit, he pulled into the low, log-cabin structure that represented the Johnson County Welcome Center, just east of town.

B.J., driving, let him get into the building before pulling into the parking lot; it was Carmody who drew the duty of trying to get in close and get an overhear.

He entered the low old place, finding it a museum in one half and a travel office in the other, with racks of maps and tourist brochures for local attractions, such as they were, and an earnest crew behind desks servicing the visitors. Indeed, the girl's dad was talking intently to an old lady, and Carmody boldly slipped near, reaching for a bed and breakfast brochure on the table, and listened.

"— so many Baptists around here, you wouldn't notice if a new one came or an old one went, I swear."

"Yes ma'am," he heard the man say. "This one would be new, I'm guessing, not a church but some kind of prayer camp. Piney

151

Ridge, I th—"

"Piney Ridge! Well, sir, why didn't you say so! Piney Ridge is where Reverend Elmore Childress had his needy child's camp in the '70s, until the, er, unpleasantness. Since then that property has sat vacant. If this new fellow wanted a place for a prayer camp, that would be the place, and who'd notice, all the Baptists around. Now my people are Episcopalian and have been, and it's nothing agin' the Baptists, but there's something a little Roman about their service if you get my drift and my sister Eula —"

And on and on the old blue-hair went, but Carmody was free of the politeness that required he listen. He snatched up the B&B brochure and, trying to keep the leap out of his steps, slid out the damned door.

"You see a ghost?"

"No sir. That bastard's already onto Pap's place."

"What? How the hell."

"Damn, I didn't get a good look at him. Well, looks like Pap may be eyeballing him himself."

He pulled out his cell, punched the Reverend's number. Meanwhile B.J. set the car in motion, eased out of the space and lot, and buzzed a little down 321 toward 61, just to be less visible when he took up the tail on

152

Old Man Swagger the next time he moved.

"Pap!"

"What is it, Carmody?"

"Pap, he knows!"

He explained what he had learned to hushed silence on the other end.

Finally his dad said, "Blasphemy! Blasphemy, damnation, and hellsmoke! That tricky bastard, what is he up to?"

"Pap, if he drops by —"

"He won't see a damn thing, that I guarantee you. Now you boys, don't you lose him. We will stay with this trickster hard and if we have to we will snuff him out. Do you hear me, boys?"

"I will tell B.J."

"You boys load up and lock but keep your thumbs on them safeties. If it comes to it, you may have to shoot fast and put him down hard."

THIRTEEN

Bob followed the old lady's instructions, drove the rental up 421 another couple of miles and found 167, with signs pointing out an airport. He turned, headed through flat farmland, though ahead a ridge of mountains rose like some kind of black wave against the surface of the earth. He passed the airport — dinky toy planes, one-engine jobs — rose through foothills, and then was in the higher elevations. The road had been engineered to find its way between the ridges, and he slid through valleys and passes, seeing many private drives off either side of the road. Then he noted his fuel light blinking and not knowing how much farther the drive would be, pulled into a grocery store. LESTER'S GROCERY, the sign said. It was a solitary white structure lodged into the slope, with a set of gas pumps out front. He filled up, decided he needed a Coke or something, and went in.

The place was dark and grubby, staffed by a lounging boy with acne and too much belly and a surly attitude. Bob got a bottle from a cooler, went to the counter, and paid.

"Say, you familiar with a Piney Ridge Baptist Prayer Camp up this way? Lady at the tourist center told me it should be along this road."

"No sir," said the boy, making no eye contact.

"How about a sudden influx of new younger men, in clumps, keeping to themselves, looking prayerful and pious? Ring a bell?"

"No sir," said the boy.

"Son, you said that so fast it seemed to me you's most interested in ending the conversation, not thinking hard for an answer. Same as last time. Here, look at me. Look at my eyes, see that I'm a human being too, try and help me out. Be surprised what good things can follow from that."

Sullenly, the boy looked over. Bob saw "boy" was the wrong word. Guy was maybe in his mid- to late twenties, though still riddled with the face blemishes of adolescence, while the features of his face had gone all lumpy with excess weight here as on his body. He made the briefest of connections, then bobbed away.

"Sometimes some fellas come in. New fellas," he finally said. "Don't seem no Baptists though. Seem more like hoodlums. Tough guys, don't know where they're from. Just show and buy up beer and Fritos and smokes and pork rinds, keeping to themselves, paying in cash, making comments about Lester's store and how shitty it is. Don't like 'em much."

"Good," said Bob. "Thanks a lot."

"Yes sir," said the boy.

Something reminded Bob of a certain kind of young marine, the loser kid who joins the Corps as a way to start over, to have a new life, to do something well and right. Some of 'em don't make it, and it's just more fuck-ups until they're gone with a new set of grudges. But now and then you find one who gets to the top of the hill and goes on to become a real marine, and maybe has a life he couldn't have imagined when he was fat, pimply, and sullen without friends and hated by everyone, most of all himself.

"That wasn't so hard, was it?"

"No sir."

"It ain't my business, but a young fellow like you shouldn't be cooped up in a nowhere place like this. And those guys, Baptists or not, are right about how shitty

Lester's store is."

"Yes sir," said the boy. "I know that."

"Can't you get a better job?"

"No sir. Can't seem to get my letters straight. Didn't do well in school, quit after two years. Don't test out good enough to get into the service. Like to be in the Air Force, work on planes. Love planes. But can't pass the tests. Lester's only fella that would have me. I think he knew my daddy."

"Maybe you got something wrong with your eyes or some little deal in your brain makes you see the letters in the wrong order. There is such a thing, you know. You should look into it."

"Yes sir," said the fellow.

"You should get yourself tested."

"Yes sir."

"Well, I can tell from the way you say it you don't mean a word of it. Son, don't give up. Take some free advice from an old goat with a limp who's been around a block or two in his time on earth. Some social service deal in town or off in Bristol or wherever will test you for free and if you have a thing wrong, come up with a way to fix it up. Give it a try. You don't need to do this shit forever."

The boy looked at him from darkest abject misery, then smiled. It seemed nobody had ever talked to him like a human being before. The smile showed surprisingly good teeth and maybe a little brainpower in the eyes.

"I will look into it," he said.

"Thatta boy," said Bob.

"By the way, that Baptist place got to be the old Pioneer Children's Camp, where I think a man hung himself when they caught him diddling little children back some years. I heard someone rented and moved in. It's four miles up on the left, black metal gate, locked all the time. They painted it over so the black is shiny but I don't think they changed the Pioneer sign."

"You do know a thing or two," said Bob.

Bob got there soon enough, and it was as the fellow had said, the gate was newly painted though the sign that read PIONEER CHILDREN'S CAMP was still shabby with age. A dirt road led off into the forest, disappearing as it wound through the dense trees in a few yards. The gate was still sticky in the August heat and it seemed a lot of bugs had landed and found their fate to be paralyzation in the thick goop someone had slopped all over. Bob looked for a way in, thought it wrong to just climb over the gate, and then saw a '70s-style intercom relay on

158

the gatepost.

He pushed the sci-fi plastic Speak button. "Hello there."

Through a rattley smear of electricity the answer was nothing more than a "Can I help you?"

"Name's Swagger," he said. "My daughter was the one nearly killed in an accident on 421 on Iron Mountain out of town last week. I'm looking into the circumstances and have information suggesting she stopped off here. Was wondering if I could talk about it to someone, the bossman I guess."

The cackly soup recommenced to jabber from the speaker and Bob thought he heard a "Certainly." A clunk of some sort announced that the lock had been sprung from afar, so he opened the gate, drove through, then closed it behind him. The road twisted through trees, then between a couple of foothills, and came finally to an open valley behind elevations that formed obstacles that were green and high but somewhere between hills and mountains. Maybe what eastern people would call mountains, but certainly not what a westerner would so label.

He saw a small, white chapel standing alone; a barn; a kind of exercise yard of pounded dirt; a schoolbus, yellow in the sun; a dormitory, and a kind of gymnasium, all of the buildings constructed with sturdy tin, tin-roofed, and a little shiny. Ballfields, basketball courts, and the crater of an old and unfilled swimming pool also used up the open space until the forest took over again, and shortly thereafter, the mountains began their skyward inclination.

He parked next to the bus in a parking lot where a lot of vehicular traffic had worn a lot of grooves. But no other machines were in sight, and as he closed his door, he looked up to see an old buzzard in some kind of powder-blue three-piece suit approaching, a cross between Colonel Sanders and Jimmy Carter, with the former's cornpone stylings and the latter's hidden hardness of spirit.

"Mr. Swagger, Mr. Swagger, we are so sad about your girl," said the man, rushing urgently to him, laying a little too much courtly southern-style bullshit on him.

Bob stretched out a hand, felt a grip stronger than you might expect, saw blue, deep eyes, pink skin; smelled cologne, saw white fake teeth and a bristle of a genteel mustache, as the older fellow announced himself to be one Reverend Alton Grumley of the New Freedom Baptist Church, Hot

Springs County, Arkansas. He was up here with a constituency of young men who wanted quiet and solitude to pursue their Bible studies. The Reverend had waves of moussed hair — possibly real but almost certainly not his own by birth — and the pinkness of the overscrubbed. He told Bob that he was welcome to stay as long as he wanted and the Reverend would answer any question.

"Sir, thanks for the time."

"Come on in, set a spell. I'll answer any question I can to put your mind at ease. Oh, the poor dear. That's sad, and a parent's pain is sad as well."

The buzzard, fretting about Nikki, led Bob to a porch that overlooked the athletic fields, and in time a well-prepared young man in a white shirt and dark trousers came out with a pitcher of iced tea, and the two men sat talking and sipping.

"She was such a nice young lady," said the Reverend Grumley.

"My first child," said Bob, "so you can see my concern."

"How is the dear girl?"

"She shows signs every day of improvement. Yet she's still in that coma. They say she could come out at any moment, or never."

"Don't mean to give you worries, but have you thought of moving her from Bristol? To a bigger city with more sophisticated hospitals?"

"Actually, I already did that. She's in Baltimore now, where they've got the best medicine in the world."

"I see," said the Reverend.

"Yes sir, the world famous Johns Hopkins."

"I have heard of it," said the Reverend. "I'm happy she'll have the best care. She's fortunate to have a father who has resources."

"The horses have been kind to me. I own a series of lay-up barns across the West, where they take their horses seriously. What's the money for, though, if not your own children?"

"True enough. Now the police say it was some unruly young man trying to be a NASCAR star that caused the accident, at least according to the paper. Is that the accepted version?"

"It is and I have no cause to doubt it. Still, I want this boy caught, so he won't do the same again to another man's daughter. Now the sheriff's department in this little county is all stretched thin because they've got to provide a detail for the big race, that plus

Sheriff Wells's helicopter raids on the meth labs that you've read so much about, which seems to be his obsession at the expense of other duties, so I worry this issue may have slid to the back burner. I am poking about to see if there's any need to hire a private investigator."

"Tell me how I can help you."

Bob said he was reconstructing that last day and was curious as to why she had come out here, given the fact a Baptist prayer camp didn't seem the sort of place to conceal a methamphetamine lab, which was the original intent of her assignment.

"She was just doing her job," the old fellow said. "She'd evidently heard reports of gunfire from out here and made a connection between guns and criminals and drug lab security, that sort of thing. But I explained to her . . . here, come with me, Mr. Swagger. Let me set your mind at rest."

They walked across the yard, then the field, and came at last to a small structure, a kind of open hut. Bob looked inside and saw a robotic-looking electric device that was like something out of an old black and white science fiction movie, with pulleys and fly wheels and an arm along one side; a stack of orange clay disks sat in a kind of magazine assembly up top. Of course he knew what it was; an electric trap for sporting clays, skeet or trap.

"It throws birds. Clay birds."

The Reverend opened up a cabinet, and inside were three over/under shotguns.

He took one, an old Ithaca, broke it open, and handed it to Bob, who looked at it as if he'd never seen a gun before.

"Many nights the boys gather here and fling birds, then try and hit them as they sail off. It takes skill, concentration, judgment, a steady hand. Philosophically, it expresses endorsement of our beloved Second Amendment, the discipline to master the gun, the wisdom to use it wisely. Discipline and wisdom, exactly what it takes to lead a life in Christ. I'd rather have the boys doing something like this than playing basketball or touch football, where they smack against each other, where strength and size count more than skill, and cliques and grudges are formed. Unhealthy."

"I see."

"And when I explained to your daughter that to the locals — we're not socializers out here, we need the silence to concentrate on the Book — that to the locals the sound of the guns in the twilight was almost certainly what they took as suggestion of some kind of drug activity, she understood in a flash. She smiled, apologized for interrupting, and went on her way."

"I see," said Bob.

"Really, that's all. Here, watch me with the gun."

He took the gun back, dropped two red cylindrical shells into it, and snapped it shut.

"Used to be pretty good at this. Go ahead, turn on the machine there, it'll throw a pair and you'll see."

Bob examined the gizmo for a switch, found it, snapped it, and the thing clacked and whirred to life; two clays descended from the stack, rolled to the arm and settled in some kind of grip; the arm suddenly unloosed itself with a spring-driven force and flipped the disks in a curving path across the field.

Smoothly, the Reverend brought the gun to his shoulder as he pivoted in rhythm to the rushing saucers in front of him, and he fired twice in the same second. Both birds dissolved in a puff of red dust.

"Ow, that's loud!" said Bob, clapping his ears.

"Sorry, should have given you plugs or muffs. Yes, the guns do make a bang, though you get used to it. The boys do it over and over. You can adjust the trap to throw birds in an amazing variety of ways."

"I see," said Bob. "Now I get it."

"Yes sir. Would you care to try a pair?"

"Thanks, Reverend, but I don't care for guns. Haven't touched one in years."

"That limp of yours, I guessed it might be from a war."

"You'd laugh if I told you. Nothing so dramatic. In Japan, a fellow who was demonstrating an old-fashioned sword. He slipped and cut me. Imagine how surprised he was at how his demonstration turned out."

"I hope you sued him but good."

"No, there was no point. He learned his lesson. Anyway, that's all forgotten."

"So, would you like to see the place? Or stay for supper? Or, I know, the 4 P.M. prayer service? Very calming, serene, a sense of connecting with God's way."

"No sir, you have solved that little mystery right swell."

"Good, sir, I am pleased. Now let me press on you something I give all visitors. It's a very nice King James Bible. We give them out quite freely. I gave one to your daughter, and she seemed grateful to receive it."

"Sir, I believe there's one in my hotel room."

"But this is a gift, and as a gift you might

someday turn to it and find wisdom and succor. You'll pay no attention to a hotel room Bible."

"True enough, I suppose."

The old man trundled off and returned with the black book in his hand. He gave it over to Bob.

"With that, I believe I have made a friend for life," he said. "I'll not beg you to read it. But some night on the road, you find yourself hungering for something, I think you'll find nourishment within its pages."

"Thank you, sir. I'll go on now, and try and locate other witnesses to my daughter's adventures. Then I've got to call the hospital to check on her."

The Reverend walked him to his car, along the edge of the grass, and it was there that Bob noticed that whoever had raked out the dust field had missed a spot at the margins, and at least twice he saw some strange tracks, wheel grooves about twelve inches apart, deep and evenly cut, indicating they had borne something heavy. It rang a bell but didn't call up an image, and he wondered where he'd seen it.

But then he was at the car.

"Again, Reverend Grumley, thanks for your cooperation and understanding and hospitality."

"It's a privilege, Brother Swagger. You're not a Baptist, I fear?"

"No, sir."

"Well, you don't need to be a Baptist to figure in my prayers, sir."

"I appreciate that, sir."

Bob headed back to town, but pulled over to the shoulder and stopped the car.

I need to get all this straight, he thought.

Do I have something or is it all co-incidence, and my own vanity has got me believing there's some deep conspiracy here because I'm so damned important?

He tried to think it out, each step at a time.

Attempt at murder by professional driver. But what's the hard evidence that it's a "professional" driver? The interpretation of two expert race people on some aerial photos. They're not professional accident investigators whose word could be trusted. Maybe they sensed my need to believe and without meaning to, fed into it, to make me happy. But they were so convincing on the subject of cornering, and clearly had a mountain's worth of experience at that arcane art. That is my best evidence.

A second though admittedly unspecific attempt at the hospital. Maybe it was, maybe it wasn't. The Pinkerton security man, who seemed solid enough, just stated that some "doctors" tried to gain entrance to Nikki's room. No one ever saw them again, no one had ever seen them before. Still memory and chaos play tricks on people's minds, and given that it was a big, busy hospital, it's easy to understand how it could have been legitimate.

The possibly missing pages and the destruction of the recorder and laptop. Also: no Bible. Again, interpretation, not fact. She could very easily have torn the pages out herself, and the electronic items could very easily have been smashed up in the crash. The Bible could have been so generic that it wasn't recorded as hers, or maybe it was thrown clear of the crash.

The odd sense of perfection at the Church camp, as if it had been oh-so-hastily cleaned up, and Reverend Grumley's seeming to fish for information on Nikki's progress while mildly cooperating. Again, it was the nature of religious establishments to keep themselves extremely tidy, although the skeet trap in the shed was an unusual touch and it might well double as a kind of subterfuge under which a lot of gunfire could be explained away innocently, just in case of curious visitors such as himself and Nikki. Not completely unlikely but again provocative.

The strange tracks in the dust. They reminded him of something, but what? And why couldn't he remember it? Where had he seen such tracks? On the other hand, why were they so strange? Could have been some kind of cart wheeled out for maintenance of the skeet trap, could have been the gardener's cart for — but a gardener's cart would be wider. Why would it be so narrow?

And finally:

The fact that he was being followed. Maybe that was the best thing. It couldn't be Thelma's department, because they didn't have the manpower to detach two boys to play tag with an annoying stranger all day long. But two boys had been playing tag with him all day long, ever since his visit to the sheriff's office. So someone in the department had a contact with someone he shouldn't have. The tail car was a Ford Crown Vic, beige. He'd yet to make direct eye contact with it, because a sniper develops instincts for when he himself is being hunted. Bob had the experience to know that you never let your hunter know that you know he's hunting you, so that in actuality, you're hunting him. So when the prayer camp showed up all clean and sparkly, it was no surprise, because the boys

170

following him in the car — they had passed him, and he knew they were waiting around another two or three turns in the road — had seen him heading down 167. They'd called ahead to the Reverend, who got his boys off on a quick and hasty clean-up, so that when he got there he'd be welcomed warmly, and nothing of suspicion would be around.

Okay, he thought, this is an interesting game, all of a sudden. So what I will do is go back to my room at the Mountain Empire and set a spell, and after dark, I will sneak out a back way, and cut open their tires, and then, unfollowed, I will head back here and see what I have got and —

His cell rang.

He answered, hoping it was Julie with good news about Nikki, but saw an unknown number in the display.

"Swagger."

"Mr. Swagger, it's Charlie Wingate, you know, at Mountain Computers."

"Yes, Charlie."

"Well, I did some work and couldn't come up with much, but I did get it to print out some script and I managed to decode a little of it."

Bob understood that the kid had somehow gotten something off the hard drive.

"Go ahead."

"Well, it was numbers, the numbers 'three-six-two.' "

"Three-six-two?"

"Yes sir. And I could tell that it was a sequence of three numbers, a dash, then four numbers. It was the last three numbers in that sequence."

"A phone number!"

"That's right. So I know a cop and he has a reverse directory and — some computer genius — I just found all the numbers by hand. There's only about three thousand people in the county — we found seven numbers ending in three-six-two."

"Go on."

"Five were just residences — I have those numbers for you — one was a day care center."

"Yes."

"And the last was a place called Iron Mountain Armory. It's a gun store on the north side of town."

"That's great, Charlie. When you write out that check to yourself, throw in a million-dollar tip."

FOURTEEN

This one wasn't stolen, it was rented, although the credit card used to rent it was stolen, by the ever-slick Vern Pye.

He'd moseyed about the mall in Johnson City, eyeing teenage girls, especially the ones with them little bubble asses. You know, no real bounce to 'em yet, but tight, kind of bursting against the cotton of the shorts and — He saw a fellow just about his own age, height, and coloring, close enough to pass as Vern in thumbnail photography but not nearly as handsome. He jostled the fellow in a knot of other shoppers leaving the big K, smiled, excused himself, and walked away with one wallet but without another one. His fingers were that fast and that good. What was that all about, you might ask? Vern knew that what gave away the stolen wallet, sooner rather than later, was the absence of the weight. So when he lifted leather, he replaced leather, usually with a few fives and ones in it. That way the mark wouldn't note the absence of the weight on his hip. Later, when he reached for his wad to pay for something, that's when he'd make the discovery that he'd been boosted. There were a few instances, though, where a guy had actually pulled the new wallet out, plucked out a five, paid, put the wallet back, and went about his business! Some people don't pay no attention at all.

The truck, yellow with two up front and eight in back, came from Penske and was a 7-stroke Ford diesel mover, as had been all the rest of the trucks (well, Fords, not movers necessarily), though this was an '06 when the others had been '04, '01, and even a '99, which Brother Richard had not been able to use because its electronics varied.

So now the three of them — Brother Richard, Vern, and his ever-present sidekick and buddy, Ernie Grumley, sat in Vern's very nice Cadillac Eldorado along a completely deserted road in the Cherokee National Forest a few miles west of Shady Valley. Vern and Ernie smoked their Marlboros, enjoying the mellowness and getting ready for the show. The yellow Penske renter sat nearby.

"Looks perfect," said Brother Richard.

"As they always are, Brother Richard, I do good clean work, you know."

Vern was anxious that he not be confused with the lower class of Grumley, whom Brother Richard was known to despise.

"Okay, I'm guessing under sixty seconds today."

"Can't bet agin' you, Brother."

"Got that stopwatch?"

"Yessir."

"Okay, watch me go."

"All set."

"You call it, Ernie."

"Yessir. Ready . . . set . . . go!"

And with that Brother Richard was off. Besides certain tools, he carried with him a strange rig that consisted of a small, green plastic box with "Xzillaraider 7.3" imprinted on it, a swirl of heavy wire with electronic interface clips at one end, with a more complex swirl of lighter wire — one for power, one for grounding — a bypass, and a switch connecter. It was the Xzillaraider 7.3 unit from Quadzilla, of Fort Worth, a truck performance shop known in the biz as the cleverest in coming up with ways to gin up the power on a diesel engine. There were other techniques, of course. You could even cut the diesel fuel in the injector by forcing propane from a tank and get a significant power swell. But who wanted to be messing with propane in the middle of a gunfight? Not Richard, no sir. So the Xzillaraider was the best for his purposes. It was a genius-level mesh of electronics that essentially took over the brain of the diesel in the Penske and increased performance parameters. It fed more fuel to the engine. More fuel meant it burned hotter, and there was your power upgrade, sometimes up to 120 extra horsepower and a torque gain of 325 foot-pounds. The problem was, you had to monitor the temp, because if you didn't, you could melt or ignite the engine. The additional problem was that Richard wasn't going to have time to mount temp gauges and all the wires of the gizmo, not in a gunfight. His problem was to find exactly how few wires he could connect and still get the maximum power boost without bothering with all the safety devices. It just had to run for a few minutes, and after that, it didn't matter if the truck burned or not.

He moved swiftly, but didn't try to push it, got to the engine of the truck, and opened the hood. Where others might have seen complexity, confusion, terror, he saw the universe of his upbringing, the nurture of experience, the thrill of God-given genius about to be engaged. Expertly, he reached deep into the engine space beyond the big architectural structures, and into the nest of wires, found the MAP sensor, directly behind the fuel filter bowl. He quickly disconnected the factory connector and connected the Xzilla harness in its place, plugging in the male connector to the harness. He cut away the wires connected to the injection pump and attached the blue wire tap to the wire closest to the engine block. From that point on, it was wire work. He had to know which wires to cut, which wires to reconnect, all of them color coded. Quickly he grounded the engine — ugh, was it really necessary to unscrew the negative terminal connection, no, not really — and then cut a hole through the rubber grommet to the right of the master cylinder assembly, and shoved the wire harness through it into the cab. He dashed into the cab, and didn't bother to mount the switch but simply began plugging the wiring harness into the module itself, that little green box, where the gods of engine monitoring lived and worked. He turned the key and watched the module's blinking LEDs finally signal success after running through the sequence, settling in the red, the highest power zone. He turned the key further, and after a grinding clunk and another turn of the key, the engine burst to life.

And, brother, did it burst. The sound was almost like no engine on earth, a guttural blast, full of implications of the explosive, and it rocked the entire vehicle. He could hear the engine revving insanely, suddenly injected with a power beyond measure, almost too much for the confines of the combustion chambers. It was on steroids! It was the Barry Bonds of truck engines!

"Fifty-seven four," yelled Vern, "a new record."

Brother Richard goosed the pedal, and the engine howled demonically, yet it didn't burst into flames.

He had it. He finally had it. And pretty goddamned near time too! Talk about cutting it thin, why the deal was only a day or so away and —

Suddenly he saw the paint on the cantilevered hood begin to bubble and crackle, and that meant flame, invisible to the human eye, had burst out of the engine.

Shit!

He rolled sideways, hit the ground, and kept rolling as he heard the tell-tale whoosh of the fuel in the tank igniting, not exploding — it wasn't under enough pressure — but flinging a blade of hot-star radiance a good thirty bright feet in the air from under

Mr. Penske's fine vehicle, bleaching the color from the day for just a second. Then the flames settled back into your normal total-toast truck burn, licking and eating and devouring, issuing the rancid odor of scorched metal, melting plastic, burning rubber.

Vern carefully backed out in the Eldorado, threw out his cigarette, turned on the air conditioner to full to evaporate the sweat on the men's brows. Soon enough they found a main road and were well gone by the time the fire trucks and poor Detective Thelma Fielding showed up.

"Lord A'mighty, that was close," howled handsome Vern, aflame in delight at the excellent adventure. "You'se almost tonight's meal."

"I'm too tough to digest, I'd keep you boys up all night with stomach pains."

"It ran good for a while, though," said Ernie.

"Yes, it did," said Richard. "I think that's it. I don't think I had it grounded right. You're supposed to remove the nut at the negative battery cable and attach the black wire. I didn't take the nut off, but just wound the black wire around the terminal. Naughty, naughty. Next time, I will take the few seconds to remove the nut. It's time well spent, and we will be close enough for government work, you'll see."

"You sure, Brother Richard?"

"Sure, I'm sure. All on that day, I'd hate to burn like a bonfire 'stead of running like a stallion."

"Burning hurts," said Vern. "Case you hadn't noticed."

"So I hear. Saw a fellow burn to death once. Lord God, he screamed. I had the distinct impression he wasn't enjoying himself a bit."

"Nor will you, Brother."

"True enough, Brother. Well boys, get that old fraud of a daddy or an uncle or a molester or whatever polysexual archetype he's playing this week to pray hard for you and me or else we'll all arrive in hell pre-fried, COD. We'll be a goddamned bucket of Colonel Grumley's chicken, extra crispy."

FIFTEEN

Bob drove through the town of Mountain City, sped along a picturesque route toward Virginia, and soon enough found Iron Mountain Armory. Of course it had a sign reading GUNS AND SURPLUS, and of course it was in an old Quonset hut with trees clumped around it with a small parking lot in front of it on Route 91 heading north. The mountains were to its left, casting late-afternoon shadows that buried the place in dimness. But he could make out a large-scale wooden .30 caliber Browning air-cooled mock-up at the apex of the corrugated steel building's curve. The old trainer showed cutaways displaying red bolt faces and chambers, which must have taught six or seven generations of machine gunners their tricks before going on the surplus market and ending up on every gun store roof in the South. The gun was rotting, though its stout four feet of mock bar-

181

rel, swaddled in cooling sleeve with the omnipresent grid of round perforations, certainly looked menacing enough. The place, like the old machine gun model, had that beaten-down quality to it, a sense of better times having gone by, interior rot under the paint.

He walked it to find what he expected: ratty old trophies of bucks and bulls long since killed, fish in waxy midleap glowing against polished wood plaques, racks of rubbery rain ponchos, utilities, BDUs, netting, shovels from half the world's armies, web gear, Chinese knock-offs of current sandbox dutywear, Multicam and digital-camo patterns everywhere, lots of gun safes, sunglass cases for that super–Tommy Tactical look, and behind the counter fifty or so rifles racked butt down for easy examination. The front case had another fifty or so handguns, mostly the black plastic stuff that was taking over the market, little of the blue steel and walnut motif that Bob and his generation had learned to shoot on except in the used box. ARs were the predominant theme, gun safes second, and hunting only a third.

Fella came up to him from the counter, older gent, heavyset, eyes dead, not your natural-born salesman type.

"Help you, bud?"

"Hope so, sir," Bob said. "You the manager?"

"Close enough."

"My name's Swagger. My daughter is Nikki Swagger. If the name's familiar, it's because she was the girl reporter from Bristol who had a bad car accident a week back on 421 coming down the other side of Iron Mountain. Someone tagged her and she's still in a coma."

"Sorry for your daughter, bud, but what's it got to do with me?" the guy said. But Bob thought he saw just a flash of dread and the beginning, soon quashed, of a guilty swallow. Maybe the fellow was just a nervous type.

"Well sir, my girl wasn't into guns or anything, which is why I thought it odd that on her laptop we came up with what appears to be the phone number of this place. I don't know why she'd call or come by, but she may have. I'm trying to track down what happened that day."

"The papers said it was an accident. What difference does it make what she did? Accident don't follow no plan. It just happens."

"I know, but there are some discrepancies in the official account. I'm just poking about trying to make sense of it all, sir. Sure it

183

don't amount to nothing, but I have to do something while I'm waiting for my daughter to come back to me."

"Well, I don't know if —"

"Here, let me show you her picture. Maybe it'll jog a memory."

He pulled his wallet, showed the man a nice picture of Nikki at last year's graduation, so beautiful, so young, so vulnerable.

The man didn't really look at it, just said, "No, no, believe me, we don't get many young women on their own in here, and I'd remember. Sometimes a young fellow comes in with his girlfriend and sometimes the wife comes along to buy the Glock for home protection, but almost never will you find a girl like that in a place like this."

"I see."

"I'm real sorry for your troubles, but I can't help a bit."

"Uncle Eddie —" came a call from a workroom behind the counter, and a kid peeped out. "You sure on that? I seem —"

"Billy, goddamnit, you git to work. You got a lot of ammo to break down and get shelved. I don't pay you to palaver."

"Yes sir."

"Goddamn kid," said the man to Bob. "Girl crazy. Catch him reading them dirty magazines one more time instead of breaking down all that .223 and his ass is gone, I don't care what Margaret says."

"I see," said Bob. "Yep, good help is hard to find these days. What about a phone call from a woman? There wouldn't be a pretty face associated with it."

"Mister, I get nothing but phone calls, some of the damnedest you ever heard. Can I rent a machine gun? Will you guarantee a deer? How come Wal-Mart in Johnson City has it for $324.95 and you got it for $339.95? Is a nine millimeter more powerful than a .38? What's the best gun for home defense? Can I buy a gun like the soldiers use? So maybe I got a call from her and maybe I don't, but I sure as hell can't answer you one way, the other with certainty. Billy, you get any calls?"

"No sir," said Billy, yelling from the back. "None that I can remember."

"That seems to be all she wrote, sir. Unless you want to buy a nice SKS for under a hundred?"

"What's an SKS?" asked Bob.

"Chinese military rifle. No, I don't think you're the type."

"Anyhow, thanks. You got me scratching another one off my list."

He turned and left.

■ ■ ■ ■

The Reverend Grumley was thinking about fucking, as he almost always did when he wasn't thinking about the next few days. He hadn't fucked in about three weeks now, and the ordeal was getting harder and harder. The images poured over him, all the holes that he had filled, all over America, how the gals just seemed to want to give a man of the cloth a reward for all the natural good he brought into the world. He was going insane! Some of the damn boys beginning to look pretty good to him! But the last time —

The phone rang, he answered it there in the office of the chapel, and it was B.J. and Carmody, reporting that goddamnit, that fellow had somehow gone straight, straight in a goddamned beeline to Eddie Ferrol's Iron Mountain Armory. How in hell he make that connection? He'd been in the goddamn county two hours and already he'd made two big connections on . . .

The Reverend got the whole story, the fellow's sit by the roadside, going over notes, then speeding off.

"He see you?"

"Nah. Carmody's too good a driver."

186

B.J. was always boosting Carmody and Carmody, B.J. because they knew in the scheme of things, they were second-stringers to the more glamorous pairing of handsome Vern and Ernie. See, that's what the Reverend hated. All that competition, the formation of cliques and rump groups and bitter outsiders. It made for bad business. And if he wasn't mistaken Carmody might actually be Vern's half brother, rather than cousin, but, hmmm, he'd have to work that one out later as these issues were never too clear. But now wasn't time for lectures on brotherliness.

"You got him?"

"Yeah, he's in there now. We're parked a good three hundred yards down the road, eyeballing him with glass."

"Okay, hang tight. This here thang's gittin' a little hard to handle. Soon as he leaves, you call me and I'll call Eddie, see what's what."

"Yes sir."

"What y'all packing?"

"I'm .45, Carmody's .40."

"Git 'em ready. May have to go to guns."

"Yessir."

"I'll try and think some plan up. You know, something —"

"There he is."

"Okay, you hang tight."

He hung up, went to his wallet to find Eddie's Mountain Armory number, but before he did, the phone rang again.

"Reverend!"

"Eddie, hear you had a visitor!"

"Goddamnit, Reverend, you done promised me nothing, nothing like this going to happen. It was clean, it was legal, it was okay, we had the paperwork and everything, and goddamnit, first that gal shows up with that cardboard piece of box top and now her goddamn father, asking questions."

"The old gray-haired guy?"

"Didn't look so goddamned old to me."

"Tell me what he asked. Tell me what he knew. Did he know much?"

"He said he'd heard she called or come out this way, it was on her laptop."

Eddie narrated the story of his conversation with Swagger.

"But he didn't seem to know nothing about what you got for me, what its possible use was, what we had planned?"

Eddie said no.

"He had no clue. He's just grasping," the Reverend said.

"Maybe not, Reverend, but he sure come close, and when this thing goes down there's going to be all kinds of commotion, and he might be the one to figure it out. So even if he don't got no idea now, maybe he will then. You said nobody could connect all this up, and goddamn it's already been connected up."

"Settle down, Eddie. I see now I got no choice. It's too close, too much is at stake. Okay, you sit tight, the Reverend will figure on it."

He hung up, repunched B.J. in Carmody's follow car.

"You got him."

"Yeah, some bad news too."

"Okay."

"Don't know what this means but he didn't go straight to the car. He went around back. He's back there five minutes. Ain't there an entrance or something? I don't know what he's looking at or doing back there, but when he come out, he made a beeline to the car, and now he's headed back into town."

"You stay with him, you understand, while I work out a plan."

"How's this for a plan. We pop him. There's the plan."

"You idiot. Why'd he get killed? You get state polices in here and they much smarter than the Johnson Smokies and the whole goddamn thing crashes and burns just a few days before. Got to come up with some way to get rid of him that don't look like Grumleys done the work on contract for something else big. That goddamn Sinnerman is out blowing up trucks with my boy Vern, and I can't use him again, like on the gal. You stay with him, you hear? Meanwhile, I'll think something up."

"Reverend, in 1993," said Carmody, evidently taking over the cell while driving, "I worked a Memphis hit where we waited till the mark was in a little store. We walked in, shot him dead, beat the shit out of the storekeep, took all the money and some peanut butter, and was gone. They never ever made it to be a hit. They may have suspected, but they never could do nothing about it. How's about that one?"

"Hmmm," said the Reverend.

"Could goddamn work. You'd get Thelma and that photo-crackpot sheriff and maybe some Mountain City fellows, but they'd be thinking robbery and they'd never link it to nothing else. They'd say, damn, this family sure did run out of luck when it come to Johnson County."

"You make certain you don't kill the clerk or any of the other witnesses. Scare hell out of them, you hear? So the cops have to wring necks just to get descriptions. Got it?"

"This one'll be fun, Daddy," said Carmody.

Sixteen

Bob went to the car, then stopped and looked back. Only one grimy window of the Quonset fronted the parking lot, and he could see that no one was eyeballing him. Maybe they were listening, so he went to his car, turned it on, gunned the engine, then turned it off. He got out, walked at an angle to a path around back, and followed it. There he found the receiving area, an open garage door and a loading dock. He leaped up some steps — ouch, the pain in his hip stabbed at him! — and slipped in. There he found the grubby assistant on his hands and knees, applying crowbar to a crate of Russian 7.62 × 39mm ammo, by which rough process he liberated twenty boxes, junked the wood, and loaded the boxes on a cart for eventual shelving.

"Howdy," Bob said.

The kid looked up, one of a type. Sallow-eyed, furtive, maybe a little brighter than the poor boy in the grocery store, back-woodsy but not an idiot.

"You ain't supposed to be back here, Mister."

"And you ain't supposed to contradict the great Eddie when it comes to remembering things."

"Sometimes I speak out of turn."

"Well maybe you have something to say worth hearing," said Bob.

"Why'd I tell you a thing? 'Round here, folks treasure loyalty."

"What I see in you is righteousness. You're stuck with a moral center. So you'll know that if it was my daughter in here, I have a right to know, and Eddie ain't got no right to clam up."

"Eddie's not righteous, that I'll say. Some things I know could — well, that ain't your business."

"But this young woman is," he said, handing over the picture of Nikki.

"She's a fine-looking young gal," said the boy. "I have to say, she deserved a lot more than getting knocked into a ditch by an ass-hole playing Mr. Dale, the senior."

"I'm looking for him. He and I have business."

"Hope you find him. Okay, here's what you want to know. Yep, she was here that afternoon, late then, near dark, like it is now. Close on closing time. I heard her voice, and knew it was a younger gal. I peeked out and got a good look and damn, she was a beautiful young lady, sir, if you don't mind me saying so."

"Takes after her mother. What was it all about?"

"Well, took a bit of squirming and I come in late on the conversation, see, I wiggled over there —" he pointed up the wall to a hazed window that separated the backroom from the store itself — "and I popped the window a bit. I suppose, I don't know, you might think bad of me, I just had to figure out what it was, sorry to say, had to get close or —"

"She's an attractive young woman. You're a young guy, you have hormones. It's only natural."

"Yes sir, thank you. Anyway, she's asking about something. The Bible, I think."

"Hmmm," said Bob. "The Bible." That Bible again. Somehow between leaving the Reverend's prayer camp and showing up here, the Bible had become important.

This connected with no theory of his daughter he could imagine.

"She had a Bible. And they'd been talking about a passage, I think that was it. I was forty feet away now."

"What passage?"

"Mark 2:11."

"Mark 2:11. And she had a Bible?"

"Unless they make other books that have black imitation leather covers and gold page edges. It was a Bible. It was Mark 2:11."

"Why'd she come to a gun store to ask about the Bible? Any ideas?"

"Well, Eddie is a lay preacher. He does know the Book. Maybe she asked someone to help her on a Bible passage and they said, hell, just down the road, Eddie Ferrol knows his Bible times backwards and forwards. Makes sense to me."

"Yeah. Possibly. And that's it?"

"Well, yep, except . . ."

"Except what, son?"

"You didn't never hear this from me."

"I never even talked to you."

"You will go away and not come back into my life."

"Yes, I will."

"Eddie's twitchy anyhow but suddenly he's real twitchy and I hear him on his cell, he goes way over in the corner so nobody can make out what he's saying, and he's like, totally twitched out, almost in tears, almost crying, almost sobbing, and then he's calmed down somehow by whoever's on the other end, he says 'okay, okay.' Then he hangs up. He comes looking for me, tells me to go home early — that's a first, let me tell you — and only time I ever saw him look like that was two years ago when his wife left him and he went on a binge. I know he binged hard that weekend, and was a grouchy son-of-a-bitch for — well, till now."

Bob knew what happened.

Somehow Nikki revealed through a Bible passage that she knew something and it scared the hell out of Eddie and as soon as she left, he called whoever he was in this with, whoever he was working for, and they called the driver fast and he raced after her, which is why he had to leave rubber up and down Iron Mountain and only just caught her, and did his killing thing then. Only she'd gotten too far down the slope and she was too good and he didn't get that roll on her, and so she survived.

Boys, he thought, I'm getting close. And then we will have our business.

But then another thought hit him.

"You go look. You tell me what Eddie's doing right now."

The boy went to the hazed window, cracked it, and peeked out.

"Just like then. He's over in the corner

talking on his cellphone and he's all twitched up."

SEVENTEEN

Now what?

It was getting dark, and the two boys on him weren't holding back anymore. They'd gotten up close, maybe two hundred yards out.

Could do a sudden turn, shake 'em.

What would that accomplish? You forestall confrontation, certainly violence, but a cost: you tell them you're onto them and suddenly you're the object of a manhunt here in Johnson County and you don't have any weapons. Maybe you don't even shake 'em, they're damned good, they run you down and that's it, you're dead, after all you've been through, some white trash peckerwoods take you down in a gully in Passel o' Toads, Tennessee, or wherever the hell it is.

No. You keep surprise on your side, make it work for you. Make them think you're an idiot. You're just bob-bob-bobbin' along, singing a song. You don't know a thing.

You're an amateur. They're the profession-als.

I need a gun.

That was what it came down to.

Without the gun, he was an old goat with a limp, a gray-haired fool in over his head. And he had two gunmen on his tail because he'd done exactly what his daughter had done, somehow cut trail on somebody's plans, even if he didn't know those plans himself or hadn't figured them out. Something would be happening soon though, else why the urgency to kill his daughter and now to kill him?

Whatever, it came to one thing: *I need a gun.* God made men but only Colonel Colt can make them equal, for without the gun the old, the young, the weak, the meek, the silly, the soft were nothing but prey to the hard and ruthless predators of the world, no matter what the rules say. Rules are writ-ten for nice people in well-guarded zones who laugh and chatter and enjoy their little jokes at cocktail parties, but here in the hard world where the shit happened fast and the blood gathered in lakes on the wet pave-ment, without the gun you were just road-kill anytime anyone decided such a thing. You lived at their whim and when they decided to take you down for whatever reason, down you went, cradle and all.

Fuck, why didn't I bring a gun. I am on the goddamned bull's-eye and I need a gun and there's no place I can go without —

He thought: Drive to the sheriff's department. Go see Detective Thelma. Spend an hour or two there until you figure out what — but they'd wait. So tell her everything. She'd laugh, then she'd be pissed, because his findings directly contradicted hers, and she'd shoo him out the door and where'd he be? They'd wait for him and take him when he was available. They were hunters, they waited for their shot.

Then he got his hard, cold Bob the Nailer mind back, and he thought, How will they do it? They can't do me with a car again, it would be too strange. It has to be a firearms thing, a shooting. What, they'll take me, put me in the trunk, drive me deep in the forest and shoot me, then bury me. It'll be days before anyone figures out I'm missing. That would be one way.

But even then, questions, things hard to control, things hard to foresee. Someone might find the car too soon, or someone might see them, someone might hear them, I might get close enough to hurt them or get a gun away from them, they don't know who I am. No, they'd much rather shoot me dead from twenty-five feet and leave me. How would they do that?

Then of course he saw how it had to happen.

He realized he had one card to play, and that was, he could control where the thing took place. And he could only come up with one answer.

He picked up the cell, tried to remember the name of the goddamned place, then produced an image of the sign, LESTER'S GROCERY, on Route 167.

He punched 411, gave them the town and name of the place, waited for the connection, and shortly enough, after three and a half rings, he heard a familiar voice.

"Yeah?"

"Is this Lester's?"

"Yeah, who's this?"

"You recognize my voice. I'se just in there two hours ago. Old guy, gray hair, limp, gave you a little lecture."

"Yes sir, I remember."

"Okay, son, you listen hard to me, son. This ain't bullshit. Okay?"

"Yes sir."

"I'm going to get there in about five minutes, maybe goddamned sooner. I will park, come straight in. As I park, you'll see another car pull in behind me. In a bit two

201

fellas will get out of it. They will have masks and guns —"

"Oh, shit," said the boy. "I'll call the —"

"You don't call nobody. Ain't time, sirens'd chase these boys, they wouldn't show, you'd look like a fool and so would I, and I'd still be dead by morning. You understand?"

The boy made a sound that sounded like a cross between a whimper and a gulp.

"Son, you listen to me and you will come out all right. You reach under that counter and pull out the gun stashed there, an old Colt I'm guessing. I know you got one there, ain't been cleaned or checked in twenty years, but it's there, and let's hope it's working. Just take it out so I can reach it easy. I will come in, take it up, and git ready. Then when the two men in masks come through the door, you hit the deck. I will take care of them."

"I —"

"We will get through this. It's the only way, and you may even get your picture in the paper and a date with Mary Sue."

He'd passed through town, turned right up 167, and by now it was full dark, and he was winding up in the hills, scooting by the odd little house here and there, otherwise alone on the road except for the headlights of his pursuers a couple hundred yards back.

"I just put the gun on the counter," said the young man.

"We will get through this."

"Oh, this is too good," said Carmody. "He's going back to that grocery store he stopped at earlier."

"Maybe he's going to visit the Reverend again."

"Maybe. But he'll stop there I'm betting and he thinks he can get something else out of that dumb clerk. Oh, this is too good. This is just what the doctor ordered."

Carmody was driving, of course, so he reached into his belt and touched the piece he always carried, just to make sure it was there. It was a SIG P229 in .40, with thirteen fast-moving, husky hollow-points tucked into the magazine and another in the chamber.

Meanwhile, B.J. was rummaging around in the glove compartment, where he came up with two balaclava hats, which could be peeled down to make face masks, either for cross-country skiing or armed robbery, depending on the Grumley mood. He got them, then drew his own weapon from his shoulder holster, a stainless steel Springfield .45. He took the safety down, performed a chamber check to make certain there was a 230-grainer nested just where it should be, put the safety back on, and reholstered the gun.

"We goin' kick some ass," he said, the blood rushing to his extremes, and his breathing grew harder and shorter.

"Yes, we are, we are for sure," said Carmody.

Bob pulled into the parking lot.

They think they're hunting me; I'm hunting them. It felt familiar and now, from somewhere, his battle brain took over. Even as he walked to the store, past the pumps, up two steps, he felt things slowing down yet at the same time enriching in color and texture, as if his vision were mutating to something beyond excellence. His muscles were turning to flexible iron, his breathing was growing nutritious, his hearing super-attuned, so that every sound was crisply isolated in the universe.

He walked down the wide main aisle to where the boy stood, awash in fear, his body rooted stiffly, his eyes too big, his lips covered in white chalk. Bob could see the gun, made it out to be an old Colt New Service and guessed that it had to be either a .45 Colt or a .44–40. It was like a gun out of an old movie, from an old America, huge, blue and gray where the finish had been eroded or spotted off by exposure to blood. It was a humpbacked thing, big for the big men who lived big American lives in the generations before, and unusually heavy for its size, possessed of an almost magic density which in turn gave it a density of purpose. He took it up, felt the checked wood grips worn flat, almost smooth, ticked open the cylinder lock and spilled out that tube to see it sustained six brass circles, glowing in the fluorescent light. Each circle wore a smaller circle in its center, the primer, and around each was inscribed .45 COLT. He snapped the cylinder shut, not hard and flashy like the fools in the movies did, but with a soft, almost gentle touch. For a revolver, even a big old boy like this one, was a gentle mesh of the strong and the delicate, an intricate, frail system of pins and levers and springs and arms that had to work in perfect synchronicity, in a very nineteenth-century sense of mission, for it was a relic of that far century. He felt it and its solidity immediately reached out and embraced him. For Bob Lee Swagger, it was like reentering a cathedral; this is where he was raised to a faith and it had never let him down and he would not let it down.

He heard the door opening, he saw the boy's eyes widening, which told him what he needed to know, that indeed, masked, armed men rushed at them.

He turned, the gun came up fast in both hands, and if he noticed a large man in black, with a blackened, hooded, furious face and a black gun coming up, he didn't have time to mark it. For in the next nano-second he pressed the big old Colt's trigger twice, and with each crank, felt the gun's complexities occurring. All the systems were in perfect mesh, as the trigger came back under the muscular pressure of his finger, the cylinder rotated under the same spring-conveyed pressure, the hammer drew back, exactly as Sam Colt or some forgotten, genius engineer working for him had planned it back in Hartford under the big gold dome and the dancing pony at the turn of the century. As the sight blade rose and became all there was in the universe, the hammer fell, and in three tenths of a second he sent two 230-grain lead fatboys on their way to somebody's low, center chest, where they tore, an inch apart, through skin, muscle, and rib and blew out large, atom-ized chunks of heart tissue that spewed crazily throughout the chest cavity.

That one went down with a thump to the

floor that sounded comic against the huge reverberation of the two powerful revolver blasts in the closed-in space before he got his own gun up.

The second guy was not dumb and, even as he knew his partner was hit fatally and that they had been the victims of, not the perpetrators of, surprise, he moved laterally, disappearing behind the rank of shelved can goods before Bob could get a fatboy into him. Bob moved back, using the shelf island exactly as his opponent did, as a shield between them, aware it was not cover but only concealment, and suddenly red spray and diamonds filled the air — everybody's ears had switched off so there was no noise — as the gunman fired three times on the oblique, guessing where Bob would be and hoping that blind shots would bring him down.

Bob was not where the fellow guessed, as he'd moved to his own left and meant to come around hard left, hunched over and just showing a little flesh along with the big piece of Hartford iron. The gunman saw his mistake and turned to correct it, when he was hit in the face with a large can of Crisco that arrived in a tight spiral and smacked him hard. He lost a step, then bent to fire, but Bob was too far ahead on the trigger curve, firing another controlled pair that sounded like one, these a little more widely spaced, one emptying quarts of coffee, Coke, and fried eggs as it tore through his stomach, exiting against the instant coffee in a puff of brown dust, the other blowing out even more lung tissue and spinal fluid as it took him on a dead central angle. He went to his knees, dropped his silver 1911, vomited blood copiously, and fell forward, his butt up in the air, in a comic kick-me pose, and in that frozen joke settled and died.

"Jesus Christ," said the boy.

"Good throw," said Bob.

"I never hit anything I threw at before in my whole life."

"Well for one second, you were Peyton Manning. Thank God it was the right second."

"I have to sit down."

"Don't have time. You listen to me. I have stood and fought with many brave men in my time, which includes three tours in Vietnam and a whole lot of other crazed stuff. You can fight with me any time and you belong with those brave friends."

"I — I — We did it."

"Yes, we did. Now quick, you take this

gun, and fire the last two shots out the door."

The boy took the gun, it seemed heavy for him, and tremblingly, he struggled with the heavy trigger and finally managed to get one, and then another shot off.

"Good work. Now you have powder residue on your hands and the police will take note of that. You see how it happened. They came in, guns out, but you drew and fired, hit the first one twice out of your first three shots, then the other one fired from behind the shelf, missed, you scooted to your left and fired three more times. Then you called the police. You got that?"

"You —"

"Me, I wasn't here. You don't know jack about anyone else. You saw masked men heavily armed, and you shot. These two may turn out to be wanted or to have paper on 'em. Any reward is yours, and anything you can get off this deal, you go ahead. You deserve it. You stood and fought. I'd pick up that can of whatever you threw, wipe it off, and put it back on the shelf. Don't need to tell nobody about that. They shot, you shot, you won. End of story. Are we clear?"

"Yes sir."

"You did good, young man. You're a hero, okay?"

"Well, I — it's, um, I —"

"Okay, I am out of here. You can get through this. You just tell 'em the same thing over and over and nobody can doubt you. Just stick to the simple story. I know you can do this thing."

"Yes sir."

"So long, now. I will call you in a few days to check up."

"Who are you?"

"It don't matter. I'm the guy in the movie who leaves without explanation, okay."

"You're Clint Eastwood?"

"If that's his name, then I guess I'm him. So long, son."

EIGHTEEN

It took a while for the news to get there. Of course, since Lester's Grocery was only four miles as the crow flies from the Piney Ridge Baptist Prayer Camp, the boys all heard the sirens wailing in the night as various police arrived at the scene. No one said a thing. It could be, it could not be. Who knew, who could tell?

But time passed and there was no news from Carmody and B.J. You'd have thought they'd call in right after, but maybe the boys went to town instead of beelining back toward the camp, and were even now carousing in some low crib they'd found out about, drinking and wailing and whoring because they knew that they'd done the Grumley work well.

But after two hours, the Reverend sent Vern and Ernie in Vern's red Caddy down 167 to see what the ruckus was, whether or not it had anything to do with Carmody and

B.J. The call came a few minutes later. The Reverend took it.

"Reverend, we are here at Lester's."

"Yes?"

"Whole mess of folks, all the cops in three counties, state boys, the works. Crime lab, that detective Thelma Fielding and Sheriff Reed Wells, maybe even FBI up from Knoxville, TV stations, newspaper and radio reporters from all three states, the whole shebang. Even civilians are pulling in, drawn by the light and the ruckus. They can smell the blood in the air. We can't get close, they've cordoned it off, but quite a crowd has gathered."

"What's the word?"

There was silence, as if neither Vern nor Ernie wanted to bust the news. Finally it was Ernie, who said, "Rumor here in the crowd is that some punk kid shot it out with two armed, masked desperados. Killed 'em both deader n' shit."

The Reverend looked for other possibilities.

"Don't mean a thing. No sir, first off, no punk kid is besting Carmody and B.J. Grumley, no sir, not now, not ever. It has to be coincidence, you know, that brought some Joe Blows into the kid's gun sights, even if Carmody and B.J.'s off roaming around to make a job on someone so as to make it look robbery-like. I know the good Lord wouldn't take two Grumleys from me, no sir, not with this big thing coming up two days off, and me needing every damn man. So you just —"

And then he sort of ran out of words.

"Sir," Ernie finally said, "thing is, I think that's Carmody's car in the lot, I can make it out. And it's impounded and they're dusting it for prints even now and a tow truck is here."

"Oh, damn. Damnation, hellish damnation, flame and spark, damnation. It just can't be."

"Sir, I am only telling you what I see."

"Was there anything about another fellow? There's a shootout, our two boys, they gone, but they got another fellow, right, tell me that's what it's about."

"Sir, ain't heard nothing about no other fellow. Only about this clerk, what a sad-sack shmo he was, only this time he came up aces, a mankiller of the first rank, chest to chest and muzzle to muzzle, he shot it out, and they're down and gone and he's a hero of the highest damned order."

The Reverend let out an animal howl of rage and pain, deep soul ache, the blues, whatever you may call it. A Grumley — no, two Grumleys — had passed. His scream so rent the air that from the rec room, where they'd been lounging, playing cards, watching TV on fuzzy black and whites, drinking, just palavering, his progeny and kin came to see him and take the message of despair and vengeance he was putting out.

"You learn what you can, boys, then you head on home," he told Vern and Ernie.

"Yes sir."

The Reverend looked up at his flock.

"We lost 'em, boys. Both 'em gone to the maker. It ain't right."

"What happened, sir?"

He told the story as he'd heard it.

"No way, uh-uh, no Grumley going down in a fight with that pudding-ass kid," seemed to be the consensus.

"Pap," a voice came, "this boy, he couldna gotten the goods on Carmody and B.J. Carmody's a good shot. He had a knack. He'd shoot the ankles off a fly."

"B.J. ain't no slouch either," said another. "Remember in 0 and 6, he shot it out with two big black dudes in an alley in St. Louis, and though he got punctured himself, he made sure he's standing and they's bagged by the time that fight's done."

Several of the wilder Grumleys wanted to lock and load and head out for hot-blooded vengeance that very second.

"We got the machine guns, we can blast the holy Jesus out of that town in a minute and a half. With that big gun we can blow down all their church steeples, we can take that fat sad clown and hang him upside down in burning tar in the town center."

It was at this time that Vern Pye and Ernie Grumley returned from their melancholy mission, and they got there in time to hear all the talk of rage and vengeance, of burning the flesh of the Grumley killer, of razing the municipality that spawned him, or wreaking biblical vengeance on the transgressors. Through it all handsome Vern kept himself calm. Finally and calmly he spoke.

"Now you listen up, boys. Listen to Vern. I am the oldest and the most experienced. I am maybe the most accomplished. I have three homes, three wives, gals, money in the bank, and know some country-western stars. So let me share some wisdom. May I speak, sir?"

The Reverend considered, then said, "Son Vern, you may speak your piece in the Grumley fashion."

"Thank you, Reverend. You boys, you's all a-rage and full of the fires of hatred and vengeance. You want to go in and flatten that place, and teach every last man and

215

woman in it the fear of Grumley justice, and I don't blame you a bit. But we are men of a certain creed who live by a certain code and have certain responsibilities. That is at our center and is as fierce to us as our Baptist faith and our willingness to shed and spill blood. So I say hold it in, cousins and brothers. Hold it in cold and tight and squeeze it down.

"Now we have a job we've contracted to do. We've worked hard on it. We've prepared and sacrificed. We've taken a stranger into our midst —" he indicated Brother Richard, who was slouched beneath his Richard Petty cowboy hat and fake sideburns at the rear of the room — "and let that stranger use his waspish words against us, as if he's some kind of high and mighty. We do that because it's part of our contract. We are professionals of a creed, brothers and cousins, and we will be true to that creed. So for now, it is my conclusion there should be no blood spilling, and that clerk should be left alone to enjoy his few minutes of glory.

"But I swear to you, and you know that Grumley to Grumley, Grumley word is holy, I swear to you that when this done finished, *then* we will get to the bottom of this. We will have a nice long chat with that lucky boy and we will find out what transpired and we will ascertain blame and we will pay out justice, eyeball for eyeball, earhole for earhole, heart for heart. We will inform the world that Grumley blood is too precious to be spilled, and when it is, hell visits in due turn."

This did not mollify the Grumleys. It was not what they wanted to hear. They turned back to their father and spiritual leader.

"Is that it, Pap? Is that what you want?"

"I have considered. I see deeper into this. It's not about that clerk. I agree he be no match for any Grumley, much less two. I see another hand at play."

He paused.

"Who, then, Reverend?" asked Vern. "Who is the master in all this?"

"I think that goddamned old man, that gray-headed fella come in earlier, the father of that gal? You seen that fella? Something 'bout him I didn't like. No, can't say I didn't like him, wasn't no issue of *liking.* Was more like, he's too calm for what he says he was. I shot a coupla clay birds for him and he said, 'Ow, it's so loud.' He said, 'Aw, I don't like guns.' He said that but he's in my vision when I'm shooting and he didn't jump none when the gun went off, as if he'd been around the report of a firearm a time or two.

And he told me this odd story about how he'd got cut up in Japan, his hip laid open, but there was no point in suing the fellow what cut him, and he told that story, which made no sense without a further explanation, almost for his own private pleasure. He's takin' *pride* in it. He's taking pleasure in some memory of some event of triumph."

"He some kind of undercover man, sir? Is that what you're saying?" a Grumley wondered.

"I don't know whose agent he is, if he really is that gal's daddy, or he's playing a game or what. But I have done this work many a year and have developed a nose for certain things. And I got a peculiar aura off him — it's what now I see is mankiller's aura. There are some born to kill with a gun. They have the steel for snuffing out life with a piece of flying lead, don't feel nothing about it. There was a breed of lawmen like that once, mankilling cops, old timers who weren't afraid of going to the gun. I didn't think there's men around like that no more. Thought the last of them died years ago when they stopped calling killing a man's job and made it like a sickness, so a man who wins a fair gunfight should feel ashamed and go into a hospital. That'll drive your mankiller into retirement or the graveyard faster'n anything. That's the only enemy he can't never beat, except maybe a Grumley boy. But this old man's one, you should know his kind has been the kind to hunt our kind since ancient days. Never thought I'd see his like again, thought that breed was vanished from the earth, but I think he's back and hunting us."

"So what'll we do, Reverend?"

"Well, only one thing to do. Now we hunt him. Grumley business come first. Without Grumley, there's nothing but chaos. Family matters most. So we must hunt and kill this bastard, and I want y'all out on the streets so as to mark him down and then we'll finish him but good. Maybe we get done in time for the job, maybe we don't. But Grumley come first."

NINETEEN

Bob realized as he left Lester's Grocery and the clerk that without his keepers, he now had a free shot to Knoxville, could check on his daughter, talk to his wife, and pick up some firepower. He turned right out of the parking lot, drove up 167, ignoring whatever mysteries lurked behind the locked gates of the Baptist prayer camp, hit 67, and soon crossed from Johnson to Carter County, on the way west to 81, which would take him south.

Immediately it was apparent that Carter was a richer county by far. It had a man-made lake, marinas bobbing with pleasure boats visible even in the dark, bars, restaurants, vacation homes, nightlife. At one point a couple of Carter County sheriff's cars roared by him, sirens blazing, lights pumping, and now and then a Tennessee Highway Patrol vehicle sped by, all of them clearly headed to the site of the shooting, where that boy had to hold his line for at least a few more days. Maybe when this straightened out, Bob would speak up, explain himself to Detective Thelma Fielding, take the kid off the spot and face what consequences there might be. But it seemed to him that there should be none, besides his leaving the scene of — well, of what? A crime? Not hardly. Fair, straight shooting in defense against armed men who had masks on who were moving aggressively toward him. Pure self-defense if the law was applied right.

Other things on the to-do list. Make sure to check the press accounts and see who these boys were. The second fellow had moved well and intelligently, brought fire, clearly a veteran of previous firefights of one sort or another. A professional, to be sure; he'd have tracks, associations, a record, all that which could tell an interested party a thing or two.

And then there's the issue of Eddie Ferrol, Iron Mountain Armory owner. Talk to him and someone tries to kill you. Who is he? Why is he in this? He doesn't seem smart enough, tough enough, ruthless enough to be a big part in anything criminal, yet for some reason he has an amazing influence on events. Why is that? What does his knowledge of the Bible, particularly Mark 2:11, have to do with anything? Why does even abstract, useless knowledge of this passage equate to an instant murder attempt? Eddie looked like the sort who'd spill his beans easily enough. But almost certainly, he'd go to ground and make himself hard to find. He certainly wasn't going back to the gun store, that was for sure.

And what was his own next move, after his time in Knoxville? Should he come back to Mountain City and continue to ask questions in hope of coming across a Mark 2:11 explanation? Would he be targeted again? Would people pick up on him, report on his presence, help a new squad of hunters locate him? Should he go on to Bristol, return to Nikki's apartment, spend some time there, at least through the weekend's big race activities, then hire a private eye, stop improvising, do this thing like a grown-up with a mind toward clearing it up and making sure it was safe for his daughter to resume her life?

He got into Knoxville at midnight, realized it was probably too late to call his wife in her motel — the call would awaken Miko and wouldn't be appreciated. So he found an Econo Lodge off the big highway and paid in cash. He hadn't realized how tired he was and that he'd been going hard without sleep or food. The food could wait. He went to bed in the small, cheap-but-clean room after a shower, and fell into a sleep full of portents of children in jeopardy and himself in various gaudy, symbolic shapes, unable to do anything about it.

You wouldn't associate the word "coma" with Nikki. She looked rosy and merely asleep. Everybody was full of hope. The doctors reported that her vital signs were strong and that she stirred, showed normal brain activity, and responded to her mother's and sister's voices. They all thought it would be a matter of days, maybe even hours before she awoke.

"She is such an angel," Bob said, holding Miko close.

"Daddy, maybe she'll wake up today."

"I hope she does, sweetie. I hope and pray she does. You and Mommy, you'll stay here and watch over her."

"Yes, and the Pinks will guard her so nobody can harm Nikki."

"Yes, honey, they're very good men."

He put Miko down.

"Now Mommy and I have to talk. Honey, you stay here for a minute, okay?"

"Yes, Daddy."

He and his wife walked wordlessly down the hall to a visitor's lounge, where they bought bad coffee in Styrofoam from a vending machine and sat at a blank table in a blank room.

The first thing he said was, "I have satisfied myself that this thing did not come upon Nikki out of something I did some years ago, when I was off doing this or that. It seems that she cut trail on some kind of plan — I don't know what it is. But somewhere in Johnson County there's a group of very bad fellows who are planning something equally bad, and Nikki picked up on some aspect of it, and they had to finish her as she was going about her business, trying to do an overall story about methamphetamine use in the county. She's innocent; she was just a young woman full of life who ran afoul of bad customers. She may not have even known what it is, but it has to be something she was close to figuring out and that's why it's so dangerous. Now I know what the clue is, and now people are coming for me."

He told her his story, each discovery at a time, each event at a time, including Mark 2:11.

When he told her he'd killed two men the night before, her gaze showed nothing. She had changed. It was her daughter; her rage and instinct had been aroused and now she understood that she could not allow anyone — *anyone* — to harm her daughter.

"You can't go to the police?" she finally asked. "Wouldn't that be the wisest thing?"

"Well, I'm not sure how they figure into it. I think this Detective Thelma Fielding is okay, but the sheriff is a pompous son of a bitch with his eye on something else. Loves publicity, won't stop talking about his time in the war. But the real problem with them is they got it all figured out to be a bad kid on a binge, looking for somebody to squash. That's all they see, that's what they want to see, that's the file it's in. They think it'll just be a day or so till somebody snitches him out, and meanwhile they got other fish to fry. So if I go to them, I have some kind of institutional inertia working against me to begin with. Then I have to explain why I ran out after the shooting, what my suspicions are, and their minds aren't equipped to deal with any of that yet. It's too much information, too fast, and it challenges the way they do business. It's like the Marine Corps used to be on snipers. They just don't want to know about it. Took a war to change their minds."

"What about the FBI? Can you call Nick

Memphis? He'd drop anything to help you. At least he can put Bureau resources behind you, and your learning curve will be much quicker."

"Hmmm," said Bob. "You sure you haven't done this before? That's a great idea. No, that didn't occur to me because I been so goddamn caught up in my own drama and not thinking straight. Yeah, I will call him first thing, and see what he can get me."

"Can you handle this? You're older, Bob. Maybe not so fast. Maybe your mind is a little slower than it once was, as well as your hands. And maybe this time you'll run out of luck, you know that. You'll end up face down, shot by some kid with a .22 who has no idea he's just murdered Achilles."

"I may run out of luck, sure. And I ain't too happy to be a hunted man once again, and to have to go to guns once again. But it's come, and I told you, I will do with it what I must. I need you behind me."

"But it seems since Japan you've had doubts, even fears. I know. You thought I was asleep, but many's the night you woke with a start, all asweat. In this kind of game, you can't have doubts. You've said that many times."

"If I was working for a government or a

sheriff's office, I might have doubts and they might get me killed on the job. But I am working for my daughter. So those doubts don't count. They went away. I have no doubts, and last night, it was the same old Bob Lee back, gun in hand, shooting for blood, making the right moves. I do need one thing. I need you behind me."

"I am behind you." She reached into her purse and pulled out a set of car keys with a Hertz emblem on the ring. "It's a blue Prism, Tennessee LCD 109953. I parked on the fourth floor, where there's fewer cars, but not on the roof, where somebody in an office could see you. You pull up to it, trunk to trunk. There are some goods inside. I went to Meachums and asked Mr. Meachum what kind of rifle he recommended for self-defense in a ranch house. He was very helpful. Didn't have any trouble on the flight. Locked case, declared firearm, the gal at the counter didn't even want to look inside. The handgun was yours, under the mattress. I bought ammunition for it and the rifle and spare magazines. It's all in the trunk. I spent last night loading magazines. The rifle is supposed to hold thirty but I could only get twenty-eight in."

"Twenty-eight is fine," said Bob. "It's better. Less pressure on the spring. More reliable that way."

"The handgun magazines loaded fine. Ten in each, ten of them."

"Thank you," he said. "Now I'm going to go. I think I have to get back to Mountain City. I can't let them think they've run me. They have to know they're in for a fight and if they're scared, maybe they'll make a mistake."

She said, "You find the men who tried to kill our daughter. You take care of them."

He kissed her, took the elevator down, went to the garage and moved his car up to hers. Satisfying himself there were no other people on the floor, he opened her trunk.

The rifle was in a Doskocil plastic travel case. He unlatched it to see what Meachum had come up with. His first thought was "Shit," because it was an M16. Well, an AR-15, as the civilian variant was called. As a man of the .30 caliber, he'd always despised the pipsqueak .223 of the classic AR platform with its tendency to bore tiny holes in people, keep going and kill the talented orphan-kid piano-prodigy while the bad guy didn't blink an eyelash and kept shooting. And he noticed it had all sorts of gizmos bolted on — an EOTech holographic sight that looked like a TV set, a forward vertical grip with a Surefire flashlight built into it at six o'clock, just under the muzzle. And the muzzle — well, it looked a little wider. He bent close, tried to make out the barrel marking in the dim light, and saw that it read DPMS 6.8mm REMINGTON SPC. As he transferred the gun and case to his trunk, he saw a few extra boxes of ammo, Black Hills 6.8, cracked one and discovered a short round that had a big bullet. Let's see, 6.8, that meant about .270 caliber. And then he remembered hearing that in the sand, the Special Operations people were so pissed at the poor one-shot, take-down ratio they were getting from the .223, some of them worked with some people at Remington to come up with a bigger, more powerful cartridge. It functioned in a system using an AR lower, and only required a new upper, thus saving the government millions of dollars. If the government adopted the cartridge, it only had to buy the top half of five hundred thousand new weapons. Maybe that would happen, maybe it wouldn't, but the cartridge had been combat-tested and was said to put 'em down and keep 'em down. That pleased him. She had done well.

The handgun was a .38 Super, his own 1911 model Kimber, a very nice gun that as he got older he appreciated more for its lack of recoil and muzzle flip in fast strings, while completely identical to the .45 in handling and operating procedures. The extra boxes indicated the load Meachum had chosen was the CorBon 130-grain jacketed hollow point +P+ ammo. His Kydex holster lay beside the case, amid the ammo boxes.

Locked and loaded, he thought. Loaded for bear or whatever.

His cellphone rang.

He looked at the caller ID and saw that it was Detective Thelma Fielding's number. He thought a bit. What do I do? Maybe that kid broke. She wants me to come in so she don't have to put out an arrest warrant. Maybe I ought to call a lawyer. Meantime, I have an arsenal in the trunk and no place to stash it. Damn, I wish that boy had lasted longer. Thought he had the stuff for it.

He could just not answer, of course. But what would that tell her?

"Hello."

"Mr. Swagger."

"Yes, howdy, Detective, what's up?" Trying to be nonchalant, just in case.

"Sir, we've had a break in the case."

"A break?"

"Yes sir. Soon's I get free and clear of an unrelated shooting took place last night, I'm going to make an arrest. Fellow named

Cubby Bartlett, a longtime meth dealer. He's the man who tried to kill your daughter. Got him cold. Someone snitched him out and I'm going to pull him in."

Swagger didn't know quite what to feel — relief that the boy had held steady and hadn't given up his name, or laughter that poor Thelma seemed way up the wrong tree and barking hard. Or maybe in some way this Cubby Bartlett fit into it.

"Sir, you said you wanted to be there for the arrest. Now if you give me your word you won't cause no trouble, I will let you sit stakeout with us tonight and watch as we bring him in."

"I'll be there," he said, and she gave him the details.

TWENTY

"You're an idiot," said Brother Richard.

"Brother Richard, if we don't do this here job, and it looks like we won't, then your ass ain't worth a cowpie in January. So I's you, I'd get myself long gone, 'cause when Grumley business be finished, my boys may remember how mean and disrespectful to them you's been. And when that happens and specially since they have the taste of blood on their tongues, maybe they get a hunger for you."

"You're an idiot," repeated Brother Richard.

"Grumley come first," said the Reverend. They sat in his office off the gym floor of the rec center. The boys had already locked and loaded and headed out, just to keep a watch and see if and when that fellow came back into town, after which point all Grumleys would coordinate and vengeance would be taken, as it mightily should be, amen.

"Don't you think you're overstating the drama of the two men you lost? Those boys were professional strong-arm men. They were begotten of and by violence. That's the life they chose. They lived high on it, scoring kills and drugs —"

"My boys don't take no drugs!"

"Yeah, you don't work with them on a daily basis like I have the last few weeks. I know Grumleys a lot bettern' you, old man. Anyhow, those two, Carmody and Blow Job —"

"Damn you to righteous flame, you bas—"

"Carmody and Blow Job had the kills and the swag and the dope and the whores and probably even a good girl or two along the way, because there do seem to be some good girls who find outlaws amusing. They lived a life of the superego unrestrained, like few men, the great thrill of the criminal lifestyle and its secret true reward. They ran hard and lived hard. It was always in the cards that at any second of any day they could run into some country cop who knew how to shoot, or take a corner too fast and smear themselves on the concrete. That's the cost of doing business in the business of violence, and it turned out that their number came up. It's an anomaly, it's unfortunate, from your twisted-sister viewpoint it might even be a tragedy, but it is what it is, and there's no money in it for any of us and we have worked too goddamned hard to give it up for some nickel-and-dime sense of vengeance on someone who, after all, was only defending himself in a square gunfight and appears to have been faster on the trigger and truer on the aiming part than your boys. Vern was right. Vern's the smartest Grumley."

"Sir, you do not understand family. And I am disappointed in son Vern."

"Sir, I *do* understand family. No man you ever met understands family more than me. Now, I'll tell you what's interesting in all this. It's my sense you have been looking for a way to fail. I believe you were coerced into this plan by someone smarter and tougher than yourself, because it is too clever for a fellow like you to think up. You're no strategist, your only product is the rawest of force. That's what you sell, that's all you know. But this thing is too cool for words and you are about to give it up not in spite of your best *instincts* but because of your best *interests*. You want an excuse to fail, to go down in some fucking massacre shootout in a blazing barn, a gun in each hand. You have 'death wish' written

234

all over you, goddamnit."

"You have fancy words, Brother Richard, and you speak cleverly but your words ain't but spit compared to the Grumley family tra—"

"What's he got on you? Bet I know."

This threat alone, of all the things Brother Richard had said, shut the old geezer up. And when that happened, Brother Richard knew he was right and bored in for the kill.

"It's gotta be a sex thing. That lizard of yours, that baby's got to feed, what, three, four times a day? You're omnisexual, polysexual, metasexual. You're unisexual. There isn't a word for what you are. It seems to run in the godhead biz. Wasn't David Koresh and that Jim guy who fed all those people Kool-Aid the same? Yeah, yeah, that's it, isn't it? You have all those kids, all those wives, all their sisters, it's all about the Reverend Alton Grumley getting his wand wet three, four times a day, even at your age. I will say, you are probably more full of sperm than any man born since Genghis Khan, father of us all, not just because you know family conspiracies are the only conspiracies that work and so you need a lot of family, but also because you have a weird gene that makes you have to fuck three or four times a day. I bet you have a cock the size of a trailer hitch, come to think of it. It all fits together — your golden tones, your soothing ways, your clank of sanctimony, your secret ruthlessness. Boy, you are one huge, perpetual-motion fucking machine. You even see it in Number One son, Vern. I picked up on the way his eyes light on the youngest, flattest, hottest, sluttiest twelve-year-old. He fixes on one of them, he's lost to the cause. You'd best hope that when the big day arrives, old Vern's got his mind on business, not on the shock-absorber-sized boner in his pocket. We need Vern's sagacity, or rather, normal Vern's sagacity, not het-up Vern's insanity."

The Reverend seemed to be getting a little crazy. The Y-veins on his forehead pulsed, his eyes sank to the size and color of ball bearings, his breathing grew harsh and shallow, and he clenched and unclenched his big hands. He looked like he wanted to strangle the life out of Brother Richard and was but a second from doing it.

"But let's leave poor Vern out of this. He's only your pattern played out, what chance did he have with a pa who was so sexed up sometimes he didn't care what kind of hole he put it in, am I right? Oh, that's the pattern, I see it now. He's got video on you and some chicken, right? Some boy whore.

Some boy-child even, one of those classic cases of the holy man who can't keep his mitts off of little Billy and Bobby and tells them God commands them to drop their drawers? Oh, that's it, I hadn't seen it till now, that's got to be it."

"Sir, you are the Whore of Babylon, the Antichrist, hiding behind a smiley demeanor and a charming patter, but truly inside, the Beast."

"Arf, arf," said Richard. "Now I see. You've been leveraged into this job, and there's nothing you can do about it. But you cannot accept it either, because the fulcrum on which it turns is your own darkest secret, the one that would destroy you in front of all Grumleys. So your attitude is classic passive-aggressive, and the longer it goes on, the longer it annoys the bejesus out of you. So now you have it: an excuse to quit, an excuse to fail, an excuse to die."

The Reverend looked skyward.

"Lord, help the Sinnerman all on that day. He has nowhere to run to. The moon won't hide him because it's bleeding, the sea won't hide him because it's boiling. With his education he comes up with terrible ideas and he contaminates those who believe. Lord God, smite him, and take him with you and give him a shaking and a talking to, so that he knows why it is you're sending him to an eternity of burning flesh in the dark and sulphurous caverns of hell."

"Who writes your stuff, Stephen King or Anne Rice? Anyhow, let me tell you: Call in the boys. Settle 'em down. We need 'em calm and collected for Race Day. We can do this thing, I tell you, and I can have my little run through Big Racing's peapatch. And we can all go home rich and nobody, *nobody,* will ever forget the Night of Thunder. Okay? Concentrate. That's how you beat your tormentor. You pull the job, you get the money, you get your film-at-eleven-minister-fingerfucks-choirboy back. Living well is the best revenge. Oh, and a few years down the line, you go back and kill the shit out of whoever was blackmailing you."

The Reverend looked at him sullenly.

Richard continued. "Apostate speak with wisdom, no, old goat? Infidel know thing or two, eh, Colonel Sanders? Think on it. Think on it, for God's sake. Now I'm going to leave. I have to get into Bristol and get a look at my little peapatch, so I can prepare my own kind of fire and brimstone for what's coming up next. I'm not even going to demand that you change your plan and call those boys in, because I know you will."

"Thou art sin," said the Reverend. "Thou

wilt burn."

"Just so I don't roll," said Brother Richard.

TWENTY-ONE

On the way back to Mountain City, Bob tried to call Nick Memphis, special agent, FBI. He had Nick's own private cell number, and he punched in the numbers as he drove north on 81 from Knoxville in the setting afternoon sun. But there was no answer, only Nick's voice mail. "This is Memphis. Leave a detailed message and I will get back to you."

"Nick, Swagger. I have to run something by you and sooner would be so much better than later. Call me on this number please, bud."

But Nick never called him back.

He was disappointed. He loved Nick. Years ago, so long ago he'd repressed it and most of the memories had vanished, Nick had believed in him. He was on the run, set up by some professionals, briefly number one on the FBI hit parade. Every cop in America was gunning for him. Then along came

Nick, who'd looked at the evidence and saw that the narrative everybody was dancing to simply couldn't have happened. By the laws of physics, too many anomalies, too many strangenesses. Nick looked hard into it, then hard into Bob's killer eyes, and believed.

Bob knew: He was reborn that moment. That was the moment he came back. That was his redemption. That gave him the strength to play it out, to go hard again, to find the lost Bob the Nailer and put the drunken, self-pitying loser-loner behind him. Nick's faith became Julie's faith became Nikki's faith became Miko's faith, all in a line, and let him be what he was meant to be, what he'd been born to be. And it let him almost, after all of it, get close to the one god he worshiped, his great, martyred father.

But Nick wasn't there. Where the hell was Nick?

So he called the number he had for Matt MacReady.

Again, he just got the machine. "This is Matt. Leave a message."

"Matt, Swagger here. Boy, hate to bother you so soon before a race. One question: Recently I saw the tracks of some kind of machine. Steel wheels, maybe eight or ten inches apart, cut deep in the dirt. Hmmm, I recall all kinds of tracks in the pits when I visited you. Any idea what those kinds of tracks could be? Sure could help me. Thanks and good luck on Race Day."

He did catch up on the news from a Knoxville twenty-four-hour radio station. According to the reporter, the two dead men in the Johnson County Grocery Store shootings had been identified as Carmody Grumley and B.J. Grumley, both of no fixed address, both known to have organized crime connections and thought to be part of a mobile, shifting culture of strong-armed men used in various mob enterprises over the years. Each man had a substantial rap sheet. Young Terry Hepplewhite, the grocery clerk who shot it out with the robbers, was being hailed as a hero, though he had yet to meet with the press and tell his side of the story.

Grumley, he thought. The Grumley boys. What is this Grumley? Another question for Nick, who could dig up a file on Grumley.

Instead of going to his motel, where he thought these Grumleys might have had lookouts waiting, Bob went to the first church he saw, which was John the Revelator Baptist Church of Redemption. Just a one-story building with a steeple that hardly went up twenty-five feet, it wasn't a mighty structure but had a rough quality, as if it had been slowly assembled brick by brick in the humblest of ways. When he entered the hushed devotional space, he first thought he'd gone astray, for two worshipers were black, and it occurred to him that their memory of large white men in jeans and boots might not be all that warm. But shortly a young black man in a suit and tie came out of a walkway and came over to him.

"May I help you, sir? Do you come to worship? You are welcome."

"Thank you, sir," Bob said. "But actually I have a biblical puzzle to solve and I thought someone here might pitch in."

"I can try. Please come this way."

The doors led Bob to a spare office with many Bibles and other books of religious persuasion occupying the shelves on one wall.

"Have a seat. My name is Lionel Weston, I am the pastor of John the Revelator."

"My name is Bob Lee Swagger, and I'm greatly appreciative, sir. This has to do with a passage that has come to my attention. My daughter was interested in it before an accident she had, and I'm wondering what it could mean."

"I'll try."

"Mark 2:11."

"Ah," said the Reverend Weston, "yes, of course. 'Arise from your bed and go to your home.' Or sometimes, 'Arise from your pallet and go to your house.' Christ has just performed a miracle. He had restored mobility to a paralyzed man. Doubters have assailed him even as worshipers have brought the sick and malformed to him. Not from ego, not from pride, but from compassion, he has restored this man's limbs to strength. It's one of the great miracles of the text. In fact, one might say those words express the pure joy of God's power, his ability to restore the infirm through faith. Does that help, Mr. Swagger?"

Bob's puzzled expression evidently communicated a truth to the minister.

"Possibly it has metaphorical meaning to your daughter. She's saying, 'I can walk.' Her sickness has been cured. She's had a revelation of sorts. Was she in spiritual or physical pain?"

"Sir, I don't think so. In fact, this muddies up the waters considerably. Could it be a code, a code word, a signal?"

"Mr. Swagger, I don't think God talks in code words. His meanings are clear enough for us."

"You are right, sir, and I am very grateful for your wisdom. I have to think on this and see how it fits in."

"How is your daughter?"

"She's recovering. I would ask her, but she's still unconscious."

"I will pray for her."

"I greatly appreciate it, sir."

"I will pray for you, Mr. Swagger. I hope you solve your riddle and straighten things out. I see you as a man who is good at straightening things out."

"I try, sir. Lord, how I try."

Leaving the church, he checked his watch and saw it was time to head to the sheriff's office. He contemplated whether he should slip the Kydex holster with the .38 Super on, and in the end concluded it would be a bad idea, a careless move, an accident. Detective Thelma would see that he was armed, which could lead to embarrassing questions, even charges.

He got there at eight, pulling into the lot.

Agh, that perpetual shroud of coal dust that hung over this neck of the woods hit him. In a second he'd have a headache. No wonder they were getting the hell out of here. Bob walked into the station and a clerk nodded him back to the bullpen area where Thelma stood by in her polo and chinos while three SWAT officers with MP5 submachineguns and AR-15 shorties were gearing up for the night's event.

"Mr. Swagger."

"Detective Fielding."

"This is our Fugitive Apprehension Team." The guys, beefy cop types. Two white, one black, in their twenties with short hair, thick necks, and the look of middle linebackers, nodded at him without making any sincere emotional commitment.

"Wow, you must be expecting some kind of gunfight. You look like you're going on a commando raid."

"You just want to take precautions. I doubt Cubby has a fix on going down hard. He's a gentle soul, as long as he isn't lit up on ice."

"I hope you're right."

"All right, sir, you drive with me, and the FAT guys will follow in their van. Let me brief you. I will park down the way and you will stay in the car; we'll wait for the van to park and the boys will take up entry positions in the rear. Then I'll signal Air and my brother Tom, who's the sheriff's helicopter pilot —"

"Your brother's the pilot?"

"Tom was shot down as an army aviator three times in two wars. The last one, in

Baghdad, was bad. He had some problems and had to leave the army. Maybe I started this whole drug-war thing, because I put through the Justice Department grant paperwork to get us the bird so my brother would have someplace to go."

"I see. Impressive. You helped him."

"I tried, but you know the law of unintended consequences. Now I worry that — oh, never mind. Let's get back to it. Tom will bring the ship in, and his copilot will work the high-intensity beam in case Cubby tries to run. I'll go in and knock and tell Cubby he's coming with me. It should go fine, but if he bolts, he'll just run into these fellows and if he goes violent on us, then we'll have to run him down. But I'm not betting on trouble."

"Okay."

"You just stay in the car. When we bring him in and book him, I'll let you listen from the next room to the interrogation. Cubby's no master criminal, believe me; he'll give it up fast and I've set it up with the Prosecutor's office to have him indicted in the morning. Paperwork's all done. Then it's just a matter of making sure Tennessee justice don't drop the ball, and I will watch that one very closely."

"I thank you for taking me along. I appreciate it."

They sat on a tree-lined street in what could never be called the nicer side of town, a run-down section east of downtown where the old houses — shacks more like it, maybe at best bungalows — leaned this way and that. And you had the sense that a lot of police action had taken place there before.

"I've been busting Cubby for ten years, off and on," Thelma said. "He'll go clean for a while, maybe as long as six months, but he's always gone back. Sad to see such a handsome man give his life away for nothing. He'll gin up a lab, he'll deal a little, he'll snitch out somebody to buy more time, just scuffling along, waiting for a way to amp the scratch to buy another bag of the stuff. Man, it's the devil's business, what it does to folks. You have any addiction problems in your family, sir?"

"Detective, I am not proud to say that I had some troubles with the bottle years back and to this day I miss my bourbon, but one sip and I'm gone. It cost me, and I finally beat it down, though now and again, under trying circumstances, I will break down and have a drink. I usually end up in the next county engaged to a tattooed Chinese woman."

She didn't acknowledge his joke.

"But my daughter's never had a thing to do with it, and only now and then drinks a glass of wine. We've been so lucky."

"Yes, you have. The wrecked families I've seen."

"Let me ask you: You're sure on this boy?"

"Sure as sure is. He has a brother who has a car that matches the vehicle ID'd on the state forensics reports, the cobalt '05 Charger. I checked this morning — it was a busy morning — and in fact Cubby had the car and in fact it's banged up where he hit your daughter. I looked at the car and I think we can make the presence of your daughter's paint in the gash along the side of the Charger."

Bob was thinking, What the hell is she talking about? Who is this Cubby? Is he working for Eddie Ferrol, or some mysterious Mister Big, the Godfather of Johnson County? How's it all connected? What does this detective know of his connections?

"You'll check on his associations once you get him locked up? Be interesting to see if he was —"

"Working for somebody. Last person he worked for was Mr. McDonald, of the hamburger chain, who fired his worthless ass in three weeks. He was never able to master the deep-fat fryer."

"Maybe he has other connections, criminal connections."

"Doubtful, Mr. Swagger, but if so, we'll find out tonight when I run the interrogation."

"Yes ma'am. Now on another thing, this sheriff's making a big splash with his chopper. But I hear the price of the stuff hasn't gone up, which you'd expect if all the labs were being closed down. What's the feeling?"

"Nobody knows. Maybe there's a super-lab somewhere, but you'd think you'd smell it, because manufacturing crystal meth in quantity produces a terrible, rotten egg smell. Or maybe it's being trucked in from somewhere. Don't know if you know it, but there's a shooting last night, some grocery clerk got lucky and killed two robbers. The robbers were interesting: real serious bad actors, your white-trash professional heavy hitter, with rumored contacts to a batch of mobs all over the South, and participation suspected in a dozen armed robberies. Them boys ran out of luck in the worst possible way last night. Anyhow, way my mind works, I'm thinking, maybe they muled a load of ice from somewhere deeper south, and that's where the stuff is coming from. I don't know what else would explain their presence here. It would go to someone who knew the area, had ambitions, and a lot of criminal skills. Don't know who that would be. You see any criminal geniuses hiding at Arby's on the way over?"

"No ma'am, but there's a shady dude at the Pizza Hut."

This got a laugh out of her, but her mind was elsewhere, really, as she scanned the shabby front of the house down the street.

"Adam-one-nine, you there?" came a squawky call on the radio.

She spoke into her throat mic.

"Adam-one-nine copy."

"Adam-one-nine, we in place. You can go any time."

"Air-one, stat. You there, Tom?"

"I read you Adam one-nine."

"Tom, you bring it on in and when you see me at the front door, you have Mike open up with the big lamp on the back of the house, you got that?"

"I read you, Adam one-nine."

She turned to Swagger.

"Please don't make me look bad. Sheriff doesn't know about this. But I figure the dad gets to watch as the fellow who tried to kill his daughter goes down."

He could tell she was uneasy, and the

breath came hard and shallow. She ran a dry tongue over dry, cracked lips, and for one second did something amazingly feminine that totally contradicted the image of a tough cop about to make a bust. She grabbed a role of lip balm from the dash, and smoothed it, dainty as an expensive French lipstick, across her lips.

"Yes ma'am," said Bob, as she got out of the car and walked slowly to the front door.

He wondered why they didn't do it bigger; ten cars, lights flashing, loudspeakers. But maybe that would spook an icehead like this Cubby, legendary maker of bad decisions, and the next thing, there'd be another big gunfight. Give Thelma the benefit of the doubt. She's done this, you haven't. You don't know so much, and as it is you are riding the raw edge of a term in jail on any one of a dozen charges.

So he sat back and watched the police theater.

Thelma arrived at the doorwell, hesitated. Her hand flew to her pistol, made certain it was where it should be and that the retaining device still held it ready and secure until the moment she drew, if she drew.

She knocked.

She knocked again.

No answer.

She slithered next to the door jamb and edged the door open. She had a Surefire in her nonshooting hand, and she used it to penetrate the darkness. He heard her yell, "Cubby? Cubby, it's Detective Fielding. You in there? You come on out now, we've got business."

There was no answer.

Don't go in, Bob thought. One-on-one in the dark of a house against a violent offender whose head is all messed up on account of the skank he eats and makes every day, who's paranoid, maybe crazy, oh lady, don't go in, it isn't necessary. Drop back, watch the exits, call for backup, let the boys in the Tommy Tactical outfits earn their dough.

But Thelma slipped in.

The moments passed, and before he knew it Bob had gotten out of the car and crouched in the lee of its wheel well, watching, waiting for shots or something.

Oh, Christ. Through the windows, he could see the beam of her flashlight dancing against the walls and ceiling of the dark interior of the small place, which couldn't have more than a few rooms.

Come on, he thought. He wanted to see her come out with the suspect cuffed, and the boys with the guns come racing around the house to take him away. Nice job, great job, good work, good old Thelma but —

From under the line of the house — it must have been a cellar window cut against a gap in the foundation — he saw someone squirm free, low crawl across the yard into the bushes lining the house next door.

Suddenly a flash-bang erupted in Cubby's house, the loud smack of percussion breaking the still of the night, and the helicopter dropped low and its light came on hard and bright. The sounds of windows breaking, doors being busted in told the story: The FAT guys were assaulting from the rear. Maybe Thelma had him or he'd clonked her and she'd just awakened and given the green light to the FAT team. But the shadowy figure that had slipped out and squirmed across the yard suddenly broke from his hiding place and began to run crazily down the sidewalk, trying to put as much distance between himself and his pursuers as he could. He raced right toward Bob, who had a sudden almost comic memory flash over him. It was so football, the running back, broken free of the line of scrimmage, scurrying down the sideline, the lone safety, the only man between him and the end zone. He knew it was a bad idea, a sixty-three-year-old man with a bum leg and everything, but it didn't matter what he knew, it only mattered what he did, which was to launch himself, run through his sudden hip pain, find the right angle, and close the distance.

At the last second, Cubby saw him and from somewhere produced a handgun. But Bob was too far gone and just plunged ahead, driving his shoulder hard into the man's ample gut, trying to drive clean through him and bring him flat to the ground, hearing some ancient coach from somewhere back in the Jurassic scream, "Drive through him, Bobby, take his legs out, give him your whole damn shoulder, explode through him." And that's what he did, textbook perfect. Both men went down in a bone-bruising crack, lights flashing through each head, knees abrading bloodily on the pavement as they tumbled, limbs flying, breaths knocked free.

He didn't feel the knee to the head. It couldn't have been planned. It was just one of those football things, when two flying bodies collide and torsos hit with the smack of wet meat falling off the table, legs and arms go screwball. And it so happened that Cubby's knee flew up in a spasm as his breath was belted out of his lungs, and the knee hit Bob flush upside the head, a little forward of the ear. It was having your bell rung, and Bob's rang so loud it knocked pinwheels of light, illumination rounds, spasms of tracers, sparks from a bonfire, fly legs and spider heads through his brain. He went to the ground all tangled with Cubby, but his limbs and his brain were momentarily dead. In a second, he came back to consciousness first to sound. The sound of running steps. The sound of a powerful helicopter engine. Then came light as the copter nailed Bob and his prey in the bright circle of thirty-five hundred lumens, and they were like as on a stage, shadowless and drained of all color except the lamp's eerie cold pure moonlight. He blinked, felt the pain, tried to breathe, and realized Cubby had linked himself to him with an arm around his throat tight, squeezing off the breath until Bob coughed and shook and the grip loosened a little.

"Goddamn you, Mister, you keep still or I will put a goddamned bullet through your head," Cubby yelled so forcefully that the message was conveyed just as eloquently by the jetstream of saliva that hit Bob. Bob saw something in his peripheral vision and felt it go hard against his head. He recognized by its circularity that it was the muzzle of a revolver.

Oh, fuck, he thought. Now you have gone and done it.

"Goddamn you, Thelma — you said — you said — Goddamn you, Thelma."

"Cubby, you hold on now. Don't you do nothing stupid. That fella ain't a cop, you got no grudge against him. You let him go and put the gun down and we'll get all this straightened out."

He could see her, about twenty-five feet away, just out of the cone of illumination; behind her, the three FAT officers had gone into good strong kneeling positions, their weapons jacked dead on the target, which he hoped was Cubby and not himself. Aim small, miss small, boys, go to semi-auto, think trigger control and breath control, he thought, gasping for air.

"Cubby, don't do anything stupid," Thelma said in a smooth calm voice, walking into the light looking calm, more like a mom than anything. "You just let that fella go. Put the gun down and we'll work our way through this."

"Thelma, *no!* You said, you said — *no,* I ain't going back to all that. It ain't right. Goddamn, oh, why this happening, why why why? I had her licked this time. Oh God, they's in my head, I hears 'em yelling. Oh Christ. *No,* Thelma."

Bob was thinking: Where's the fucking sniper when you need him? Did he have a Little League game to coach or something? A good man on a .308 and a solid position could send 168 grains of Federal's best match load through Cubby's eye and into his ancient snake brain and end this thing in the time it took the bullet to fly at twenty-three hundred feet per second to its target. But there was no sniper, just the woman cop and the three young Tommy Tacticals looking shaken as they crouched, trying to keep good muzzle discipline.

Thelma took another step. She had guts and how. This screwball could pop one into Bob and whirl and fire and take her down before she cleared leather. Of course the three Tacticals would each heroically dump a magazine into him, but both he and Thelma would be beyond caring. Why had he done such a stupid thing? Where could Cubby have gone anyway, cranked as he was on the ice that ate holes into his brain? But his grip on Bob and the force of his wrist against Bob's throat was iron, and Bob struggled again for air, while smelling his rank body odor, and feeling the fear and craziness vibrate through Cubby's flesh.

"Don't you move goddamn you," said Cubby, pressing the gun muzzle so hard against the thin skin at the crown of Bob's head that he cut it. A trickle of blood oozed out, and Bob felt the warmth of the liquid and then the sting of the wound.

"Cubby, you just calm down. Nobody has to get hurt now, I'm telling you."

"But you goin' send me back. Don't know why I did it, Thelma, don't remember none. I don't know, I been so high for so long don't think I hit no car, but goddamn I got voices saying you hurt a girl you hurt a girl. Wouldn't hurt no girl, Thelma. Like them girls sometimes they nice to me. God, they in my head — it hurts. I can't go back — I can't go back. It ain't right — I didn't do nothing, I don't want to hurt nobody. God, Thelma, it just ain't right — I can't do this no more — it's just no good no more. Oh, Thelma, you said you'd help me — I am so sorry I can't —"

Bob heard the oily slide of the hammer against the constriction of the frame, as Cubby drew it back, then the slight vibration as it locked. The gun was now cocked, his finger on the trigger, just a single-action jerk away from firing.

"Thelma, I will kill this boy — you go way — y'all go way — put down your guns, let me go. Don't want to hurt nobody. *Please, please,* it don't have to be this way, but goddamn I will squeeze on this here boy — you just lay down your guns and —"

Thelma drew and fired with a speed that was almost surreal. Bob had never seen a hand move so fast, so sure, so smooth, so clean. It was like a trick of physics, a speed beyond the influence of time, that seemed to come from nowhere, elegant, controlled, blazing. It was professional shooting at its finest.

He saw the flash, saw the slight buck of the automatic as its slide jacked in super-time, saw the spent shell flip away, caught in the light, and even felt the simultaneous vibration as whatever she'd sent off hit its target. The sound of bullet on flesh is always the same, dense and wet and full of the sense of meat splattering and bone shatter-ing, yet compressed into a nanosecond. He actually felt Cubby die instantly, the vivid vital flesh in supertime again alchemizing to dead, directionless weight, pulled on by impatient gravity. As Cubby fell, his draped arm brought Bob down with him harshly, and they landed in a heap and the handgun, still cocked, bounced away.

Bob wriggled free and saw that Thelma'd hit him left of the nose, maybe an inch, and that the bullet had drilled a perfect round black hole, which, in another second, began to release a surprisingly thin gurgle of black fluid. Then his nose began to bleed, not copiously, just a trickle of black as blood under pressure sought escape. The man's eyes were open, and so was his mouth. Behind him, a ponytail fanned out on the sidewalk in the harsh light, and a puddle of exit-wound blood, black in the illumination, began to delta outward through the hair. That must have been a hell of an exit. He wore a cut-off Ole Miss T-shirt, a pair of tight jeans, and was barefoot. His feet were dirty with long, animal-like toenails crusted with grime.

Bob stood up.

"Mr. Swagger, are you all right, sir?"

"I am fine, Detective. That was some shooting," he said.

"I am so sad I had to drop him. Only had to do it once before and it shook me up for a year."

"I am glad you were over your shakes tonight, Detective."

The other three officers had gathered around, and Thelma put her pistol away, and knelt next to the fallen man. She pried the gun from his fingers — a Smith K-frame, probably in .38 — decocked it, and expertly popped the latch open, letting the cylinder rotate out.

They both looked into it.

"Empty," she said. "Well, I couldn't wait. I had to put him down."

"You made the right decision, ma'am."

"Thelma," one of FAT kids said, "you didn't have no choice. You did the right thing."

"That's right, Thelma," said another. "Don't you worry about it. Nobody could fault you."

"You sure you're okay, Mr. Swagger? Maybe when the medical people get here you might want to have them look at you."

"I'm fine, I'm fine. Maybe it'll hit me later, but right now it just seems unreal. Detective, where'd you learn to shoot like that? I never —"

"Thelma's three-times running ladies' USPSA champ of the Southeast Region, Tennessee, North Carolina, and Kentucky. She could go pro, she's that good, Mr. Swagger. Para-Ord sponsors her. You're lucky she's here. She's probably the best shot of any law enforcement agent in this part of the country. Maybe the whole damn country."

A cruiser, its lights running hard, pulled up, and then another and another, so on until general delirium took over the scene.

TWENTY-TWO

The thing was, you couldn't smoke. He might see a lit cigarette glowing in the otherwise-darkened interior of Vern's red Cadillac El Dorado, then bolt. *Agh.* So both Vern and Ernie, in cranky moods, sat grumpily scrunched down in the car in a dimly illuminated zone of the parking lot of the Mountain Empire Motel. Neither had had a cigarette in hours. It was a little after midnight.

"I might sneak out and run around back for a smoke," said Ernie.

"You will not, cousin, no sir. And take a risk he pulls in just as you're in his lights? That's how it'll happen, you know it is, that's how it always happens when you give in to your hungers on a job. You be a good bad guy now, and do what Daddy has said. We may get a kill out of this tonight and then we can smoke our asses off."

"Vern Pye, I don't mind saying, I didn't

enjoy your tone with me just there. Didn't say I'd do it, now, did I? No sir, said I *might*. Just talking. You're so high and mighty, I see your eyes go all buggy anytime a piece of hot under the age of fifteen with no tits goes on by. Please watch that tone, Vern."

"Well, excuse me, sir, I'm just trying to get the job done right and proper so I can go back to my regular line of business. And what kind of gal I take a fondness toward ain't nobody's business. I will say, this here stay in scenic Mountain City has been as hard on me as it has on you, cousin."

"You don't even want to be here, that is why you are in such a punky mood."

"No, I don't. This is not the right move. But if the old man says do it, I have to do it and so do you, even though you agree with me and not him."

"All I know is, he says go, I go. That's how it is."

"Even now in this car alone you are afraid to defy him."

"Maybe I just respect the rules, is all. And if you don't, no cause to turning all crabby on me."

But then a car pulled into the lot. Both squirmed down a little, both noted that it was indeed a small Ford or Toyota, the sort the rental companies generally provided. It prowled, looking for spaces, and found one close to Room 128, which they knew to be the hit's.

"Could be," said Vern.

"Pray to God," said Ernie. "Or maybe it's a teen-age gal in short-shorts and a halter with the new issue of *Tiger Beat*."

"Asshole."

The fellow got out, slid around to the trunk, opened it, took something out, and held it tight under his arm, looked about for signs of something not in place, and then moved gently toward the room. But it was the limp that gave him away for real. It was like he had pain in that right hip from more than a single wound. He was also moving stiffly as if bandaged in a dozen or so places. He paused, took a look around the lot again, satisfied himself that it was all clear, then bent to open the door, slipped in, and locked the door behind him.

"Hot doggies," said Vern. "I can taste that Marlboro right now."

"He's the pilgrim, all right. Can't believe a old gray-hair like that dusted Carmody and B.J., but now's the night he learn it don't pay to poke at Grumley."

"That's holy Baptist writ, right there, cousin."

Vern slipped his Glock .40 from the

shoulder rig and edged back the slide to make certain a shell lay nested in the chamber, while Ernie, a wheel gunner with an engraved El Paso holster on his belt, did the same with his 2.5-inch-barreled, nickel-plated Python full of .357 CorBons.

Vern had figured it out.

"I say we wait a bit. Let him get settled in. Brush his teeth, check the lot through the window, make his calls, maybe have a sip or ten on that bottle of bourbon he done brung into the room, get all settled and snuggly, then we kick the door and empty our guns into the guy on the bed who won't know what hit him, and then we head out fast. You okay with that, cousin?" Vern asked.

"Sounds like a plan," said Ernie. "Should we call your daddy?"

"Don't know about that. You look more like him than I do. It's in the nose and the mouth."

"I don't like powder blue. It don't bring out the color in my eyes. And I don't wear no white fright wig so's to look like that chicken-pushing Confederate colonel. My ma never said he was my daddy. He's the only one."

"Ooo, doggie, I see I done touched a nerve."

"Hell, cousin, he's probably *both* our daddies by both his sisters. Now what's that tell you about the old man's judgment? So why'd we want to call him?"

"I think my ma's his daughter, not his sister. He do like to stir the soup, don't he? Anyway, I'm thinking we ought to bring other boys in. Maybe someone with a shotgun to blow the door, then step aside."

"He brings that shotgun, he ain't gonna want to step aside. He's going to want to put a couple of double-oughts into the guy in the bed, watch the fur and feathers fly. Then we ain't done nothing but been good little scouts. It don't do me no good. 'You hear, someone dumped two Grumleys and old Vern Pye hisself went after and put the man down hard.' I want that said about me, and I want a reward for three hours without a cigarette."

"That's cool by me."

They settled in, waiting as the seconds dragged by. What, another hour? An hour was too long. Half an hour would do. But as the time crawled by, doubts appeared.

"You sure you don't want to call the old man?"

Vern said, "He'd just want to come out hisself. Then we got to wait on him. We got to wait while the whole thing comes together. That's two more hours without a smoke."

"Or a poke."

"You see anything pokable here now? No sir. Anyhow, I say, we do it, we're gone, it's over and it's smoke time. Then we get back, then we go on the main job, then we get our swag, then we go about our business and put this here time in the prayer camp behind us. You can go back to your job in the warehouse, I can go home to one of my three wives, or maybe a stripper, or maybe pick me up something new and fresh."

"Somewhere in there, can we throw in a shot of tequila? A shot of the worm, damn, that'd be just swell."

"Yessir to that."

"Yessir to the worm."

But a few minutes later, it was Vern who said, "Hell. I just don't know what's nagging at me. Too long without a pop, my nerves are shot. Don't want to make no mistake. Call him. Make certain."

"Okay."

"Keep it quiet now."

Ernie slipped his cell out, ordered it to call the Reverend, and heard the rings, one, then two, then a thir—

"What is it, boy?"

"Sir, we got him. He just come in. Been in his room 'bout half hour now. Vern and me's fixin' to visit and leave hair and brains on the wall. Just want —"

"No, no, no," said the old man. "Haven't you heard? Already a shooting in town tonight, some meth dealer got wasted by Thelma. Man, you go and shoot the town up, it's going to be like Dodge City here and we get the state cops and the FBI and all them other boys. They already here, I'm betting."

"Daddy, I can *nail* him in ten —"

"No, boy. I changed my mind. Too much of a risk. We have a big job. Now here's what I want. You and Vern, you head on into Bristol. I'm betting he's staying at his girl's apartment, and I got that address. You set up over there. After the big job is done, he'll be there. *That's* when you hit him and finish this business but good, in the Grumley way."

"Yes sir. Does that mean, if we don't go on the big job, we don't git our share of —"

"No, it does not. You get full share. You just don't meet up at the camp 'cause we'll be long gone and spread to the four winds after Race Day. You call me a week down the road, and I'll have your share for you. Just as promised."

"Thank you, Daddy."

"You follow me?"

"I do, sir."

Ernie clicked off.

"Well?" said Vern.

"Smoke 'em if you got 'em," said Ernie, lighting up a cigarette.

Twenty-Three

Swagger awarded himself a good night's sleep, as he'd been running without it for two or three days. He'd gotten back from giving a deposition at the sheriff's office around midnight. He jammed a chair under the doorknob to hang up any unexpected intruders, stuffed his pillow under the blankets to represent a fellow sleeping on a bed, and took his rest in the bathtub, boots on, with the Kimber .38 Super as a pillow. He had good, deep sleep, slightly broken by dreams where his father told him how disappointed he was in the man Bob had become. But this theme presented itself so often it didn't bother him. It went with the privilege and the luck of being Earl Swagger's son.

He awoke at ten, took a shower, rebandaged the cut on his knee, checked on the swelling around his eyes to see that it had gone down a little, took three ibus, then changed into new jeans and a new polo shirt. Next, rather than breakfast, came coffee brewed in the room's coffee maker. Then he got down to it. His first call was to his wife.

"Well howdy," she said, and he sensed from the joy in her voice something good had happened.

"Is she awake, Julie?"

"She was. For almost a whole minute. She sat up in bed, looked at me, and said, 'Hi, Mom.' Then she smiled at Miko and said, 'Hi, little sister.' Then she lay back down and went back to wherever."

"Oh, great! Oh, that's the best news! What do the doctors say?"

"It's how they come back. It's never, 'Hi, what's for breakfast? Let's go to the movies.' It's a slow swim out of the dark place. She may have short periods of wakefulness for a few days going before she comes out of it completely. So they're very, very optimistic. Sometimes the victims don't remember a thing, but she knew who I was and who Miko was. Oh, it's such good news. Can you come soon? It'd be so good if you were here when she really came out of it."

"Well, damn, I'll try. There are some things, some issues, I have to deal with."

"There was more shooting last night out there."

"I didn't fire a shot. In fact, my gun was still in the trunk. I come through it all right, except for a cut knee and a swollen forehead. They're even calling me a hero and some TV station wanted an interview. I told 'em to call my PR rep. Anyway, I'll call back in a bit. It still ain't — isn't a good idea for you to call me. I just don't know where I'll be and the sound of the phone might not do me any good."

"Okay. But please come soon. Oh, I am so excited."

"The news is great, honey."

The next thing he did was call Nick Memphis again. Nope, no answer. Where the hell was he? It wasn't like Nick to disappear. Maybe he was overseas or something. Anyhow, Bob just left the same message. Then he called Terry, the grocery clerk, to see how he was doing, but got no answer. He left a message. A second later the call-back came.

"You all right?" Bob asked. "Holding up?"

"Sir, it's been great. I been on the TV a bunch of times, I got calls from some producers in Hollywood, I been in all the papers. Is that okay? Am I handling this correct?"

"You ride this for all it's worth, you hear.

You owe me nor nobody nothing. You leverage it for all you can get out of it. If you want, I won't never call again, Terry."

"No, no, sir, call me. I want to know what's going on and I may need your advice. Also, I feel guilty being called a hero —"

"Which is the true mark of a hero. All heroes feel that way. I've known a few. But don't kid yourself, you stood and fought against two armed men, you took one of 'em down, put him on the floor and really won the fight while all I did was squeeze a trigger a few times. You are a hero, son. Even if you don't believe it. The rest is meaningless details."

"Yes sir."

"Now I can't tell you anything about the entertainment field. It's full of sharpies and you'd best keep your hand on your wallet is all I know. But you do call me if you have any trouble, you see anyone dogging you. And be careful. These fellas was working for other fellas. You hear me?"

"I do."

The next call was to Charlie Wingate, the boy genius in the computer store.

"Any more for me, Charlie?"

"Mr. Swagger, this hard drive is totally fried, near as I can tell. I only got that little bit, I'm afraid to say. Won't charge you a thing for that."

"Oh, yes you will. You charge me for a full day's work at topscale, consultant level, and not a penny less, you hear?"

"Yes sir."

"Now I want that brain of yours working on something else. Know anything about the Bible?"

"Not much."

"Well I don't either. But something's come up involving a biblical passage, Mark 2:11. It's where Jesus cures a crippled man and says to him, 'Get up, go home.'"

"'Mein Fuhrer, I can valk,'" said the boy.

"Yeah, something like that," said Bob, not even close to getting it. "So what I want you to do is analyze it from any perspective you can think of. Is the number significant, the two-eleven? Is the page on the Bible significant, don't know what it would be. What do the commentators say about it? What are the different interpretations? Is there some word translated differently from the original language, whatever the hell it was."

"Aramaic."

"Yeah, fine. Could it be a code, what are its other citations or usages in history or whatever? Are there paintings or something based on it? All that stuff. You're smart, you know what I mean."

"I'll try."

"You know the town?"

"Been here my whole life."

"Okay, maybe there's some connection between it and this town. I don't know what, but be creative, think outside the box, make it fun, a puzzle. Who knows what you might come up with."

"Yes sir."

He disconnected, and almost before he could put the phone down, it buzzed again. He checked the number and realized it was the private number of Matt MacReady, the young NASCAR racer calling him! Wasn't tomorrow the big race?

"Yes, Matt?"

"Hello, Gunny. How are you?"

"Only a week older'n last time I saw you, but it feels like a hundred years."

"Time do race, don't it? Only thing goes faster than my USMC Charger."

"Only thing."

"Anyhow, been thinking and looking and maybe I have something for you."

"Go ahead, son."

"Wheel marks, metal close together, part of the NASCAR racing operation? Well there is something. You see it all the time in the pits, it's everywhere, what's the word, upbequious?"

"Hmm, don't know that word."

"Red says it's 'ubiquitous.' That's what it is, ubiquitous."

"Well, damn. Hope I don't forget it. Ubiquitous. Everywhere."

"What it is is, it's the track of our hydraulic jacks."

"For tire changing?"

"Sir, yes sir. It ain't all the driver. Part of the art of winning at this game is teamwork on the car. I have a good crew, Red's got 'em trained up real good. They get me gassed, watered, maybe oiled, and re-tubed in less than fifteen seconds. It's like choreography, the way they work a car in the pits on Race Day. And the key to the tire change, of course, is the jack. It's a big heavy dog, solid steel and it's hydraulic, built of cylinders full of lube. Weighs about fifty pounds. Runs on steel wheels about an inch wide. You have your biggest, strongest stud as your jack man. He gets it over the wall, guides it fast to the wheel well, jacks the car off the ground. Meanwhile, your air-wrench guy de-lugs the tire even as the jack is lifting it high enough to clear. The wrench guy clears out, a guy comes in and grabs the lugs; that's his job, his only job, to keep track of the lugs. Two other boys, the tire men, pull the burned-out tire off the axle, roll it away, and slam on another one, which two other boys have rolled to them. The wrench-man airblasts the lugs tight, and the jackman lowers the car, and the whole team of them crash hell for leather to the next tire and repeat the same thing. They can get the car re-rubbered in fifteen seconds, and if you look, after a race, win, lose, draw, or crash and burn, their hands and wrists and especially fingers are all cut to hell. But they're tough boys, they don't much care."

"Got it. And they roll that thing through oil and water and it leaves tracks, maybe six to eight inches apart, everywhere on the tarmac, in the pits, everywhere?"

"I'd be willing to bet, sir."

"So if you saw a tangle of 'em, you'd think, someone's practicing a wheel change?"

"Well, that's what I'd think."

Hmmmm. Swagger tried to press this new information into the pattern he'd assembled. Tire change. Someone was practicing a speed-tire change, after the fashion of NASCAR. Now why the hell would that be? The boys setting this thing up weren't racers, weren't running a pit crew. What'd they need a speed-tire change for? What vehicle came with the wrong tires in place and had to be re-rubbered fast? What would be the point of the new tires? Well, only way it makes sense is if the first set of tires is burned out. Now what would burn out a set of tires? Were they going to steal a racing car? Those babies were expensive but he didn't —

Then he thought, no, no, it's not burned out. You change the tires in order to change the performance profile of the vehicle. It's tired-up one way, for one purpose, and now you re-rubber it and you use it for some other, presumably unusual purpose. Maybe that somehow linked with this fit of exploding trucks around the area? Maybe they were deviling up the engine as well for that purpose. But what truck could it be, what new purpose could it have?

"You still there? Does that help?"

"It sure does. Can't see just how yet, but I'm getting pieces in a row and pretty soon a pattern will be there. Now let me ask you something. This here's a long shot. Does the biblical passage Mark 2:11 about Jesus curing a crippled man mean anything to you? Would it fit into anything along these lines?"

"We really weren't people of the book, Gunny. Some drivers are but not us. So no, it doesn't mean anything to me, and I don't think it connects to Big Racing in any way."

"Okay, well, thanks. Really appreciate your taking the time with all you got do do. You're a good fella, I can tell."

"My pleasure."

"All you must have to do and you gave me a hand. That's marine all the way."

"Fact is, we don't do much day before. We'll run the car this afternoon for a last minute check, I have a signing at my retail trailer in NASCAR Village that'll be a madhouse but will move a lot of souvenir hats, and other than that it's just relaxing and trying to keep the mind clear."

"Well, good luck. I know you're good enough, I just hope the breaks go your way."

"Can't control that, so never worry about it," said the boy.

Bob sat, ruminated, took notes. Nothing. Then he realized he was hungry, slipped his .38 Super into the Kydex holster, locked on his belt after checking it for the millionth time to be certain it was cocked and locked, and eased out the door. Nothing seemed to be moving in the blazing August heat. A few cars were in the lot, but it was mostly dead space. A couple of stores down the big road was a Denny's, so Bob headed down to it, completely in Condition Green, giving his world a three-sixty every few minutes on the hunt for anything unusual, looking into shadows, looking for irregularities like the exhaust from a parked car or the same hat showing up on different people, that sort of thing. But it was just a hot day in small-town America.

He ate breakfast, though it was nearing one, and halfway through the meal had an idea of something proactive to do. He would read the entire Book of Mark, and maybe that way he'd get a feel for verse 2:11, see something in it that might have given his daughter some insight that would turn Eddie Ferrol and his associates homicidal.

So he spent the afternoon in his room reading the Bible, enjoying it more as a story — it was a great story, the way Jesus could have run and didn't want to go up on that cross, reminding him of too many marines who could have run and didn't and stayed to die — than as anything else. When he was done reading the chapter the second time, he had nothing.

Think. Another thing to do was to look up Eddie Ferrol's home, then visit it well after dark. Almost certainly Eddie wouldn't be there, but who knows what clues he might have left behind. Then there was the Carmody and the B.J. Grumley cousins;

maybe by now, more information on them had emerged. But he'd have to get that through Nick, as calling Thelma and betraying an unusual interest in that case would not be an intelligent move. But Nick hadn't called either. Bob called again, and the same thing happened — no answer. And there was no call from the kid in the computer store.

He was tired and felt room-bound and restless at the same time. After a good start, the day was turning out to be worthless. He'd learned nothing, made no progress and —

He knew the sound, the almost liquid sloshing of a heavy airborne engine that could spell only one thing, and that was helicopter. He'd ridden in enough of 'em, and one had saved his life in Vietnam by getting him to the field surgical hospital at Dak To before his life signs slipped away after a Russian sniper had blown a hole in his hip. This one was no Huey, but a larger, more powerful craft and it grew louder and louder, signifying close-by descent.

Bob went to the window, looked out, and saw a large ship settle in the empty parking lot, its rotors a heavy blur that stirred up whirlpools of dust and debris for a hundred yards. It was a Blackhawk no less, much weathered by the winds of wars here and there across the planet but now wearing the starred emblem of law enforcement and the announcement, SHERIFF'S DEPARTMENT JOHNSON COUNTY TENNESSEE across its nose. A handful of grit flew into Bob's face, and the force of the air beat him back, but he saw the chief Tommy Tactical of them all, Sheriff Reed Wells, drop heavily from the large cargo hatch and head his way.

The sheriff wore a black Nomex jump suit that was hung with belts containing gas grenades, flashbangs, knives, and radio gear. A low slung holster was strapped to his thigh with a tricked-up, cocked and locked .45. His upper body was encased in a stiffly uncomfortable armored vest, with SHERIFF in white letters across the front. Both his knees and his elbows were protected by thick plastic and foam pads. He had a black baseball cap that bore the star emblem of his department, tear-shaped shades, and carried a shorty M4 with a 30-round P-mag, a suppressor and a couple of thousand bucks' worth of optical sights, flashlights, lasers, and maybe even a can opener bolted onto various rails that ran around the gun's forearm and receiver top. Lord, the man looked war.

Bob stepped back to let the warrior king

clamber in, all rattley and clanky, as if he'd just gotten off his horse sometime in the fifteenth century. But it wasn't a raid, and the sheriff gestured to Bob to sit, while he himself sat heavily on the bed. Bob saw immediately that the sheriff couldn't put the M4 down because it was looped to him by a single strand of sling that ran diagonally around his body. But he laid the gun in his lap and took off his hat and glasses. Outside, the noise of the Blackhawk lowered as the pilot shifted to an idling pitch.

"Mr. Swagger, I am beginning to grow annoyed. Your daughter's case is closed. Thelma closed it last night. We here are very sorry about what happened, but I took it for granted that you'd move on out of here today."

"Yes sir, don't mean to overstay my welcome. I'se just going over some loose ends and was going to type 'em up and send 'em off to Thelma. She did damned well, by the way."

"She saved your life as I recall. Or at least at the time, it certainly seemed she did."

"Long as I live, I will never forget the sound of that hammer being pulled back and the speed of her draw. The gal is superfast and shoots straight. I was a lucky man and will be forever grateful."

"Let me ask you about a few loose ends myself. What you went through last night would send most men to the hospital. At the least, they'd be throwing up in the grass for a week. They'd also be changing underpants right away, to be crude but truthful. And that's just the hostage situation and the trigger pull on the empty chamber. On top of that, you saw a man killed at close range, his brains blown out, and the bullet that took his life passed within six inches of your head. Again, a source of major psychological trauma. When people see people shot, it robs them of sleep for weeks, sometimes months, sometimes years. But from all reports, you hardly noticed and were up and perky in seconds."

Bob realized he'd misplayed the scene last night. Some macho twist in his mind made him make certain that Thelma and the three FAT officers understood he was as much man as they were and his close call was meaningless to a man who'd had thousands of close calls. Duh! Stupid. Now they were curious about his fortitude. Where did it come from, what did it mean? He should have thrown a weeping jag and pretended to be too distraught to continue. But it hadn't occurred to him. Another foolish old man's mistake.

"It was so fast in the happening and so unreal. I still can't believe it happened. Maybe my rough times are all ahead of me, and that's when the sleep goes away."

"I suppose. That would be one explanation. But another occurred to me. You're not a professional? A gunman, some kind of commando veteran, a former SWAT officer, military with a lot of combat, something like that? That's how you operated."

"I told you, I had some military experience years ago."

"We ran your record. Clean. No indictments, no felonies. I'd pay that ticket you owe the Boise police, though. And I hope you get the drainage issue on your Pima County barn settled. You don't want trouble with those environmental groups."

"Yes sir. I have a lawyer working that one now."

"See, I can't help notice that you show up and suddenly this little sleepy village becomes Dodge City. Two nights ago, some kid clerk outshoots two hardcore bad guys. I mean really outshoots 'em, absolutely the way a trained professional with a knack for gunwork and a commando's sense of aggression might have outshot 'em. You're nowhere connected to that, except that I do have an unverified report of a dark sedan, probably a rental, leaving the grocery store in the immediate aftermath of that shooting. We can't crack that kid, but I do note you drive a dark green Ford rental sedan. Ain't that one interesting?"

"Sheriff, I'm just a dad trying to figure out —"

"And yesterday you take down a fleeing armed man. You're sixty-three years old and walk with a pronounced limp, yet you have no fear of going one-on-one at top speed with an armed drug addict. I have twenty-five-year-old, two-hundred-forty-pound deputies who wouldn't do that. Then, when he takes you hostage, you don't even sweat. When he cocks the hammer —"

"I didn't hardly have time to react to that, sir. It happened, and Thelma fired almost in the same second."

"And when our officer drills him beneath the eye, you don't even notice. You're hardly curious. You don't breathe hard, you don't become agitated or nothing. It's ho-hum. Another day in Mr. Swagger's life, yawn. Another head-shot, another dollar. Yet your record is curiously, curiously clean, as if some professionals had taken care of you for whatever reason, and there's no paper or reports of any kind on you. Did you work for CIA or something?"

"I have known an officer of that agency, a very fine lady. Also some assholes. I am friendly with a highly placed FBI agent as well, from events years back. But there's no paper on me because I'm just a lucky businessman from outside Boise. I was in the marines for a time. There's no story there. This ain't some kind of thriller book where everybody's somebody else and everybody knows how to shoot."

"I hope you're telling the truth."

"Should I get a lawyer sir? Am I a person of interest? Would I be better off with legal representation?"

"I suspect you'll always be a person of interest, Mr. Swagger. No, you don't need a lawyer, what you need is a full tank of gas and a good westward destination."

"Yes sir. I never argue with a man who has a machine gun. But I have paid my night's rental and it's now dark, so I have no particular interest in driving the far side of Iron Mountain at this time of night. Suppose I leave tomorrow, bright and early, hoping to beat the Race Day traffic. I'll finish up the report at my daughter's and send it to Detective Fielding. Is that acceptable?"

"Somehow I doubt you're afraid of the dark, sir."

"It's not the dark. It's what's in the dark."

"I heard a very capable Green Beret say the same thing. All right, Mr. Swagger. Tomorrow you're gone or we will meet again at Booking. Over and out?"

"Over and out, Sheriff."

TWENTY-FOUR

Brother Richard looked so much like Richard Petty you'd have thought he'd get arrested for impersonating a hero. He had that befeathered, straw cowboy hat pulled low over his ears, the tip and tail of its rakishly cantilevered brim cranked beneath eye level, its Indian festival of secretly meaningful charms and amulets flopping insouciantly in the breeze. His eyes were shielded behind glasses that would have looked equally good on the authentic King Richard or Jacqueline Onassis. He had Richard's scrawny, twisty, muscular body and he wore a NASCAR T-shirt with a pack of Marlboros rolled up in the sleeve. He wore tight jeans and comfortable Luchese boots.

The reason he didn't get arrested or beaten up or mobbed by teenage white gals was that where he was, every other man looked just the same. It was like a carnival of Richard Petty look-alikes, that being but one category. Others chose the Kurt Bush paradigm, and still others the Dale Jr. Huck Finn, the Tony Stewart, the Juan Montoya, the Mike Martin, the Matt MacReady, and there were even, hard to believe, a few Jeff Gordons, though they had to be from California. This was the crowd at NASCAR Village, that gridwork of cult and retail sites just outside the mighty Bristol speedway, which towered above them all, while providing a steady deafening roar as the weekend's cars whizzed about it a few last times to run the engines at speed for a final checkout.

It was Friday, the start of racing weekend, under a hot August sky, in a Shenandoah Valley that at this moment was plastered with cars, tents, Rec-Vs, SUVs, everything short of armored personnel carriers. The vehicles rode the gentle hills like a gigantic carpet, as the hundreds of thousands came to worship, live, experience glory and fear vicariously, drink, smoke, shove, fuck, hoot, and have a hell of a good time. Most of them were beyond bliss; there was so much happiness in the meandering beast of the crowd you couldn't but crack a smile at the heat of the joy. It turned you a little red in fact.

But none of them were as happy as Brother Richard, as he let the crowd push him this way and that through what really amounted to a NASCAR Casbah. The streets weren't lined with gold, not, that is, if you were buying, though maybe if you were selling. For NASCAR people were spenders. They had to take something of the great Night of Thunder home with them. They bought pendants and T-shirts and cup-holders and beer caddies and hats and thick leather jackets and sweat shirts and polo shirts and pictures and die-cast models and bottled water, beer and bourbon and corporate propaganda. Chevy, Ford, Toyota, and Dodge, the four sanctioned automobile suppliers, had gigantic pavilions, and all four had a pedestal inside. Atop each pedestal was a street shell of the hand-made, custom machine that would, tonight and especially tomorrow night, roar four hundred then five hundred times around the stiffly tilted half-mile where dreams could die in seconds, sometimes in flames, sometimes in the crunch of collapsing metal. The track where guts and grit and luck played against each other at 140 per until one boy was smarter, tougher, braver, and luckier than all the others, and crossed the line first and tasted, however briefly, godhood.

Each of the boss drivers had a long-haul

trailer set up in the village, which they'd converted to a dedicated sales outlet. There the hero's image or number or both had been imprinted on everything, books and videos were added to the swag, hats in a hundred variations were on display — and for sale — and a crew of cashiers lined up to take your bucks. The cash flow must have been amazing; the twenty-dollar bill was the new one-dollar bill, and although the modern cash registers didn't *ka-ching* like the old mechanical marvels from Dayton, you could tell yourself that you heard a heavenly choir of *ka-ching*ing, even if it weren't necessarily true. Brother Richard looked at all that money flowing one way and one way only and briefly considered what might have been but never was, and stifling a choking sound, he took another hard blast on the Bud he carried (like everybody else) in a bright red foam caddie.

You could tell who was hot by the crowds. Both Kyles were doing swell and of course everybody had a thing in their heart for the wonderful Dale Jr., inheritor of the mantle and now driving for the beloved football genius Joe Gibbs; there was little business at Jeff's, the eternal outsider's unit, where only malcontents and self-proclaimed mavericks gathered. But the hot one just now was the young redhead, Matt MacReady, just twenty-two, already with a handful of major wins at Sprint venues, in the hunt for the big cup itself still this late in the season.

Somehow, Richard felt himself pulled by torrents of enthusiasm, even love, toward the MacReady locality. In a second he realized why there had been such a current in the crowd. Good Lord, the boy himself was there.

Brother Richard halted and held back. He considered it for a second, then realized that after his surgery and in his currently repackaged King Petty mode, he would stir no old memories, not to the boy, not to Red, not to any of them. So he ambled close, slipping in and out of the whirls and eddies of pilgrims, and by not pushing it too hard, he got pretty close. No, he wouldn't get in the line, where Matt was dutifully signing posters, hats, T's, anything, with a Magic Marker, accepting goodwill wishes and even love-horse-powered thumps on the back with grace and ease and charm.

Richard didn't want to halt, for motion was the law of the crowd. He let it sweep him on by and saw Matt's calmness — Matt always had that — and his decency — Matt really had that — and it made him realize with surprising bitterness that Matt was really the beneficiary of all the madness of eleven years ago, though nobody could have known it then, for Matt was just a boy from the second, the trophy wife. He was good-natured and unassertive, all eyes and ears to the excellent adventure the fates had decreed would be his life.

"Yes ma'am," Richard heard Matt say in that soft voice of his. "Be happy to." And he took a three-year-old upon his lap and smiled for a pic. Then it was time to go and the thousand still in line had to be disappointed. Matt rose and said into a mic, "Folks, I have to get my beauty rest and keep my arm loosey-goosey for all them left-hand turns!" And of course everybody laughed.

Matt waved. Then he and Red left the venue as a golf cart arrived, and Richard saw how thin and muscular the young man was, how lean and graceful. He had the racer's perfect body, the body that the great ones had, short and slender so there was no crowding in the driver's seat, with muscular forearms and a longish neck, which gave him eerie pivoting ability for peripheral vision left and right, legs able to reach pedals without cramping, in short, the whole package.

The golf cart speedily vanished behind the

cyclone fence that marked off the driver's compound, that is, the fence that marked off the aristocracy from the peasantry.

Richard watched it go until it disappeared, and he imagined where it took Matt: to a luxury Rec-V customized for travel, a beautiful woman or four or six, a crew of adoring hangers-on, an accountant, maybe rock or movie star pals, the big life as imagined by America at this moment in history.

Again, melancholy came across him, a fleeting image of the eternal What Might Have Been. He'd steeled himself to believe to the contrary that, given certain behavioral dynamics within himself, there was no What Might Have Been, there was only a What Never Could Happen. It wasn't in the cards; he didn't have Matt's go-along-to-get-alongness, his mellow ways, his charm. He was too fucking outlaw, he had to have it his way. He was also too smart, too self-aware. Like all athletic and warrior enterprises, NASCAR tended to reward unconscious genius. If you had irony, had read a book or two, had a taste for surrealism and grotesquerie, if you hated structure and had a natural guerrilla's heart, it could never be for you. You saw through it too easily. It was like a church, and you were born with a nonbeliever's heart. And even if you felt tremendous nostalgia for it, the honest, bitter goddamned truth was that it was never going to be and could never have been for you. For Matt it was maybe just perfect, given his perfect blend of talents and limits. For Richard it was too much, given his blend of talents and limitlessness. No matter what, he would have destroyed his inheritance, crapped in the church, and gone his own outlaw way.

That's why he was the Sinnerman.

He turned his iPod way, way up until his anthem blasted melancholy from his brain.

Sinnerman, where you gonna run to?
Gonna run to the sea
Sea won't you hide me?
Run to the sea
Sea won't you hide me?
But the sea, it was a boilin'
All on that day

Now it was on to business. He looked up at the towering speedway, its circularity gone this far under its shadow, so that it was just a wall of girders and walkways on the underside of the steep auditorium seating. Next to it, silver in the August heat, was the faux-streamline building of the speedway headquarters, which looked to him like a Greyhound station in about 1937. It sat atop a shelf of land, and down here, beneath it, was the grid of lanes of NASCAR Village and all its little retail outlets. A gully, some kind of drainage arrangement full of dirty water, split NASCAR Village in two. But there were two bridges across the channel. He took out a pen and a notepad and carefully drew a map, and on it traced the quickest way from the roadway to the bridge. Oh, that would be the fun part.

He moseyed over to the far side of the gully and found exactly more of the same for another square mile or so, the tents and booths, the walkways, somewhat tackier here, the sense of bizarre for the pilgrims where everything was a holy relic of the faith, all for sale and not cheap. Beyond the village was the hill that lay at the end of a long scut of ridges trending down from the north. He let his gaze fall upon the tip of the hill probably a mile off and six hundred feet up, through mud and inclined forests. He knew that, as in many old fables, paradise lay atop the mountain. I have been to the mountaintop, wasn't that it? But before you got to the mountaintop you had to cross a river and a plain, bringing fire and destruction along with you. What was this, the Bible?

Ah well, he thought, continuing with his map: Fuck 'em if they can't take a joke.

TWENTY-FIVE

The caravan left at 4 A.M. to avoid Race Day traffic and observant eyes and to get set up early. It consisted of the Reverend Grumley in the lead car, Brother Richard driving, and two senior Grumleys, a Caleb and a Jordan, both of whom promptly fell asleep, in the back. In the second vehicle, a truck which bore the name PINEY RIDGE BAPTIST PRAYER CAMP carried most of the heavy equipment the long day's toil would demand. The third, a van also bearing the name of the camp, consisted mostly of man- and firepower. The fourth, a pickup, bore as its loads the tents and over ten thousand bottles of water, as well as ice, coolers, NASCAR hats, T-shirts, King Richard cowboy straw Stetsons, Kyle Busch caps, and other NASCAR trinkets that would justify their presence at the location. The fifth, another van, contained more men, though these were the humbler Grumleys, the tire-change team, and others with various and sundry little tasks, according to the master plan.

The five vehicles moved through a desolate, almost-unlit Mountain City, across Iron Mountain — the spot where Sinnerman had almost taken out Nikki slid by without comment — through Shady Valley, past the last long abutment, Holston Mountain, then full into the Shenandoah for the next eighteen-odd miles to Bristol and its famed speedway.

There was no chatter. Brother Richard drove with his usual deft touch, the car alive in his hands, while the Reverend stared glumly into the darkness.

A cellphone rang to the tune of "Hail, Hail, the Gang's All Here."

The Reverend took the phone from his powder blue suit jacket and examined the caller ID.

"His master's voice," said Brother Richard. "Who else'd have the number and call at this hour?"

"Yes," said the Reverend into the cell.

He listened.

"Yes, again."

He listened some more.

"Absolutely."

A few more seconds passed.

"I guarantee it. They are well prepared. I myself am here to lead. It will happen exactly as planned. Pray to God our luck is high, but it should be, as the Lord favors the bold. I prayed hard last night and again this morning and so I am confi—"

Brother Richard could tell he was cut off.

Finally he said, "You have my assurances. And I have yours. Then I will see you when we are home free and ready to celebrate."

He put the phone away. His dark mood was not alleviated.

"That's the big boss," said Brother Richard. "That would be the gent that actually thought this up, as it clearly lies beyond the Grumley IQ pool. He's got his doubts about you, Reverend, I can tell. He wants reassurances, guarantees. A big pair of dice are about to be rolled and, nervous as a cat like the rest of us, he just wants to make certain you have covered all the bases, right?"

The Reverend was silent.

"Sure would like to know who's on the other end of that phone. Got my ideas. Yes, I do."

"I ain't at no liberty to discuss certain business arrangements with a rogue like you, Brother Richard. Don't think I didn't notice your head went unbowed during my

302

words with the Master before we left. That is a ticket to damnation, sir."

"I am already thrice damned," said Richard. "Which ain't nothing to you, old man, you are probably thirty-eight times damned or some such, for all your sinning. Here's what intrigues me. Do you actually believe the Baptist bullshit you sling, or is it just a performance sustained so long it's become second nature? Are you a con man who's come to believe in his own con?"

"Hellfire," said the old preacher man. "Damnation Road. Streaks of fiery lightning. Endtimes. That's your fate and you will rue it when Satan opens the door with his big smile and welcomes you to the flames of eternal torture."

"Hoochie mama," said Richard. "I *like* it. The sea be aboilin', the moon be ableedin', and the Sinnerman don't got no place to run. I embrace it. That's why I like myself so much more than I like you, Reverend. I am what I am and I know it. I am not a hypocrite. I took the cards I was dealt, made my decision, played the hand hard to this moment. You hide behind some kind of self-delusionary veil, claiming the Lord's interest while you're just a common murderer and thief, and you lead a tribe of neopagans to loot the earth, rape, burn, pillage, and move on without a glance back. You're actually pre-Christian. A PhD could make a career studying the Grumley way and its roots in the Germanic swamps. What was the original, Grummelechtenstein?"

"We be Scots-Irish border-reiver heritage. This talk does us no good."

"Did he remind you he had video of you and —"

"Shut your mouth," snapped the Reverend.

"Them boys back there, cousin or brother or both at once, are sleeping the sleep of the purely innocent. Nothing weighs on the conscience-free mind."

"Nevertheless, shut your mouth."

"Touchy, touchy. But I did learn something interesting today. Yes, I did. I see now the nature of your relationship with the fellow who runs you."

"You know nothing."

"Tell me if I'm wrong. He's somebody you knew before. He's somebody close to you. He may even be family. First off, I hear something troubled in your voice, and I hear you let him cut you off, when no one other than me ever cuts you off. So he is familiar to you. An old sponsor? Someone who saved your life? A cellmate? Someone who's profited off you as you've profited off him over long standing? I hear intimacy. Damn, who'd a thought? But that ain't all."

"Do tell, Brother. You are so full of yourself. Pride goeth before the fall."

"Sir, I done already fallen, which is why I consort with your likes. The second reason is, when this is done, there's got to be a transfer, almost like a dope deal. You will deliver him the swag, he will take his lion's share, you and the boys will squabble over what's left. This is a tricky transaction, I know, I've driven kingpins to and from enough buys. Usually there are a lot of guns involved for security, paranoia is running hot and feverish, and at any moment for any reason it can all go broken-cuckoo-clocks, the guns come out, and you got yourself a goddamned major firefight. All that cash, just there for the taking. Yet that does not frighten you, does it, Dr. Grumley?"

"When a Grumley give his word, his word is ironclad."

"Except when it's not. Oh, there's the leverage, the pix of the Rev and his boy toy —"

"Richard, I warned you."

"— but somehow no one is concerned about the exchange. That means it isn't a problem, everybody, way up front, is okay with it. Damned interesting. Would it be another Grumley? So the leverage ain't mean-spirited, more like a suggestion than a threat. Everybody's all cozy with it, especially the gun-crazy, giant gonads sleeping in the van."

"Richard, I ain't speaking to you no more. When this is done, I hope never to see you no more never again. You been paid upfront, so my advice is to do your job and disappear."

"I always do."

"Pappy," said Caleb from the back seat, "what's 'paranoia'?"

By six, the caravan had decamped and unloaded. The boys worked swiftly, for here was labor hard and simple. With strong arms and backs, they sank the tent pegs and drove the poles deep into the ground. With stout hearts, they unpacked and unfolded the tables. With dead earnestness, they stowed certain boxes containing certain pieces of equipment underneath the tables, arranging and stapling the table cloths so that their skirts covered the items beneath. Then they got the coolers out, packed each with ice, and began to load the bottles into them, each one holding about fifty, so the liquid would be readily cold for pilgrims as the sun rose and pulled the temperature with it. They stacked the remaining cases behind the tables, almost forming a revetment which would keep anyone from noting what they were up to in its dark shadow.

As they worked, of course, they were not alone. All along the Volunteer Parkway this close to the venue, merchants of various stripes were setting up their wares. For this road to and from the speedway would carry, by ten in the morning, a slow-motion parade, as cars crept along its jammed lanes and pedestrians coming from vehicles already parked streamed in the thousands toward the mighty coliseum. Next to the Grumley installation, for example, was PHIL'S FINE NORTH CAROLINA BAR-B-Q, where Phil and his sons had already lit the coals under the broad-bottomed grills that would hold the meat put atop them, allowing the juices of Phil's secret mix of sauces and herbs to permeate it, so that by noontime, damn, the whole place would smell of hot pig and sweet bubbly brown sugar. On the other side, a tall Mr. Stevens had an elaborate tent that offered a line of extremely fine woven mats, some showing drivers standing before their sleek vehicles, some showing the flag or Elvis or the Iwo Jima memorial or the Twin Towers (NEVER

FORGET!) or the flag of the departed Confederacy or F-15s blazing across a sky or horses rearing proudly against a western mesa or Osama in the crosshairs of a sniper's scope, all made, of course, in China. And on and on it went, down the parkway that linked the speedway and the city of Bristol twelve miles away. The parkway that on Race Day would be a near-frozen river of automobiles moving an inch at a time.

But the Grumleys had gotten the best spot of all, and it took some doing, as the permit for this space had been held for a number of years by another Baptist church, which used to sell souvenirs as well but had been persuaded to turn over its permit in receipt of a large donation. So the Grumleys had set up almost at ground zero of the NASCAR explosion: directly across from NASCAR Village, on the other side of parkway, just a bit down from the driveway that led to the parkway from the speedway headquarters, an admin building in art moderne aluminum. As they labored and the sun rose, they could see across the way the hugeness of the speedway itself, dwarfed only by the mountain beyond NASCAR Village that topped the wall of the racing structure.

They were all done by eight: bottles, hats,

T's, and so forth, all displayed under a large banner that read, PINEY RIDGE BAPTIST PRAYER CAMP WATER $1 HATS $10 T'S $15 and in smaller letters, SEND A STUDENT TO PRAYER CAMP TO LEARN THE WAY OF THE GOSPEL AND THE TRUE MEANING OF WORSHIP.

It was, at long last, Race Day.

■ ■ ■ ■

PART II
RACE DAY

■ ■ ■ ■

TWENTY-SIX

Vern knocked on the door. He heard awkward, reluctant shuffling, sensed doubt, perhaps even fear, but finally the door popped open about two inches, held secure by a chain lock, and he and his partner faced a pair of ancient Asian eyes in an ancient Asian face. Mama-*san* looked to be in her seventies, without much English, and quite insecure.

Vern, with his gift of gab, his easy ways of persuasion, his cheap good looks, was on the case from the start.

"Ma'am," he said with a smile and warmth radiating from his eyes, "sorry to bother you, but we are official inspectors. We have to inspect, you know? Only take a moment."

The woman's face collapsed into confusion. Suddenly a much younger Asian face, possibly no more than fourteen years old and belonging to a very pretty child, leaned beyond the door. Well, hello, hello, Vern thought.

Her skin was fair, her eyes almond, her hair drawn back. She was smooth as a peach and tiny as a fairy princess.

"My grandmother doesn't understand. What is it?"

"Sweetie," said Vern, kneeling to the girl, "we are official inspectors. From the Department of Official Inspection. Here, lookie this."

He showed her an Alabama driver's license in the name of Horton Van Leer.

"See that star. Means it's official. Just need to come in a second and we'll be gone. Have to make a report. You wouldn't want to get in trouble with the department now, would you?"

The child said, "There's no such thing as a department of inspections. That's an Alabama driver's license, not a badge or an ID. Go away." Then she shut the door.

Alas, working quickly, Ernie had already knocked the hinge bolts out, and when she slammed it, the door almost toppled in. Catching it, Vern scooted forward, while Ernie held the door, secured at that moment only by the still-attached chain lock. To give his pal some leverage, Vern smilingly unhooked the chain, as if to say to the two terrified women, "See, that's all there is

314

to it." He actually managed an expression that suggested he expected some kind of congratulations. Having entered the apartment, Ernie swiftly and expertly remounted the door on its hinges, replaced the bolts, then closed and locked it. The two women stared at the intruders, horrified. Whatever visions of American evil they secretly held, these two men now liberated.

Meanwhile, Vern slipped across the room, peered through the sliding doors that opened, as if onto a balcony, but where there was no balcony since this was the first floor. Instead, they opened onto the parking lot. Across the lot stood another building like this one, an undistinguished, three-story brick structure with four outdoor stairwells, and six units per stairwell. The unit directly across from them was Nikki Swagger's, which they'd discovered by checking the mailboxes.

"Is it okay, Vern?" called Ernie, who was more or less just intimidating the prisoners with his presence and his baleful, charmless stare.

Vern said, "Yeah, it's fine. We can see him good, no problem."

He turned to the two Asian women.

"Sorry, gals," said Vern, "but what's got to be's got to be. Now, no need for nobody to git excited. We are very easygoing, long as you cooperate."

Without violence but with a force that suggested the possibility of violence, Vern herded the women into the living room.

"Now, little lady, since you're so damned spunky, and Granny here don't talk the lingo, looks like you'll have to answer the questions. No holding back now, little dolly." He put his hand, friendly-like, on her frail shoulder, feeling it stiffen.

"Are you thieves? We have so little but take it and go away. My grandmother has been ill. A shock could kill her. Look at her, she's scared to death."

Vern hugged Grannie.

"There, there, Mama-*san,* it ain't nothing. You just relax now, okay. Just sit down on the sofa and relax. Watch a show, do some knitting."

"She likes Sudoku."

"Yeah, then do that. Meanwhile —"

He took the smaller girl back into the bedroom. She was one of those scrawny-beautiful scrappers, with eyes that glittered fiercely. Twelve, maybe. No breasts. Short, a T-shirt, some running shoes. The T-shirt said HANNAH MONTANA '08 TOUR and had a picture of another kid. The child had no sexuality but she was hotter than hell nevertheless, as the smart, feisty ones always are. She'd never back down from nobody.

"Sweetie, please work with me on this. It's better for everone. How many people live here? Where are they? When they gonna be home? I don't want no surprises, and if I'm surprised, you ain't gonna be a happy camper."

He showed her the grip of his shoulder-holstered Glock.

"In case you don't get it, that's a real gun. I am a real bad man and I have to be here for a time. I ain't gonna hurt you. You ain't a witness, because my name's already on a hundred circulars. But I am the real thing, and there ain't no heroes no more, nobody's coming to save you, so you do what I say, exactly, or there will be some problems. And I'm the easy one. That guy, Ernie, with me? He is a true bastard. I'm the only thing between your family and him."

He loved the perfect tenderness of her beautiful little ear: so tiny, so precise, like some kind of exquisite jewelry.

"You're an ape. Why are you doing this? We have nothing."

"I am not an ape. Well, maybe a little. Sweetie, we're here because we're here and we'll be gone when we're gone. What are you, Chinese?"

"Vietnamese. My grandfather's with the hospital, a researcher. My father's dead, my mother works. My brother and sister will be home by four, Mom at five. Please don't hurt us. We don't have a thing, we haven't done a thing."

"There you go, sweetie, talking about hurting. I told you, nobody gets hurt long as I get smooth cooperation. Here's how it's gonna be. Grandma's in here with you. You can watch TV, go to the bathroom, whatever. You can fix food. But that's it. We're going to be outside in the living room, looking out the sliding doors at the building across the parking lot. Don't know for how long. If we're still here when the other folks start arriving, it's your job to keep them from going nuts. You tell them what's what. You cool them down. You have to be a grown-up today. How old are you?"

"None of your business, you ape."

"Wow, you do have snazzle. I like that. Think somewhere I got a gal your age. Hope she's got the same snazzle. Anyhows, go ahead, hate me, I'm used to it. I kind of like it, truth is. Maybe that's why I turned out so rotten. Anyhow, you got responsibilities. You have to please God. I am God. Please me and you'll come out happy."

"You're not God. You're an ape bastard

318

bully with a gun."

He saw he was never going to make any headway with this one, which of course made him really like her a lot. Maybe too much. An idea was starting to form. He could get her in the bathroom and she had to do what he said or he'd hurt her family so she'd have to do it. He saw her fear, her little body, the trembling. It excited him.

"I'll go get Grandma. Oh, and one other thing. What do you want on your pizza?"

TWENTY-SEVEN

For some reason, like an old bear, he needed sleep. So he violated his promise to the sheriff by sleeping through the clock radio, awaking at ten-thirty and thinking first of all, Oh hell, where am I?

That moment of confusion, familiar to men beyond sixty. His eyes flashed around the banal motel room and he had no idea what he was doing there, what time it was, why he was so late, why in his dreams people seemed so disappointed in him. It came back, of course, but not quickly enough, and he needed a good ten minutes for the blood to somehow reach his brain and revive his short-term memories. Quickly he took up the Kimber .38 Super, made a quick recon of the parking lot of the Mountain Empire Motel and was satisfied to see it largely empty, no sheriff's cars in sight. He started the coffee, took a shower, pulled on his last clean Polo — there had to be a washer and dryer at Nikki's — and began his calls.

The first, of course, was to his wife.

The news was great.

"Bob, she's awake. She's back, our baby is back."

Bob felt the elation blossom bright, like a flare in the night, signaling that reinforcements were coming in.

"Oh, thank God. Oh, Christ, that is so great. When did it happen, how, what's her condition?"

Julie tumbled through the story. At about eight-fifteen, Nikki opened her eyes, sat up, shook her head groggily, and said, "Hi, Mom. Where am I?"

Doctors came and went, tests were made, Nikki gradually seemed to focus, and particularly benefited from her little sister's incredible joy. The two girls sat on the bed and talked for what seemed hours, while all the fuss went on about them. Now she was getting further tests.

"She doesn't remember anything about the incident, but everything else seemed all right. How's Dad — oh my God, how much work have I missed — oh, I have to call my editor — when can we leave — I'm hungry."

"Oh, that's so great," said Bob. It doesn't get much better than the moment you hear your kid has pulled through a tough one. His first impulse was to race to the car and beeline to Knoxville to be with his family at this precious moment.

"The doctor says the signs are good. She'll get more memory back over the next few days. Our little girl is going to make it."

Miko came on, delirious, and he talked to the second daughter for a while, in the language of fathers and daughters, both intimate and silly. But at a certain point it came back to him. Yeah, she's fine, she's okay, it's all right, there's a happy ending . . . *if.*

He realized that she'd make it *if* the boys didn't come back to take her out again. She was much more dangerous now that she was conscious. Unconscious, there was always the thought that she could pass; now, revived, she was a threat.

"I'd like to come back," he said. "I wish I could come back."

"But you can't," Julie said. "You have work to do."

"Yes, I do. I want the security tightened."

"Bob, I've already called Pinkerton. They're upping the manpower. It'll cost us a fortune, but I don't care. What's happening there, where are you?"

He told her, summing things up, wishing

he had a definite next step in mind, or that a solution would somehow soon be at hand. But it remained amorphous. Strange men tried to kill Nikki, tried to kill him for looking into it. The sheriff's office didn't have a clue. Nick Memphis hadn't returned his phone calls.

"I'm going to go to Bristol now, to her apartment. That's where they'll know to find me."

"Bob, be careful."

"Maybe I can turn a thing on them. If not, I'll wait a few days until after the race, then I'll sneak back here and sniff out Eddie Ferrol. If anyone knows anything for sure, it's him. He and I'll have a little conversation, and then I'll be up to speed."

"Can you find him?"

"I think I can."

He saw his cell light blinking, informing him another call was coming in.

"You know, I have to go. I'll get back to you when I'm in Bristol."

"Love you."

"Love you."

He called up Received Calls and recovered Charlie Wingate's number. He punched Call and the phone was answered in two seconds.

"Charlie?"

"Mr. Swagger, did you hear?"

"No."

"They found the owner of that gun store dead. Eddie Ferrol, the guy who owned Iron Mountain Armory. Someone shot him. They found the body off the interstate."

Bob blinked, took a swallow of the coffee.

"Yeah," he said. "And before he and I could chat."

"Remember, I gave you the number from your daughter's laptop hard drive. Did you see him? I don't —"

Bob suddenly saw how it might have looked to the kid.

"You think I tracked him down? You think I'm some kind of hit man? No, Charlie, it's not that way. I saw him and asked him some questions about my daughter. He denied ever having seen her, but I learned that was a lie. I was going to see him again, but the next thing I know, I'm the one who's targeted. Long story. Been more or less laying low ever since. But anyone concerned about me would know that Eddie's the man I'd have to get back to. If they couldn't get me, they could get him. Especially since they can't have had any confidence in his ability to stand up to tough questions. The fastest way out of that jam is a bullet in his head."

"Yes sir. Um — am I in any danger?"

"Don't think so. Only way would be if whoever I'm looking for has very sophisticated phone intercept capability. Government quality. No, not these boys. Smokeless powder is about as sophisticated as they get. It ain't the CIA or even the mafia. It's some boys who aren't sure the wheel is going to last. Charlie, I'm about to leave town. You keep working on what I told you, and I'll check back from Bristol, okay?"

"Yes sir. This is kind of cool."

After disconnecting, Bob tried Nick again. *Agh!* Where was he?

He called Terry Hepplewhite, the clerk at Lester's, about whom he still worried. But he found Terry in fine spirits with nothing to report. He had half a mind to pay for a vacation or something, but saw in an instant that wouldn't work. Thelma'd be all over it if Terry suddenly vanished. No, Terry had to sit it out, at least until whatever happened happened, his case was processed, and police interest had moved elsewhere. Bob thought, That was another mistake. I shouldn't have involved that kid, I should have stuck around and taken the heat. Man, am I losing it? I have made a batch of bad decisions on this one, and maybe I am just making things more difficult than they are. But there was nothing left to do but get out

325

of town, so that sheriff didn't drop down in his Blackhawk again.

He threw his laundry into his duffel, and went to the car. He drove aimlessly, hoping to smoke out anybody following, but his sudden turns and reverses uncovered nobody. For all of it, he was in the free and clear.

The route took him up and down Iron Mountain on 421, across Shady Valley, where he stopped and refueled and got a bite to eat. He then crossed Holston Mountain and, twenty miles out of Bristol, almost immediately hit the Race Day traffic he'd sworn to avoid by leaving early. That plan lost, he settled in for the long haul: the drive across the valley, a backup at the approach to the bridge over Holston Lake, and then into really heavy stuff as he got close to the speedway itself, which was twelve miles outside of Bristol. He hated traffic. He was too old for traffic. Traffic was no fun. The only good thing about traffic was that nothing bad could happen in it, because nobody who did anything bad could get away. There was too much traffic.

He looked at the map, thought maybe he could figure out a way around the mess. It might be longer in miles but it would keep him driving and engaged instead of crawling. That was always his theory in other situations: it's better to drive at speed even if it takes longer than to endure the frustrations of the slow stop-and-go.

But none of the other routes really offered much in the way of possibility. He had to remember that hundreds of thousands of people were on the march, and that every single route would be slowed down. It was just physics: That many cars on those few roads computed to simple congestion no matter what. You had to accept it, not let it screw you up.

So he just tried to stay relaxed, giving himself up to the radio, running from country western station to country western station, occasionally nesting on the Knoxville 24/7 news station, hoping there might be new information on the two Grumley boys who'd tried to kill him. But there wasn't. That story was dead, as was the killing of the meth addict Cubby Bartlett. Nothing lasted more than a day in today's news cycle.

Why didn't Nick call? With Nick's help, he could find out in minutes who these Grumleys were, what their involvement foretold, and who, possibly, they were connected to or working for.

But Nick didn't call.

Finally, around four, he hit the city limits, and forty minutes later crawled past the speedway itself. It was the same, only worse. The huge structure dominated the valley, but it was aswarm with crowds. Traffic just crawled, and people wandered through it en masse. Most of the husky fellows who herded families through the merriment seemed to carry coolers full of beer on their shoulders, and NASCAR ball caps were perched on every head from the youngest to the oldest. The pilgrims were dressed any old way, mainly in cut-off jeans and tank tops, and everybody smoked or had a beer in a caddy. The women wore flip-flops, and a few even seemed to have bras underneath their shirts, but mainly it was down-home as it could be. Not a tie or a jacket anywhere in sight, just thin clothes, heaving flesh, a sense of complete ease. This was the night of nights, the Night of Thunder.

On both sides of the road — he'd turned from 421 to the Volunteer Parkway — even more booths had been set up, so that the strip appeared to be a vast bazaar. There wasn't hardly anything NASCAR you couldn't buy, except possibly body parts or DNA samples, and every merchant seemed to be doing land-rush business, all of it cash. Smoke hung in the air from the barbecue grills, and even the tee-totaling Baptists were selling water bottles to raise money for their prayers.

Bob found it hard not to feel the joy these folks felt, and he connected with it. His daughter was all right. She'd come back. She was okay, she was going to be fine. He again felt rich in daughters and possibilities and wished he could just enjoy it a little.

But there was the worm. Someone had tried to kill her, might try again. They'd tried to kill him; they'd kill anyone who got in the way, even if that person didn't realize they'd gotten in the way. Mark 2:11. "I say, arise from your pallet and go to your house." Crippled man, arise, you are cured. I give you your life back. That fellow would feel some joy too; the sensation leaking into his legs, the strength burgeoning, the psychological burden of self-loathing, of imperfection, of isolation, all of that gone. Rejoin the world, son. Welcome back to the land of the whole. That's how he felt when the word came that Nikki was awake — he'd risen from his bed, able to go to his home again.

What could it mean? *What could it mean?* The thing weighed like an ingot on his brain, so much so that he hardly noticed that the traffic had thinned and — glory be! — that he could accelerate, stoplight to stoplight, because he was now inside the destination. It was the lanes on the other side of the median that were so impossibly jammed up.

He sped through downtown Bristol, found the right cross street, looked for the Kmart that was his tipoff, managed a left, and wound through the little, hidden neighborhood and up a hill into the complex that ultimately yielded her apartment.

He parked next to a red Eldorado — wow, don't someone have extravagant taste in transporation! — and stopped to look around, see if there was a chance anyone had stayed with him through the endless hours of traffic. Nope. Funny, though, he had a strange feeling of being watched. He had good instincts for such. Kept him alive more than once.

He looked again, saw nothing. A parking lot longer than it was wide, on each side of it low four-story brick buildings, typical American apartments, lots of balconies. Down the way some kids played, but no one new pulled into the lot. He looked for activity in the cars, for any sight of activity on the balconies and no, no, there was nothing.

Gunman's paranoia. Going a little nuts in my old age. Mankiller's anxiety. All the boys

I put down are coming after me. Happens to the best of them.

Satisfied no sign existed of threat, he climbed the stairs, opened the door to her apartment, and stepped in.

As he did, a man stood up from her sofa.

Hands flew to guns.

The weapons came out, fingers on triggers, slack going out, killing time was here. But then —

"Nick Memphis, for Christ's sake."

"Hello, Bob. You sure took your time getting here. Didn't think you'd *ever* make it."

Twenty-Eight

"Vern, dammit, I can't do this alone, git over here. I might miss something. I have to pee."

That was Ernie sitting in the dining room chair at the drawn sliding doors, peering at the building across the street through a sliver of open curtain.

But Vern didn't answer.

Instead, he asked the young Vietnamese girl in the bedroom, "So, what's your name?" while the grandmother looked on with angry eyes. She clearly did not think his attentions were appropriate, and the way he kept looking over to her and grinning with his big white teeth got on her nerves. But then she had never understood these strange white people anyway. What was wrong with them? They were so stupid about so many things.

"What difference does it make?" asked the girl.

"Well, if it don't make no difference, might as well tell me as not. I'm guessing Susan. You look like a Susan."

"I do not. I look like a Hannah. Hannah Ng. Pronounced 'ning.' "

"Hannah Ng, my name is Vern Pye. This ain't the way I'd have arranged it, but I sure do think highly of you. You're about as cute as they come. I'd like to hang out with you."

"You're trying to *date* me? My mother doesn't even let me date boys my own age. Plus, you smell like a smoker. You must smoke eight packs a day."

"I ain't that much older'n you. Only two packs, and I'll be quitting real soon."

"About sixty years, it looks like to me. And you smell like eight packs. *Ugh.*"

"You're what, fifteen?"

"Fourteen."

"Well, I am forty-four. That makes me only thirty years older. And I have the constitution of a much younger fellow."

"You're really delusional. Really, you're sick."

"You are so cute. I like your ears. Your ears are so tiny. You're like a little doll. Anybody ever tell you how cute you are? We could have some fun together, you bet. You'd git some cool new clothes out of it. We'd go to the mall, git Hannah Ng any damn thing she wanted. New jeans, new T's, new tank tops, new hoodies, new sneaks. We'll have a hell of a swell time, sweetie, Vern promises."

The child shivered.

"This is getting creepy."

"If you didn't fight against it, it wouldn't seem so hard, honey."

"Vern, goddamnit, get over here," yelled Ernie.

"Now don't you worry about a thing. Vern's got some work to do, then we'll talk some more."

Vern left, went to the living room, and pulled a chair up to spell Ernie so he could go pee.

" 'Bout time. What you been doing?"

"Just talking to the kid."

"Vern, we got a damn job. You stay away from her while we work, you hear. The Old Man'd be plenty ticked if he knowed you'se been mooning on that damn kid when you'se supposed to be man hunting."

"When it comes, it comes. Sometimes you don't get a second shot. You got to take it. Things is swell here."

"I'm going to piss."

Vern sat dreamy-eyed and disconnected at the window. He didn't see the cars across the parking lot or the building they fronted, or the steps up to the doors. He saw himself and Hannah Ng in the bathroom, he saw his easy way with her, how he'd have his way, how good it would feel. He told himself she'd like it too. The more he thought about it, the better it seemed.

Ernie came back.

"Goddamn, Vern, there he is!"

Vern snapped out of the hot and sleazy place his brain was in, and reentered the known world. There indeed, not twenty-five yards away, was the tall, older man named Swagger who was their quarry. He'd parked, now he got out and peered about carefully, making certain he was unfollowed and unnoticed.

"See, he's a careful one."

"Yeah, he is. He ain't no pushover."

"But he'll go down hard, like any man."

The man then went to the stairwell, climbed past second- and third-floor landings, and on the fourth, took out a key, opened the door to an apartment, and stepped in.

"Now we really got to watch. Vern, you can't —"

"I know, I know."

"Better call the Old Man."

"Yeah, yeah," said Vern, taking out his cell. He punched in the number.

"What, Vern?" asked the Reverend.

In the background, Vern could hear hub-bub, as the boys sold water and Reb hats and T-shirts to pilgrims going to the race. Vern could tell that business was land-rush scale.

"Reverend, he done showed. Just arrived. He's there."

"Oh, that's good, that's fine, that's swell."

"Yes sir. We could go over there right now, kick in the door, be in, out in five seconds, and it'd be done."

"No, no," said the Reverend. "You never can tell. Long as he's in there, he ain't doing us no harm. You just watch and wait. If he don't never leave, you wait till we go at eleven or so, then you go. That way, what the hell, the laws have situations at both ends of town with a massive traffic mess in between 'em. They won't never git it sorted out. That's when you do 'em. Or, if for some reason, he decides to go somewhere. You see him come out and go to his car. Then we can't know where he's going, then you go out and while he's in that car starting up, you pop his ass good and hard. Drop that hammer. Nail that boy to the wall. Yes sir, bappity-bap-bap and you all done. Then you go. It's so far off, no laws will figure it has nothing to do with anything else. But that's my second choice. Best wait till our fun commences before y'all go settle Grumley accounts. Got that, Vern?"

"I do, Pap."

"God," said Ernie, "this is turning into an Adam Sandler movie. Dopey-stupid and crazy. Someone else just arrived. What's next, the circus?"

The two boys watched as, indeed, someone went up the four landings and knocked at the old man's door. After some time the door was answered, and an awkward transaction took place.

"Them guys always come at the wrong time," said Ernie as the UPS man walked down the steps and returned to his brown van.

TWENTY-NINE

"Well, you look older and dumpier," said Bob. Nick had indeed thickened some, and let his crewcut grow out a little. The years of service had engraved wary lines in his face, and now he wore glasses, horn-rims. He still wore the uniform, the black suit, white shirt, and red tie, and if you looked you saw his handgun printing high on his right hip. He now replaced it, as Bob replaced his.

"So do you. What's with the hair? You must have seen a ghost."

"Reckon so. It just went in two weeks. I had a rough spell in Japan. These folks kept trying to cut me down, so to get their attention, I cut them down. I'd tell you more about it except you'd have to arrest me."

"Since I haven't seen any Interpol circulars on them, you seem to have gotten away with it again. By the way, do you have a license to carry that gun?"

"No."

"Good. Same old Bob. Just checking."

"How's that tough little wife of yours? She still want to put me in jail?"

"More like a mental home. Anyhow, Sally's with the U.S. Attorney's office in D.C. now."

"She never liked me much. But then few do, why should she be any different?"

"I never liked you much either, if it matters."

"Well, what I liked about you was, you'se so far down the totem pole, I could say 'ain't' and 'it don't' without any career harm. And, by the way, what're you doing standing in the middle of my daughter's living room?"

"How is she?"

"You know what happened to her?"

"As of two days ago, pretty much everything. I know she's awake with a groggy memory, which is why there's no sense talking to her. But I will. And that's why even as we speak, a team of U.S. marshals has taken over security at her hospital. She's a valuable federal witness, even if she doesn't know it."

"Looks like we've got a spell of talking to do. Mind if I get something to drink?"

"You shouldn't drink and carry. Not a

good idea."

"Don't mean that kind of drinking. Drink as in fruit juice or a nice Coke, something wet. You want one?"

"No, I'm fine."

Bob got himself a fruit juice from the refrigerator and when he got back, Nick had sat down on the sofa. He reclined in a chair.

"Okay, old friend. Let's talk. By the way, I'm really glad you're here. This thing is very complex, and I ain't got it half figured out. But why didn't you call me back?"

"Because I'm looking for a very smart guy. I don't know his capabilities, but he's a highly organized criminal with amazing technical skills. He might know about the task force and he might have penetrated it. Just a precaution."

"The driver, right?"

"Yeah, the driver. The guy who tried to kill your daughter. The car guy."

"He came damn close."

"You don't know how lucky your daughter is. This is a very bad actor. He's killed nine federal witnesses and six federal officers over the past seven years. He did a family in Cleveland three years back. The father was an accountant who was going to testify against a teamster local, money laundering and extortion. Never happened. The driver hit them and they were gone in a second. Mother, father, three kids. He may even have more kills that we don't even know about; he also freelances for various mob franchises, even some overseas outfits — we have Interpol circulars on him. But we're in this because of the federal angle."

"You have a name?"

"We don't have a name or even a face. All we have is a modus operandi, and it took years before we were even on to that. What we've been able to learn is that he's some kind of genius with automobiles. Genius driver, genius mechanic, genius car thief, genius on automotive electronics. He can break into any car he wants in about six seconds, drive off in three more. He seems to like Chargers. He'll steal a car, plates, and so forth. He sets the car up with a heavy-duty suspension, tunes the engine for max power. Then he scopes his quarry out. Waits till they're on the highway. He understands the physics of the accident, what it takes to knock a car out of equilibrium, where to hit it, which angle to take, that sort of thing. It usually takes only one pass. He hits 'em hard, they overcorrect to keep control, and they lose it. The car flips. It rolls, it bounces, and everyone inside is whiplashed to death in seconds. He's gone

341

in a flash, the car is never found, there's no prints, no DNA, nothing. Just paint samples that lead back to a stolen car."

"You don't have any idea who he is?"

"There's stories. Some say he's a rogue NASCAR guy who killed another driver in a fit of rage and had to make himself scarce. We have seven names like that, all of them accounted for. Some say he pissed off Big Racing by fucking one of the family's daughters, and they made sure he'd never race a sanctioned event again. Some say he's just pure psycho, with a gift for automotives. It could be any of those, all of them, none of them. We just know he's good, very thorough, highly intelligent, the fearless, classic psychotic. But when we heard about Nikki, we set up a task force out of Knoxville. Something's up, we think."

"I do too."

"So what have you got?"

"Well —"

Someone knocked on the door.

The two men exchanged looks.

"Were you followed?"

"Don't think so."

"Expecting anyone?"

"No."

"Let's be real careful on this one."

Nick slipped to the right of the door, SIG

in hand, tense, ready.

Bob went to the left of the door, drew the Kimber, held it behind him, thumb riding the safety, ready to push it off in a second.

"Yeah?" he demanded loudly.

"UPS," came the muffled reply.

"Just a sec," said Bob. He looked through the peep hole.

"He's in brown. I don't know, maybe they're so far into this they have fake UPS uniforms."

"I don't know," said Nick.

"Can you just leave it?"

"Need a signature, sir."

"Okay," said Bob.

He opened the door two inches until the chain restrained it, even as he peeled away from it in case somebody fired through it.

But instead a thin cardboard box slipped through the two-inch opening in the doorway. Bob grabbed it, shook it, and tossed it on the floor.

He opened the door, signed his name with a stylus on the computerized notepad, and watched the fellow trundle off, slightly absurd in his short pants and brown socks.

"Those guys always arrive at the wrong time," said Nick. "They have a gift for it."

They sat down again, and Bob told the whole story, from start to finish, his arrival in Bristol after his daughter's accident, his investigation, the sheriff department's investigation, the opposing conclusions of each, the two critical incidents that left three dead, Bob's remorse about leaving poor Terry Hepplewhite alone back there as the supposed shooter, the death of Eddie Ferrol, the police politics of Johnson County, the situation as it now was with Nikki awake.

"So let me sum up your findings," Nick said.

He ticked them off.

The strange economics of methamphetamine in Johnson County.

The Baptist prayer camp, run by an Alton Grumley.

The driver.

The tire-change jack and possible exercises to refine that skill.

The night firing of guns.

The attempts on Bob's life by Grumleys as he tried to investigate.

"Grumleys are a southern crime family, headquartered near Hot Springs," Nick explained. "Kind of a family training camp for the criminal skills. Been around for generations. They produce all kinds of mischief, force-based mainly, but also confidence, bunco, extortion, and kidnapping. Very tribal group of bad guys. If they're involved, I'm suddenly seeing a lot of dough."

Bob took it in, then continued.

The missing pages in his daughter's notebook, the crushed car, crushed recording devices.

The trip to the gun store.

And finally, Mark 2:11.

"That's it," said Bob. "Now here's my take. Somehow Nikki picked something up. So she visited the camp but saw through the Reverend. She poked around on her own and she found something. Clearly these Grumleys were involved. But what she found made her think of — I don't know, here's where it gets blurry, guns or the Bible or both? She wouldn't call me to ask about the Bible, that I guarantee you. So maybe it is about guns. She tried to call me but I was out in the horse ring. So she went to the first Baptist minister she heard about, who turned out to be Eddie Ferrol, and asked about Mark 2:11, thinking that fella would know."

"And the fact that he owns a gun store is coincidental? I don't buy coincidences that big."

Bob stopped. "Yeah, this is where it comes apart: the bullet or Bible issue. And she called me first, and I don't know jerk about

Bibles. But the fact that he claims she didn't go there, and we know that's a lie . . . She drives home, and that guy, who's later killed, somehow gets to the driver, and he's sent after her. Now he had to be close. So he was clearly at the prayer camp run by old man Grumley. We have his tracks as he raced down 421 to catch up to her."

"That sounds right. Okay, we don't have Mark 2:11, but what do we have? Here's what I'm getting. It seems to me what they're planning isn't a conspiracy, a murder, a scheme, a plot. That doesn't sound Grumley. It's more of a caper, a one-time thing, some kind of raid or operation. Maybe a robbery. That's the urgency. That's why everything has to happen fast, 'cause they're up against a tight deadline, and what happens happens soon. They have to go at a certain moment, not before, not after. And that information has to be protected. It's so fragile that even the suspicion of something going on would screw things up. Their plan must depend on total surprise, and even minimum-security upgrades would defeat it. That's why they go after Nikki. Even if she knows nothing, she might make phone calls or ask questions, and someone else might figure something was up and those upgrades would be made and their plans would be screwed."

Bob thought, Yeah he's pretty smart. That's good for government work.

"Could it be a code, a signal? Let's Google it again. Maybe we missed something."

But they came up with nothing except the endless and seemingly fruitless biblical references.

"Let me call this kid Charlie. He's real smart, maybe he's come up with something."

Bob called Charlie; the boy was apologetic, self-doubting and disappointed because he hadn't come up with anything.

"I even ran it by a guy I know who specializes in codes. He looked at it for numerology, misplaced letters, anagrams, displacements, upside down writing, backwards writing, and he came up zilch."

"Okay, Charlie. Thanks."

"Sorry I couldn't do better for you, Mr. Swagger."

"Well, you actually cross out a lot of possibilities, son. So that's of some help. It ain't a code, it ain't nothing from the Bible or the numbers or letters in the Bible. That cuts it way down."

"I won't charge you."

"Charlie, how many times do I have to say this: Charge me!"

Bob disconnected.

"Nothing. And if you're right, if they have some kind of caper going on against a deadline, here we sit with nothing to show for it, no progress made. Could it have to do with the race? The big race?" He looked at his watch. "Hell, eight-thirty. It's started. Could it be a rob . . ."

But he let it trail off.

"It doesn't make any sense," said Nick. "How could they rob something in the middle of the biggest traffic jam in Tennessee this year? How could they get in, get out? I suppose they could go on foot, but how much could each man carry? I just don't see any reasonable methodology here. Those roads are going to be like parking lots for hours. Nobody's going anywhere."

"I am at the end of the road."

"Man, I'm about to say, call it a day. Maybe tomorrow I can run it by the analysts back in D.C. and get some genius to look into it and see what we don't. I do need a drink, a real one. But let's ask: What do we know the most about?"

"The answer is Nikki. I know Nikki. I know how her mind works and what a stubborn little cuss she can be."

"So let's think along with her. Take us through her thoughts on that last night. You know she's called you."

"She calls me . . . but I'm not answering. She gets a burr under her saddle, she's got to get it out. She calls me, I ain't there. What does she do? Call someone else? Who else would she call? She's been to a gun store, she had a Bible she got from the Reverend, she can't find no satisfaction, she calls me, I'm not there, who else does she call? It's early evening, most places are closed down. Who does she call? The newspaper? Could she have called the newspaper?"

"But you said she didn't."

"That's right."

"Maybe she didn't call anyone. Maybe she just up and left for home and the driver caught her and —"

"No. Gal wouldn't give up. That's not how she was taught. She'd want to do something positive, achieve a sense of progress. So somehow she'd continue to search. So, who's open that late? Who never closes? Who has information on anything on tap even if you're in the woods in rural Tennessee in the dark?"

They looked at each other.

"She had a laptop, right?" said Nick. "Wireless, right? She went to the Internet. She tried to Google Mark 2:11 and came up with what we came up with — ten thousand explanations of how Jesus cured the cripple and sent him home, and she couldn't make any sense of it. Who does she call next?"

They looked at nothing and then they looked at each other again.

They looked at the package that Bob had just dumped on the floor. It said AMAZON.

"She buys a book!"

THIRTY

Vern's cell rang.

"Yes sir."

"What's the word, Vern?"

"Ernie, what's the word?"

"Ain't no word, goddamnit, Vern, and you'd know that if you done your job. Don't know how you can take money for tonight, just sittin' there hammerin' on that poor little girl and her family."

Vern sat next to the little girl on the sofa, his big hand draped protectively about her. Gently he'd been caressing her arm for about and hour, whispering softly into her ear.

"Well, sir, Mr. Holy Water, I will do my job, same as you, and earn my money, same as you."

He went back to the phone.

"Sir, I —"

"Vern, I heard discord. I told y'all I didn't want no discord. Discord is what makes things fall apart, that I know true and straight."

"Sir, Ernie and I are fine. We just ran into some unexpected situation is all. As for that old man, he ain't peeked out a bit. Ernie kept a good watch on him, yes he did. There's no move or nothing."

"Okay, we are about to let hell out of the jar here. The race'll be over in a little bit — they're up to lap four eighty or so now — and they'll let the traffic build a bit, and then they go and we jump. Like I said before, that's when you go up, you bash in the door, you hit him with both barrels, a lot of shooting, it don't matter, no po-lice getting there for six hours with the mess we making here. Then you git gone but good. I'll call you later so's you can pick up your swag."

"That is a good plan, sir."

"Boys," said the Reverend, "I just want you to know, you're doing Grumley work tonight, but more important, you are serving the Lord."

"Sir, He has rewarded me. I have met the gal of my dreams here tonight, yes sir!"

THIRTY-ONE

Bob tore open the Amazon package.

It was *The History of Sniping and Sharp-shooting* by Major John L. Plaster, a sniper expert and former SOG ᵥ ᵗog in Vietnam, who Bob actually knew.

"Sniping," said Nick. "So she was trying to find something about snipers?"

"She couldn't have found a gun. Nobody loses a gun. She'd found, I don't know, a piece of equipment, a gillie hat, a range book, or maybe some shell-related thing. The shell itself, the box, a piece of carton, a manifest, a bill of lading, something with a shell designation on it. But it had to be something unusual. The girl is my daughter. She'd been around cartridges her whole life. She knew the difference between a .308 and a .30-06 and between a shell, a cartridge, and a bullet."

"And it had to be arcane then, if she didn't know it right away and sought someone with more information — the guy in the gun store, you, finally the book."

"Let's try Mark 2:11," Bob said.

He went to the index. Damn! No Mark 2:11. But he was so close now, he could feel the answer almost as a palpable presence, floating just out of focus in the corner of the room.

"Damn," said Nick. "I was so sure it —"

"Wait," said Bob, "I think technically they abbreviate 'em. And we never saw the word 'Mark' written in her own hand. Don't know if it really was a Mark or some kind of abbreviation. I think the military uses '*M-k* period' as its abbreviation, left over from the old days. But I don't see —"

"Go back to the index."

Bob found the designation "Mk.211, 622."

Bob turned to page 622 and immediately saw a photo of a group of long, big, mean-looking cartridges, missiles really, their sleek brass hulls propped upright as they rested on a rim, while at the top, a bullet like a warhead promised speed, precision, and destruction. The conical, streamlined-to-death-point thing itself was sometimes black, sometimes blue, sometimes red, sometimes tipped in these colors, all a part of the complex system of military enumeration, by which armies on the prowl in far dusty places could keep their logistical requirements coherent.

And there, finally, it was: Mk.211 Model O Raufoss, with green-over-white painted tip.

They read. The Mk.211 Raufoss is a dedicated armor-piercing .50 caliber round, meant to penetrate light steel, of Norwegian manufacture (NAMMO being the name of the firm) and design, in play in specialized roles in the American war effort in the Middle East. It consists of a tungsten core buried in the center of the 650-grain bronze bullet and was designed so that the bullet itself, traveling at over twenty-five hundred feet per second and delivering four thousand foot pounds of energy at impact, would bore through the armor of the vehicle. A nanosecond later a small charge would explode, thus releasing the tungsten rod within, which being heavier and harder, would fly into the crew compartment, shatter and fragmentize, quickly wounding, disabling, or simply slaughtering the human beings and any delicate electronic equipment inside.

"It's for light armored vehicles," said Bob. "Not a tank, but an armored personnel carrier, a Humvee, a car, a radar screen, an aerial, a mobile command center. Or maybe a bunker or barricade, a helicopter, a plane on the ground, a wiring junction, a stoplight, a camera or infrared scope, any number of military applications which are classified 'soft targets,' anything short of the real, big mechanized stuff. I'm betting they do a lot of damage wherever they're deployed."

"The .50 caliber. That's the big one?" Nick wanted to know.

"They call the original gun the Queen of Battle. Ma Deuce, from the heavy machine gun designation which is M-2. You rule the battlefield with it in certain situations, say on a hill way out in bad-guy land. We used a lot of 'em in 'Nam. We loved 'em. But this here's the newest wrinkle. It ain't for a machine gun. See this Mk.211 shit's for a rifle built by an outfit called Barrett, a big son of a bitch, just barely man-portable. Six feet long, forty pounds or so, off a bipod. Looks like an M16 on hormones for Arnold Schwarzenegger. You couldn't carry it in a holster to rob a store. But placed with a trained operator, you could use it to snipe at over a mile to take out trucks and lightly armored defensive positions, you could rain havoc and brimstone on your target zone with pinpoint accuracy. You could take down people, low-flying planes, missiles on their launch pads, radio and radar installations, anything. You could use it on the president with that ammo. It ain't the gun, it's the ammo. It's strictly military-only, banned from civilian use, and I don't think even the NRA cares about that. It's for blowing up stuff, for multiplying the killing force, for bringing down planes or choppers. That ammo'll go through anything and cut the shit out of what's on the other side."

"So that's what she found," said Nick. "Some evidence of a .50 caliber rifle with deadly, military-only ammunition in criminal hands, presumably being readied for some kind of kick-ass caper. And that's why they wanted to kill her, and when you found out, they had to try and kill you. But what would the caper be? Can you guess? And when is it going down?"

"Could it be a kill?" said Bob. "That's what you could do with this. The president, I don't know, the governor, some big guy, he's in a box watching the race. They're on the mountaintop which just barely might give you a vantage point on the speedway or somehow they've gotten into the speedway itself, though with a gun that big, I don't know how. Maybe he can zero the big guy's box, put ten Mk.211s into it, kill everybody in two seconds, I'm guessing. Or it could take out an armored limousine.

Turn it to Swiss cheese."

"The president isn't there. The governor of Tennessee is, but . . . the governor of Tennessee? I suppose. I just —" Nick ran out of words. "Somehow, it doesn't seem Grumley. It's not their style."

"No, no, this is good, consider it," said Bob. "They're hired by some mob who knows their one value isn't sophistication but silence. That's what they're selling. So maybe the governor is organizing some new anti–organized crime task force, got 'em all scared. They contract the hit to the Grumleys who bring it off with their usual crudeness and violence but also a refusal to snitch 'em out if caught."

"The tires, Bob. You were the one that discovered the tires. Were you wrong on that? How would that fit in?"

"Ahhh —" Bob thought, clinging to his thesis. "Yeah, yeah, they could count on their being an SUV there in the crowd, but not with off-road tires. Yeah, after the hit, which takes maybe two seconds, they chase a family out of its Bronco, speed-change the tires, and take off cross country, maybe to the top of that hill. A chopper picks 'em up. It sounds pretty good to me, partner."

"But maybe you have biases. You're a

sniper. Everything to you looks like a sniper job."

"From ten feet with a .50 Mk.211, it ain't much like sniping. It's like blowing stuff up real good."

"Okay, I think we have to alert this command structure somehow. They've got to get people into the area, put a hold on all VIP transit, and maybe — I still don't like it. It just doesn't seem Grumley. Does it seem Grumley to you?"

"Until today, I didn't know a Grumley from a dandelion."

"Could they shoot up the race? From up above, fire the ten shells into the lead three cars as they move through the pack on a turn? You'd get a massive crash, cars all over the place, the race would be a catastrophe, they'd stop it, cancel it, something."

Bob saw through that.

"And if someone laid money against the one-in-a-million shot there'd be *no* winner to the Sharpie 500 — well, that person would win a fortune. But he'd get a visit from the Vegas mob enforcer to make sure his win was on the up-and-up, and since it wouldn't be, he'd get a swim in Lake Tahoe with a pair of cement socks."

"And it doesn't seem to need a driver, a speed-tire change, or any of the other stuff.

It just doesn't seem to make any sense," Nick said.

"And just to make it more ridiculous, the race is almost over. It's near eleven. They start at eight and do the five hundred laps in about three hours. Man, I am so buffaloed. Come on, Nick, you're supposed to be smart. Figure it out."

"I'm tired, I'm old. I feel older than you look."

"Okay, go back to basics. What do we know, absolutely."

"We know, absolutely, they have acquired a .50 caliber rifle and a supply of armor-piercing incendiary rounds of a sort the government categorizes as 'antimatériel.' "

"So," said Bob, "let's pursue this particular line. What is matériel?"

"Okay, I'd answer like this: light armor. Limousines, sure. Or, given this environment, power lines, TV trucks, light safes, radio installations, I don't know, McDonald's signs, news helicopters, race cars, race car trailers, propane barbecue tanks. It could be any of those. I'm afraid we're stuck with —"

"Just make the call. You don't have to designate a target. You just have to flood the zone with law enforcement and security and —"

"What zone?"

"I guess the race zone."

"Yeah, but, hello, it's full of three hundred thousand happy campers. Too bad there's not a nice armored car in the middle of this, chock full of cash. Now *that* would make some sense. Okay, I'll make the call and —"

It lay there in the room for a while. Each man considered what Nick had just blurted out. Yes, armored car. Seemingly impregnable, full of cash, stuck in traffic, yet easily taken down by such a tool as an Mk.211.

"What you just said," said Bob, "now that makes some sense."

"It does, doesn't it?" But he had to fight it. "Why would there be an armored car in the middle of all this? It doesn't track, it's a bad idea, a red herring, it —"

Nick took out his cell, punched a number. "I'll call a state police captain I've worked with. He might know something," he said.

When he got through, Bob heard him say, "Hey, Mike. It's Memphis, sorry for the late call. You've been watching the race? Cool, is it over yet? No, I could call back, it's almost over, but let me just lay something on you. I'm here in Bristol myself. Sorry but it's important."

He said to Bob, "Now he's turning the TV down. Ah, okay, Mike, we have intelligence that some very bad actors are on scene here with a piece of ugly work called an Mk.211 Raufoss antimatériel round. And a .50 caliber rifle to fire the stuff. They could use it to do all sorts of things but the more we think about it, this group seems criminal, not political, and we're trying to figure out if there's a target they could unzip with it. I know it sounds ridiculous, but I'm thinking how ideally suited the ordnance would be against some sort of armored car. Is there an armored car in play here that you would know anything —"

He listened as far-off Mike told him all about it.

Then he said, "All right, can you patch through to your command center? I'm going to try to reach them from my end. I'll try and get a Bureau SWAT team deployed from Knoxville by chopper, and then we'll move on site fast as we can. Ten-four."

"Well?" said Bob.

"Come on," said Nick, "we don't have time. I'll explain on the run."

Bob threw on a light khaki sports coat to cover the gun in Kydex and mags arrayed in clip holders along his backside.

"It's the concession money," said Nick. "All of it, cash, small bills, a week's worth of souvenirs and baseball hats, plus tickets for tonight, hot dog money, beer money, all the money from that NASCAR Village operation. He says it's a six to eight million take. Now I should say, if you rob a bank and get two million, you've really only stolen $200,000 because you've got to move it to an overseas cartel, they've got to launder it and get it back to the U.S., and they'll only pay out one on ten. That's universal — except for this. Eight million small bills — maybe eight hundred to a thousand pounds of deadweight — is eight million. No one for ten. Straight one-for-one. You can start spending immediately, no one can track it."

"It's in an armored car?" asked Bob.

"More like a truck. They gather it up during the race and haul it to speedway headquarters. But there's no vault there. So they bale it up and load it aboard that armored car. When the race is over, that vehicle, with a driver and three or four guards, moves out into the traffic and begins the long crawl to Bristol where it's vaulted at one of the big downtown banks. The traffic jam, that's supposedly the security. No one would hit an armored car in a traffic jam, because there's no way out. But I'm guessing they've figured some way —"

It was suddenly clear to Bob.

"I see it. No, they don't take the swag. They blow open the car, kill or incapacitate the crew. It takes ten seconds with an Mk.211. They set up perimeter security to deal with the cops who will have to fight the tide of panicked fans in the thousands to even get there. This team changes tires fast. Why? Because they ain't driving down no road. The roads are jammed. They go off-road, they just mounted some kind of powerful off-road, heavy-tread tire. They go off-road, they grind through the most open area, which is that NASCAR Village, they just smash through it, nothing could stand up to the power of that truck. Maybe they've amped the engine somehow, to get a lot more power for a few minutes before the engine seizes or catches fire. That's something the driver could do; he could figure it out."

"Yeah, but where does that get 'em?"

"It gets 'em to the mountain. The hill, whatever. Up they go, and for that ride they'd need the best driver in the world, someone who'd won hill-climbs and truck demo derbies, the whole nine yards. They crank up that hill five minutes and fifty dead citizens and cops after they first hit the car. Up top, that's the only safe place for that chopper pickup I came up with earlier. The chopper comes down the mountain range, way out of reach or even sight of any police firepower on scene, it picks them and the dough up, and they're gone in seconds. They run through the dark low without lights, and nobody will follow them, because a) they can't see 'em, and b) even if they could, they're afraid of that .50 caliber, which will easily take a chopper down."

Nick took up the narrative. "They chopper out of the area, land, split the swag, and they're gone by dawn. We won't even find where they'll land."

Bob made his choice at that moment. He knew where they'd land. But he had business there too.

"I have to move," said Nick. "I'm going to try and get a chopper in here and get out there. You don't have to —"

"Oh, yes I do. You need guns. I've got one."

Thirty-Two

The race was over. It was a jim-dandy. Junior won, just beating Carl by shedding him in a pile of the lapped but persistent tail-enders on the last half of number five hundred, when Junior went low, slipped through a gap between Food City and Bass Pro Shop, buzzed dangerously around the blue-green Dewalt reading the apex of the curve — which he knew better than his girlfriend's inner thighs and which he dreamed of more often — and hit the last straight in FedEx's wake, slingshotting off the suck, and hitting the checker maybe six feet ahead of Carl's Office Depot. Carl got caught behind Cheerios — damn him! — then caught a gap and some sling action of his own, but just couldn't overcome Junior. If it had been a five hundred-lap-plus-thirty-foot race he'd have done it. Okay, so? It's only one race.

The boys were all cheering, all up and

down Volunteer Parkway outside the gigantic speedway structure, where the rug merchants all waited for a last shot at the johns and their families. Less sincerely, the Grumleys lurked, waiting for their big moment.

"Where'd USMC 44 finish?" asked Brother Richard.

"They haven't read off the order yet — wait, here it is —" and Caleb listened hard to his little radio in the darkness. Then he said, "Fourth, he finished fourth."

"Cool," said Brother Richard.

A half-mile off, the speedway was still a source of immense noise, even with the engines finally turned off as the hot and smoky cars were rolled to their garages. It was the roar of the tribe. It was immense, the NASCAR animal in full throat, and above the stadium one could see the illumination not merely of the lights that made night racing possible but the thousands upon thousands of flashbulbs pricking off to record the moment when the young Dale the junior took his trophy.

"Okay, boys," said the old man, "time to git 'er ready. Say a prayer for fortune if you're with me, if you are a secret nonbeliever, that's okay, 'cause I will say a prayer for you and as I am close to Him, he

367

will look out for you."

The boys began to prepare. Caleb quietly slipped under the table, pulled two large plastic bins out and withdrew into the dark space made by the tent above and the revetment of water bottles behind. There, in privacy, he removed two large constructions of metal, the upper and the lower of a Barrett .50 caliber M107. Expertly, he fitted the two together, finding the machined parts connected in the perfect joinery of the well-engineered. Pins secured the two units into one solid mechanism. Completed, made whole, it looked like a standard M4 assault rifle after six years in the gym, the familiar lines where they should be, but the whole thing amplified and extended, thickened, lengthened, densified, packed with strength and weight. Another Grumley — he couldn't see who in the darkness — handed him a heavy magazine with ten Raufoss armor penetrators locked in and held tense under extreme spring tension. He himself slid the heavy thing into the magazine well, heard it click solidly as it found its place. He drew the bolt back, his great strength helping, let it slip forward, moving one of the quarter-pound, 650-grain, tungsten-cored big guys into the chamber, and locked it.

All up and down the line, the Grumley boys were cowboying up. Most wore bulletproof vests, and the guns were a motley of junky but effective Third and Fourth World subguns from various organized crime arsenals around the South, plus some functional American junkers. The inventory included a couple of Swedish K's; a couple of Egyptian Port Saids (clones of the K), some beat-up Mk-760s from small American manufacturers after the original S&W variant, which was itself a K clone; an Uzi; a kicked-to-shit West Hurley Thompson; a full-auto AK-47. With all the clicking and snapping as mags were locked in, guns were cocked, belts of spare mags were strapped on, body armor was tightened and ratcheted shut, it sounded like chickens eating walnuts on an aluminum floor. But in a few seconds or so, it was done.

"We all set, Pap," said Caleb, more or less the sergeant.

"Good, you boys stay back there in the dark, the crowd's coming out now. Lord God Almighty, there's a vast sea of people."

And there was. The first of about one hundred fifty thousand people slithered out of the speedway gates, spread when they hit open air, and fanned across the available ground. It was an exodus from the church that was NASCAR, and now these good folks had nowhere to go except back into the dreary real world and no way to get there except to take the slow-motion parade in the opposite direction of the afternoon's slow-motion parade. A few runners made it to their cars early, began to pick their way out of the densely packed lots. Meanwhile, seeming to materialize from nowhere, the police in their yellow-and-white safety vests with their red-lensed flashlights moved onto the roadway to govern or at least moderate the huge outflow of people and vehicles. Dust hung in the soft summer air, shouts mostly of joy, the clink of bottle on bottle, the pop of cans being sprung to spew brew, the friendly jostle of people of the same values, the hum of insects drawn by the lights, the acrid drift of cigarette and cigar smoke, the occasional boastfulness of the young and dumb, the wail of a too-tired baby, a whole human carnival of happy yet exhausted people.

In just a few minutes gridlock had set in; so many cars, so many folks, so few roads. Honks filled the air, but mostly the crowd had made peace with the ordeal of the egress. In short order, the lanes immediately in front of the Piney Ridge refreshment station were jammed with cars full of citizens, bumper to bumper and door to door in either direction, frozen solid. The people in the cars unaware that a commando force, heavily armed and full of aggression and craziness, lurked just a few feet off in the shadows.

Ain't you folks gonna git a thrill in just a minute or so, thought Richard.

He was behind the skirmish line, unarmed. No reason for him to be up front and get himself shot up in the early rush. He wouldn't venture out until the truck was taken down, the guards either surrendered or murdered. He licked his lips, which were dry, and his tongue was also dry. He pulled a bottle of water out, now warm, popped the cap and slugged some down.

"Go easy, Brother Richard. You don't want to have to pull over for a piss in the middle of all this."

Everybody laughed.

"Why, Cousin Cletus, if I do, you hold 'em off while I empty the snake, okay?"

More laughter. That Richard. What a joker.

The minutes dragged on, the boys sat patiently, a Marlboro or Lucky firing up in the darkness, the drift of the smoke through the tented space.

"I see her," said the old man from out

371

front. "Yes sir, here she comes, trying to edge her way in."

Richard saw it. The vehicle, technically called a "Cash in Transit" truck, was a Ford F-750, probably from Alpine, the biggest of the up-armor specialty firms. It wore a bank emblem on its flat sides and doors, and was a boxy thing, ten feet high and twenty-two long, with the grace of a milk truck from the '50s blown up to be a parade float. White, it gleamed in the cascade of lights, the rivets in their grid all over the damned thing cast tiny shadows, so unlike the smooth skin and bright primaries of the civilian vehicles, this big, sluggish baby had texture. Its grill was a meshwork of slots that looked like, but weren't, gun slits, and if the thing was armored to the hilt at the highest upgrade it could withstand anything — except what the Grumleys had prepared for it that night. Squared fenders, a stout body, everything acute-angled off, vault-like, it was made to convey the impression of invincibility, of a moving fortress atop the upgraded shocks and suspension.

Richard could make out the two doomed drivers, blandly sitting behind the three-inch-thick windshield glass, unaware that hell was about to arrive in spades. The two men slouched, like the others having made peace with the ordeal ahead, and the big thing edged its way down the road from speedway headquarters to the merge with Volunteer. As it advanced, waiting in a line to get in another line, it edged ahead ever so damned slowly. People poured around it, sloshed around it, some even clambering on its bumpers as they progressed, the whole thing eerie in the brownish lights of the vapor-mercuries up above. It demanded respect. Twice, vehicles with better position moved aside to permit it entrance, because it was in some sense magical.

But everything was rapidly collapsing into a phenomenon of lights with no one feature predominant, because there were so many sources of illumination, those merc-vapors up top, the lights from the cars in the various lines in the various lanes, the bobbing strobes of the cop monitors, the overhead fast movers that were affixed to various news helicopters and a police ship or two. Beams cut the air this way and that — was it a lightsaber battle from *Star Wars VII: Attack of the Baptist Killer Redneck Hell-Raising Natural Born Killers?* — and zones of illumination played on the surface of the clouds of dust or smoke that roiled heavily, the whole thing punctuated by sounds of the America of 2008: cars, kids, squeals, shouts, taunts, laughter. In the scene the humans were insubstantial, almost flickering ghosts and shadows.

"Damn," said Richard to nobody in particular, "is this a great country or what?"

"Hell boys," said Caleb, "time to git some."

"Here he comes. Caleb, you ready?"

"Yes sir."

"Remember, you move with purpose like you're doing what you're supposed to be doing. Remember, not through the windows, we need that bulletproof glass on the way up the hill."

"Yes sir, Pap."

"I loves you, son. I loves all you boys, you goddamned brave Grumley boys."

"We love you, Daddy."

"Brother Richard, I even love you."

"Reverend, will you take a shower with me after this is over?"

Grumley laughter.

"Such a Sinnerman," said the old man.

Now it was Caleb's move. He stepped onto the roadway with the heavy, lengthy weapon — thirty pounds, fifty-eight inches long — and boldly walked across the lanes, dipping in and out, once waiting patiently as an SUV full of kids pulled by, two in the backseat bugeyed at the unbelievable image of a blond hulk in a heavy metal T-shirt, a Razorbacks baseball hat, plugs in his ears, body armor clinging to his upper torso and six feet of the gunliest gun ever made in his hands. But no one could really put it together. He seemed calm because he was calm. He got right up close to the sluggishly moving F-750, at almost-point-blank range, the muzzle three feet from the steel door, the guards looking lazily not around but up the road at the jammed-up lanes of cars and their blinking, on-again, off-again brake lights that yawned before them, and then Caleb fired.

THIRTY-THREE

Vern removed the girl from the bedroom with an insincere smile to her cowed family and took her into the bathroom. He sat down on the toilet, his arm draped across her shoulders. The door was closed.

"Now, sweetie."

"I don't like this," she said, her eyes looking nervously around.

"Now, sweetie, you just calm down. Does Vern look like a man who could hurt a cute little thing like Hannah Ng?"

"Please don't hurt me."

"Sweetie, I would never hurt you. In fact, to relax, I want you to think about ice cream. What's your favorite flavor?"

"I don't know. I can't think."

"Strawberry. Mine too. Now what do you do with a nice big pink strawberry ice cream."

The girl had shut her eyes. He held her by the arm.

"You *lick* it. Isn't that what you do?"

He forced her to her knees.

"You lick it, nice and hard. *Ummm,* good. Now, Hannah, let's pretend we got us a nice ice cream right here right now —"

"Let's go," called Ernie from the living room.

Damn!

Vern leaned down and gave the little Asian girl a kiss on the cheek.

"I'll be back for you. We got some fun ahead."

He raced through the apartment, out the open sliding doors, crossed the lawn, and caught up with his cousin just as Ernie hit the parking lot. They slipped between cars, and Vern saw ahead of him two men coming down the building steps on the other side of the parking lot, lit in the glow of the stairwell. Who the hell was the other guy? Too bad for him, he's dead too. He indexed his finger above the trigger guard of his Glock for fast application, and he and Ernie described a straight line on the interception of the two targets who, heading on the oblique, were obviously going to a car somewhere farther down in the lot.

Didn't matter. Was easy. Them boys didn't know a thing, didn't have a prayer or a hope. Bang bang, it'd be over. He watched them, as everything seemed to accelerate in time, noting one was the lanky, gray-headed older guy, a Mr. Swagger Pap said, who had been their quarry so many times before and who Pap said killed Carmody and B.J. The other, a beefier guy, police beef in a suit with a thatch of hair, who was talking into a phone.

The Grumleys had their guns out, but the rule was, get close as you can, then get closer, get close enough to touch, get close enough so missing isn't on the table, shoot 'em fast in the guts, shoot 'em down, then lean over 'em for the head shot, blow their brains out, shoot your gun empty, then get the hell out of town.

It was happening now, it was happening fast, his gun came up, his finger flew to trigger, it was so easy, they picked up their speed on the unsuspecting marks, almost running now.

"Look out," came a cry from behind, "they're killers, look out!"

It was a young girl's voice.

As they raced down the stairwell, Nick held a slight lead and Bob could hear him talking urgently into his cell.

"Officer, this is Special Agent Nick Memphis, FBI, Fed ID 12-054. Lancer, you've got to patch me through to the speedway command center, whoever's in charge. We believe there's going to be a robbery assault at your location. No, no, I've got SWAT operators inbound from Knoxville, but it'll be a time before they're on scene. This is a heavy ten-fifty-two by an armed team, maybe with automatic weapons, all units should be alert and ready to move on the sound of the gunfire, somewhere in the speedway vicinity. Please patch me through to your command center, and I will need airborne transportation to the site and need a rendezvous point and —"

They cleared the building, slid through the darkness to Nick's car, though Bob didn't know which one it was, and seemed almost to be on the run when Bob heard a voice from across the way screaming, "Look out, they're killers, look out." In that same second he saw two hunched men rushing at him, guns out, guns upfront. A gun flashed, there was no noise, but the brightness of the muzzle flash displayed the urgent mug of a handsome-ugly guy and Bob knew Nick was hit. Stricken, he muttered an animal noise, lost a step and all rhythm, and was struggling for his own gun.

It happened fast, faster by far than the speed of coherent thought, faster almost than the pulse rate that was in any event suspended by blood chemicals, and each of the four at close range in the dark devolved into creatures of instinct and training, and the victory would go to the one with the best instinct and the most training. The determining factor was distance; up close, skill counted for nothing, but at ten feet out in the dark, it wasn't just who shot fast, but who shot best, who had the knack to hit movers in bad light on the fly.

Bob's hand flew at a speed which could never be known or measured, so fast that he himself had no sense of it happening, he just knew that the Kimber .38 Super was locked in his fist, his elbow locked against his side, his wrist stiff, the weird, maybe autistic brainfreak in his head solving the complexities of target identification, acquisition, alignment that had been the gift of the Swagger generations since the beginning, his muscles tight, all except the trigger finger, which — you get this about ten thousand repetitions into your shooting program — flew torqueless and true as it jacked back, slipped forward to reset then jacked back again, four times, all without disturbing the set of the gun in his hand. Brass bubbles flew through the air, as spent shells pitched by the Mach 2 speed of the flying slide as it cycled, all four within an inch or three of the others, and Bob put four .38 Super CorBons into the center-mass of the fellow closest to him, who immediately changed his mind about killing.

Nick fired. Bob's opponent fired finally, but into the ground. The man on Nick fired twice more from a smallish silver handgun, though crazily, and Bob vectored in on him and fired three more times in that superfast zone that seems to defy all rational laws of physics. The night was rent by flash. From afar it must have looked like a photo opportunity as a beautiful star entered a nightclub, the air filling with incandescence, the smell of something burned, and the noise lost in the hugeness of all outdoors. But it was just the world's true oldest profession, which is killers killing.

It was over in less than two seconds.

Bob dumped his not-quite-empty mag, slammed a new fresh one in and blinked to clear his eyes of strobe, then looked for targets. The guy he hit second was down flat, arms and legs akimbo, his silver revolver three or four feet away, weirdly gleaming in the dark from a random beam of light. The other fellow, hit first, was not down but he had dropped his gun. He walked aimlessly about, holding his stomach and screaming,

"Daddy, I am *so* sorry!"

Bob watched as he went to a big car and settled next to it, his face resting on the bumper. The lack of rigidity in the body posture told the story.

Bob knelt to Nick.

"Hit bad, partner?"

"Ah, Christ," said Nick, "can you believe this?"

"No, but it sure happened. I'm looking, I don't see no blood on your chest."

"He hit me in the leg, stupid fucker. Oh Christ, what a mess."

By this time, people had come to their balconies and looked down upon the fallen men.

"Call an ambulance, please. This officer is hit. We are police!" yelled Bob.

But in seconds another man had arrived, a smallish Indian with a medical bag.

"I am Dr. Gupta," he said, "the ambulance has been called. Can I help?"

"He's hit in the leg. I don't think it's life threatening. Not a spurting artery."

The doctor bent over, quickly ripped the seam of Nick's suit pants with scissors, and revealed a single wound about an inch inboard on his right thigh, maybe off-center enough to have missed bone. The wound did not bleed profusely, but persistently. It was an ugly, mangled hole, muscles puckered and torn, bad news for weeks or months but maybe not years.

"Tie," said the doctor.

Bob quickly unlooped Nick's tie and handed it to the doctor, who wrapped it into a tourniquet above the wound, knotted it off, then pulled out and cracked open a box, removed a TraumaDEX squeeze applicator and squirted a dusting of the clotting agent on the wound to stop the blood flow.

"Don't know when the ambulance will arrive in all this traffic. Can you give him something for pain?"

"No, no," said Nick, "I am all right. Where's that damned phone. Oh, shit, we can't get a chopper in here. Oh, Christ, I need to —"

"You ain't going nowhere," said Bob, "except the ER."

"Oh, Christ," said Nick. "I hope they got my message." But even as he said it, he knew it was hopeless, as did Bob. The shooters would bring their weapons to bear, the cops were strung out, the situation was a mess, nobody would know a thing, it was —

"I'll get there," said Bob.

"How, you can't —"

"My daughter's bike. It's over there. I can ramrod through the traffic. I've got some firepower. I know where they're going. I can intercept them at the hill, put some lead on them, maybe stop them from that chopper pick-up."

"Swagger, you can't —" but then he stopped.

"Okay," said Bob. "Who, then? You see anybody else around? You want these low-life fucks to get away with this thing, and the contempt it shows for all law enforcement, for civilians, for anything that gets in the way? You see anyone else here?"

But there wasn't anybody else around. Funny, there never was.

"Here," Nick finally said, "maybe this'll stop the cops from shooting you." He reached into his shirt and pulled out a badge on a chain around his neck. "This makes you officially FBI and there goes *my* career. Good luck. Oh, Jesus, you don't have to do this."

"Sure, why not," said Bob. "I got nothing better to do. It'll be my kind of fun." Bob threw the chain around his neck so that the badge hung in the center of his chest, signifying, for the first time since 1975, his official righteousness.

He rose, walked through the gathered crowd. He walked across the parking lot to his car, but next to it, came across the curious scene of a Vietnamese family standing in a semicircle around the gunman who had fallen against the bumper of his red Cadillac. One of them was a pretty young girl in a Hannah Montana T-shirt.

"You yelled the warning?" he asked.

"Yes. They were in our apartment all day, scaring my family to death. Horrible men. Monsters,"

"Can on co em. Co that gan da va su can dam cua co da cuu sinh mang chung toi," he said.

She smiled.

He walked to his car, popped the trunk. He withdrew the DPMS 6.8 rifle, and inserted a magazine with twenty-eight rounds. He looped its sling, held by a single cinch, diagonally across his body so that the gun was down across his front with enough play to allow him to get it either to shoulder or a prone position. He looked at the monitor atop it, that EOtech thing that looked like a '50s space-cadet toy, figured out which of several buttons turned it on, so that if he had to do it in the dark, he'd know which one to use.

He threw on the vest Julie had provided, in which he'd inserted, in dedicated mag pouches, the other nine magazines, all full with ammo.

Slamming the trunk, he walked back to the stairwell where Nikki's bike rested under a tarp. He ripped the canvas free and climbed aboard the Kawasaki 350. Shit, the pain in his hip from Kondo Isami's last cut flared hard and red, but he tried not to notice it. He turned the key to electrify the bike. It took three or four kicks to gin the thing to life, but he saw that he had plenty of fuel. He heeled up the stand, lurched ahead, kicked it into gear, pulled into the lot, evaded the gawkers, and took off into the night, running hard, disappearing quickly.

Nick, his leg throbbing but feeling no pain, watched him go.

Lone gunman, he thought, remembering Lawrence's words defining the American spirit: "hard, stoic, isolate, and a killer." But on the Night of Thunder, so necessary.

Thirty-Four

The muzzle flash of the Barrett 107 was extraordinary, a ball of fire that bleached the details from the night, so bright that it set bulbs popping in eyes for minutes. Caleb, who was holding it under his shoulder like a gangster's tommy gun, felt the heavy surge of the recoil as the weapon rocked massively against his muscle, almost knocking him from his feet, while at the same moment fierce blowback from the point of impact lashed against his face. Without glasses, he'd have burned out his eyes. The muzzle blast, expanding radially at light speed, ripped up a cyclone of dust from the earth beneath; it seemed a tornado had briefly touched down, filling the air with substance.

The 650-grain bullet hit the steel door two inches below the window frame, blowing a half-inch-size gaper and leaving a smear of burnt steel peeling away from the actual crater. It took both driver and assistant driver down, spewing a foam of blood on the far window inside the cab, after the tungsten core, liberated from the center of the bullet by the secondary detonation, flew onward at several thousand miles per hour and ripped them apart.

"Jesus Christ," said Caleb, himself awestruck and even a little nonplused by the carnage he had unleashed.

"The rear, the rear," screamed the old man.

Caleb lumbered around behind the truck with the heavy weapon in his hands, locked under his shoulder, as the Grumleys fanned out to surround the vehicle, while at the same time gesturing with their submachine guns to frozen passengers in the jammed cars to abandon ship and run like hell.

"G'wan, git the hell out of here, git them kids out of here, there's going to be a lot of goddamned shooting."

Caleb closed his eyes, fired one more time, point blank, into the rear of the truck from dead six o'clock. He even remembered to crouch and hoist the weight to orient the gun at a slight upward angle so that the tungsten rod it flung wouldn't continue forward, exit the end of the armored box, shred the dash, and end up chewing the bejesus out of the engine. That would have been a mess.

Again, the fireball blinded any who happened to observe the discharge from within a hundred yards, though most civilians had abandoned their cars and were running en masse in the opposite direction. Again, the muzzle blast unleashed a cyclone of atmospheric disturbance. Again, the recoil was formidable, even if slightly dissipated by the give in Caleb's arms and body as he elasticized backward from the blow. This time, for some reason, the noise was present in force and Caleb, even with ear plugs in, felt his eardrums cave under pressure of the blast.

A crater ruptured the upper half of the rear door.

A Grumley leaned close and yelled into the hole, almost as if there were a chance in hell anyone inside could hear, "You boys best open up or he'll fire six more in there."

There was a moment, then the door unlatched. Two uniformed men, with darkened faces from the blast, their own blood streaming from ear and nose, someone else's splattered randomly about them, eyes unseeing for the brightness, staggered out, fightless and dazed. Instantly the Grumleys were on them, disarmed them, and shoved them to one side of the road, where they collapsed and crawled to a gully to try and forget the horror of what they had just seen — the third member of their crew, who'd evidently taken a full injection of flying tungsten frontally, vaporizing the upper half of his body. His legs and lower torso lay on the floor, like the remains of a scarecrow blown down and scattered by a strong wind; the plastic bags of baled cash stacked on racks now wore a bright dappling of his viscera.

"Damn thang means business," a Grumley said.

"Go, go, boys, git going, no goddamned lollygagging," shouted the old man, a kind of cheerleader, amazingly animated and liberated by the violence. "Watch for them coppers."

A Grumley took up a position at each of the four compass points around the truck. The idea was to try and locate approaching police through the lines of cars, and engage them far away, because with their handguns the cops couldn't bring effective fire from that range. Meanwhile, other Grumleys set about their business. One dragged the second half of poor Officer Unlucky out of the truck, and dumped him. Another flew to the bags and began to pull out the ones containing change, which he dragged out and dumped. No need for extra weight on the upcoming hill.

Now it was Richard's turn.

"Tire guys, go, go, get it done," he shouted, and as they had so often practiced, a Grumley team of three hit the rear axle of the vehicle, got the heavy power-jack underneath, and with swift, focused strength jerked the thing atilt. Meanwhile, from roadside, two heavy tires with off-road treads meant to bite and tear at the earth in maximum, tractor-pull traction, trundled out, driven by Grumley power to the site of the armored truck, and the changing commenced.

Richard raced to the engine with his trick bag, not looking at the cab, not wanting to see what remained of the crew; he'd let Grumley minions clear that mess out. A Grumley struggled against the locked hood, then fired a blast of tracer into it. The bullets tore and bounced and in seconds had reduced the metal to tatters so that the hood could be lifted and hoisted high.

Richard set to work, as flashlights beamed onto the chugging complexities of the engine. He waited till a Grumley turned it off, and it went still. It was exactly as he expected, a Cat 7-stroke diesel, producing around 250 horsepower, which is why the big truck would always move sluggishly, underpowered for the extra weight of the armor. Quickly, he plunged into the nest of wires, found the MAP sensor, disconnected it, and reconnected the Xzillaraider wire harness. Plug and play was the principle. As the Grumleys held the flashlights, his fingers flew to the right wires, cut them, and quickly and expertly clipped in the new wires. He grounded the assembly, this time taking the time to unscrew the negative terminal, carefully wrap the grounding wire against the plug, then rescrew the cable terminal, making sure everything was nice, tidy, and tight. He paid no attention to what was going on around him, and so maximized was his concentration that he missed the crash of a helicopter brought down by Caleb. Then he leapt back to the rear of the engine compartment, pulled a knife, and cut through the rubber grommet and stuffed the wire harness through into the cab.

Ugh. Now the unpleasantness. When he got to the F-750's cab, however, the bodies were gone and some Grumley with a thoughtful touch had thrown a wad of NASCAR T-shirts on the blood and flesh matter that the Mk.211 had blown loose from the drivers. It wasn't so bad; no hearts or lungs or heads lay about, it only looked like several gallons of raspberry sorbet had melted.

He got to work, linking the harness of wires to the Xzillaraider module. He quickly wired the unit to the fuse box, then slid behind the wheel, paying no attention to the three gunshots that ricocheted weirdly off the three-inch glass, leaving a smear, nor to the fact that the whole scene appeared to be lit by an orange glow, as the crashed helicopter blazed brightly in the middle of NASCAR Village. Under normal circumstances, who would not stare at an aviation disaster such as that one? But these weren't normal circumstances, and Richard was much more fascinated by the blink sequence on the module. Yep, as he turned the key, the lights went through their positions and ended up in the red of high power.

He turned to see the Reverend, a Peacemaker in his hand and a cowboy hat on his head, and Brother Richard said, "When the tires are finished, old man, we are good to go."

While Richard worked, the old man had been commanding Grumley defenses. His gunners peered three-sixty, looking for targets, and when a poor police officer approached on foot, illuminated by his traffic safety jacket, a Grumley put a burst of 9mm tracer into him. The tracers were a wonderful idea: they made manifest the strength and invincibility of the Pap Grumley firepower.

Pap watched as a sleek streak of 9-mils raced down the corridor between abandoned cars, struck the poor officer, who had not even drawn his pistol, and flattened him. Those that missed their targets spanged off the cars on either side, pitched skyward into the night air. Hootchie mama, it was the Fourth of July! It was Jubilee! It was hell come to earth, fire, brimstone, the whole goddamned Armageddon thing.

"Good shooting," he yelled, "that'll keep their damned heads down."

Then someone poked him in the ribs and he looked down and saw a black hole in the lapel of his powder blue Wah Ming Chow custom suit. Fortunately the armored vest underneath stopped the bullet, but it meant some cop had fired from nearby up on the hill to the right.

"Over there," he commanded, and two Grumleys put out a blaze of noon light in the form of a half-mag apiece. If they got the cop or not, nobody could say, but the bullets sure chewed the hell out of an SUV in line to get out of a parking lot. Fortunately for all concerned, it had been long abandoned and so if anyone died, it would only have been a copper.

The sound of shots rang out everywhere as Grumleys on the perimeter either saw or thought they saw policemen slithering closer, and answered with long, probing bursts of tracer. Now and then something caught fire, including the rear of a Winnebago, a souvenir stand whose supply of T's and ball caps went up in flames, a propane heater for a barbecue stand. These small disasters added yet more hellish illumination to flicker across the already incredible scene, part monster movie (the citizens flee the beast), part war movie (the noise, the tracers, the screams of the wounded), and part NASCAR documentary (the tire crew operates at top speed, well choreographed and rehearsed) as the Grumley tire team, having gotten one of the off-road tires rigged, switched sides of the F-750, and went hard to work on the other.

But then a new source of illumination shocked all the Grumleys with its relentless quality. It was a harsh beam of light from a state police helicopter thirty feet up and fifty yards out, catching everything in high, remorseless relief.

"Drop your firearms," came the amplified order, "you are covered, drop your firearms and —"

"Caleb, take 'er down," yelled the old man.

"Pap, you sure?"

"It's copper, boy, they about to fire."

"Got it."

Caleb set up the Barrett on the hood of an abandoned car next to the F-750. He shouldered the weapon for the first time, drew it tight to him, and put his eye to the scope — he had no idea, but it happened to be a superb Schmidt & Bender 4×16 Tactical model — and in a second, as he adjusted his eye to the focal length, saw the black shape of the helicopter behind the blazing radiance of the light which was quadrisected by the cross hairs of the scope. He fired. The gun kicked so hard it broke his nose.

"Ow, fuck," he screamed, thinking, Wouldn't want to do that again, goddammit.

He put a 650-grain Mk.211 into the helicopter, right through the engine nacelle, and the bird climbed upward abruptly as the pilot realized he was under heavy fire. But then all his linkages went, and from aircraft the thing alchemized into sheer weight, beyond the influence of anything except gravity, and it simply fell from the air, straight down into NASCAR Village, nose forward. There it hit, its rotors chawing up a circle of dust from every bite. It seemed to die like an animal for a few seconds, still and broken, and then it exploded, an incredibly bright, oily, napalmesque four-thousand-degree burn. It lit the scene like day, exposing the fleeing masses, the fallen and trampled, the occasional crouching police officer popping away ineffectively with a handgun from two hundred yards out. Then the glare dulled and subsided, and all detail was lost.

"That'll keep them boys far away," yelled the old man.

"I'd like to git me another, Pap," said Caleb.

"You just wait on it, son, goddamn, them other birds is far away." And it was true, for a mile out, a number of choppers had settled into orbit.

"Tires done," yelled a Grumley.

"Richard, we are set to rock out of here."

"Okay," yelled Richard from the cab. "Git the boys aboard, all that want to come."

"Time to go, fellas."

With that, the Grumleys descended upon the F-750. That is, the armed Grumleys. The tire boys had been well prepped and knew there wasn't enough room aboard for all of them. Instead, they moseyed to the edge of the cone of light, and there, in darkness, peeled off armored vests, put on new baseball hats, and melted off into the trees. There were a few Grumley cars hidden in outlying spots to which they'd have no trouble proceeding, and would rendezvous later for their split of the swag. But now it was left to Richard and the shooters to get the load out of there.

Richard, in neutral, rode the pedal as his gunmen jumped aboard. Pap climbed into the other seat.

"Four minutes," he said, looking at his watch. "By God, we are ahead of schedule, don't think we've taken a wound, much less a kill, and nothing left to do but to drive on out of here, Richard. Let them boys shoot at us all they want, ain't going do no damage."

Richard shifted from neutral, gunned ahead, battered the car in front away until he had maneuver room. He turned the truck, found an angle between two abandoned cars pinning him on his right, and smashed between them. They fought the strength of his vehicle. The clang of vibrations loosened everyone's dentures, the metal screamed, but the cars yielded to the pumped-up CIT vehicle. Freed, he turned left, rode the shoulder for fifty feet, then turned right down an access road toward the speedway. This road took him to a bridge over a gully, and he pulled across it. Before him, pristine but not quite deserted, lay the heart of the kingdom, the confluence of courage for sale, engineering genius, soap opera, family feud, grudge, redemption, and failure, along with hats and shirts and signed portraits, the trailers turned to shops, the industrial pavilions, the souvenir and bric-a-brac outlets, the beer joints, and the cash machines that were NASCAR Village. It was the only thing between them and the mountain a mile away.

THIRTY-FIVE

Swagger had no trouble at first, and raced through the streets of Bristol, skewing and fishtailing around curves, zipping in and out of the traffic, as most people were off the streets or, if in their cars, intent on the racing news that had turned into robbery news. But the traffic began to thicken as he got through downtown and headed out the Volunteer Parkway toward the speedway and the civic disaster that engulfed it.

Signs of the disaster were everywhere as he buzzed at eighty down the road; it seemed that signal lights pulsed from every direction, and the traffic soon began to coalesce into something dense and motionless. He diverted to the shoulder but found that congested with fleeing citizens. He veered back onto the roadway and found the lane between jammed cars also impenetrable because of the panicked crowd.

He pulled up, looking for an alternate

route from the mess of fleeing civilians and abandoned cars that solidified the parkway before him, when a cop on foot materialized from nowhere and started screaming, "Buddy, get that goddamn thing out of here, do you know what's —"

But then Bob offered him the magic talisman of the FBI badge, and the man's eyes slid quickly to the assault rifle Bob wore crosswise down the front of his body, and his eyes bugged.

"You got an update?" Bob said.

"Well, it's a real bad ten-fifty-two, lots of shots fired, officers down all over the place. They got some kind of cannon or —"

"Can you get through to command on that thing?" He indicated the radio unit pinned to the man's lapel.

"It's a mess, I can try."

"Okay, tell them FBI recommends they get their SWAT units to the mountain overlooking the speedway. They're going to try to take that truck up there and go out by helicopter."

"What truck?"

"It's an armored-car job. They want to take all the baled cash to Mexico or wherever and anybody who gets in their way gets shot up. Now make the call."

"Sir, we can't move nobody in there now.

It's a mess, with thousands of civilians in the immediate and we can't get through 'em."

"Are there secondary routes to the mountain?"

"Not really. Lots of little streets, but nothing straight that ain't jammed with cars."

"Okay, advise SWAT to get as close as possible then move out on foot. It's the only way. Now someone has to intercept them and I don't see anybody around so it looks like it's me. You tell me my next move."

"You're it? You're the whole FBI? A guy on a bike?"

"Better yet, an *old* guy on a bike. We have people incoming by chopper, I'm advised. Look, we're wasting time. How do I get to that mountain? Up ahead's no good."

"Okay, sir, I'd fight my way down Volunteer best as possible. Too bad you don't have a siren on that thing."

"I liberated it from a civilian."

"You go down and about a mile before the speedway, you'll hit Groverdale Road. You left-turn on that, follow it to something called Cedarwood Circle. You can cut through somebody's yard there and you want to find Shady Brooks Drive, it's not much, but it curls around behind some houses that have probably given their yards up to parking, and that'll take you alongside the hill before it heads back to the parkway. You may want to leave the road when you're next to the mountain, as I'm thinking there's nothing up there except fields and stuff and maybe you can move faster. I'm guessing that's the only clear way."

"Got it."

"You want my body armor?"

"Thanks, officer, I don't have time."

"When this is over, I'll have to cite you for no helmet and driving off roadways."

"You do that. Mr. Hoover'll pay the fine."

"Who?"

"Never mind, son. You get on that squawk box and try and get SWAT where I told you."

"Yes sir. Good hunting, Special Agent."

"Thanks."

With that Bob spurted ahead, trying to ease his way between fleeing citizens, at last finding a fairly clear path between cars on the wrong side of the road. He never got into third gear. Up ahead the disaster played out; it seemed all the squad cars in the world were on the perimeter while the sky above was filled with the lights of orbiting choppers. He became aware of glare against the darkness which could only signify something burning hot, eating up aviation fuel, and that stench seemed in the air as well. He could hear no shots because of the sound of the engine, and now and then a hard-moving foot patrolman would try to wave him down and get him out of there, but the FBI badge made these phantoms depart.

At last he hit Groverdale, which took him down a road lined with modest houses, where each homeowner had turned his land over to parking use. The rate, he saw from the remaining signs, was a hundred dollars a night. Most people had been glad to pay it, and now most of them were in cars, caught in a thermal stew of light, dust, exhaust, cigarette smoke, and body odor, the cars locked bumper-to-bumper. But Bob made pretty good progress just along the edge of the shoulder where the road dissolved into grass and the walkers had moved up a bit, giving him room.

He found himself in a bright cul-de-sac, where the illumination blocked out all sense of what lay beyond. He had a sense, possibly from a new, dead quality to the echoes, possibly from the imposition of a kind of dampness on the sultry air, of a mountain, a huge, green obstacle, close at hand. Between the houses he could see glimpses of NASCAR Village, jiggles of flame, and everywhere, it seemed, emergency service vehicles trying to penetrate the gridlock of wreckage, but hopelessly behind the curve, unaware of what was happening to whom. He thought it was better he had no radio contact with any of this, for the network would have been a crazed blur of garbled facts, glaring misinterpretations, wrong advice, command ego, reluctance. It was like radio traffic during a big attack in that far off fairyland called Vietnam, all but forgotten these days but still the crucible that burned in Bob and made him the man he was.

He cut between two houses, almost put-putting along, riding the throttle grip and clutch grip and the gears between first and second, really defying the bike's true nature, which was to rush ahead, faster and faster. He skidded, found himself in a backyard where folks clustered around a radio and looked at him fearfully. A shotgun or two seemed to come his direction.

"FBI!" he yelled, holding up the badge. "Which way to the fight?"

A fellow in Bermudas with a beer in one hand and a Remington 870 in the other gestured onward, the direction he was headed.

"You go get 'em," he screamed. "Let me

finish this beer and I'll be right behind."

"You'd best sit this one out, sir. You need to protect wife and family and in-laws."

"Yes sir," said the guy, settling into a lawn chair. "FBI with a machine gun on a Kawasaki in my back yard. Goddamn, ain't I seen everything now."

Bob lurched ahead, through a line of bushes, into another back yard, the bike grinding and chawing through a garden. Threading between houses, he found himself on a still-narrower road — this had to be Shady Brooks Drive, which was really only wide enough for one car, and which was jammed with them, all going the way Bob wasn't.

But there was room on the shoulder, and he got all the way up into third for a while, at last running free of cars. Then he saw why. The road wound back to the right, toward the parkway, toward NASCAR Village itself, and that small metropolis now blazed like London in the blitz. Something had ramrodded through it, strewing wreckage and ruin everywhere.

But Bob saw clearly that proceeding in this direction would prove nothing, for it would take him only where his enemies had been.

He looked to the left, saw trees in pale illumination and saw that it had to be the base of the mountain. His thought now was to run the edge of the incline and see if he could cut trail, and where the boys had gone up, follow them.

It seemed to take for-goddamned-ever. He couldn't run full out — the way was tough, and he had to wiggle this way and that off-road and around natural obstacles. He couldn't see far enough ahead to make any speed at all, and though the land looked flat, it yielded up a bumpiness concealed in the height of the grass.

He came at last to some sort of installation in the lee of the mountain, a complex of corrugated tin buildings sealed off by cyclone fence, its approach from some other angle. He prowled around the perimeter and came upon a gate that had been smashed in. No lawman had made it this far. He pulled open the gate, found himself at last on level roadway, and followed the tracks of a heavy vehicle with born-to-raise-hell treads on the tires that had churned its way back beyond the buildings. At last he found an archway in the trees where a much-disturbed dirt road and dust in the air signified the recent passing of a major vehicle. The road had to lead up.

Bob circled, backtracked a hundred or so

yards, then gunned his engine and jumped gears. He hit the road in a fishtail of spewed mud, slithered around a boulder, penetrated heavy woods, and began the stark upward climb, his bike fighting the mud below and the gravity that pulled it backward.

THIRTY-SIX

Brother Richard paused for a second, feeling the thrill of the moment, feeling the low hum of vibration running from the amped diesel to his foot on the pedal, feeling his fingers in barest contact with the truck through the wheel, feeling all the million little tingles of tremor and jiggle and bounce that signified a vehicle with a load, a lot of fuel, and a wide open road.

"Richard, boy, goddamn, time's a wasting," said the Reverend.

"No, no, just look for a second. Look at it now to fix it in your mind."

"What you talkin' about, boy? All this here don't matter a frog's fart, just get us to the mountain!"

"It matters to me, old man." He smiled, turned and looked at the old man, and the Reverend saw for the first time how insane Richard was. He swallowed. The driver was one twisted visitor from beyond Pluto with his superiority, his mechanical and driving genius, and now this, his weird and furious insistence of enjoying the ride as if it were sex.

Richard winked.

"Remember Slim Pickens in *Strangelove*?"

What the hell the boy talking about? The Reverend thought this was crazyman talk.

"Remember 'Yee-haw,' the ride down to Armageddon, the sheer joy of it all? Well, old man, it's yee-haw time!"

Richard punched it. With a lurch even its toughened-up shocks couldn't soften, the heavy cash truck surged forward. First up was some sort of Jack Daniels tent, the center of which was a huge construct of whiskey bottles and cases. Richard aimed and hit dead zero. He felt the flimsy canvas yield without a whisper, devoured by the roaring bull of the truck, and the whiskey bottles shattered in a spew of brownish chaos, asparkle with the light, blown this way and that by the big vehicle's velocity. It was a whiskey explosion. He emerged from the mess with a truck bathed in eighty-proof Jack, good for curing colds, relieving virgins of their burden, burying grudges or exposing them, as well as causing the ruin of many good men of high birth and low, and being a boon companion on a long flight through lightning.

"Richard, goddamn boy, you just git us to the hill. Don't you be smashing things."

But Richard had another agenda, and the Reverend now saw that this thing here, this glory-run through the civilization that was NASCAR, this was the point.

"See them feathers fly?" Richard shouted, eyes lit by the glare of superego blitzed on brain chemicals. "Well, they shouldn'ta run!"

He was truly insane, particularly to the narrow mind of Alton Grumley, who didn't realize Richard was channeling Bo Hopkins from the first shoot-out in *The Wild Bunch,* nor that he had morphed into both Holden and Borgnine.

"Let's go," he said. Then he answered himself, "Why not?" and let a little sliver of psycho's giggle escape, just as Borgnine's Dutch had in that movie all those years ago.

"Richard, Richard, we don't have the time."

Richard then hit the pedestal on which an orange Toyota Camry, Daytona subvariant, was mounted twenty feet above all as part of Toyota's very polished pavilion. He didn't hit it straight on; it was more of a glancer, the point being to knock the car to the ground. In this humble desire, he succeeded, and the sleek vehicle pitched nose first into the mud, then toppled like a flipped turtle onto its back. Richard continued his war on the Japanese by clipping the corner of the Toyota structure, a piece of airport-like architecture meant to suggest the future, and his blow was so well considered that half of the roof went down, shattering glass and burying display cars in rubble inside.

He accelerated, took out this or that little place, the details were unimportant to him, saw people flee before him in both terror and glee and — *oh, boy, fun, fun, fun till Daddy took the T-Bird away* — found himself lined up perfect dead-on zero angle for the concourse of driver retail outlets, those trailer-truck souvenir shops where each of the big guys had heroic portraiture, replica clothing, ball caps, leathers, books, and related vanities on sale.

Richard revved the truck, enjoying himself. It was here he noted with amusement a certain base human truth. It was not he alone who looked upon the organization of commerce, the standardization of currency, the capitalist system, and had a violent impulse to destroy it all. He liked to crush things, sure, but so did lots of Americans. Yep, and it seemed that there were hundreds, maybe thousands, watching him. The moms and the kids and the old guys had fled. Not the young ones, the key NASCAR demographic of fourteen to thirty-six, southern, male, employed, tattooed (at least three), smoker, drinker, carouser, fighter. These guys, in the thousands, had somehow sensed that a show was about to begin.

"Can you hear it, old man?" Richard asked.

The Reverend could. It was soft, a murmur at first, but it picked up, the chant, "Go, Go, Go," until it became *Go, Go, Go!* and Richard was nothing if he wasn't the fellow who knew how to play to a crowd.

He punched. The roar rose, the windshield blurred with speed, then jolted with impact after impact, pitching this way, then that, tossing stuff through the air either whole or in many pieces. He fishtailed and jackrabbited his way in a perfect, high-test zigzag of destruction, hitting and smashing the truck trailers, which yielded by tipping or jumping or simply collapsing in shame. In thirty loud seconds Driver's Row looked like Battleship Row after the first wave of Japanese dive bombers. For good measure, samurai Richard-*san* pounded the snot out of a cash machine at the end of the formation, and dollars flew everywhere.

Richard heard the cheer of the crowd. He looked in his side mirror and was saddened to see that he had started no fires, though he'd knocked down some electric wires and they bled sparks in a few places, dangerous and beautiful and spectacular at once. Then suddenly one of them ignited something and the fire rose and leaped, at least on one half of Driver's Row, and soon enough flames consumed a great many of the battered retail installations.

Damn, that was good! Do it git better?

"Richard, my poor Grumleys in the back. They ain't got no seatbelt."

"Their heads are too hard for injury. You can't hurt a Grumley by hitting him in the skull. But okay, let's go."

He came next to a little bridge across a gully, initially cut off by traffic blocks set in the earth. But a less important Grumley job had been to wander down there during the race itself and pull them out. Richard rumbled across the bridge, pulled up an incline, and came again to flatness and temptation. Now the speedway was half a mile behind him, the mountain half a mile before him, and the structures on this side of the gully less substantial.

"Go, Richard," shouted the old man.

This wouldn't be as fun. It was all ticky-tack, tents and ramshackle lean-tos, all of it held together by aluminum and canvas and tape and twine, representing the lower end of the NASCAR money pyramid. Not corporate power but scavenging entrepreneurial nomadism.

"Ho hum," said Richard. "Don't think nothing'll burn or electrify, sorry to say."

"Richard, you don't got to narrate everything. This ain't a damn movie."

"Oh, it is, old man. You're Tommy Lee Jones, avuncular and charming, but now old and weary. I'm the mean Kevin Costner, not the sensitive Kevin, Caleb is Marky Mark, and maybe somewhere there's a hero who'll bring us down, but Clint retired and nobody took his place, so I don't think so."

After these important comments, Richard finally consented to do his job, and roared through the lesser precincts of NASCAR with much less pizzaz, as if he'd grown bored, having the attention span of a gnat. It was just snap, crackle, and pop, as the flimsy structures were eaten alive by the power of the Cash in Transit truck, and no pile of hats or Chinese Confederate flags or funnel cakes or barbecued ribs and sausages could stand against the onrush. Beer exploded, tables of goods were splattered, tents billowed as their ropes were cut, signs fell, but it lacked the FX grandeur of the previous few minutes' work. As spectacle, it had fallen. His esthetic sense somewhat blunted, he glumly soldiered on.

But as tactical enterprise, the genius of the plan soon became evident. There simply was no way any four-wheeled vehicle could have followed them, because Richard left behind him so much more damage than had been there before, and whether or not planned, the dynamic of the crowd, ebbing this way and that, opening before him, then solidifying behind him, precluded penetration. Then too, of the few roads around NASCAR Village, all were impenetrable, because all were jammed with civilians headed out, not in. Many of those people had abandoned their cars upon seeing the panicked crowd and hearing stories of machine guns, armed guerrillas, terrorists, Klansmen, militia. So in the vast mess, only the armored truck had any maneuverability, purely on the strength of its ruthlessness. It could and would drive through anything, it could and had driven down anybody, it was without conscience, a Moby Dick on land, or a Godzilla or a Beast from Twenty Thousand Fathoms that regarded humanity as insects to be crushed. It was just diesel nihilism on four tires, driven by venality and psychopathology and the fury of sons who'd disappointed their fathers, and it was unstoppable.

Richard drove on, he flattened, folks danced in delight, some throwing beer bottles at him, not so much to stop him but to participate in the wanton pleasure of the evening. Now and then a police bullet sounded a pitiful ping as it bounced off the heavy armor but failed to penetrate. At the far end, the anticlimax arrived with a whimper. Richard found a dirt road that led to a gated installation in the lee of the mountain, built up some nice speed and fragmented the cyclone gate with his Ford cyclone, and roared along the edge of the mountain, which presented itself to him as an incline swaddled in trees.

"There 'tis," shouted the old man, and indeed, up ahead, an archway in the trees revealed a dark portal, behind which lay the serpentine of a switchbacked track to the top, glistening with perpetual mud from a dozen mountain springs, its existence all but forgotten, a relic left over from logging days. "Here's where you earn all that goddamn money we done paid you!"

"Think there's a man in America who could get a rig this heavy up a road this steep and sharp? Well there ain't but one, and he took the Pike's Peak hill climb three times running and some other up-hills as well, and has done the trick on bikes and go-carts and destructo jalopies and tractors and big-daddy trucks and hell, even a kiddie cart or two."

"You'd best have it, boy."

"Hang on, Grandpappy. The elevator is reading Up."

He plunged ahead.

A lesser man would have wept. Not Caleb. His shattered nose blossomed blood, and he felt like a piece of popped corn in a corn popper, floating this way and that, a hard trick with a thirty-pound rifle in his hands.

"Goddamn him, that sumbitch, gonna whip his ass!" screamed another flying Grumley, immediately before hitting the goddamned wall or sharp shelf or any of the dozens of hard surfaces inside the box.

"The fucking little prick, he doin' this 'cause he thinks he's special, it's his little trick on us poor dumb Grumleys."

"He thinks we ain't human!"

It was, in other words, no fun in the box. The five boys each were made clumsy by submachine guns, their body armor, their spare magazines, the darkness, the claustrophobia. It was like a submarine undergoing a depth-charge raid by the Japanese. They were tossed this way, then that, without visibility. On top of that, shrapnel, in the form of thirty-pound bales of bills in tamper-evident plastic bags flew around the interior like really heavy pillows. They fucking hurt when they hit you, and they could hit you at any time from any angle. Then there was a lunch box or two, maybe a few cans of Diet Coke, and who knew what else afly in the dark atmosphere of the steel box and though the shocks supporting it were thick and strong, they did little to protect against the vicissitudes of crumple and crunch that Richard produced as he wreaked vengeance on NASCAR for the crime of being NASCAR. Back here, a hero was needed, a man of strength.

But these were Grumleys, greed-driven and sensation hungry, the brains scientifically bred out of them, so they had no hero. No calm voice took over and soothed, not even Caleb's, as that unhappy warrior simply sat as still as possible, clutching the huge Barrett .50, trying to breathe through blood, while dreaming of driving the Barrett's butt into Richard's strange, disguised head and watching it shatter. The rest got through the ordeal of the ride on the strength of their considerable sheer meanness, their similar hunger to pulp Richard when the day was done, and dreams of swag and whores and drugs and other cool Grumley things.

It was dialogue. It was not oration, still less a lecture, and least of all some kind of pontification. No, it was chat, conversation, attention to nuance, cooperation, and teamwork. This is how you climb a hill that doesn't want to be climbed in a big vehicle that doesn't want to climb it. Richard listened and talked with the components of the adventure. He felt the traction in each tire, not a chorus, but the voice of each as the expression of a personality; he felt the play between torque and transmission even in the crude containment of the automatic gear shift as these two dynamisms bartered their way through the complex transaction. He felt the tremble of vibes from the shocks, the subtler orchestration of announcements from the enhanced diesel as the Xzillaraider had blown out the parameters of the performance package, and the diesel fuel burned hot and long and fierce, turning its own chambers a molten red, threatening to go volcanic at any second. On top of that, through the imperfect vision cones of the illuminating headlights, Richard read the curves, finding the ideal line in each, read the texture of the mud in the road, divining where its gelid smoothness contained strength and where only watery treachery. He sensed which logs could be crushed, which knocked aside and which, still strong, had to be avoided. It was a complex negotiation, and he was right that few men in the world could have done it, and few would have wanted to.

It seemed to take forever, and Richard at a certain point felt his muscles locked against the wheel as if the wheel was the enemy and the addition of his human strength could make a difference. He cued himself to relax, and felt the iron melt from his neck. Though bathed in sweat, he felt at last a kind of relaxation, because it occurred to him that that which he feared most — a sucking pool of mud that would engulf him to above the hubcaps — would not befoul him.

"Jesus Christ," said the old man, "I think you done it, boy. I think we going to make it."

The truck broke from gnarled, mythic wood into a kind of grassy meadow and it suddenly occurred to Richard that there was no more hill to climb.

He brought the truck to a stop. He opened

the door and almost fell out, limp with exhaustion, spent and wasted and hungry for vacation. He sucked coolish air, felt coolish air against his brow. He looked, saw stars, pinwheels of ancient energy, dancing light years off. Jesus, what a fucking thing.

"We here, boy, we done it," sang the old guy. From behind came an outpouring of Grumleys as the boys liberated themselves and had a moment of pure bliss. They were on top of the world. Ma, we're on top of the world. From hating Richard, they flew to loving him. Richard had never been so admired in his life. He felt like a rock star as hard Grumley hands pounded him on the back.

"Okay, boys, you git that dough on the roof," yelled the old man, and then turned to speak on the cell, "Tom, get that bird in and get us the hell out of here. Time to go home."

As behind him, the Grumleys set about to move the money bales to the roof of the truck so that they could be tossed into the hovering chopper, Richard moseyed off a few yards and came to a vantage on what he had done.

He looked down from a thousand feet on the vast structure of the speedway and the NASCAR civilization that had spread forth and put roots down upon the plains.

He saw wreckage. He saw fire. He saw a thousand emergency service vehicles spitting out goobers of red light. He saw smoke, drifting this way and that in the wind, he saw the crushed, the broken, the smashed, the atomized. He saw pain, disbelief, destruction, disaster. He saw the beast wounded. He felt in himself an insane pride in the ruination. Sure you could have detonated a bomb like some A-rab boy-fucker, or opened up with a Glock like a sad, sick Korean kid, or any of another dozen methods of high-octane takedown, but to drive through it, to smash and grind and pulp and express the ultimate contempt in traction and horsepower — say, that was pretty fucking cool. It was so Sinnerman. He felt a sense of profound fulfillment.

Fuck 'em if they can't take a joke.

But then he heard it. They all heard it. The sound of a motorcycle as it churned up the same hill they'd just mounted.

"It's the goddamned Lone Ranger," somebody said.

Thirty-Seven

Bob hit the hill hard on his Kawasaki. The bike slid upward, attacking, sliding right and left, inclining on the sudden hairpins, spitting mud, churning dirt, sliding this way and that as it fought for traction. Up he went, feeling between his legs the throb of the pistons beating as he rode the line between second and third, foot alive to the quickness of the necessary shifting. He smelled gas as it was eaten in 350-cc gulps.

But he knew it was time to dump the bike when the tracers came floating his way. Whoever these boys were, they weren't well schooled. They fired too early, counting on the display of neon death floating parabola-like through the trees (and rupturing wood where it struck) to drive him back. He might have been a different fellow, but Bob had taken tracer before, even fired batches of it, so panic was not what he felt, even as random bullets began to kick up stingers and puffs of mud near him.

He cranked hard, put the bike over, feeling it bite against the mud as it plowed furrows. Before it was even still, he'd scrambled off, found cover in the trees, and begun his assault. He had no targets yet, but still his finger flew to the EOTech gizmo atop his DPMS rifle, and pressed the button that was protected against accidental tripping by a plastic sheet across it. He nudged it, felt it give, brought the gun to his shoulder and saw, to his surprise, a bright orange circle on the 2×2 screen. You didn't need training, so simple was the concept; you put the circle on what it was you wanted, you pushed the trigger, and you ventilated. He slithered upward, safety off, finger indexed along the top of the guard, and forty yards out saw two men hunched over weapons on a crestline, peering hard for target.

"I think we put him down, Pap," came a cry. Bob put the orange circle on the center of mass, and fired three times. This damn gun was no poodle-shooter; it bucked, more by far than a .223, but not so much that it was beyond control. With superb trigger control and a stout shooting position, Bob knew he scored all three and he watched the unfortunate recipient jerk when struck, then fall to the left. Bob came over, wasn't quite fast enough on the pivot, and by the time he got around, the second guy was down under cover. Gunflashes gave away his position, and so did the tracer burst which vectored like splashes of liquid weight toward Bob, bending as it arched toward him and tore into trees and ground. And suddenly other boys were on the line and the hill was alive with the sound of death. The guns buzzsawed hellaciously and ripped, and the world turned all nasty and full of frags and flying debris and the spritz of near-supersonic wood chips. Bob squirmed back, aware that they were shooting toward sound rather than actually acquiring a target.

He waited a bit, moved a little more but delicately, put his rifle up and waited patiently. Soon enough a scout popped up to see if he could see a thing, and just as quickly Bob put one into him, center mass again, the gun beating into his shoulder with its upward torque, the muzzle flash bleaching detail from his night vision, illuminating a spent 6.8 shell as it flew to the right. Another one down, but another cycle of mega-blasting came abanging as the rest of the boys dumped their mags at him.

He waited them out. Would they have the guts to flank? Would they put people off on his right and his left, triangulate and take him out? He bet not. They weren't trying to hold the hill for but a few more minutes, and nobody wanted to miss the big bus out.

And indeed, here came the bus; it floated out of blackness, its rotor kicking up a cyclone, huge and messy, blowing clouds of dust everywhere. He couldn't get a good shot at it, however, and when it had settled in, it was hidden behind the angle of the incline and he could only hear it, see its column of rising disturbance. Then another posse of tracer came his way, lighting up his world and almost hitting him. One came closer than any round since fifteen years earlier, and he had a moment of fear. Even he, the great Bob the Nailer, victor in a hundred gunfights against impossible odds, felt the terror of the near miss, and he slunk back, happy just to be alive.

The phone rang.

Odd time for a phone call. But it rang, some chipper computery tune calculated to alert and annoy, the sound fortunately buried from his antagonists by the roar of the chopper. Astounded that he would do such an amazingly stupid thing, he obeyed the human rule that no matter what, phone calls take precedence over all reality. Maybe it was FBI, or maybe Nick had given the number to local authority.

"Swagger," he said into it after plucking it from inside his vest and slipping it open.

"Mr. Swagger, it's Charlie Wingate," said the voice.

"Charlie? Well —"

"I think I figured Mark 2:11 out. It took a thousand hits on the Net but it's actually 'Mark,' as in military or industrial model designation, capital M, small k, period, then just two-eleven, no colon, and it refers to a .50 caliber armor-piercing munition that —"

At that moment the tree trunk behind which Bob had slithered exploded. It atomized as something weighing 650 grains with a secondary explosive and a tungsten core, traveling at twenty-five hundred feet per second, hit it at zero angle, detonated, and sent a shockwave through it that all but liquefied the wood structure itself. It toppled, but could not find room among the other trees to actually hit ground, and lay suspended at an angle.

"Thanks, Charlie," said Bob, "I'll get back to you." He flipped the phone away, slithered even farther down the hill. Good old Charlie. Better late than never.

Two more .50 Raufosses arrived, but the gunner had no target. This time, not hitting wood, he did not get his secondary detonation, but only plowed into the dirt, kicking up a huge, dusty geyser of earth and leaves, each blast a bit farther from Bob, the thrust of the recoil taking him away from his target with each shot. Bob rolled to the side, came up in a good kneeling position, put the red circle on his target and, guessing that he was body-armored, shot him in the head.

Now, he thought, get to the top, get some rounds into that bird, cripple it, then fall back and live happily ever after. Let the real FBI take over.

Each thirty-pound, twenty-by-twenty-four-inch, plastic tamper-evident bag contained approximately twelve thousand bills, as baled carefully in the counting room at Bristol Speedway headquarters. The distribution of bills was predictable, even immutable: 10 per cent of them were ones, 15 per cent fives, 25 per cent of them tens, 40 per cent of them twenties, 5 per cent of them fifties and 5 per cent of them one hundreds. Each bag contained about $226,000 and all thirty-five of them — roughly $8 million in small, unrecorded bills — weighed a thousand fifty pounds.

The Reverend needed men. So he sent only two gunners to the crestline to search for the ranger on the motorcycle, figuring the two could handle it easily enough. That left three to unload and hoist, and one on the roof to stack the bales in a neat pile for easy tossing into the wide-open chopper door. If that goddamned Richard were here, it would help, but the boy had disappeared.

The Grumley inside tossed the bags out to a Grumley beside the truck's open rear door, and he in turn — husky Caleb, bloody nose and all — heaved it up to the Grumley atop the truck. When all the bags were out, all the Grumleys would climb up top and toss the bags into the chopper hovering above. It seemed to be going pretty well, given that the rotors of the helicopter were tossing up hell and gone, when someone wandered up groggily, holding his ear.

"Pap," he yelled, "he goddamn hit me three times and the last one bounced off the vest and tore off my ear."

"Oh, Lord," said Pap.

"Pap, I'se hurt bad. Git me out of here. That boy can shoot a lick."

The Reverend made a decision.

"Caleb, you no nevermind that, you git over there, you boys too, you put this fella down."

So the whole goddamned team quit their loading and ran to the edge of the hill.

Pap waited as the guns blazed, the helicopter hovered, and nothing seemed to be happening except time was passing. What was taking so long?

"I'm getting worried hanging here," said the helicopter pilot through the phone. "They git heavy guns up here, they can bring this thing down in a second. You said wouldn't be no shooting."

"Some damn hero trying to win a medal," Pap said. "Hold her just a second."

He looked about. Richard would sure have been a help around now. But no Richard.

Suddenly the boys was back. They'd dumped their mags, filled the woods with slugs, tore shit out of it no human man could live through, and left Caleb to hold the fort.

So it was Pap himself who climbed up top the truck from the hood, and started lifting and tossing the bales into the chopper. Hard to believe, each chunk of weight was about a quarter mil in swag, untraceable, immediately spendable, investable, hell, a feller could have himself a great weekend in Vegas with just one of 'em. And goddamn, he was getting two, the boys one each and —

He found superhuman strength in the power of his greed and tossed them aboard. The pilot helped by walking the chopper down the length of the truck so the distance wasn't far, and the thirty-five bags went aboard fast. Then each scrambled in, all helping to get the wounded man aboard.

"Where's Caleb?"

"Sir, he ain't coming, don't believe. We seen him go down just a second ago. We ought to —"

But the old man didn't need to be told. He twisted from the news, looked through the entryway from cargo hatch to cockpit where a pilot looked back at him, and gave the thumbs up.

Too bad for Caleb, but that were the Grumley way, and even though the bird was no rocket, they all felt some kind of low g-force as she zoomed skyward, straight up into the black, with four Grumleys and eight mill small unrecorded aboard.

Whooooeeeee, Pap felt himself gush as the bird climbed and began its outbound jaunt, running low, hard and without lights.

Nothing could stop them now.

Bob hadn't even made it out of the trees as the bird — it was a Blackhawk, no less — took off for the moon or other parts ethereal. It climbed high until it was damned near invisible, and it was out of range in seconds. He didn't have a shot.

Shit, he thought.

Then he cursed himself for chucking away the phone as he now saw he might have been able to get a call through, somehow have gotten word to somebody that . . . but he saw that was impossible. Nah. The airwaves were still a mess, nobody knew anything, no —

Mark 2:11. "Arise from your pallet and go to your house."

Mk.211, Model O, Raufoss armor-penetrating incendiary.

It was time to let Jesus speak for himself.

Swagger ran to the fallen man, who lay in a fetal position, his head bent and crushed by a 6.8 Remington. But that wasn't the point. The point was cradled in dead hands. Bob picked up the goddamned Barrett rifle, all thirty pounds of it, and ran back with it to the armored truck. He set up over the hood, after performing a quick check with the bolt to make certain a shell lay in the chamber and seeing that it did, he found a good supported position, the heavy thing on its bipod legs. He drew it to his shoulder, aware from Japan that he'd find speed in no speed, he'd find attainment in no attainment, he'd find it all in smooth, and in smooth he ticked them off: spotweld, check, trigger finger, check, breathing discipline, check, bones locked, check, mind numbed to stillness, going, going, going on toward nothing.

The last time he'd fired through a scope was months ago, and what was this scope, what was its zero, who set it up? Well, the bad boys didn't set it up, because they used it close in, and the shooting they'd done was from the hip, at distances of twenty feet or less, as witness the beefy guy who'd tried to hipshoot him. They'd left it alone, most likely, fearing it a little. What was the origin of the gun? Was it a privately owned weapon, used by some rich gun guy for hitting targets a mile out? No way, too beat up for that, not well enough cared for. Had to be from the same source as the restricted Raufoss ammo, that is, from some Justice Department/Defense Department equipment program, meaning it was a military gun, maybe refurbed by Barrett after use in the sand, declared surplus and turned over to law enforcement cheap for use in the war against drugs and somehow coming all the way to Mountain City. Bob tried to feel its last real shooter and came up with a man like himself, a marine NCO, hard and salty and given to the mastery of the technology, his imagination enflamed by the possibility of doing bad guys a mile away and saving the lives of young marines who'd otherwise have to close and do it at muzzle-blast range.

He's a mile out, he thought, and whoever set this up, he fired at a mile, that was his pride, his power. He knew with certainty: The scope is zeroed at a mile.

Bob settled behind the reticle, indexed on his approximation of the angle at which the bird had headed, and there it was, illuminated in the light of the speedway its occupants had just looted, the bird in blur, three-quarter profile, bisected in the milliradian-designated crosshairs, and it all came together in the kind of stroke only someone who'd done the deed under pressure a thousand or a million times on training fields and in bad places where they shot back could make happen — smooth and beyond attainment or speed or ambition.

He didn't even feel the recoil in the nanosecond the bird crossed the crosshairs of the scope, though it may have been ferocious, even as he gave with it, rolled backward, and let the gun resettle for a second shot. He didn't see the blinding muzzle flash as the huge missile with its tungsten core flew onward at well past the speed of sound, he didn't feel the noise, which was immense, he didn't sense the disturbance all those hot, roiling gases unleashed.

He looked again when the show was complete, but he couldn't find the bird. Where had it gone, what was it —

He saw it sliding out of the sky. He watched through the magnification of the scope and caught the thing in its downward gyre. It wasn't smoking or burning, but its internal rhythms were psychotic and the fuselage rotated wildly, whipping ever faster, until it was just barely flying, and at the last the pilot, whoever he was, got some control, and the thing hit with a smash against the empty seating of the speedway, its tail boom shearing off and going for a tumble, smoke rising now from a dozen different areas. Then Bob saw men spilling crazily out of it, even one, from this distance, in blue.

Then a glare spotlighted him.

He looked up to see another bird just a few feet up. He felt himself pinned, silhouetted in the harsh light. He raised his hands, holding Nick's badge up for all to see.

The bird got even lower, and in its own light he now saw KFOX-TV written on its boom.

He climbed up to the roof of the truck and the chopper came even lower. He got a foot on the runner, launched forward, and eager hands pulled him in.

He was aboard next to a guy with a fancy haircut and a guy with a camera, both so excited they looked about to pee. But he wedged past them, knowing all too well the interior of the Huey, and leaned into the cockpit.

The pilot handed him a set of earphones, which he slipped on, finding a throat mic at the ready.

"I'm with the FBI," he said, gesturing with the badge.

"Yes sir."

"Listen, can you run this baby south to 421, then follow 421 all the way over Iron Mountain out to Mountain City?"

"Sure can."

"When we get there, I'll talk you in the rest of the way. You drop me where I say, and then you make tracks."

"Read you, Special Agent."

"Then let's rock and roll the fuck out of here."

THIRTY-EIGHT

The boss waited. Radio reports were incoherent, inclusive, communicating only chaos and conflicting intelligence. Choppers down, but Caleb had to bring a chopper down. How many? One? Two, three? Hard to say. In the end, it was pointless to listen, and so the boss turned off the unit.

The boss checked the time. After midnight. Here, so far away, the night was calm, the sky full of radiance, the temperature at last bearable, and a sliver of gibbous moon let low gleam smear the southern hemisphere. When the hell would it be here? Why wouldn't the hands on the watch move more quickly? Why was breath so hard, neck so stiff, mouth so dry?

Suddenly, there it was. The boss felt immense relief. It felt so good. They were here. It was done.

The black bird, running low over the mountain crest, finding this unlit field behind the prayer camp without a problem. He was such a good pilot and now he could be taken care of too.

The boss lit a flare, the only signal necessary.

It's done. They said it couldn't be done. But I did it. Now I'm free and clear and rich and untouchable. I'm a legend. They'll wonder for a hundred years what became of me, what I did with all that money. They'll tell of the boss who beat the game.

The helicopter set down, pitching up a whirl of wind and dust and leaves, blowing and bending the grass away from its roar. But Grumleys didn't jump out. That old man in his blue suit didn't leap out, dancing as was his way when gleeful, and there were no Grumleys shouting and pounding and strutting as was expected, everybody hungry for their share of the swag, neatly pre-cut into bales of cash, one for each boy, two for the old man, and the rest for the boss, as planned. Then the boss would jump aboard the chopper, and it would continue its run in the dark, low and unfollowable, another hundred miles to an obscure rural field where an SUV waited along with some phony passports. They'd be in Mexico in a day.

But no, none of that happened.

No Grumleys got off.

Just one old man: Bob Lee Swagger.

"Howdy, Detective Thelma," Bob said. "Nice to see you."

"Swagger," she said. "Goddamn you."

"I do annoy people."

She saw the badge.

"You were FBI undercover all the time?"

"No, ma'am. I am Nikki Swagger's father, pure and simple. But I have a great friend in the Bureau and we linked up. Now I'm working for him. But I'm still working for Nikki."

"It wasn't personal."

"It never is."

The two faced each other in the flicker of the flare as the helicopter skipped away into a high orbit.

"No way that hayseed gun store gets hold of imported Norwegian Raufoss armor-piercing rounds without someone running a request on police stationery through Justice under the sheriff's signature, the sort of thing someone running an anti–meth lab program might have, right, Thelma? But who runs the department? That matinee-idol sheriff? He's so dumb he doesn't know how many feet he's got. They'll figure that out down there soon enough. I already did."

"Swagger, don't make me do this. I see I have to run hard now, and I can't waste time here with you."

"There ain't no rush, Detective Thelma. I don't think you're going nowhere. Hmm, let's see, what else? Oh, yeah, sure, I'm betting the superlab is in the coal yard next to the sheriff's office, under the stink of all that coal where nobody can sniff it out, most of all that sheriff. Boy, you made some monkey out of him. But that's why you got to go, isn't it, Thelma? OSHA's closing down the yard and y'all are moving the department. You can't run the lab if they're closing down the whole zone. You've run meth in Johnson for three years now. You fed the sheriff the intel, let the sheriff take out the competition, and you manufactured the stuff by the bagful right under his nose, slipstreamed behind him, kept the cost of meth the same. That network of snitches you're so proud of; those are your dealers. That poor boy Cubby Bartlett you shot was a dealer and he was so cranked he didn't have any idea what was going on. You grabbed the gun because when you showed up at his place that afternoon and pumped him full of ice, you found his piece, unloaded it. So you had to grab it to justify your prints all over it. The upshot is, you used the profit to set up this operation, to turn an awkward million you shouldn't have had into eight unmarked free and clear. Hell, the pieces were already in place for you; the helicopter, its pilot being your banged-up gone-to-hell brother. And I know you got him the job. The Barrett rifle already in the inventory, the inside dope on the cash movement, the inside dope on how tied in knots law enforcement was. All you had to do was get the sheriff to sign off on the Raufoss. Then off you go, laughing all the way. What you got on old Alton to leverage him like that? Something pretty, I imagine."

"Damn you, Swagger, how'd you get so smart? He likes boys. He come chicken-hawking up here, and I heard and set up a sting and got video on him. In his circles, that's ruination. So he does this job, and we're quits."

"You are a bad girl, Thelma. But we ain't quite at the end. You knew Grumley before. You got some strange connection to Grumley. Grumley don't trust no outsiders. They'd just roll over you. What is it, Thelma. Who are you?"

"Born Grumley. Maybe Pap's, maybe someone else's. Grumley blood. They got rid of me. Too smart. Raised in an orphanage. But I backtracked and found 'em. Pap could never bring himself to shed Grumley blood. End of talk. Time to go. Swagger, you are way overmatched. You have seen me draw. You know how fast I am, and how I don't never miss. I have to leave now. If you try to stop me I will kill you. Who do you think you are?"

"Who do I think I am? You never got it, did you? Y'all thought I was some old coot from out West, no match for Grumley killers and armed robbers and crooked-as-hell detectives. I am Bob Lee Swagger, Gunnery Sergeant, USMC, eighty-seven kills, third-ranking marine sniper in Vietnam. I have shot it out with Salvadorian hunter-killer units and Marisol Cubano hitmen and a Russian sniper sent halfway around the world. I even won a sword fight or two in my time. They all had one thing in common. They thought they were hunting me, and I was hunting them. Faced many, all are sucking grass from the bitter, root end. Here're your choices: You can come easy or you can come dead."

Thelma drew.

She was way fast, she was so smooth, her hand flew in a blur to the Para-Ord in the speed holster, it came up like a sword stroke, invisible in its raw speed.

Bob hit her twice in the chest before she even got the safety off.

She spun, hurt so bad, and the heavy gun fell from her hand, the two CorBon .38 Supers enabling the ritual of drainage that would take her life from her as they opened up like sharp steel roses. She gasped for air, finding little, and turned to look at the old man with the pistol in his hand, just as the flare died.

"By the way," he said, "I was also Area 7 USPSA champ five years running. Nobody ever called me slow."

■ ■ ■ ■

PART III
LAST LAP

■ ■ ■ ■

THIRTY-NINE

It took some sorting out, and the politics were enormously complicated. But the final law enforcement debriefing on the incident of August 23, 2009, Bristol, Tennessee, managed to get through its business in less than six hours. All participants — the FBI, the Tri-cities Law Enforcement Task Force representing the municipalities of Sullivan County, the Tennessee Highway Patrol, and the appropriate federal, state, city, and county prosecutor's offices — remained cordial and tempers were more or less controlled throughout.

It helped that though the Grumley mob had fired over 750 rounds of ammunition — this was the number of cartridge casings picked up by the FBI Evidence Recovery Team on site at the Bristol Speedway the day after the incident — no civilians were killed, though eleven were wounded, one critically. It helped that Bristol police officers caught the main perpetrators — actually had them signed, sealed, and delivered when the hijacked Johnson County Sheriff's Department's helicopter crashed conveniently into the speedway itself — without difficulty. It helped that law enforcement casualties were quite low too: a Bristol traffic officer was seriously wounded by 9mm fire as he approached the site of the takedown, a state police helicopter pilot was badly burned when his aircraft was shot down by Caleb Grumley early in the firefight, and his copilot broke an ankle pulling him out of the downed machine in the seconds before the fire erupted. The real tragedy was the three employees of Cash Transit Service of Tennessee killed outright. It seemed to bother no one that three perpetrators — Caleb, another Grumley gunman on the hilltop, and a corrupt Johnson County law enforcement officer — were killed by FBI agents. Two other Grumley gunmen were killed earlier in the evening by another FBI team.

If anyone could be said to have won the engagement and emerged in extremely positive light, it was the Bureau, with its intrepid penetration of the conspiracy, its rapid response and deployment, and its heroic SWAT actions during the incident itself.

Task force director Nicholas Memphis, wounded in the first shooting relating to the events of that evening, was singled out for special praise and would almost certainly win another decoration. The undercover agent he supervised was never identified to law enforcement personnel — the Bureau is notoriously reluctant to share operational details, even with other agencies — though many believed the tall, anonymous older gentleman who accompanied the Bureau contingent to the meeting might have been that fellow himself.

Some oddities and disappointments became clear. Though in fact FBI initiative closed the attempt down, it was clear from even the most preliminary study that the real failure factor in the criminal enterprise was the odd route the driver of the hijacked Cash in Transit truck took to the helicopter pickup point. Had he not diverted to cause maximum damage to NASCAR Village, the felons would have made their escape easily. Running low and without lights by helicopter, they would have been impossible to locate. They could have split the $8 million cash take, and dispersed almost instantly. That's how close the bad guys came to getting away with it. That led, in turn, to the one disappointment: the failure to apprehend that particular fellow, the mysterious driver who had somehow slithered away in all the craziness.

As for the Grumleys themselves, they were as they had always been: tough, silent men who did their crime and were willing to do their time, even if, as in the case of Alton Grumley, he would certainly perish in prison before that time was over. They named no names, snitched out no others. Besides Alton, three shooters were taken alive and would not name the other Grumleys who had helped in the vehicle takedown and then melted away, remaining unapprehended. The pilot, former major Thomas Fielding, United States Army, would have sold anybody out, but he knew nothing. He was a wounded combat veteran who had been shot down three times in two wars. His last tour of duty had been very rough, leading to a history of drinking and other personal problems. He quickly turned state's evidence, though he had little to offer except to point out to any and all that he should never have listened to his little sister.

Finally, it was over, though adjudication remained, the inevitable process by which things get processed in the justice system. It would involve many of the cops, further investigation, much sworn testimony and court time, generally inconveniencing everybody and using up millions of dollars. But all that was in the future, and the heroic Nick Memphis, sure now to become an assistant director, left with his party, including the quiet older agent who said nothing but watched all.

The two of them walked to Nick's car and they were a sight. Bob still limped and would always limp from the deep cut across his hip and down to his steel replacement joint. Nick was on crutches and hobbled along as best he could.

"If we had a drummer, we'd look like Yankee Doodle Dandy," Bob joked at one point. They got across the parking lot of the Bristol Police Department, where the meeting had taken place. It was another sultry day in the South, with a low, gray sky and a threat of rain in the air. Nick turned to Bob.

"I have to say, partner, you are some kind of cowboy. We don't have a guy who could come close to you, and we've got some damn good guys. What's the secret, Bob? What explains you? No one knows you better than me, and I don't know a thing."

"My old man was the real hero. I'm just his kid, trying to live up to him, that's all.

That plus good old USMC training, some kind of natural skill, and what can only be called Gunfighter's Luck. Wyatt had it, so did Frank Hammer, Mel Purvis, Jelly Bryce, D.A. Parker, all those old boys. I seem to have just a touch myself."

"You have what they have for sure, and it isn't luck. It's something else. Arkansas boy like you ought to know the term for it. 'True Grit' ring a bell? If not, try Japanese: 'Samurai.' Sound familiar? You were there. Marine Corps. 'The Old Breed.' Bet you heard that one. Or go back to the ancient Greeks: 'Spartan.' Any of it mean a thing?"

"Don't know, Nick. Maybe it's just stupid luck. And maybe it's just who I am, that's all."

"Okay, go home, rest, enjoy. You've earned it. Get fat. Have more kids. Die in bed in forty years."

"I intend to. First though, I'm heading back to Knoxville, to pick up my wife and daughters. Boy, am I sick of that damned drive down and back. After I git quit of this part of the country, ain't never driving that I-81 spur again. Sorry you didn't get your bad boy, that driver. That one must sting."

"We'll get him. If he was expecting a cut of the cash, he came up short, which means he'll have to work again soon. We know what to listen for this time."

"Bet you do get him, too."

"If Nikki remembers — you know, anything, but a face would be best. You have my number. This time I'll answer."

"You don't think —"

"He's long gone. Believe me, this guy is not hanging around when there's all this law enforcement buzz."

The two said goodbye with a little hug — the sort masculine men not given to emotion but feeling it nonetheless are given to perform — and then Nick climbed awkwardly into the seat, and his driver took him away. Bob watched his closest — maybe his only — friend go, then turned, and headed to his own car, now much-loathed, the little green, rental Ford that had hauled him so many places. He had half a mind to buy a really nice Dodge Charger, blood red, the big V8 engine, spoilers, the works, to celebrate surviving another one of his things.

Feeling the omnipresent pain in his hip, he negotiated his way to the little vehicle to see, astonishingly, that someone had pulled up in a brand new Dodge Charger, his dream vehicle, though this one was death black and gleamy. The door opened, and a familiar figure stepped out. It was that young Matt MacReady, who'd taken USMC

44 to a fourth in Bristol.

"Howdy, Gunny. Heard about this meet, thought I might find you here."

"Well, Matt, how are you? Congratulations on your run."

"Sir, it wasn't nothing compared to your run, what I'm hearing. I just drive in circles and nobody's shooting."

"Well, most of what I did was crawl in circles, hoping not to get shot."

"Sergeant Swagger —"

"Bob, I told you, son."

"Bob, Big Racing won't ever say a thing, but I came by to thank you just the same. If that thing had come off, it would be a stain. You stopped it. A cop told me you stopped it alone. So, no stain. No ugliness. No memories of bad things. In fact, in some perverted way, I think everybody who didn't die or lose their business kind of enjoyed it. But the race is still the thing."

"Thank you, Matt. Everybody seems to think I was an FBI agent and now even the FBI's pretending to that one, so it looks like it'll clear up okay for me and I can get back to my front porch."

"I doubt anything'll keep you on a front porch. But there's one more thing."

"What's that?"

"This guy, the driver?"

"Yep."

"Think I know who he is."

This got Bob's full attention.

"All right. That puts you ahead of everyone else in this game."

"He's the man who murdered my father. On the track, twenty years ago. Ran him hard into an abutment, killed him, everybody knew it was murder, but there was no investigation because Big Racing didn't want an investigation and a scandal. They just ran him out of the game and made sure he never got on another track again."

"So he was a racer?"

"The best. Would have been a god. Trained by the hardest task-master, made hard and cruel by a hard and cruel mentor, trained to show no mercy, to intimidate, to win or die trying. A monster, or maybe a genius, or maybe the best racing mind and reflexes ever put in one body. Who knows what he might have been? I grew up hearing rumors about him — anytime there was some strange guy winning an unsanctioned event like a coast-to-coast or a mountain climb or some slick driving in a bank robbery getaway, I always thought it was Johnny."

"You sound like you know him."

"I do. I once loved him. I guess I still do, no matter what. He's my brother."

FORTY

"So let me get this straight, Dad," Nikki said. "In my own newspaper it reports, 'An FBI unit pursued the robbers to the top of the hill, killing two and bringing down the fleeing helicopter.' "

"That's what it says, so it must be true," he answered. "They don't put it in the paper if it ain't true, as I understand it." He was pushing her in a wheelchair down the hallway from the release office at the Knoxville hospital. She wore blue jeans, a polo shirt, an FBI baseball cap that he had brought her, and a pair of flip-flops.

"But that FBI unit — that was one guy, and he wasn't even in the FBI. That was you?"

"I have no comment for the press."

"And this," she added, reading more from the paper, " 'Other federal units converged on Piney Mountain Baptist Prayer Camp, where they encountered Johnson County

Sheriff's Department Detective Thelma Fielding with evidence that she planned the robbery, Tennessee's most violent since the 1930s. Fielding resisted arrest and was shot dead.' That was you too."

"I don't honestly remember."

"Aren't you a little old for all that cowboy stuff?"

He laughed. It was so good to have her back. His chest swelled. Who said snipers have not hearts or that mankillers are isolate and stark? Through her, he was connected to it all. She was all: civilization, democracy, honor, civility, loyalty, the radiance of sheer life itself. He felt so damned good!

She looked wonderful, her eyes bright with the furious Nikki-intelligence that had always marked her presence on earth. Her face had color in it, her blonde hair was pulled back in a pony tail, and she had that cut-to-the-chase directness he'd always loved so much. She was quite a kid and he thought anew how lucky he was to end up rich, most of all, in daughters.

"Once cowboy, always cowboy, I guess. Didn't know I could move so fast, nor be so lucky still. I suppose I'm supposed to feel bad about putting those people down, in the modern fashion, but then I remember they targeted my daughter, so I can't work up no tears."

"*Any* tears."

"Any tears."

"What boy who loves me can ever compete with you?"

"Nah. You'll meet him and forget clean about the old goat. That's the way it's supposed to be, and just getting you back into the world to meet him and have a great life and contribute wherever you go, that's enough for me. Now let's go, Mommy's waiting in the van. We have to get you back to Bristol."

He pushed her to the elevator, then the lobby. People waved at Nikki and she waved back, and then he took her outside, into sunlight and southern heat. The clouds had broken, the sun shone, and the trees flashed green as their leaves played in breeze.

"It's so stupid," she said. "I can walk perfectly fine."

"These hospitals have rules. You don't go home on your own two feet, honey."

They waited, and then Julie pulled up in a rented red Ford passenger van. The door popped open, and Miko hopped out and threw herself at Nikki. The two daughters embraced.

"Your daddy," said Nikki, "your daddy is still a tough old bird, sweetie. I fear for the boys you start bringing home in a few years."

"I don't like boys," says Miko. "I like my daddy."

"She'll sing a different tune pretty damn soon," said Bob.

Gingerly, Julie and Bob got Nikki, still a little fragile despite her protestations, into the backseat of the van. Julie got in next to her, got her seat belt on, and Miko got into the front seat. Bob climbed into the driver's seat, engaged the engine, and pulled out for the long, last trek up I-81 from Knoxville to Bristol.

Brother Richard watched them, listening to his iPod.

Sinnerman, where you gonna run to?
Run to the sea, but the sea it's aboilin',
Run to the moon, but the moon it's
    ableedin',
Sinnerman, where you gonna to run to,
All on that day?

He was parked two blocks back in a recently stolen Dodge Charger, 6.7 liter Hemi V8, the car idling smoothly, giving no evidence of the 425-horsepower beast under its hood. He'd been on the Swaggers for three days now, knowing that sooner or later Nikki would leave the hospital. He knew they'd rent a van, and he ID'd the handsome woman who was the mother of the girl he had to kill.

Now he watched the little scene at the hospital doors, so sweet, the theme of family wholeness after an ordeal, the subthemes, the heroism of the father, the faith of the mother, the weird special talent of the daughter, the innocence of the younger child. But he wasn't thinking about the family or themes; he was thinking tactically, of details involved in the action ahead. He knew that no matter how well the van was driven by this extremely competent man, it was too tall, too slow, too stiff, had too high a tipping point, to stand up to the assault of his Charger.

He knew so much. He knew which route they'd have to take to the I-81 ramp, and he knew exactly where he'd take them, right after Exit 66 and its outlet mall, where the traffic would be thinner, the road straight, the embankment low, and the precipice steep, and the jolt would force the van over and down it would go, bouncing, bouncing, snapping the spines of all inside.

I never meant to do a family, he thought, but I am the Sinnerman, and that girl has seen my new face and when she remembers, I am done. That's what the Sinnerman does. He does what is necessary.

Bob drove through traffic idly, looking neither left nor right, paying no particular attention to anything. He turned a corner, then had a sudden inspiration.

"I could use a nice chocolate Softee," he said.

"Daddy, you'll get fat."

"I'll get a Diet Softee then," he said, laughing.

He pulled into the immediate left, a convenience store parking lot.

Julie said, "Okay, everybody out."

"Mommy, I —"

"No, no, just out, *out,* fast."

There was something new and hard in her voice.

She shepherded the two girls, but not into the store for the treat, but instead into another rental, a car, where she directed them to lie low.

"Mommy, I —"

"Do it, honey. Just do it *now.*"

She turned back into the cab of the van, where Bob had cinched his seatbelt tight.

She made eye contact with him, and spoke not with love but with the mission-centered earnestness of officer to sergeant.

"This time, *get him!*"

All of a sudden, they turned right, just as he was himself caught in an unexpected snarl of traffic. *Agh!* They're getting away. Brother Richard felt a spurt of anger. He could control so much, but not traffic. But just as swiftly it cleared up, and he darted ahead, took the right-hand turn and saw that they'd pulled into a convenience store, probably for a Coke or something, and were now pulling out, back on the road. He idled by the side of the road, let the van put some distance between them, then cut back into traffic and began his leisurely stalk.

He stayed far behind, occasionally even losing visual contact. But he reacquired the van as it pulled up the ramp to I-81 North. Again without haste, he let some distance build, took the ramp, and slipped into traffic. There it was, maybe half a mile ahead, the red van, completely unaware of his presence. He accelerated through the gears, the Charger growled, shivered at the chance to show off its muscularity and all 425 of its horses, and Brother Richard felt that octane-driven bounce as the car flew ahead, pressing him into the seat.

The miles sped by, the van always in the

slow lane, holding steady at fifty-five, Richard a mile back, forcing himself to keep his power-burner at the same rate. He'd lose the target on hills or turns, but it was always just there, ahead of him, easily recoverable. The exits ticked by, until at last, almost an hour later, Exit 66, with its much-ballyhooed promise of consumer paradise at cut rate, took the majority of the northbound cars.

We are here, he told himself. We are where we have to be. We are Sinnerman.

He had them. The road was clear, no Smokies had been seen in some time, the odd trailer truck or SUV dawdled in the slow lane, now and then a fast-mover passed too aggressively in the left-hand, speeder's alley, but not with any regularity.

He turned up the music on his iPod, that continual loop of the old spiritual, with its image of Armageddon, its sense of the endings of things, its image of the Sinnerman in all his glory, finally facing his ultimate fate, the one this Sinnerman was now about to make impossible by destroying the one living witness to his deeds and face.

He hit the pedal. The car jacked ahead. Clear sailing, only the red van stumping along across the ridge lines of the bland North Tennessee landscape with its anonymous farms and low hills. The car sang as it ate up the distance, alive under his touch as all cars always had been. He closed fast; they had no idea the Sinnerman was on them.

It was just like all the others: the blind-side approach, the perfect angle, the perfect hit just beyond the left rear quarter panel, the satisfaction of the thump as metal hit metal at speed, possibly a flash of horror as the doomed driver looked back, even as, predictably, he overcorrected as he felt control vanish and the side of the road beckon, not realizing that the overcorrection was the killer. Then the weirdness visible in the rearview mirror as the car twisted and lost traction, always seemingly in slow motion, and began to float as it separated from the surface of the planet. Once it floated, it pirouetted, almost lovely for a thing so full of death. Then it hit, as gravity reasserted its command, and bounced, jerked, spun, disintegrated, throwing up heaps of dust. Possibly it disappeared, going off a precipice or down an incline, but it didn't really matter, for the velocity-interruption of the strike of car to ground produced more torque than any human body could withstand, and spines, like toothpicks or straws, snapped instantly. If the car hit a tree, hit a rock, hit an abutment, burned, shattered, splintered, erupted, it didn't matter. Its cargo was corpses by the time the ultimate worked itself out.

He had them he had them he had them. He was in the blind spot, he found the angle, he veered for the fatal smash —

Where you gonna run to, all on that day?

A curiosity. Unprecedentedly, before he struck, the van disappeared. No, it didn't disappear, it braked hard but well, instantly jettisoning its speed, and in a nanosecond was out of the kill zone as he oversped. But as it disappeared, it also revealed. That revelation was *another* vehicle, just ahead, so close to the first that it had been hidden by the height of the van. In another nanosecond Brother Richard discovered that it was a Dodge Charger like his own, only glistening black, the V8 6.7 liter Hemi, 425 horses raring to go.

In that second, too, he recognized the profile of its driver. It was his brother, Matt, the NASCAR hero, whom he'd always adored but whom he also hated, for Matt had the life that he, Johnny, so wanted.

Matt nodded.

The Sinnerman knew what would happen next.

Matt slid inside him, came left hard, hit him just beyond the rear quarter panel, and he felt the traction going as the car floated left. Before he could stop himself, he over-corrected, and the car launched at 140 miles per.

Where you gonna run to, all on that day?

You're not going to run anywhere. There was no place to run.

He was floating, his tires lost contact with the surface of the earth, the moon was bleeding, the sea was boiling, the car was rolling, all on this day.

ACKNOWLEDGMENTS

This one began the second I saw the Speedway at night, loaded with fans, frenzy, and happiness. I thought: What they need is a good gunfight! I recommend a trip to Bristol whether it's a racing weekend or not, for that view of the hugeness of the structure in the greenness of the valley is shocking and somehow awesome. It stands for man's monumental imagination and his ability to impose his will on nature. On the other hand, if those aren't your values, you'd better stay away. Anyhow, I was down there visiting my daughter, Amy, who, like Nikki, is a reporter for the Bristol *Herald Courier,* and she's just as gallant and intrepid as Nikki, even if I'm a far cry from Bob Lee Swagger. Without giving it a thought, I had bumbled into the most fantastic American spectacle I'd ever seen and knew I had to do something with it.

The confluence of daughter and setting

suggested a plot, though it took a while to get it all straightened out. In the early going, the story was going to revolve around an attempt to fix a race and would have required penetrating NASCAR culture to a far greater extent. Ten minutes into a race convinced me that "fixing" was impossible, so I diverted to something more gun-centric and fireworks-intensive. Had a hell of a good time doing it, too.

Thanks to the usual suspects and some newcomers as well. Thanks to Amy for inspiring it, thanks to NASCAR for being so much fun to write about, thanks to the millions who attend NASCAR events, for their good humor, enthusiasm, charisma, and consumption of beer in epic quantities. Thanks to Gary Goldberg, who became a sort of majordomo of the book, and figured out, among so many things, how much $8 million in small bills would weigh. Thanks to John Bainbridge for proofreading, to Lenne Miller, Jay Carr, Frank Starr, Mike Hill, and Jeff Weber for good counsel and morale. Thanks to Jean, as usual, for going along on my mad flights with a good spirit. Thanks to Folk Village, and XM-15 for playing "Sinnerman" at the precise moment I was trying to get a handle on the driver. Thanks to Ylan Q. Mui at *The Washington*

Post for her help with Bob's Vietnamese.

Thanks to the professionals: my agent, Esther Newberg, my publisher, David Rosenthal, and my editor, Colin Fox. Thanks to Kimber, DPMS, and Black Hills for inspiring all the hardware. Thanks to Dodge for the Charger, a piece of work and a half. Most of all, thanks to you for entertaining my efforts.

ABOUT THE AUTHOR

Stephen Hunter has written fourteen novels. Recently retired as chief film critic for *The Washington Post,* where he won the 2003 Pulitzer Prize for Distinguished Criticism, he has also published two collections of film criticism and a nonfiction work, *American Gunfight.* He lives in Baltimore, Maryland.

The employees of Thorndike Press hope you have enjoyed this Large Print book. All our Thorndike, Wheeler, and Kennebec Large Print titles are designed for easy reading, and all our books are made to last. Other Thorndike Press Large Print books are available at your library, through selected bookstores, or directly from us.

For information about titles, please call:
(800) 223-1244

or visit our Web site at:
http://gale.cengage.com/thorndike

To share your comments, please write:
Publisher
Thorndike Press
295 Kennedy Memorial Drive
Waterville, ME 04901